HOME ON THE RANCH:
REDEEMING THE TEXAN

———————— ⚒ ————————

PATRICIA THAYER

Previously published as *Luke: The Cowboy Heir* and
The Lionhearted Cowboy Returns

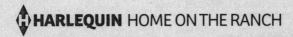

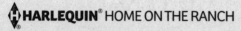
HARLEQUIN® HOME ON THE RANCH

Recycling programs
for this product may
not exist in your area.

ISBN-13: 978-1-335-00869-5

Home on the Ranch: Redeeming the Texan
Copyright © 2020 by Harlequin Books S.A.

Luke: The Cowboy Heir
First published in the U.K. as The Black Sheep's Proposal in
2008. This edition published in 2020.
Copyright © 2008 by Patricia Wright

The Lionhearted Cowboy Returns
First published in 2010. This edition published in 2020.
Copyright © 2010 by Patricia Wright

This edition published by arrangement with Harlequin Books S.A.

For questions and comments about the quality of this book,
please contact us at CustomerService@Harlequin.com.

Harlequin Enterprises ULC
22 Adelaide St. West, 40th Floor
Toronto, Ontario M5H 4E3, Canada
www.Harlequin.com

Printed in U.S.A.

Suddenly the rain grew heavy, pounding against the tin roof, breaking the spell between them.

"Looks like we're not going anywhere for a while."

"Then it's good Dad's asleep." She went to the door and squeezed through the small opening to the outside.

Luke was at a loss for what else to do for her. He hesitated...until he heard her quiet sobs.

"Tess..." He touched her shoulder. Tess turned around, her head lowered. "It's okay. Let it go."

She shook her head and frantically swiped at her tears. "I can't. My family...needs me."

Luke had no idea what that was like. He'd never gotten so involved with anyone they would have to depend on him. This was different... Tess was different. He wanted to be there for her.

"What about you, Tess? What do you need?"

In the shadowed darkness, he could see her tearstained cheeks. Her eyes revealed so much— her need...her desire.

"I can't need anything," she said.

"Then let me offer it," he told her. "Let me help you, Tess."

CONTENTS

Patricia Thayer was born and raised in Muncie, Indiana. She attended Ball State University before heading west, where she has called Southern California home for many years.

When not working on a story, she might be found traveling the United States and Europe, taking in the scenery and doing story research while enjoying time with her husband, Steve. Together, they have three grown sons and four grandsons and one granddaughter, whom Patricia calls her own true-life heroes.

Books by Patricia Thayer

Harlequin Western Romance

Count on a Cowboy
Second Chance Rancher
Her Colorado Sheriff

Harlequin Romance

Tall, Dark, Texas Ranger
Once a Cowboy...
The Cowboy Comes Home
Single Dad's Holiday Wedding
Her Rocky Mountain Protector
The Cowboy She Couldn't Forget
Proposal at the Lazy S Ranch

Visit the Author Profile page at Harlequin.com for more titles.

LUKE:
THE COWBOY HEIR

To Hence, thank you for sharing your life, the wonderful stories and your family.
I'll miss you, friend.

1909–2007

Chapter 1

He'd sworn he would never come back here.

Luke Randell hadn't been left with a choice. He released a long breath and climbed out of his BMW. His gaze swept the area that had once been his childhood home. The Rocking R Ranch.

Large oak trees shaded the green lawn. A concrete walkway led to the wraparound porch of the big, well-kept Victorian house. A recent coat of white paint covered the two-story house where he used to live, more than twenty-seven years ago. A rush of feelings—sadness and a lot of bitterness—hit him as he glanced toward the large barn, outbuildings and corral. They, too, had been well cared for.

Not what he'd expected when he'd left Dallas to return to San Angelo, Texas. A warm breeze brushed against his face, and he caught a whiff of the ranch's earthy smells, causing a flood of more memories— memories of his pony, Jazzy, then his horse, Bandit, the chestnut gelding he'd been given for his fifth birthday.

Damn. He'd loved that horse.

Tightness gripped Luke's chest as he thought about the painful day his daddy had sold the animal…. That same day everything had changed. No more perfect family. For a six-year-old kid it had been the end of the world.

He quickly shook off the foolish sentiment and walked along the path to the porch, then up the steps. His gaze caught the wrought-iron branding symbol of the Rocking R nailed next to the door.

Another memory hit him before he could push it away. He couldn't keep doing this. Not if he was going to live here in his childhood home. The heavy oak door had been opened inward, leaving a wood-framed screen door to keep out intruders. He shrugged. It was the country, not downtown Dallas.

"Hello… Anyone here?" he called.

He waited for an answer. When none came, he walked inside the large entry hall. The hardwood floors were polished, showing off their honey color. The front parlor, as his mother used to call it, also sparkled with polish and a lemony scent. There were several antiques, but the dark brocade sofa and chairs still looked uncomfortable.

Who cares? he asked himself. With any luck, he wouldn't be here that long. Right now he needed to find Ray Meyers. Suddenly a sound interrupted his thoughts.

On the open staircase that led to the second floor he found a black kitten with white paws.

"Well, at least someone's here to welcome me."

He got another meow as he walked over and picked up the kitten. "Maybe you can tell me where everyone is."

The cat meowed again just as muffled voices came from upstairs. "Looks like I got my answer." He started up the steps, carrying his new companion. He walked along the hall past several rooms, one of which used to be his. He ignored it. No sense stirring up more memories.

Luke continued on toward the open door to the master bedroom. Once across the threshold, he found the source of the voices. He leaned against the doorway and enjoyed the view.

A woman was on her hands and knees with her head buried under the large four-poster bed. He couldn't help but notice how well she filled out her fitted jeans. Next to her was a little girl not more than four or five.

"Mommy, we have to find Jinx. She gets scared when she's all alone." The child's long, blond hair was pulled back into a ponytail. Her worried look didn't take away from her cute features. Just then the woman's head appeared, and Luke's heart shot off racing. The little girl definitely got her good looks from her mother.

Her wheat-colored hair was pulled back in a ponytail, also, and was a shade darker than the child's. Her profile was near perfect, along with her creamy complexion. He cursed silently for noticing, and cursed again for wanting to see more.

"Excuse me," he said.

The two females swung around toward him. Okay, both mother and daughter were gorgeous. Somehow he managed to find his voice. "Could this little guy be who you're looking for?"

"Jinx!" The small child jumped up and ran to him. "You found my kitty."

Luke handed the furry bundle to her. "I think it found me." He brushed his hands off and glanced at the woman.

Tess didn't like being caught off guard. Over the last several months her entire life had been turned upside down, and she suspected this stranger was the big reason.

He walked toward her and extended a hand. "Luke Randell."

She climbed to her feet. "Tess Meyers." She shook his hand. It was not rough like a rancher's, but his grip was strong.

"This is my daughter, Olivia."

Her daughter looked at Mr. Randell. "But everybody calls me Livy, and this is Jinx."

"Well, hello, Livy…and Jinx."

Tess drew his attention back to her. "We weren't expecting you for a few more days, Mr. Randell."

"My plans changed." His gaze bore into hers. "Is there a problem?"

"None whatsoever," she lied. "I just wanted to make sure the house was ready for you." No way was she ready for this man with his dark good looks and silver eyes. Just what San Angelo needed. Another handsome Randell man.

He glanced around. "I didn't expect any of this, but I appreciate it. Thank you."

"Outside of needing linens on the bed, the house should be livable."

He nodded toward the fresh sheets on the bare mattress. "I think I can manage to make up a bed."

She nodded. No doubt he could mess up a bed, too. She groaned. Where had that come from? "Oh, I plugged in the refrigerator, but I'm afraid there isn't any food in the house."

"Not a problem. I stopped by the grocery store and bought some staples."

She couldn't help but stare at the man dressed in his knife-pressed jeans, navy polo shirt and topsider shoes looking like the last person anyone would expect to take over a cattle ranch—a ranch she and her father had put a lot of work into, which, there was a good possibility, could be taken away from them. She had to be very careful. This man held her future in his hands.

"Okay then, I guess we'll be going and let you get settled in." She started for the door. "Come on, Livy."

"But, Mom, I didn't ask him yet." She stood rooted in the middle of the room, gripping her kitty. "Do you have any little girls I can play with?"

The new owner looked surprised by the question, but finally he said, "No, sorry, I don't."

"Oh…" Livy looked disappointed. "That's the reason I got a kitty because I don't have anyone to play with." She held up Jinx. "Mommy said she wasn't going to have any more babies…and I got him so I won't get lonely."

"Olivia Meyers," Tess said, mortified. "It's time we let Mr. Randell move in."

"Okay." Her daughter complied and walked to her mother. "Goodbye, Mr. Randell."

"Goodbye, Livy… Jinx." He looked at Tess. "Mrs. Meyers."

"It's Miss Meyers." She didn't know why she corrected him. "Ray Meyers is my father, not my husband."

Livy chimed in once again. "Yeah… Mommy doesn't have a husband, and I don't have a daddy."

Thirty minutes later, Tess sat at the kitchen table in the foreman's cottage.

"I was mortified, Bernice," Tess said.

Her aunt shook her head. "The child sure has a mind of her own." She carried their lunch plates to the sink. "Now, tell me, is Luke Randell as handsome as his cousins?"

Bernice was her dad's younger sister. In her late fifties, she'd lost her husband a few years ago. When Ray Meyers first took ill last year, Bernice didn't hesitate to come and help out.

Tess shrugged. "If you like the preppy look. He's definitely not a rancher. I doubt he's capable or has any desire to run this place."

"He could learn," Bernice told her. "My goodness, he has six cousins who do some sort of ranching. It's in his blood."

"What if he doesn't want to ranch, but instead sells the Rocking R?"

Those soft hazel eyes met hers. "Doesn't he have to wait for his brother to show up before he could do anything?"

She nodded. "They do own it jointly."

She'd been notified of Sam Randell's death by the lawyer, who also let them know that the ranch had been left to his two sons, Luke and Brady.

"Maybe Brady Randell wants to sell, too. He's a pilot in the air force. Why would he want a ranch?"

With a shrug, Bernice filled the sink and added some liquid soap. Tess picked up a towel to dry. "And maybe those boys will decide to continue to lease the Rocking R to you."

"Sam Randell leased the land to Ray Meyers. And we both know Dad can't run this place any longer."

Sadness crept in as Tess leaned against the counter in the small kitchen. She'd grown up in this house. Back then it had been just her and her dad. Now it was pretty crowded with Bernice and Livy added into the mix.

That's why Tess had moved into her daughter's bedroom. It was more convenient for everyone to have Bernice move into Tess's room.

She knew this setup was only temporary. His disease was progressing, and his good days were becoming fewer. He hardly ever left his room. It made her sad to think of her father's mind slowly erasing memories of his life…and that he was not always able to remember his daughter, or his granddaughter.

Tess shook away the sad thoughts. "I need to talk to

Mr. Randell. I need to know what he's going to do, so I can make some plans." She was hopeful she could stay on and continue to lease this house, along with barn space for the horses. She needed to make a living for her family. And there was her father's cattle operation. Although small, she didn't want to sell the calves yet. Roundup wasn't for another few months.

But if the worst happened and they had to leave, she'd get another place. She doubted she could find as good a setup as the Rocking R Ranch. Her father had built several of the horse stalls in the barn. The large corral had been Ray's handiwork, too. That had been the reason the lease agreement was so cheap; her dad had also been the caretaker.

They'd had such big plans as partners. The Meyerses were going to breed and train quarter horses. And her bay stallion, Smooth Whiskey Doc, was going to be their cutting champion. So far she had made something of a name as a trainer and rider. But she wanted and needed the money that her future champion stallion could bring in. She wasn't thinking about herself, but Olivia. She was her sole parent.

Her aunt's voice brought her back. "What?"

"Go work Whiskey," Bernice said. "That always calms you."

She shook her head. "Dad will be up from his nap soon."

"Go. I can look after Ray." She turned her niece around and nudged her toward the door. "Take a break, Tess. You need it."

Tess didn't argue, just headed for the door. She found Livy on the porch playing with her dolls and the kitten.

"Hey, sweetie, I want you to stay on the porch. It's too hot to go out in the sun."

"Mommy, can I go see Grandpa? I'll be quiet. I promise."

It was so sad. Livy and her grandpa Ray had had a close relationship since the day she was born. Now most of the time he couldn't speak to her. "I think he'd like that. But maybe you should leave Jinx in the box in our room."

"I will, Mommy. I know Grandpa doesn't mean to, but he sometimes squeezes too hard."

She knelt down in front of her daughter. "You know Grandpa's sick. He doesn't mean to squeeze too hard."

Livy's blond ponytail bobbed up and down. "I know, Mommy. I wish he wasn't sick."

"So do I, sweetie." Tess had to fight her tears. "You're my best girl."

Livy smiled. "And you're my bestest mom."

They exchanged a kiss and then Tess started off, but her daughter called to her. "Are you going to go see Mr. Randell?"

"No, honey, Mr. Randell is busy. I'm going to work with Whiskey."

Livy's eyes narrowed. Tess knew her daughter was cooking up something else. "He's a nice man. Maybe we should bake him a cake to welcome him home."

Butter up the enemy. That was an idea. "We'll talk about it later. Remember, don't leave the porch." She turned and walked toward the barn, knowing that ploy wasn't going to work for long. She had to come up with something to keep Livy from intruding on Luke Randell.

Putting her wide-brimmed cowboy hat on her head, she glanced toward the large Victorian house. Perched on a hill with a grove of pecan trees lined up on either side for shade and protection from the elements, it was a sight to behold.

She'd heard stories that Mrs. Sam Randell had been so humiliated when her husband's brother, Jack, had been sent to prison for cattle rustling, she insisted they leave the area. It had been twenty-seven years since anyone had lived there.

"Your father did a wonderful job with the upkeep," a man's voice said.

Tess swung around to find Luke Randell. "Oh, Mr. Randell…"

"Please, call me Luke."

"Luke, and I'm Tess," she said, a little breathless.

He'd changed into a long-sleeved shirt and a pair of boots. Cocked on his head was a worn cowboy hat, giving him a rugged look.

"Do I fit in a little better?"

Tess was tall at five-nine, but had to look up at him. Stand back was more like it. "You fit in dressed like you were before, but this is more practical for the ranch."

"Especially if I'm headed for the barn." He smiled, and it caused her pulse to race. Great. She was acting like a teenager.

"You want to see the barn?"

He glanced around. "Actually, I was looking for your father. Is he around?"

Oh, no. She wasn't ready to discuss her father's... situation yet. "I'm sorry, but he isn't feeling well right now." She rushed on to say, "I'm sure I can answer anything you want to know."

"I just wanted to let him...and you—know that my arriving early isn't meant to disturb your operation. You still have another two months on your lease. As the lawyer informed you, I'm just living in the house until a decision is made about the property."

A decision? "What about your brother?"

Luke still had trouble getting used to that term...for Brady. "Half brother," he clarified. "Brady is a pilot in the air force, and the only information I've gotten from the military so far is that he's overseas. I left word for him to contact me here."

"So your plans are to sell the ranch?"

Luke sighed. If only he could, it sure would solve his immediate problems. "There are a lot of things to consider when or if this place goes on the market." His gaze locked with her rich blue eyes and it caused him to get temporarily distracted. He quickly glanced away. He wasn't about to let that happen...again.

"I know you and your father need more information than that," he told her. "But it's all I can give for now."

She nodded. "Of course, Dad and I would love to continue the lease arrangement we have now." She gave him a sideways glance as they started walking toward the barn. "Are you considering staying on...and running the ranch?"

He frowned. "Technically I've never ranched before. I was just a kid when we moved away."

"But you still have a lot of family here. I'm sure they'd help out."

They came to the barn and he slid open the large door. "So you know the Randells?"

Tess nodded. "There's something else. The lease arrangement your father had with my father could continue…or if you'd like to raise cattle under your own brand, we could stay on as the foreman." She shrugged. "It's just something to think about."

Not waiting for an answer, Tess walked into the cool interior. Although the barn was clean and well organized, the smell of hay and horses was prevalent, and she liked the earthy scent. She headed down the concrete aisle, passing several empty stalls. She was hoping to have them filled by now, but without her father's help she couldn't board any more horses.

There were two quarter horses here she'd been working with, but her main focus was still on Whiskey. Taking the time, she greeted the valuable equines before she reached the last stall. Her bay stallion greeted her with a soft whinny, and he nuzzled her hand.

"How's my favorite guy?" she crooned. "You ready to work?" He bobbed his head.

"This is Smooth Whiskey Doc. He's the future cutting champion."

With an ease that surprised Tess, Luke walked up to Whiskey and stroked him. "Hey, fella, how you doing?" Whiskey took to the attention and moved closer to the stranger. "You sure are a beauty."

"Don't give him too much praise. It'll just go to his head."

"So you breed horses?"

She nodded. "Been working on it. I've had a lot of help from Chance Randell. He also breeds quarter horses. I've done some training and competing with my mare, Lady. I helped out Chance with training, in trade for his stallion, Whiskey Pete, to breed with my mare, and as a result we got Smooth Whiskey Doc."

"You're partners?"

She couldn't help but laugh. "Hardly. Chance doesn't need me. He's made quite a name for himself on his own. He just did me a favor." She patted the horse's neck. "And I appreciate it. As neighbors we all kind of help each other out."

"So you and your father aren't running cattle any longer?"

"There's just a small herd now."

Here was her opportunity. "Cattle isn't our main focus anymore. Like I said, we've been breeding and training cutting horses for competition. And if for any reason, you and your bother decide to stay, I'd—we'd like to continue to rent the foreman's cottage and rent barn space to board the horses."

Luke Randell just stood there for a long time, then finally spoke. "I can't say one way or the other what will happen now. I have no plans to ranch at this time. To be honest, I never planned to come back here…ever. So as soon as it's possible for me, I'll be leaving."

Tess was angry. "And the hell with us."

He blinked at her bluntness. "You have two months to relocate."

The man didn't have a heart. "The Rocking R has been my father's and my home for well over twenty years. My daughter hasn't lived anywhere else." She hated that she sounded so desperate. But she was. "It isn't so easy to move a family and livestock." Or a father who barely remembers his name, she added silently. She studied the stubborn look on his face. "Besides, how can you be so anxious to sell land that's been in your family for generations?"

Luke Randell stiffened, then glanced away, but not before she saw a flash of emotion. "Maybe because that family deserted me a long time ago."

Chapter 2

An hour later, Luke leaned against a post on the back porch. He held a long-neck bottle in his hand as he watched Tess Meyers work her quarter horse in the corral.

Impressive. He took a thirsty drink of beer. She looked strong astride the powerful stallion, and the two together were as graceful as a ballet, moving in perfect unison in their performance.

There were a half-dozen steers in the pen, and she and Whiskey easily separated a calf from the others, then drove it back into the herd. Even from a distance, he caught her smile as she patted the horse's neck affectionately after he completed his task.

Once again his body stirred. For the second time in hours this cowgirl had him wondering about things he had no business thinking about.

Luke sat on the porch swing and propped his booted feet on the railing. What the hell was he doing here? He never wanted to come back to this place. The home he'd once loved, where he'd been part of a family. That had ended when his parents divorced, his dad went back into the military and his mother took him to live in Dallas.

He closed his eyes and he could still hear the fights late at night. Doors slamming, his dad starting the car and driving off. The worst sound was of his mother's crying. He hated his father for that. Most of all he hated Sam Randell for deserting them.

Now, all these years later, he had no choice but to come back here. The perfect scenario would be to sell the place, make some money and start over.

He doubted he could go back to Dallas. Thanks to a bad deal, his reputation had been destroyed in the real estate business. Because of a woman, Gina Chilton, he'd gotten involved with the wrong people. Her daddy, Buck Chilton, had invested money in his real estate venture.

In the end Luke had barely escaped criminal charges, and it had cost him everything. His employees hadn't fared much better, but at least he'd been able to give them a severance package. That meant there'd been nothing left for him. Everything he'd worked so hard to build was all gone now. Just some personal things, his clothes and the car remained. And he had to sell the luxury vehicle so he'd have some money to live on.

Well, at least he had a roof over his head…for now.

"Hey, mister. Are you sleeping?" a young voice said.

Luke opened his eyes and saw little Livy Meyers

standing on the porch step. She was wearing jeans and a ruffled pink blouse, holding her kitten.

He dropped his feet on the floor. "No, just doing some thinking." He glanced around to see if Tess Meyers was around. "Does your mother know where you are?"

Looking sheepish, the child moved to the top step. "Kinda." She shrugged. "She said not to bother you 'cause you were moving in. Are you finished?"

With what was left of his furniture in storage, he had only a few suitcases to empty. "Yes, I'm moved in."

She smiled at him, and something tightened in his chest. She strolled to the swing and sat down. "I'm glad. And I'm glad you came here to live, too. You want to hold Jinx again? He likes you."

"You think so, huh?" He couldn't help but take her offering. He doubted many people could resist her big blue eyes and dimples. The kitten immediately curled up against his chest and closed his eyes.

"Hey, mister, see he likes you." She studied him. "So do I."

"Well, I like you, too. Maybe you could call me Luke."

She frowned. "Mama says I can't call big people by their first names 'cause it's not 'spectful."

"Respectful," Luke corrected gently.

She nodded. "Yeah. Maybe I can call you Mr. Luke."

Luke wasn't used to being around kids. But Livy Meyers didn't seem to notice. "Sounds like a good idea."

Her smile widened, and he saw the resemblance to her pretty mother. But the smile suddenly disappeared when someone called Livy's name.

They both turned to see Tess coming out of the corral. "Oh, no. I gotta go." She grabbed her kitten and went to the edge of the porch. "I forgot to ask you something." She came back. "What's your favorite flavor of cake?"

He blinked. "I guess it would be chocolate. Why?"

Livy leaned forward and whispered, "It's a surprise." Giggling, the little nymph ran off toward her mother.

Tess approached her daughter, and he didn't have to hear to know that the child was getting a lecture. With a nod, Livy started for the foreman's house while Tess headed his way.

Luke stood, feeling a little rush of excitement on seeing her graceful strides, and those long legs encased in jeans and covered with worn leather chaps. She wore a Henley-style shirt and her battered cowboy hat on her head. Suddenly he couldn't remember why he swore off women. He adjusted his own hat and went to meet her.

"I want to apologize for Livy bothering you," Tess began. "It won't happen again."

"She wasn't a bother. She asked if I was busy. So please don't let her think I'm some sort of ogre." Why did he care what a five-year-old thought?

"Well, she still shouldn't have come here. I told her to stay on the porch."

"Technically she was on the porch."

Tess jammed her hands on her hips and frowned. "Not her porch. And with you living here now, she especially needs to know boundaries. There are too many things that could happen to her around a ranch."

"I understand." He nodded. "But there's also no reason for us to avoid one another."

"Of course." She sighed. "I'm sorry, Mr. Randell—"

"Please, it's Luke."

Tess hesitated. She didn't want to get too friendly with this man. "Luke… It's just that there's never been anyone living in the house."

"Like I said, it's temporary. And I don't want or plan to disturb your operation."

"So you aren't giving any more thought to staying and going into ranching?"

Not in the last hour. "I've never given any thought to staying permanently," he said stubbornly.

Tess couldn't understand how he could walk away from this incredible property. "Maybe you should talk to your cousins before you make a decision."

He arched an eyebrow. "Oh, yeah, the notorious Randell brothers."

She didn't miss the resentment in his voice. "Your family runs several successful businesses. There's the guest ranch…along with horse breeding and a cattle operation. Not to mention being a supplier of rough rodeo stock."

"Don't forget my uncle who was arrested for cattle rustling and cousins who were juvenile delinquents. My uncle and my daddy were well-known womanizers."

Tess tried not to react, but it was hard. "Those are old stories. Chance, Cade and Travis have all but erased that bad reputation with their work in the community. You should give San Angelo a chance."

He blew out a long breath. "That still doesn't make me a rancher."

Here was her chance. "But I am. I could run this place for you."

He stared at her for a long time. "You're asking to be my foreman?"

She fought the blush coloring her cheeks. "It's not as crazy as it sounds. I've worked alongside my daddy as soon as I could climb on a horse. I was three years old when we first came here."

Tess recalled her father's stories about how he'd used her mother's life insurance money to buy the first herd. She thought about her father now and she grew sad, knowing he was going to have to leave here, anyway.

Luke's gray eyes filled with mischief. "So you think you can make a rancher out of me?"

Her pulse raced as she looked him over. "You are a Randell, so I'd say it's already been bred into you."

Two mornings later Luke was still thinking about Tess Meyers. She'd managed to interrupt his thoughts sporadically in the past forty-eight hours. Although he'd spent most of the time in solitude, and his meals had consisted of frozen dinners he put into the small microwave he'd brought with him, he still wanted to eat in peace. The crazy thing was, he actually had thought about her offer…all of thirty seconds.

Luke sipped his coffee and leaned against the kitchen counter. The room was huge with built-in cupboards that lined the walls. The countertops were a golden-hued Mexican tile, and the floor was covered in terracotta brick.

He smiled. He remembered it vividly since he used to eat breakfast here as a child. The very same table was placed by the row of windows that overlooked the barn and corral. Back then there were ranch hands around, helping his father run the place. Sam had gotten out of the military...and he was finally home with his family.

Luke had just turned five and gotten a new horse for his birthday that summer. He rode Bandit every day until he went off to kindergarten. Life could have been better, but it could get a lot worse. Parents could fight and decide to end a marriage...destroy a family. And a boy might never see his dad again.

Luke shook away the thoughts. Damn. Stop it. He was an adult now. He'd gotten over all that long ago. He'd moved on. Or had he?

There was a knock on the door, pulling him back to the present. He looked through the screen and saw Livy and an older woman.

Surprisingly he was happy to see her. "Morning, shortcake. You came back."

"It's okay, I'm 'posed to be here now."

"I'm glad." He opened the door. "Who's your friend?"

Livy giggled. "She's not my friend, she's my aunt Bernie."

"Bernice Peterson," the older woman said, and offered a warm smile that crinkled the corners of her hazel eyes. "Please call me Bernice."

"Nice to meet you, Bernice. I'm Luke. Would you come in?"

Both females walked into the kitchen. "I hope it's not too early, but I wanted to bring you some biscuits while they were still warm from the oven."

"Of course it's never too early if you bring food," he said. "You must have heard my stomach growling all the way to your house." He took the basket, placed it on the counter and dug out a soft, steaming biscuit. He took a bite and groaned. "Delicious. I could get used to this."

"Thank you." She grinned. "I do appreciate a man with an appetite."

"And I appreciate home cooking. Would you like some coffee?"

"No, thank you. We need to get back to the house."

"Yeah, we can't leave Grandpa by himself," Livy told him. "And Mommy's in the corral working Whiskey. He's gonna be the NCHA champion some day," she announced proudly.

"Olivia, it's not nice to brag," Bernice said. "Now, ask Mr. Luke before we wear out our welcome."

"My mom, Aunt Bernie and me want to invite you to supper tomorrow night." The child's eyes widened. "Will you come? Aunt Bernie is making our favorite, pot roast with those tiny potatoes. And there'll be a surprise…"

This child was a charmer. So different from her mother's no-nonsense attitude. "Well, how can I turn down an invitation like that? I'd love to come. What time?" "Say six o'clock," Bernice said as she started for the door. "Come on, Livy, we need to get back to Grandpa."

"I hope Mr. Meyers feels better soon."

Livy looked up at him, her eyes sad. "Grandpa is really sick. He doesn't even read me stories anymore." Her gaze widened. "Do you read stories, Mr. Luke?"

Tess stood in her father's bedroom. "It's okay, Dad. I can do it for you."

"No," Ray Meyers argued, pushing her hand away. "I can button my own damn shirt."

Tess stood back, but watched protectively as her aging father worked at the simple task. Today was one of his more lucid days. And she was grateful.

His fingers were clumsy but he managed the job. The sixty-five-year-old one-time rodeo cowboy, horse trainer and rancher looked used up. She brushed a tear from her eye. His thinning hair was more white than gray. His lined skin was liver spotted and his blue eyes were tired…and sad. To her he was the most wonderful man in the world. And soon he wouldn't remember her…or his granddaughter.

"Hey, Dad, you want to sit outside today? It's not too hot yet."

"I don't want to sit on the porch… I need to check the herd." He glanced at Tess and a strange look came over him. "Mary Theresa, why aren't you in school?" he asked, suddenly agitated "You don't want me to get into trouble again do you?"

"No, Daddy. I don't." She knelt down next to his chair. "You know I love going on roundups with you." She wanted to store up all the memories she could, no matter if they were decades old.

"And I love you with me, too, baby girl. But you

need to go to school." He brushed his hand over her head and cupped her cheeks. "You're so pretty…just like your mama."

A tear ran down her face. "I love you, Daddy."

"I love you, too." Then the look in eyes changed to confusion and Tess knew she'd lost him.

"How about if I turn on the television and you can watch *The Price is Right*?" She didn't wait for an answer as she pressed the remote to the game show, then left the room.

Bernice looked up from her crossword puzzle at the kitchen, but Tess didn't want to talk right now. She needed an escape for a few hours. She turned to Livy who was playing with her cat on the back porch.

"Hey, sweetie, how would you like to go riding?"

It was late morning, and the August sun was beginning to heat up by the time Tess saddled the horses. Her dad's gelding, Dusty, was ready for Livy. The old buckskin hadn't been ridden much lately, and the exercise would be good for him. She led Whiskey and Dusty out of the barn. That's when she looked up and saw Luke pull his car up at the back of the house and get out.

"Mom, look it's Mr. Luke." Before she could stop her daughter, the child took off running. "Hi, Mr. Luke," she called.

"Hey, shortcake," he called back and started toward the corral. He was in a pair of faded jeans and a chambray shirt and boots. He sure didn't look like a businessman.

Tess watched her daughter beam as she approached him. "We're going riding."

"Seems like a nice day for it," he said as he caught up to the child. His gaze met Tess's and offered an easy smile.

Ignoring the funny tingle, she touched her finger to her hat and nodded. "C'mon, Livy. We need to get going."

The child seemed hesitant, then said, "Mommy, can Mr. Luke go with us?" She turned back to the man in question. "You can ride Dusty…he's real gentle."

It wasn't a good idea. "Livy, Mr. Luke probably has a lot of things to do today."

The girl looked up at her new hero. "Do you?"

Luke slipped his hands into his pockets. He wasn't sure what to do. He didn't want to sit around the house all day…again. He shrugged, but felt his excitement grow. "No. I'm free. I wouldn't mind seeing a little of the ranch."

The child grinned. "See, Mommy. He wants to see the ranch."

He watched Tess struggle with her decision. He couldn't blame her, he was a threat to her family's future.

She finally said. "Okay, you can ride Dusty, and, Livy, you'll have to double up with me."

Livy jumped up and down. "Oh, boy." She grabbed Luke's hand and nearly pulled him to the corral.

Tess tied the reins to the railing. "You'll need to adjust the stirrups."

"I think I remember how."

He went to work as she boosted Livy up on Whiskey.

Then she went around to the other side of Dusty and helped him with his task. Finished with the one stirrup, Luke came around to the other side. Standing next to her, he caught the soft scent of soap and shampoo. He stole a quick glance at her face to find her skin scrubbed clean of any makeup, revealing a dash of freckles across her nose. She looked like a teenager.

"That should do it." She squinted up at him. "Just give Dusty his lead, and he'll do the rest."

Luke nodded, happy to have something else to concentrate on. He jammed his boot into the stirrup, grabbed the horn and boosted himself onto the horse.

Excitement went through Luke as he walked the buckskin away from the corral gate and tested some basic commands.

"How does it feel?" Tess asked.

"Good." He glanced at her and smiled. "Real good."

"Okay, let's go," Livy said.

"Hold your horses," Tess said as she climbed up behind her daughter.

The child giggled. "That's funny, Mommy."

Luke couldn't take his eyes off Tess. She easily handled the stallion. The animal danced away, but she got him under control with expert hands and soothing voice.

They started off toward the south. Once in the open meadow, Livy turned to her mother. "I want to go faster, Mommy," the child urged her.

Tess smiled. "You do, do you? How fast?"

"Really, really fast."

She gave a sideways glance at Luke. "We'll be right back." She made a clicking sound with her mouth as she squeezed the horse's sides. Whiskey shot off in a run, then gradually began circling the pasture.

Luke didn't like being left behind, and neither did Dusty. "What do you think, boy? Should we try to catch them?"

The horse bobbed his head. The instant Luke touched the heel of his boot against the animal, he took off. Awkward at first, Luke soon found the rhythm as he followed the female duo.

Tess spotted Luke coming toward them. He didn't look bad on a horse and more than capable of handling Dusty. She also couldn't help but notice his broad shoulders and taut body. So the hotshot businessman was playing cowboy.

She pulled on the reins to slow Whiskey so the other horse and rider could catch up.

"Mommy, let's show Mr. Luke the ponies."

"The mustangs? They still around here?" Luke asked, pulling up beside them.

Tess nodded. "They are." It wouldn't hurt to show him what he was giving up. "Are you up for the ride?"

"Sure."

About fifteen minutes later, they reached the edge of the Rocking R property, a large section of land called Mustang Valley. There were three other ranches that bordered this area, too. She slowed her horse, and Luke rode up next to them.

"You did pretty well," she told him, and patted Dusty's neck. "And this guy sure needed the exercise."

Luke pulled off his hat and wiped his forehead on

his sleeve. "Yeah." He blew out a long breath. "But I think I'm a little out of shape, too."

No way. Then Tess chided herself for noticing. "Riding takes a lot more stamina than people think."

"I'm learning that the hard way."

"We have to be very quiet, Mr. Luke," Livy warned as her voice lowered. "So not to scare the ponies."

"Okay, I'll be quiet."

They continued over the rise down to the creek and Luke couldn't help but look around at this special oasis. Vague memories flashed back to him as they passed through the large grove of aged oak trees, shading their journey. When they reached the bottom he heard the sound of water. Soon he saw the creek that ran along the edge of the trees. Tess stopped and climbed down, then helped Livy. He followed, and together they led the horses to the water, allowing them to drink.

"You can drink, too," Tess said. "The water is very good."

Luke crouched down, cupped his hands into the stream and drank the cool refreshing water. When he glanced up he caught sight of a small buckskin mare. Her mane and tail were long and shaggy, but she was a beauty.

Whiskey sounded off with a loud whinny and began to dance around nervously. Tess immediately gripped the reins to hold on to the horse.

"Whoa, boy. Slow down." Luke went to her aid as the stallion reared up. He came behind Tess and grabbed hold of the reins closer to the horse's mouth and held on tight. The powerful animal fought, desperate to answer the call of nature.

"Whoa…fella," Tess crooned, her voice low and sultry.

Luke kept his mouth shut, knowing Whiskey was her horse. Finally the cries softened as did the fight. But it was Luke's turn to feel the excitement. Tess's body was pressed against his, and their arms still entwined. Her hat had fallen off, and his face against her ear.

Damn, she smelled good.

Suddenly Whiskey's whinny brought him back to the present and the situation.

The buckskin answered back, but she wasn't alone. Off in the distance was a gray stallion. Even from far away, Luke could easily see the battle scars on the animal's hide as he pranced around nervously. Then suddenly rearing up on his hind legs, he gave a piercing whinny that echoed through the silence valley. There was no doubt who was the alpha male in the herd. The little mare turned and ran off toward him. Whiskey gave one last neighing sound, then slowly calmed down.

"Sorry, fella," Luke said. "I think she's already taken." He glanced down at Tess. "You okay?"

She looked up at him with those deep-blue eyes. "I'm fine. Thanks for your help."

"Glad to be of service." He nodded to Whiskey. "I'd hate to see anything happen to this animal."

Taking full control of the reins, she stepped away. "That buckskin has…been around many times. But I've never seen Whiskey so…excitable before. She must be in season."

Luke couldn't help be grin. "By the attitude of the gray stallion I'd say so."

"Mommy. The pony is running away with the other ponies."

Whiskey had settled down enough, she tied him to the tree. "That's her family, sweetie."

"Oh… I thought she wanted to play with Whiskey and Dusty."

"Not today. Remember when we talked that there are times when horses mate…and make babies?"

The child nodded.

"Well, see that big gray stallion? That's the buckskin's mate. And if I let Whiskey go out there, they would have fought and one or both might have gotten hurt."

Livy seemed satisfied with the answer. She wandered down to the creek and walked along the edge.

"That was interesting."

She absently rubbed the stallion's neck. "I didn't expect to find a mare in season, or a stallion eager to fight."

Luke glanced around. He didn't remember too much about this place, but it was beautiful. A five-year-old did most of his ride around the corral. "I've heard stories about the alpha males in the herd. How sometimes they fight to the death."

"That's how it is in the wild. And I also think that's what makes this place so beautiful…so untouched…"

"And why you don't want to leave it," he finished.

"Can you look at this beautiful place and tell me that it should be destroyed. Homes constructed…roads built…and the traffic—"

He held up his hands. "Wait a minute, I never said

anything about developing this land." There wasn't anyone in the business that would give him the time of day, let alone invest any money in another project with his name on it.

She turned her back to her daughter and glare at him. "You're in real estate," she said, her voice low and controlled. "Isn't that why you're so eager to sell it?"

"I *was* in real estate," he said. "Besides, I can't do a damn thing right now."

"You haven't even tried to make a go of the Rocking R. I'd say that's giving up before you give it a chance."

"But I've never ranched before in my life."

She crossed her arms over her breasts. "So, you could hire people."

"Meaning you and your father?"

Something flashed in her eyes, then it was quickly masked. She shrugged. "It's just something to think about."

He studied her for a long time. He couldn't help but think back to another persuasive woman, one who ended up making a fool of him.

"All I'm thinking about right now is finding my brother…"

He paused when he saw two riders coming over the rise from the other side of the creek. They must be friends because Livy was waving at them.

Tess sighed. "Well, looks like it's time you met some of the neighbors."

"Who?"

"Well, Randells of course. Looks like your family has come to welcome you home."

Chapter 3

Hank Barrett had lived along the Mustang Valley all of his seventy-plus years. And he'd been a neighbor of the Randell family for that same amount of time. Three of the now-grown boys, Chance, Cade and Travis, were like sons to him. Hank had been lucky enough to raise them after the loss of their mother, and their daddy had been sent to prison.

He slowed his horse as he caught sight of the couple across the creek on Rocking R property. He recognized Tess Meyers right off, and her young daughter, Livy, playing by the creek. The tall, well-built man was a stranger, although nothing made him think she was in danger as the two stood by their horses.

A closer look had Hank seeing more. The familiar

way the man carried himself, the slight tilt of his hat. He smiled. So Sam's boy had returned to the valley.

Chance rode up beside Hank. "Who's that with Tess?"

Hank gave him a sideways glance. "Take a closer look."

Chance's eyes narrowed. "From a distance I'd say he looks a little like Travis. But he's in San Antonio to interview a new veterinarian."

"I'd say it's Sam's boy. Your cousin."

Chance smiled, and tiny lines fanned out around his eyes. That was about all that gave away his age of forty. The expert horseman was in top shape. He needed to be to keep up with his young family, his lovely wife, Joy, and two young daughters, Katie and Ellie, and his baby son, Jake.

"That's Luke? That skinny kid who looked like he'd cry if you said anything to him?"

Hank looked back at the couple across the creek. "I'd say that was because you and your brothers did your share of intimidating that youngster."

Chance rested his forearm on the saddle horn. "So you think he's going take over the ranch?"

Hank shrugged. "Not sure, but as head of the family, you should welcome him back."

Luke barely remembered any of his Randell cousins. Only that he was too young to hang around with them.

"Who's the old guy?"

Tess smiled. "Hank Barrett. And you better not let him hear you call him that."

Luke recognized the name. "Isn't he the one who took in my cousins?"

"And raised them. He's also your neighbor. The Circle B Ranch borders the other side, but now it's owned by Chance, Cade and Travis."

Tess smiled and waved as the two rode across the creek. "Hello, Hank. Chance."

"Tess. How are things going?"

She stood alongside a calmer Whiskey. "Can't complain."

Hank climbed down, along with the other rider, and removed his hat. Sparse patches of white hair covered his balding head. He had a friendly smile and clear hazel eyes.

"Hank, Chance, I'd like you to meet Luke Randell."

Hank was the first to respond as he offered a hand. "I knew you had to be Sam's boy." His smile disappeared. "Sorry to hear about your daddy's passing."

"Thanks." Luke shook the hand.

Next came Chance. "It's been a while, cuz."

Luke nodded. These people were strangers to him. "I've been gone a long time."

"Sorry about your father. Was he sick long?"

"I wouldn't know, I hadn't seen him in years."

"Sorry to hear that, too," Hank said, then glanced at Chance. "It's nice that you're back."

"Mr. Hank! Mr. Chance!"

They turned to see Livy come running toward them. The child couldn't get there fast enough.

"Well, if it isn't the prettiest five-year-old girl in the valley," Chance said.

Livy blushed. "What about Kate and Ellie?"

"Well, Katie is eight, and Ellie is almost six." He reached out and touched her nose. "So that leaves you."

The child turned shy and leaned into her mother. "Did you know that Whiskey almost runned off with that horse?"

"So that's the commotion we heard," Hank said, he turned to Tess. "Was it that little buckskin?"

"Yeah…that little tease," Tess said. "She finally went back to the herd. We had a devil of a time trying to calm Whiskey."

"Yeah, he bucked and whinnied but Mommy and Mr. Luke held on tight."

Chance walked over to the bay quarter horse and rubbed his neck as he looked him over. "Man, he's a good-looking son of a gun. How is he working out?"

"He's a great horse, Chance," Tess told him. "Easy to train." She paused. "Come by the ranch and see for yourself. And I wouldn't mind some advice."

He smiled at her. "I got plenty of that, not sure if it's any good though."

For some strange reason Luke was feeling as territorial as that alpha stallion. That was crazy.

"I wouldn't even have Whiskey if it wasn't for you… and your generosity," Tess told him.

Chance pushed his hat back. "Okay, then pay me back by winning the NCHA title."

"I'm working on it. But with Dad sick, my time been limited."

"If you need any help with the herd, let us know," Chance told her. He exchanged a glance with a nodding Hank.

"The boys have taken over running things," Hank said. "These days I mostly sit around. So I've got nothing but time. I could move the herd, or help with the roundup." The old guy looked at Luke. "Son, I bet you could help some, too."

"Sure," Luke agreed. "I wouldn't mind helping out."

Chance grinned. "So city living hasn't made you soft, Luke."

For some reason the teasing rubbed Luke the wrong way. "Maybe some, but then again, I'm a lot younger than you are."

Hank burst out laughing. "You definitely are a Randell." He nudged Chance. "Come on, old man, let's get you home to your rocker." He waved, then tossed over his shoulder. "We'll stop by when you're settled in, Luke."

"Mr. Chance, will you bring Katie and Ellie to come see me?" Livy called.

"Sure, they'd like that." The men climbed on their horses and rode back up the rise.

Livy looked at her mother. "Oh boy, I get to play with Katie and Ellie."

Tess needed to calm her daughter's excitement. "Yes, honey, but Chance and Joy are pretty busy. I'm not sure how soon they'll be able to stop by."

The girl's smile disappeared. "I never have anyone to play with."

Tess knew it was lonely growing up on a ranch, but she couldn't let her daughter feel sorry for herself. "Isn't that why you got to go to the animal shelter and get Jinx?"

"I guess," the child admitted.

"And in a few weeks, you'll be starting school. You'll make all kinds of friends."

She brightened. "Will Katie and Ellie ride the bus, too?"

"I'm sure they will. And there will be other five-year-olds going to kindergarten."

Livy glanced at Luke and smiled. "And I got to go riding today. Did you have fun, Mr. Luke?"

"Yes, I did," he told her. "Thank you for letting me ride your horse."

"He's not mine, he's Grandpa's." She shook her head. "He can't ride anymore."

Tess saw the curious look on Luke's face. "I'm sorry to hear that. I hope he gets better soon."

"So do I. I miss him."

Tess didn't want to do this now…if ever. "Livy, we should get back to the house."

"Yeah, I've gotta help Aunt Bernie with the…surprise for tomorrow. You're still coming for supper, aren't you?"

"I wouldn't miss it," Luke assured her.

The child beamed. "I'm glad. And you know what else? I'm glad you came to live here, and I can see you every day."

The next day, Luke paced the kitchen, his cell phone against his ear. He'd been on the phone with Hill Air Force Base in Utah for the last twenty minutes. After getting the runaround, he'd finally reached his brother's commanding officer.

"What do you mean that you can't tell me where my brother is? Don't you know?"

"That's affirmative, sir. We know the location of Captain Randell. Since it's a…sensitive mission, he can't be reached at this time. As soon as he returns we'll give him the information."

Luke sighed. "Please, tell him it's a legal matter and urgent that he contact me. You've got my number?"

"Yes, Mr. Randell, I have it. Good day." Then the line went dead.

Luke cursed. He was tired of getting nowhere with the military. Why couldn't they just tell him his half brother was on a mission…and when he'd be back? What was strange was Brady had been notified about inheriting the ranch. Didn't he care enough to make a simple phone call?

Luke went to the window. Well, they had to settle this somehow. Was this land valuable enough for a profitable sale? Would the other Randells be interested in buying the place? Surely they'd want to keep the Rocking R in the family.

He blew out a breath. He'd never had much family to rely on. Just his mother…and she'd had so much bitterness over the divorce, it had made him gun-shy. Sam hadn't cared much about fatherhood. Luke couldn't help but wonder if it was just being *his* father?

There was a soft knocking on the screen door. He turned to find Livy standing on the porch. She had on a bright-yellow print sundress, white sneakers and ruffled socks. Her hair was up in a ponytail tied with matching ribbon.

"Mommy said I can come and get you."

"Well, hello." He held open the door, allowing the child inside. Livy didn't have a father in her life. "Mommy has no husband, and I have no Daddy," she'd told him the day he arrived.

"My, don't you look pretty as a June bug. So you're my date for the evening."

She giggled. "I can't date. Mommy said I can't until I'm older. Aunt Bernie said I'll be ready when I don't want to play with my dollies anymore and I get breasts like Mommy."

Too much information, Luke thought. "How about we just pretend for tonight?"

"'Kay. Let's go."

Luke picked up the flowers and wine off the counter. "Here, you can carry these," he said as he handed the bouquet to the wide-eyed girl.

"Oh, they're pretty."

"You can share them with Bernice and your mother."

They headed for the foreman's cottage as Livy chattered away. It was amazing how much the child could talk. What he noticed the most was how happy she seemed with her simple childhood. What about the girl's father? Did he ever visit her…or her mother? Did Tess still love the man?

Luke glanced at the simple white house the Meyers lived in. It was small, but well kept with a neatly cut lawn and colorful flowers edging the porch. Several years back another bedroom and bath had been added onto the structure. Still, it had to be crowded for four people.

"I helped Aunt Bernie plant those flowers," Livy said as they reached the front door.

"And they sure are pretty."

Livy looked up at him with those big blue eyes. "But your flowers are pretty, too."

They stepped into the living room that looked lived

in, with a worn, comfortable sofa and chair. In front was a coffee table with magazines neatly stacked on the top. There was a small television in the corner.

"C'mon, Mr. Luke." She waved him on.

At the kitchen entry he was hit with mouthwatering aromas, and his stomach growled. A long table was set with simple stoneware, and steaming food was already arranged for the meal.

"Aunt Bernie, we're here." She rushed to her aunt. "Look, Mr. Luke got us flowers."

The older woman wearing an apron turned with a smile. "Well, land sakes it's been years since I've gotten flowers." She held up the multicolored bouquet. "Welcome, Luke, and thank you. They're lovely."

"Thank you for inviting me."

He suddenly felt awkward as he lifted the bottle of wine. "I also brought wine for dinner."

"Oh, my, this is a treat. I just wish I had something fancier than pot roast."

Luke grinned. "Your pot roast smells fantastic, and it's one of my favorite meals."

Bernice smiled. "Well then, let's open the wine." She went to the cabinet drawer, dug around and produced a corkscrew. "We'll celebrate your homecoming."

"Dad, please, you need to eat," Tess said as she handed him a fork.

"I'm not hungry," her father argued firmly. "Why are you always trying to get me to eat?"

Because you're losing too much weight, she screamed silently. "Because you need to keep up your strength."

"Why?" He turned those lost blue eyes on her. "I ain't goin' nowhere."

Tess blinked. Her father had been lucid most of the day. "You could go outside, or we could go for a walk." She knew that Luke had arrived, but she could skip dinner. "Want to go out to the barn? You could visit Whiskey and Dusty."

She saw a little spark in his eyes, then it quickly died. "No!" he said curtly. "What I want is to be left alone."

She tried to remember it was the illness that caused her father's erratic moods, but it still hurt her feelings.

"Okay, I'll leave you alone." Tess got up and walked to the door.

Outside in the hall, she paused, listening to the laughter coming from the kitchen. She brushed off imaginary wrinkles from her dark slacks and burgundy Western-cut blouse. With a toss of her hair off her shoulders, she put on a smile and walked in.

Her daughter was the first to see her. "Mom, look, Mr. Luke brought us flowers and wine. Aunt Bernice is drinking some, but I'm too young so I got grape juice."

"That's nice."

Luke stood. He looked so fresh in his new jeans and starched cream shirt. His inky black hair was combed back and his square jaw was clean shaven. He smiled at her and she couldn't seemed to catch her breath.

"Would you like a glass, Tess?"

She started to turn him down, then decided why not? Shouldn't she enjoy the evening, too? "That would be nice."

He filled one of her mother's crystal goblets and handed it to her. "I hope you like it."

"I'm sure I will." Those silver eyes met hers as she took a sip. Her heart leaped as the fruity liquid slid down her throat. "Very nice," she managed, and began to relax.

"Don't let it go to your head, Mommy."

They all burst into laughter.

"Well, Aunt Bernie said that she didn't want it to go to her head."

Tess looked at Luke and felt her body warm. The wine wasn't her problem…. "I'll try not to, honey," she told her daughter.

"Since we're all here, why don't we sit down to supper," her aunt suggested.

Luke helped Livy to her seat. "I'm sorry to hear that Mr. Meyers isn't well enough to join us."

Tess glanced at Bernice. "No, he's not feeling well this evening."

"Grandpa has been sick a long time."

Bernice set the rolls on the table. "Livy, will you say the blessing tonight?"

She held out her hand. "Mr. Luke, you got to hold my hand and Mommy's hand. So God will know we're all praying."

"Okay," he said.

Tess felt a strange tingle go up her arm as Luke grasped her hand. She blamed it on the wine.

"Close your eyes," Livy coaxed. "Lord, please bless our food you gave us, and thank you for taking care of Grandpa and bringing Mr. Luke here. Amen."

Everyone else said, "Amen." Then the food started around the table. Tess watched as Luke helped serve Livy. The girl thrived on the male attention. Maybe more so since her grandfather hadn't been around.

Tess took another sip of wine. The last thing she wanted was her daughter getting attached to a man who wasn't going to stay around. Tess couldn't, either. She'd survived one man leaving…never again.

More laughter broke out, and she shook away her thoughts. She took the bowl of potatoes and dished up a large helping along with meat and gravy.

"Bernice, this is the best pot roast I've ever eaten," Luke told her.

Her aunt blushed. "Oh, I bet you tell all the ladies that."

Luke arched an eyebrow. "Not about their pot roast, I don't." He got up and retrieved the bottle off the counter and added to their glasses.

Bernice laughed. "You're a sweet-talkin' rascal, Luke Randell."

Tess couldn't believe her aunt's behavior. She was actually flirting with the man. She glanced at Livy. In her little-girl way, her daughter was doing the same.

Luke lifted his glass. "I'd like to make a toast. To three of the loveliest ladies I've ever had the pleasure of dining with."

Livy climbed onto her knees and clinked her glass with Luke, Bernice and then to her. "Mommy, you do it, too."

Tess turned to the handsome man to find him watching her as she touched her glass with the other three.

Accidentally her fingers brushed Luke's and she felt the strangest sensation. Warmth went through her and suddenly her stomach did a flip. It's the wine, she told herself as she quickly went back to her meal. She had no business having any feelings whatsoever for this man.

A few minutes later Livy spoke up. "Aunt Bernie is it time yet?" she asked. "I ate all my food."

"Okay, it's time." The two got up from the table and went to the covered cake pedestal on the counter. Bernice removed the lid to reveal a chocolate masterpiece. With Livy's assistance, her aunt carried it to the table.

"Look, Mr. Luke, it's chocolate, your favorite. Aunt Bernie and me baked it for you."

"It sure is. And the prettiest cake I've ever seen. And I can't wait to taste it."

Livy beamed, and Tess couldn't help but feel sad that she'd denied her daughter a father. Even if it wasn't her fault that the man she'd thought she loved didn't love her or his child.

Tess quickly shook away the memories. This evening was too nice to think about anything bad. "I can't wait to taste it, too."

"Mommy, did you know that chocolate was Mr. Luke's very favorite?"

"No, I didn't," Tess said. "Aren't you a lucky girl, because isn't chocolate your favorite, too."

The child nodded at Luke. She was obviously enamored by the good-looking Randell. So was her mother, but at least Tess knew enough to keep her distance.

Bernice cut everyone a piece and handed them out. She picked up another plate.

Luke took a bite. "This is wonderful."

Livy put a forkful in her mouth. "Mmmmmm. It's good."

Luke grinned at her, then turned and winked at Tess. "You should try some," he urged.

She managed to take a bite. The rich flavor melted in her mouth. She had to fight back a groan. It was a sad state of affairs when a grown woman who was nearly thirty got her pleasure from eating a piece of cake.

She stole a glance at Luke. She bet he knew how to give a woman pleasure. She gasped, realizing the dangerous direction of her thoughts.

Thirty minutes later, dressed in pajamas, Livy was snuggled in her single bed covered with a Little Kitty comforter. The matching lamp sent off a soft glow, just enough to read some of her daughter's favorite story.

Already the child's eyes were drooping. "I'm too tired for a story, Mommy." She fought a yawn. "I like Mr. Luke."

"I'm glad," Tess said, knowing she hated to see her daughter get attached to a near stranger.

"I'm glad he came to live here."

Tess wouldn't go that far. Luke Randell's arrival would change their life, but she couldn't explain that to a five-year-old. "You've had a busy day. It's time for sleep."

"I can't yet. I forgot to say good-night to Mr. Luke."

Tess recognized her daughter's familiar pout. "Mr. Luke has probably already gone home, sweetie."

Livy blinded at tears. "No, he didn't, he's helping Aunt Bernie do the dishes. Please…"

Tess knew she shouldn't let her daughter get away with having her way, but it was late. "Okay, I'll see if he's here." She got up and went out to the kitchen. That was where she found Luke and Bernice standing by the sink, laughing.

She realized she was a little jealous of their relaxed and easy banter. It was something she was never good at…especially with men.

Tess started to back away when Luke looked at her. His smile faded. "Is Livy asleep already?"

"She's in bed, but if you don't mind, she wants to say good-night."

He smiled. "Of course not." He set the towel on the counter. "I'll be right back, Bernice. So don't try to put away that heavy platter."

He walked toward her and Tess felt a warming sensation rush through her. Please…let it be the wine. She turned and he followed her down the narrow hall.

Luke stopped at the partly open door. He gave a quick glance at Tess. He could see how protective she was of her young daughter. He didn't blame her.

"She's nearly asleep."

"I won't stay long," he assured her and walked into the room. He went straight to the small bed. At first he thought the child was asleep, but her eyes opened.

"Oh, Mr. Luke, you came."

He eased down to the side of the bed. "I couldn't leave without saying good-night to you, shortcake."

She smiled. "I like it that you call me that name."

"Okay, then I'll keep calling you that. Shortcake." He took her hand. "Now, I think I better leave before your mother chases me out. Good-night, Livy. Thanks for inviting me." He couldn't say why he leaned down and placed a kiss on her cheek.

"'Night, Mr. Luke." What he didn't expect was that the little girl would kiss him back and wrap those tiny arms around his neck. His chest tightened with emotion. How had she managed to sneak in and steal a piece of his heart in just a few short days?

He stood and left the room to find Tess waiting for him. "She's a special little girl."

"I know," Tess said. "I'm protective of her, too."

Luke didn't blame her for that. "Is that because of her father?"

Tess straightened. "He's never been a part of her life. That's fine with me. It's just been me and her… and my dad."

"My mother raised me alone, too. I believe everyone knows of my father's affair." Hell, why was he bringing this up now?

"There are a lot of single mothers out there," Tess said.

Luke knew he was crazy for letting himself be drawn to this woman. Yet, nothing he did seemed to stop it. He took a step closer to her. "The guy must have been out of his mind to let you go."

He heard her quick intake of breath as her blue eyes widened in surprise. But before she could speak, Bernice appeared from the other end of the hall.

"Ray's not in his room," she announced.

Tess moved away from Luke, trying to remain calm. "It's okay. He probably just went outside."

Bernice nodded. "His window was open. He must have climbed out."

Luke came up behind her. "Is there a problem with him going out?"

Tess sighed, trying desperately to clear her head. "Dad can't be left alone. He has the early stages of Alzheimer's disease."

Chapter 4

Tess's heart pounded in her chest as she took off out the door and ran around the house and yard. With no sign of her dad, she widened the search area. She heard her name called out, but refused to stop.

Dad was out there…alone, and she had to find him. Only the porch light and gathering clouds overhead helped illuminate the familiar path to the barn. The wind had picked up and it smelled like rain.

Not good. She was trembling when she reached the barn. She struggled with the heavy door when suddenly Luke's steady hands took over the job.

"Tess…we'll find him," Luke assured her. For some strange reason his words reassured her. "I'm going to help you."

"It's okay, he's probably in the barn with Dusty," she lied. Anyway, her dad was her responsibility.

"Has he wandered off before?"

She shook her head, and started the trek down the aisle. An overhead light guided the way. She hated to share her private life with a virtual stranger.

"He had hip surgery about a year ago and was laid up. That's when we discovered the other problem." The horses stirred, and she knew something had disturbed them.

"Dad!" Tess called as she reached Dusty's empty stall and another wave of fear hit her. She swung around and hurried out into the corral. A security light came on, but the area was deserted, too, and the gate was open.

Tess cupped her hands around her mouth. "Dad!" she yelled into the windy blackness. She ran into the field, trying to control her panic, but how could she when her dad was out there all alone. He could fall in a ravine or…

Luke caught up and grabbed her arm. "Tess, wait."

She tried to break his strong hold. "I've got to find him."

"You can't, it's black as pitch out there."

"And my dad is out there somewhere."

Luke gripped her other arm and shook her slightly. He had to calm her down. "I know he is. But you can't go running off."

"I know the land."

"And when you find him you'll probably need help to bring him back. Besides, he's on horseback." It was too dark to see her fear, but he felt her tremble. "Do you have any idea where he could have ridden off to? A favorite place?" He was frustrated he couldn't do more. "Is it possible your dad saddled a horse?"

She shook her head. "Dad's riding Dusty bareback. The bridle was missing from outside his stall. That's all he needs since those two have been partnered for twenty years."

"That's good. Maybe Dusty will bring him back," he said, trying to encourage her.

"I'm more concerned about Dad falling off the horse. He isn't real strong these days."

"Okay, then we should call for help."

"Please, don't call the sheriff, yet. I'm going to look for him."

He nodded at her stubbornness. "Okay. I'm going with you."

"No. You don't know your way around the ranch."

He followed her back to the barn. "Take it or leave it, Tess, because I'm not letting you go by yourself. If Ray did fall off Dusty and is hurt, you can't manage him by yourself."

Tess blinked at threatening tears. This was all her fault. She should have watched him closer. "Okay, but you better keep up."

"I will. He followed her into the tack room. She assigned him a saddle for Lady. Luke took it from the stand and went to the mare's stall. When they finished, Bernice and Livy came in with rain ponchos and flashlights, plus a pair of jeans and riding boots for Tess. Hats for both of them.

Bernice looked worried. "I saw you in the corral

alone so I called Hank Barrett to help. It was lucky that Chance, Cade and Travis were there for supper."

Tess sighed in frustration. She didn't usually ask for help, but this was her father. "Where are they going to meet us?"

"Hank said they'd start from the Mustang Valley and spread out until they reached you." She also handed her niece the cell phone. "I programmed in Chance's number, and he has yours. They'll call if—when they see anything." Aunt Bernice hugged her. "It's going to be all right. And you've got Luke to help you."

"Thanks, Bernice." She went back to the tack room to change.

Livy tugged on Luke's hand. "Mr. Luke. Will you bring my grandpa back?"

Luke crouched down to be eye level with Livy. He definitely wasn't the hero type. Yet, seeing the child's pleading look, he knew he'd give it everything he had. "I'll do my best."

"Here's some licorice." She pulled out a small bag. "It's Grandpa's favorite."

"I'm sure he'll be happy to get this." He stuffed the sack into his shirt pocket and stood, then grabbed Lady's reins and headed outside.

Tess came out of the tack room, said her goodbyes, then together they walked the horses out and mounted them.

"Your mare will stay close to me," Tess told him and glanced up at the sky. "Let's hope the rain holds off for a while." She gave Luke her cell number in case they got separated.

They exchanged a long look. Luke's chest tightened, feeling protective toward her...more than he had a right to. Finally she glanced away and they went through the gate.

"We're going to find him, Tess," he recited the mantra. "We'll find him."

She nodded as they rode through the trees. "Dad's going to hate us coming to look for him. He's very proud."

Luke heard the tears in her voice, he also heard the love in her words. "He sounds like quite a man. I can't wait to meet him."

Luke prayed he'd get the chance.

About twenty minutes later they met up with Hank about a mile from the creek. A light drizzle had begun and they'd put on their rain ponchos.

"Hi, Hank."

"Tess. Luke." He sighed. "I hate to say it, but we haven't seen any sign of Ray." He raised his hand. "The boys are still sweeping the ridge on both sides."

"We came straight here," Tess told him. "I've whistled for Dusty several times, but nothing." She wiped the back of her wrist over her wet face. "I can't believe Dad could have gone this far. He was only left alone while we were eating supper."

"You can't watch him every minute, Tess," Hank said, leaving any other comments about Ray Meyers' rapidly progressing illness unsaid.

Suddenly a rider came over the rise leading a horse. "It's Dusty," she said hopefully.

It was Travis Randell who arrived with the riderless gelding. "I found Ray's horse, but there's no sign of your dad. Sorry. Cade is still looking, and Chance is out there, too."

He looked at Luke. "I take it you're Luke?" He held out his hand. "Hi, I'm Travis."

Luke shook his hand. "Nice to meet you. Wish it was under better circumstances."

Travis nodded. "We'll stay out here as long as it takes."

"Where did you find Dusty?" Tess asked.

"That strip of north pasture bordering Chance's ranch. It's about a mile from here."

Luke turned to Tess. "We should ride out there," he suggested.

"Yeah, I want to go." She took Dusty's reins, but before she could leave, Hank reached over to stop her departure.

"The weather is only going to get worse, Tess," he told her. "I think we better call in the sheriff."

Tess tried not to think about the danger, but she had to. "Okay, but I'm going to check the old shack up in the foothills. If he isn't there, I'll call the sheriff myself."

"Are you talking about Jake Randell's old shack? I didn't know the place was still standing." Hank looked at Travis. "Did you or your brothers come across a shack?"

"No, we didn't see anything."

Luke sat back in his saddle feeling useless. Suddenly he remembered a small cabin along a little creek. It was his grandfather's place. "I think my dad took me there once."

"I know exactly where it is," Tess said as Whiskey danced anxiously. "We'll call you when we get there."

Hank nodded. "We just want this to be a happy ending. Let us know if you need more help."

Luke looked at Travis. "Thank you both, and thank your brothers for us."

"Not a problem." The young Randell smiled. "It's a pretty tight community here. Ray and Tess would do the same for us. Good luck."

Tess rode off leading Dusty trailing behind. Luke right behind her. The rain had grown heavier, but it didn't slow their pace. Luke was glad he'd been able to keep up. He glanced at Tess. He knew she was stressed, but she hadn't lost her composure. She was the most self-sufficient woman he'd ever met. Not to mention stubborn, headstrong…graceful…beautiful. Why would she lead him to believe that Ray only had a temporary illness?

Was she hoping to renew the ranch lease, and she thought he'd discriminate against her because she was woman? Man or woman, he wasn't planning to renew the Meyerses' lease.

With that decision, he'd be throwing out two women, a small child and a sick father. Why not? Hadn't he done it with investment properties in Dallas? He'd gotten into the real estate business to make money, not to be charitable.

He tried to tell himself that he needed to make a living. When had he gotten so greedy? Now there was nothing but this ranch.

It was funny that the last place he'd ever wanted to

return to was the only home he had left. He looked at the woman ahead of him. Technically it was Tess's home more than his. And right now she had a lot more to lose.

Tess slowed her horse as they approached a group of trees. Luke wiped his eyes and saw a small structure. He took out the flashlight to guide them the rest of the way. They reached the shack and climbed down, then tied the horses to the old hitching post under a sagging lean-to. It was good enough to keep them out of the weather.

Luke took the one step on the landing and pushed open the stubborn door. He shone the flashlight inside to find an old table and chairs placed by a potbelly stove. He moved the light along the wall and that was where he saw the huddled form on the bunk. An old man held up his hand against the glare from the light. "Shut that damn thing off."

"Dad!" Tess cried running to him, stripping off her poncho as she reached the bunk.

Luke set the flashlight on the table, giving Tess more illumination to check her father's condition.

Ray Meyers was a slight man with thinning, white hair plastered to his head. His face was lined, no doubt by hard work…and life.

"Dad, are you all right?"

The shivering man refused to look at her. "I can't find my way back."

"Dad, it's me, Tess." Her gaze scanned over him, making sure he wasn't hurt. "You're safe now, and I'm going to take you home."

"Home?" His eyes searched her face, then suddenly

he blinked and gripped her hand. "I can't go back there. Elizabeth is gone."

Luke looked at Tess to see her tears as she stroked her father's hand. "Oh, Dad, Mom's been gone for a long time."

The old man's eyes widened in recognition. "Tess... Oh, Tess... She got sick." Suddenly he shook his head and began to sob. "I couldn't help her. I miss her."

"I know, Dad. I miss her, too." Tess climbed up on the bed and wrapped her arms around him.

Emotion clogged Luke's throat. He moved back, then stepped outside to give them some privacy. He busied himself checking the animals, then he untied the bed rolls and brought them into the cabin. Inside he checked to be sure the blankets were dry and handed one to Tess.

Taking the extra flashlight, he went back outside and found pieces of wood stacked under the lean-to. Sorting through the bundle, he found some wood chips dry enough to burn.

On his return trip, he found Tess cradling her sleeping father. "There are matches in my saddle bag," she said softly. "I need to call Hank and Bernice."

"I can do that for you," he said as he took her cell phone. He went back outside and made the call. He thanked Hank again and assured him they could get Ray back to the house without help. Could they? Would the man be lucid enough for the ride back? He then talked with Bernice and let her know the situation.

Carrying an armful of wood inside, he placed it in the ancient stove, then added some wadded-up newspaper from the floor. There was no doubt that someone had been using the cabin recently. He lit a match and tossed it into the stove, and the paper caught fire instantly. After it got going, he closed the grated cast iron door and pulled off his plastic poncho. The rain had caused the temperature to drop ten to fifteen degrees.

Luke also lit the kerosene lantern on the table and glanced across the room to find Tess watching him. Seeing her sadness caused his chest to tighten. He wanted to go to her, take her in his arms. "This should help take the chill off," he told her. The fire from the stove and lantern had helped illuminate the tiny cabin.

He doubted the warmth he felt was from the wood burning. Suddenly the rain grew heavy, pounding rhythmically against the tin roof, breaking the spell between them.

He glanced overhead. "Looks like we're not going anywhere for a while."

"Then it's good Dad's asleep." She lifted Ray's head and slid away from him, gently laying him down on the dirty mattress. The old man curled up in a fetal position and began to snore softly.

Tess looked at Luke, but avoided his eyes. "I know it's not exactly sanitary, but…he needs to rest. And he's warm." She went to the door and squeezed through the small opening to the outside.

Luke was at a loss for what else to do for her. He went to the door and hesitated…until he heard her quiet sobs. He stepped out under the overhang.

"Tess…" He spoke her name and touched her shoulder.

She turned around, her head lowered, trying to hide her weakness. "It's okay, let it go."

She shook her head and frantically swiped at her tears. "I can't. He…needs me. My family…needs me."

Luke had no idea what that was like. He'd never had much family. He'd never gotten so involved with anyone so they would have to depend on him. This was different… Tess was different. He wanted to be there for her.

He knew she was too proud to ask for help. "What about you, Tess? What do you need?"

She finally raised her head. In the shadowed darkness, he could see her tear-stained cheeks, her sadness. Her eyes revealed so much: her need…her desire. It also made him realize how long he'd been alone.

"I can't need anything," she breathed.

"Then let me offer it," he told her. "Let me help you, Tess."

He took a step closer and drew her against him. He closed his eyes when her luscious body pressed into his. She resisted at first, but then her arms slipped around his waist and she buried her face in his shirt. Then she let go and cried her heart out.

He blinked his own tears away in the dark and rain. She was losing her father…piece by piece. The man who'd raised her by himself. Maybe Luke was feeling his own pain, too, about the loss of his own parent.

Her crying slowed, then stopped as she looked up at him. The darkness hid her vulnerability, but not the intimacy created between them.

"I'm sorry," she whispered. "I guess I lost it."

He cupped her cheek. "It's okay, Tess. I've got you." Unable to stop what was happening, he lowered his head…and his mouth caressed her lips. Her soft gasp drew him back for more. His mouth touched hers again…and again, until she joined in. She raised up and wrapped her arms around his neck, parting her lips so he could delve inside to taste her sweetness.

He groaned and widened his stance, pulling her closer. She made him hungry…so hungry. He sipped from her, unable to think about anything else but her taste, her touch…her body pressed against his. It would be so easy to lose himself in her.

Finally she broke off the kiss and they were both breathing hard.

Tess finally stepped back. "I've got to check on Dad." She rushed inside.

Luke took another calming breath and released it, hoping the cool air would help him. It didn't. He suddenly realized that not much could help him when it came to Tess Meyers.

Two hours later the rain had lessened some, but there was no way to bring a vehicle into the area. So they were stuck here until the rain stopped. Probably dawn.

Tess sat on the opposite end of the bed covered with the other blanket. Dad was still sleeping soundly. There was no chance for her, not after her foolishness. How could she let Luke kiss her? She couldn't blame him alone; she'd participated in that kiss, too. What she needed to concentrate on was her future, not start something with the new ranch owner.

She stole a glance across the room at Luke who was seated on the floor by the stove. His head was tilted back against the roughly paneled wall. His eyes were closed, but she doubted he was sleeping, either.

"You should try and get some sleep," Luke said, his voice sound so intimate in the small quarters.

"I can't… I worried about Dad."

"I think it's more than that." There was a long pause. "It's okay, Tess," Luke began. "We're consenting adults and unattached. There's no sin in sharing a kiss."

"It still shouldn't have happened." She paused. "I don't want you to think that it will lead anywhere."

He hesitated, then said, "You mean like you sneaking off in the dead of night to my house…and me having my way with you?"

She heard the amusement in his voice. "In your dreams, Randell."

Luke wasn't smiling. She'd been in his thoughts and daydreams since he'd first found her in his bedroom. Tess had ignited something in him he didn't want to analyze. And the kiss they'd shared told him he should definitely back away…far away. "Don't worry, Tess, it was only a kiss," he lied, knowing he'd intended to offer comfort but it had turned out to be much more.

"Just so you know, all I want is a business relationship."

He snorted as he thought back to his past experiences. He might be cynical, but people take advantage if they have the chance. "Good. That should get us through the next few months."

Tess needed to concentrate on her dad, not on the man across the room who'd awakened feelings in her, feelings she thought had died when Ben had walked away from her and his child. Worse, she'd let Luke distract her from her responsibilities. She couldn't let that happen again.

Her dad stirred on the bunk and sat up.

"Dad, are you okay?" She reached for him, but he pushed her hand away.

"I'm just dandy." He threw the blanket off and scooted off the bunk. "I just need to go outside a minute."

Tess followed him. "I'll help you."

"No, I'm not an invalid yet, girl. And I don't need any help to answer the call of nature."

Before Tess could answer, Luke climbed to his feet. "You know, I need to take that trip, too. You mind if I go with you?"

Ray looked up. "Who the hell are you?"

"Luke Randell. I arrived at the ranch a few days ago."

Her father studied him. "You Sam's boy?"

A smile appeared. "Yes, I am. It's nice to meet you, sir." Luke held out his hand to shake her father's hand and helped him to his feet. She was grateful for Luke's kindness. Her father hated being babied by the women of the family.

"You resemble your daddy. There's plenty of Randells around these parts."

Luke nodded. "I think the rain has let up so we shouldn't get too wet."

Her father looked old and stooped next to the tall well-built younger man. He also had a slight limp from his hip surgery last year as they made their way to the door.

After they answered the call of nature, Luke helped Ray back onto the porch. He hadn't had any experience with Alzheimer's patients, but as far as he could tell, for the moment anyway, Ray Meyers's mind was clear.

The older man hesitated at the door and glanced toward the horses. "Mr. Randell, could you do me a favor?"

"Only if you call me Luke."

Ray nodded. "Could you tell me how I got out here?"

"It seems you wanted to go for a ride on Dusty." Luke turned to the older man. "Do you remember anything?"

He looked frustrated. "Just bits and pieces. Did I hurt Dusty?" At the sound of his friend speaking his name, the horse bobbed his head and neighed.

Luke smiled. "Dusty's fine. We were worried you might have taken a fall, though."

"I feel all right…but I sure as hell don't remember getting here." He wiped his hand over his face. "Oh, man, I probably scared my girl half to death."

"The main thing is that you're safe. That's all she cares about."

"I'm worthless like this. I can't even stay on a horse."

"I know Tess doesn't think of you like that. I'd say you're a lucky man to have three females who love you so much."

"I should be taking care of them, not the other way around. Maybe she should just put me in a nursing home."

"That's something you need to talk over with your family. Right now, I think we better get you back home."

Just then Tess came out of the cabin. "Luke's right. I want us to get home. You can ride Whiskey, since he has a saddle. I'll take Dusty."

Luke watched Ray start to argue, but then he nodded. "I wouldn't mind sleeping in my own bed."

They put out the fire and closed up the line shack and finally were on their way. The rain had stopped and the clouds moved out, giving them a moonlit sky and a clearer path back to the ranch. They still moved slowly.

Once they pulled up in front of the small house, Luke helped Ray off his horse, tied them to the post, then walked up to the porch. Bernice met them at the door.

"Well, it's about time you got home," she said. "You worried us all to death."

Ray frowned. "See what I have to put up with?"

"I'd say you've got it pretty good."

They continued down the hall and into the bedroom. Luke started to leave when little Livy stepped out of her room. She was wearing a nightgown and holding a raggedy stuffed animal.

"Hi, shortcake." He bent down. "Shouldn't you be asleep?"

She nodded. "I want to thank you for bringing Grandpa home." She threw her arms around his neck and hugged him tight, then she placed a kiss on his cheek. "'Night, Mr. Luke." She turned and disappeared into her room.

Before Luke could recover Bernice appeared. "Thank you, Luke." She hugged and kissed him, too, then went back into Ray's bedroom.

He didn't quite know how to handle this. Then Tess appeared. Those blue eyes bore into his and he began to ache. He knew the feelings she could create in him...

if he let her. "I guess you're next," he teased lightly, but wanted that kiss and hug more than he could admit.

She strolled past him. "You'll get a thank you from me," she said. "Anything else— Like I said earlier in your dreams, Randell, in your dreams."

Chapter 5

Smiling, Luke followed Tess out of the house. As she started to lead the horses to the barn, he took Lady's reins from her.

"What are you doing?" she asked.

"It's called helping out."

"You don't have to, I can do it."

"I know. You're superwoman." Leading the horses, they walked side by side toward the barn. "It's okay, Tess, if someone helps you."

"It's the middle of the night, and you could be in bed."

He didn't need her using that terminology. "So I get there a little later. I can always sleep in." He had nowhere to go…no job. "You, on the other hand, will have to be up in a few hours to feed the stock."

Tess didn't respond as he slid open the barn door and they escorted the horses to their stalls. She removed Whiskey's saddle and wiped him down, then went to Dusty. She glanced over to see Luke following her actions with Lady. Once finished, they carried the saddles into the tack room.

Tess didn't know how to handle this. Luke Randell was nothing like she'd had expected. She'd figured he would arrive here, live in the big ranch house and keep to himself while he decided what to do with the place. She never expected the man to get involved with her... problems...her life.

With the tack put away and the horses settled, they headed out of the barn to the house. It was where Tess would feel safe. After tonight, she felt so exposed to this man. In just the few days that Luke had been at the Rocking R, he'd learned far too much about her—about her dreams...and now her family secrets. He hadn't flinched, even when he learned about her father's illness.

Then he had to go and kiss her. Big mistake on her part. What she needed was to keep her concentration on her family and her horse breeding business. Not on another man who would eventually walk out of her life.

"You know, there are programs out there that might help your dad," Luke said.

"Dad has been resistant about doing anything but sitting in his room. Until tonight."

"Maybe if he spent more time outside doing things."

She stopped at the porch. "Look, Luke, I'll do about anything to help my father, but I also have to work with the horses. If he's outside there's a lot that can happen to him. He could get hurt." She hated people coming around and telling her how to handle the illness. "As you can see, I did a lousy job tonight."

When she turned away, he reached for her. "I wasn't judging you, Tess. I can't imagine how you do all you do on your own as it is. I just want you to know there's help out there.

She tensed. "I'm not putting him in a nursing home."

He raised a calming hand. "I'm not suggesting that. But there are other options. There are exercise programs and medications that might help him."

She sighed and closed her eyes. She was tired. "I plan to talk to his doctor tomorrow when I take him in."

Luke smiled and she felt a warm tingle rush through her. "Good. Now if you leave instructions on feeding the horses, I can handle that for you."

It would be so easy to lean on him. "That's okay, I can do it."

"I know you can, but that doesn't mean I can't help. 'Night, Tess."

Tess watched him walk off the porch and head toward the big house. She didn't go inside until the shadowy figure disappeared, fighting the urge to call him back. She wasn't used to depending on anyone but herself and her family. And never a man she could fall hard for...that was far too dangerous.

At dawn Luke left his house and headed for the barn. Once inside he checked on the horses. All three were valuable animals and seemed to have fasred well during the rain-soaked night.

"You're glad to be back in your dry stall, huh, fella?" He patted Whiskey and was happy the stallion seemed comfortable around him. They also expected him to fill their feed buckets.

"Sorry, you have to wait for the boss lady."

At that moment the door opened and Tess strolled in. Dressed in jeans and a navy-blue Henley shirt, she looked fresh from the shower with her blond hair pulled back into a ponytail. She had just enough of a sleepy-eyed look to stir his body and make him wish for another activity this morning.

If she was surprised to see him there, she didn't show it. "If you're going to help, then you better come with me."

Luke followed her as she went to the plastic bins where she kept the grain. She instructed him on the amount of feed for each of the horses. Then she showed him a wheelbarrow and a pitchfork and sent him off to start mucking out a stall. He caught her surprise as he went off to do the job. About an hour later they'd finished all the chores and were headed back to the house.

Luke started toward his house when Tess called to him. "Bernice would shoot me if I didn't ask you in for breakfast."

He grinned, feeling his strained muscles and his hunger. "We can't have that, can we?" He hurried to catch up with her, and they headed through the back door.

Bernice beamed at him. "Good morning, Luke."

"It is a good morning, Bernice." He pulled off his

hat and hung it on the hook as did Tess. He went to the sink and washed his hands. "I hope you don't mind me coming by."

"The way you helped out last night, I wouldn't mind you coming by every day."

Luke dried his hands on a towel and took a seat at the table. "I wouldn't want to wear out my welcome." He smiled, glancing at a stoic Tess. "But you might be able to persuade me with some of your cooking."

"You charming devil." She placed a stack of pancakes in front of him. "I'm surprised some woman hasn't snapped you up."

"Maybe I haven't found the right woman." He took a bite and groaned. "Oh, my, I think I have. Bernice, you have to marry me."

Laughing, Bernice waved a dismissive hand. "Oh, yeah, you're definitely a charmer, just like all those other Randell boys."

An hour later, with his stomach full, Luke walked back to his house. Funny, for a man who'd pretty much been a loner most of his life, he found he didn't want to leave the Meyerses' kitchen. Even Livy and her grandfather had joined in the meal.

He walked through the back door and was hit with silence. He'd noticed it before, but more so now after spending time with a family. This house was big…and empty.

All these years his mother had insisted that no one live in her house. He understood some of Kathleen Randell's resentment over her husband's affair, but why would she want to hang on to a place that reminded her of so much unhappiness?

It also made him realize how empty his life was. He'd lost everything, and there weren't many people who cared. His thoughts turned to Gina. She was supposed to have loved him. Yet she bailed out…when her father pulled out of the deal. She took off six months ago, and he realized he didn't even miss her. It made him wonder if he'd ever loved her.

He walked down the hall through the formal dining room with the dark wainscoting and paneling and oversize furniture. At the stairs, he went up to the second floor and the master bedroom where he'd been sleeping since he returned home. There was a four-poster bed and dresser, but there weren't any personal things left in the room that had once been his parents. He hadn't checked the drawers, knowing his mother's will stated that all the contents of this house were his. Since her death, three years ago, Luke had never wanted to come back here. Now he hadn't had any choice.

He tugged his shirt out of his jeans, knowing after the workout in the barn, a shower would be a good idea. He pulled out clean clothes from his suitcase in the corner and headed for the bathroom.

Ten minutes later he returned to the bedroom. He had other things to do, but nothing would take his mind off Tess and her dad. He wanted to go with her, but he knew she wouldn't ask for help. He told himself that he was just trying to help out a nice family. That wasn't entirely true. There were so many reasons why he should keep away from her.

Their relationship was supposed to be business only. He needed to remember the woman who had helped destroy him. Good old Gina.

"You need to focus on rebuilding your career...your credibility," he reminded himself. Besides, he was nearly broke. He owned half a ranch, but couldn't locate the brother he'd never met. Not exactly a perfect life.

He walked to the bank of windows that overlooked the barn and corral. The worst part was he was beginning to like it here. And he couldn't let that happen. He didn't do home and family very well.

His attention was drawn to a late-model truck coming through the gate. It stopped by the barn, and a tall man climbed out. He smiled to himself. Looked like one of the Randells had come for a visit.

He headed downstairs, grabbed a hat off the hook and met Chance on the back porch, surprised to find the big cowboy was holding the hand of a little girl. Pretty and petite, she was dressed in blue jean shorts and a white shirt with ruffles. Her long blond hair was pulled back with clips.

"Hey, how are you doing this morning?" his cousin asked.

"I'm fine."

Chance nodded. "Luke, this is my six-year-old daughter, Ellie. Ellie, this is our cousin Luke."

The cute child smiled at him, but stayed close to her father. "Hi." She looked up at her dad. "Can I go play with Livy now?"

"She's a little shy with strangers," his cousin told

him as they both watched until the child reached the cottage and went inside.

"Tess isn't here," Luke announced. "She took Ray to the doctor this morning."

"I know. I talked to her earlier."

Luke frowned. Had Tess called him for help?

Chance sighed and pushed his hat back, revealing his brown hair. "It's a rough situation all around. I wanted Tess to know that we'll help her out whenever she needs us."

Luke figured Chance meant the entire Randell family. "I'll pass on the word to her."

Chance smiled. "I'll be here to tell her myself, since I'm going to work Whiskey this morning."

Luke couldn't even speak as Chance took off toward the barn, then stopped at looked back at him. "If you want, you're welcome to come along." His cousin gave him the once-over. "Last night you handled yourself pretty good on a horse."

Luke's competitiveness had him hurrying after his cousin. "I hadn't ridden since I left here."

"Some things are bred in you. Like I said, you did real well." They paused at the door as Chance said, "You know, all the wives are asking about you."

"Really. What are they asking?"

Chance shook his head. "I'll let them ask you the questions," he said. "I'm just to pass on an invitation to a barbecue to you and of course, the Meyers family, too."

"When?"

"Tonight." Chance grinned. "You might as well get

it over with. The women in this family can be relent-
less when they want something."

"What about Ray?" Luke walked through the barn
door. "I'm not sure he could handle the big crowd."

"Then we'll bring the get-together here."

Luke blinked.

"Don't worry. We'll bring everything we need, including a barbecue grill. So come on, you can ride
Dusty. He's a pro at cutting."

Luke was swept along but had a feeling Chance had
it planned that way. He'd give his cousin this one, but
he'd get even. After all he was a Randell, too.

Tess returned from the doctor just before noon. She
sat while her dad had lunch, and listened to Livy and
Ellie talk about their adventures that morning.

Thirty minutes later she was on her way to the barn
to see what else had gone on while she was away. No
one was inside…and Dusty and Whiskey were missing
from their stalls. She went out to the corral, and that
was where she found them.

Standing in the shadows, no one noticed her as she
watched Luke. The one-time city guy surprised her as
he worked Dusty. He sat relaxed in the saddle while
the horse went through the maneuvers of cutting a calf
from the dozen in the herd.

Chance was a horse breeder and trainer by profes-
sion, and he was excellent at both. He called out instructions and encouragement to his cousin, and Luke did
exactly what was asked of him. Surprisingly, he had an
easy command of the horse and they worked well as a

team. Luke sat relaxed in the saddle, his hands on the horn and the reins slack. He was letting the horse do what he was trained for.

"Use your legs to give the commands," Chance instructed.

The deep concentration showed on Luke's face as he never took his eyes off the anxious calf. Finally the yearling relented and the task was complete.

"Good job, cuz," Chance called out as he rode up to him. "What do you think, Tess? He got the makings of a cowboy?"

Caught, she had no choice but to come out of hiding. Tess straightened, stepped out into the sunlight and walked toward the men on horseback. The calf scurried back to the herd across the pen. "He might have some potential," she called out over the bawling of the cows.

Luke looked pleased at her back-handed compliment.

"Not bad for a city boy," Chance teased.

She rubbed Whiskey's neck. "What do you think of this guy? Did you get a chance to work him?"

"I sure did. He's something, all right. I think it's time you put him to a real test. Enter him in a show."

Tess's heart raced with excitement. Those were the words she'd wanted to hear. "He's ready, huh?"

Chance nodded. "I wouldn't say it if I didn't think he was ready. At least see how Whiskey does in competition. He's got to learn how to handle the crowds. Start locally at the San Angelo Rodeo and work your way up."

Luke saw her hesitation. "Isn't this what you wanted?"

Tess straightened. "It is, but I have other concerns right now. Dad needs me."

Both Chance and Luke climbed off their mounts. It was Chance who spoke first. "What did the doctor say, if you don't mind my asking?"

She glanced at Luke, then back at his cousin. "No, I don't mind." She released a breath. "After I told him about Dad wandering off last night, he was concerned, especially about Dad's depression. The doctor wants him to come back Monday for a series of tests. Right now he said Dad needs to get out of his room and get more exercise."

Chance didn't hesitate. "Okay, that sounds good. What can we do to help?"

Tess shook her head. "You've already helped plenty."

Chance pulled off his hat and wiped his forehead. "You're as stubborn as your dad. I seem to remember when you played good neighbor and helped clean up Joy's house before we brought our baby home from the hospital."

"There were a lot of other church ladies there, too. Besides, Joy is your wife."

Chance arched an eyebrow. "She wasn't then. She was a stranger here. Come on, Tess. Let us help you. We all owe Ray."

Once again Luke found he was envious of Chance having known Tess all those years. "I can help out, too," he added. "I can feed the stock."

"Yeah, my cuz here is just lying around." Chance slapped him on the back. "Hey, come to think of it, I can use you over at my place. I've got several stalls that need to be mucked out."

"Sorry, I'm busy," Luke answered.

"Oh, yeah, you're having about thirty people over tonight." He leaned forward. "The Meyers family is invited, too."

Tess looked at both men in surprise.

"It's just a little Randell get together," Luke told her. "It seems I'm being welcomed back into the family."

Four hours later Luke had watched as truckloads of Randells arrived at the Rocking R. Every family member, either by blood or adoption, had come to see him. They'd set up tables and chairs in the shaded yard. The Randell women worked efficiently together, organizing the food while six brothers supervised the lighting of the barbecue grill. The children, fifteen altogether, looked after each other, with the older ones in charge.

Hank Barrett was the family patriarch. It was obvious that Jack's sons, Chance, Cade and Travis, loved and respected the man, as did their wives, Joy, Abby and Josie. Josie was Hank's biological daughter, whom he hadn't found until she was an adult and came here looking for him.

What a crazy family; and Luke envied his cousins even more because they'd had Hank to bring them up, after their father, Jack Randell, deserted them.

"It's a little overwhelming," Hank said as he came up beside him.

"The noise takes a little getting used to."

A big grin appeared on the old rancher's face. "It's great." He took a drink from his long-neck bottle. "And I love every minute of it."

Luke turned his attention to the crowd and spotted

Tess holding one of the babies. She took great care to support the infant's head as she showed him off to Livy.

"That's Chance's boy," Hank commented with a nod. "Jake Michael. I was wondering if he was going to spend his life surrounded by beautiful women. He's still outnumbered by two daughters, Katie and Ellie."

He glanced over at the smiling father. "He doesn't look too unhappy."

"That's because of Joy. A good woman can change a lot of things. Just ask any of my boys. They've been lucky enough to find love."

"Just one big, happy family," Luke murmured as he continued to watch Tess. A tall, teenage boy came up to her. They seemed engrossed in conversation. The boy's body language told Luke that the kid had more than a passing interest in Tess.

"That's Brandon, Cade's oldest," Hank said. "He didn't get to know his real father until he was nine years old. Cade and Abby were lucky to find their way back to each other. They married and have another son, James Henry, and a little girl, Kristy. Brandon didn't want to leave the ranch, so he goes to college locally.

"Wyatt Gentry came here a few years back to find his father, Jack, but instead he found Maura and her two kids, Jeff and Kelly, living in the old house he'd just bought." Hank took another drink, before he continued the story. "He owns the other part of the Rocking R Ranch. His twin brother, Dylan, an ex-bull rider, came to live there, too. He married Brenna, and they have Sarah Ann and Nicholas. The two brothers raise rough stock for rodeos. They're also part of Mustang Valley Resort and Retreat."

So far Luke had kept up with all the brothers. "So everyone is involved with the Mustang Valley business."

Hank nodded. "Any family member who wants to add to the many services are given consideration." Hank watched him a long time. "You give any more thought to staying?"

"I am staying…for now.

"So you're still planning to sell?"

"I can't do a thing until Brady shows up. I have to say I'm intrigued. I believe that parts of the Rocking R are valuable, especially the strip of land along Mustang Valley."

Hank shrugged. "It would be a shame if the land went to someone outside of the family."

Luke couldn't help but think about it. "Like I said, I'm just hanging out."

"If you get bored let us know, there's plenty to do."

He turned to look at Tess. She was rocking the baby against her breast. She raised her gaze to him, and their eyes locked in a silent gesture that had Luke oblivious to anything else but her.

Hank's voice suddenly broke through his reverie. "She's a special woman."

"Who?"

"Tess. She's special, all right. I've known her since she was Livy's age. You couldn't find anyone as kind and loving. She's had some rough knocks in life, but she's managed to come out of them. It's a shame about Ray."

Luke wanted to ask about Livy's father, but he doubted Hank would say anything. "Yeah, that's rough."

"I'm glad you'll be around for a while. She doesn't ask for help much."

"She doesn't need to ask. Not as long as I'm here."

"That's nice to know, son. That's nice to know."

Twenty minutes later Chance called out that the steaks were ready. Everyone cheered and headed to the tables.

After the blessing everyone began passing food around the long table. Luke quickly realized that it was difficult to carry on a conversation. He sat back and listened mostly. Then he realized that he was the only Randell who wasn't a couple. Even Hank and Ella were together.

Luke had heard the story that Ella had been Hank's housekeeper for years and helped raise Jack's boys. He finally admitted his feelings for her and they married a few years ago. She officially became Grandma Ella.

Tess glanced across the table at Luke. He looked overwhelmed by the large group, all the questions. She was feeling a little of the same, but she'd been to Randell barbecues before and knew what took place.

It was different for Luke. This was his family. Did he accept that, or was he crazy enough to push them aside and walk away?

"Hey, cuz," a grinning Travis called out. "I hear you're a hotshot real estate developer."

Tess watched Luke tense.

"Not so much anymore. As you might know, the real estate market is in a slump."

Travis called out, "So, does that mean you're going to try your hand at ranching?"

Chapter 6

Six Randell women had invaded his kitchen, but Luke wasn't about to chase them out, not after seeing the row of pies on the counter.

The seventh woman was Hank Barrett's wife, Ella, a handsome older woman dressed in jeans and a plaid shirt. Rumor was she wasn't the best cook in the kitchen, so she organized things and left the preparation to the younger women.

Chance's wife was petite, but she managed to keep up with Cade and Chance's wives, Abby and Josie. As rowdy as the Randell men were, their wives seemed to be able to handle them. That included the half brothers' spouses, Dana Trager, and Maura and Brenna Gentry. They'd all come here to find their roots and found a spot in the Randell family, too. It sent a longing through Luke like he'd never experienced before.

He backed out of the kitchen slowly, not wanting to answer another fifty questions from the women. Outside he found most of the men at the corral. He wandered over to see twelve-year-old Jeff Gentry on Dusty, and nineteen-year-old Brandon on Whiskey. They were cutting calves from the small herd.

Cheers of encouragement came from the group of spectators perched on the top of the fence. The oldest Randell grandson, Brandon, looked as comfortable in the saddle as if he were in an easy chair. The younger one didn't look bad, either.

"Hey, Luke," Cade called out to him. "You want your turn with the junior group?"

Luke was as competitive as the next guy, but he wasn't about to be bullied into something he wasn't sure he could do. Before he could turn down the offer, Chance spoke up. "Luke worked Dusty this morning with me. I have to say I was impressed by the way he handled him."

"Then I guess we need to sign him up for the Circle B rodeo next month," Cade suggested.

Goodnaturedly the rest of the Randells started pitching to Luke about entering Hank's annual neighborhood Rodeo in a few months. The talking quickly died out when Tess emerged from her house escorting her father.

Hank and Chance went over to greet Ray. He smiled as they all exchanged handshakes. Luke could see that they'd been more than just neighbors over the years; they were friends, too.

Luke watched the touching scene and realized he couldn't name a single one of his neighbors in Dallas. He discovered that the only socializing he'd done had been for business.

Ray spotted him and nodded as he continued to walk in his direction. "Hello, Luke."

"Ray. It's good to see you out."

"I might not be enjoying this day if you hadn't helped Tess the other night."

"Not a problem, sir. I have to practice my riding."

"Well, from what I could see, you handled yourself just fine."

Hank nodded his approval as he guided Ray on toward the corral, but Cade and Chance hung back. "Nice going, cuz," Cade said. "You're okay in my book."

Luke got slaps on the back from both men before they trailed off after Ray and Hank.

Luke felt a strange tightness in his chest. Why had his cousins' remarks meant so much to him?

Tess stayed behind with Luke and they watched Ray's enthusiasm over the cutting competition.

"The doctor started Dad on a new medication," she began. "Along with some vitamin supplements. There's a study program that Dad might qualify for."

He nodded. "It's good to see him outside."

"Hank had a talk with him. He told him he's wasting a lot of good times he could be enjoying with his family and friends."

"Good for Hank."

They stood there for a long time. His mother would have hated this. She wasn't fond of the Randell cousins.

Luke couldn't help but think about what he'd missed when his parents moved him away.

There were times since his return that he'd wanted to fit in with the rest of the Randells. Was the Rocking R the place he should be? He glanced at Tess, remembering the kiss they'd shared at the cabin. There was no doubt she'd drawn him in a way no other woman ever had.

But they both had other commitments. Tess had her family to think about, and he had no money…and a sketchy future. Right now everything was on hold, and a relationship was the last thing he needed.

Tess's voice broke through his reverie as they wandered away from the large crowd. "I want Dad to have the best care…. But the thought of putting him in a nursing home kills me.

"If you could have known him before…even a year ago. He rode in the rodeo circuit. That's where he met my mother. They fell in love and were married a few months later. Dad came back to Mom's parents' ranch, and he learned to train cutting and reining horses." She smiled. "Then I came along. I thought life was pretty great until I was about Livy's age, when my mother got sick. She had cancer…and died about a year later."

"I'm sorry."

She sighed as they strolled toward a shady area and away from the noise in the corral. "I did better than Dad," she told him. "He was lost for a long time, until we moved here. He seemed to thrive, working his own place. Dad started running cattle, but he also bred horses—saddle horses back then. But he knew good quality. And he taught me everything I know." She looked at him, her blue eyes sad. "I can't just abandon him."

Luke's stomach knotted. And he might be the bastard who was taking everything away from her. "No one wants you to. Is there any other family?"

"No, just Bernice and Livy. Bernice moved here right after Dad was diagnosed."

"So what were your plans if your father hadn't gotten…sick?"

"Renew the lease on the ranch," she told him. "Whiskey was going to be a NCHA Champion. And we were going breed other cutting horses."

He couldn't help her on the first one. "How long are you able to run this place by yourself?"

She stopped walking when they reached the tree in the yard. "I can't handle the cattle operation without help. For now the Randells are helping out, then I'll sell the herd off after the roundup next month. I can teach riding and help Chance with some horse training." She paused. "Now, if you're planning to stay on and live here permanently, I'd still like to stay on as your foreman…."

"Do you really see me as a cattle rancher?"

She shrugged. "Maybe not, but you have prime acreage along the valley, and that's worth a lot to the other Randells. I'm sure they'd want that strip of land, if only to protect their nature resort…and the mustangs."

He needed to tell her his situation. "To be honest, Tess, I need the money from this place. And that seems to be the best part of the Rocking R. If I were to de-velop that land—"

She gasped. "You'd build in the valley? But what will happen to the mustangs?"

"I may not have a choice. The ranch is all I have left. And I have to share it with a brother I can't seem to find. I have to do what I can just to survive."

"What if your brother wants to keep the ranch?"

He was so tired of talking about Brady. Seems his fu-ture hinged on what his brother wanted. "I guess you'll have to wait until he gets here. Who knows, maybe you can cozy up to him and work out some sort of deal." The second he said the words and saw Tess's hurt look, he wanted to take them back.

Luke reached for her. "Tess, I'm sorry. I have no right—"

"No, don't." She pulled away and walked off. He started after her but quickly stopped. He didn't want to have this discussion in front of the Randells.

Suddenly there was more commotion up by the house. A late-model black Mercedes parked by the back door, and a tall brunette climbed out. Luke's heart sank, and dread overtook him when he realized it was Gina Chilton. He wanted to disappear, but she'd already spot-ted him and called out his name.

What the hell was she doing here?

Seemed as if everyone else wanted to know the same thing. She smiled and hurried toward him as fast as she could in high-heeled sandals. He glanced over her cream-colored skirt that hit just above the knees, and a silky, royal-blue T-shirt. Her dark hair was cut in a straight blunt line, just above her shoulders.

Luke waited to feel some kind of emotion as his former business partner's daughter, and his one-time lover approached…but he didn't. He didn't want her here, intruding in his life.

Luke tensed. "What are you doing here—"

Gina stopped his words when her mouth covered his in a kiss.

Two hours later all the Randells had packed up and gone home, leaving Luke to deal with Gina. He hated being caught off guard, but he was definitely curious about why she showed up unannounced. There had to be a good reason, because Gina never did anything unless it benefited her. That was for damn sure.

And he couldn't wait to hear it.

After her own tour of the house, Gina floated into the kitchen. Her clothes left little to the imagination. She was a man's dream woman. Just not his. These days he was more into women in fitted jeans, T-shirts and dusty boots.

"Oh, Luke. This is a beautiful house. It's so quaint. Of course it needs work, but your mother's antiques are exquisite. And there's a beautiful hand-carved jewelry box…." Her eyes lit up. "I wonder what treasures could be inside?"

Luke ignored her rambling. "After all this time, you're here talking about this house."

"Oh, but this would be a perfect property to turn into a dude ranch."

He ignored her comments. "Why are you really here, Gina?"

She put on her best smile and gave his boots, jeans and Western shirt the once-over. "I missed you, of course." She sauntered up to him. "And I have to admit, I like your new cowboy look."

He wasn't buying it. Actually, he found he was immune to her. "And this visit…it was because all of a sudden you started thinking about me? You didn't have any trouble walking away when daddy called you."

"I thought about you…a lot," she admitted.

He folded his arms over his chest. "Funny, I couldn't seem to find you or Buck four months ago when I was fighting for my financial life."

She looked sad. "We had to get out, too, Luke. Daddy had a lot more to lose in that deal."

"So you both left me to take the loss on everything."

"That's why I came here, to tell you I'm sorry." She slipped her arms around his neck. "And to make it up to you."

Gina's perfectly made-up face suddenly seemed cold and hard. Why hadn't he noticed it before? He decided he preferred the fresh-scrubbed look better. Tess.

He removed her arms and stepped back. "There's no need to, Gina. You've already let me know where you stand."

She pouted. "Don't be that way, Luke. Daddy sent me to help you."

He laughed. "No, thanks. I've had your help before and I can do without it." He wanted her gone. "So please leave."

She looked surprised. "At least hear me out. It's a great deal. You can make up everything and more of what you lost."

Luke was curious. "Okay, talk."

She grew serious. "It's a great property. We can develop it with luxury homes and horse property in a gated community. We can even put in an executive golf course."

Not that he was thinking of partnering with Gina ever again, but he couldn't help but ask, "And where do we get the backing? My reputation and credit is in the toilet."

"That's the best part, sweetheart. You already own the property."

"The Rocking R Ranch."

She smiled. "It's even got a great ring to it, The Rocking R Estates…located in Mustang Valley."

"Mommy, why was that lady kissing Mr. Luke?" Livy asked as she put on her nightgown.

Tess didn't want to know. It was none of her business. "Mr. Luke said she was a friend that he used to work with."

"But Brandon told Jeff she was a hot babe. What does that mean?"

"That means you shouldn't have been listening to other peoples' conversations."

"I didn't mean to. The words just sneaked into my ears. Do you think Miss Gina is going to move into the house with Mr. Luke? I hope not 'cause I don't think she likes little kids." Livy climbed into bed and Tess pulled the covers up.

"Maybe it would be a good idea for you to not go to the house for a while."

"Are you mad at Mr. Luke, Mommy?" her daughter asked.

"No, sweetie. I'm just tired." But she was sad she'd let herself care for a man who ended up hurting her.

After a kiss on her daughter's cheek, Tess left the bedroom and walked out to the living room where Bernice was watching television.

"I'm going to check on the horses," she called as she walked out the back door.

She needed the solitude of the lone walk, hoping to clear her head of the sight of that woman kissing Luke. She hated that she cared, but she refused to look toward the house to see if Gina Chilton's car was still there.

She'd been such a fool to think that Luke Randell might want to fit in here. That he might stay and let her continue the lease agreement. Any hope of that, and her dream of breeding horses, was dimming quickly.

She stepped inside the barn and started down the aisle illuminated by soft light. After the amount of exercise the horses received today, she didn't expect any of them to be restless. The stalls were quiet, but she still wanted to check Whiskey.

The stallion raised his head over the gate and greeted her. "Hey, fella, had a lot of fun today, didn't you?"

The animal bobbed his head and nuzzled her for more attention. "You're just like all men, can't get enough." She smiled, but it faded quickly.

Was Gina the woman in Luke's life? Would she take him back to Dallas? Tess shook away any thoughts of the man. She wasn't going to waste her time.

"Tess…"

She glanced up to see Luke standing in the aisle. He had on his jeans, but his shirt was unbuttoned and pulled from the waistband. His hair was mussed as if his fingers combed though it…or someone else had. "Bernice said you came out here. Is everything okay?"

"It's perfect." She turned away and paid attention to Whiskey. "Just checking on the horses. What are you doing here? Don't you have a houseguest?"

He walked to her. "I don't have any guests, invited or otherwise. And Gina wasn't invited."

"It's not my concern who your friends are." She grabbed the halter off the gate and walked off.

Luke was tired of stubborn females, this one especially. He went after her, following her into the tack room. "Well, I need you to hear me out about Gina."

"I don't need to hear anything," she told him, hanging the halter on a hook.

"Too bad, you're going to listen," he said. "I didn't invite Gina, nor did I know she was coming here. I never expected to see her again."

"Well, she seemed to think that you'd welcome her with open arms."

Luke was tickled that Tess cared that much. "At one time I would have…but not anymore. She knows that now, and she's headed back to Dallas."

Tess paused, then murmured, "It matters if she took your heart with her."

Luke didn't want Tess to think Gina was still part of his life. "Looking back… I think Gina bruised my pride and destroyed my ego, but my heart…not so much." He moved closer to the woman who had gotten his attention. "I guess I wanted something so badly. I started fantasizing about a perfect life. Now, I think Gina and I used each other and it cost me…a lot."

Tess looked at him. Her gaze locked with his, and he had to fight not to take her in his arms. "I think I'm starting to realize I want something different now."

There was another long pause. "What about you, Tess Meyers? One man broke your heart, so you keep us all at arm's length?"

She swallowed. "I have too much at stake to have a casual relationship. Livy being the most important reason."

He couldn't help but be curious. "Has her father ever been in her life?"

She shook her head. "He had another family he'd conveniently neglected to tell me about." She stole a glance at him. "I was just a naive college student who fell for her married professor. Although at twenty-two, I should have known better. Believe me, I wised up quickly. After Livy was born, I had him sign away all rights to his daughter."

Luke cursed, then suddenly reached for Tess, taking her in his arms. "Good riddance," he whispered, closing his eyes at the incredible feeling of her body pressed against his. He felt her tremble, or maybe it was him. "You deserve so much more, Tess. Livy deserves more." He drew back and looked at her. "You're a beautiful woman." He couldn't let her go. "There's a man out there who would love you and your child."

Tess didn't believe in pretty words anymore. "Yeah, they're just pounding down my door." She managed a weak smile. "I'm not looking, Luke. All I want is to make a good living for my family."

And yet, she wanted to bury deeper into Luke's embrace. Just for a little while she wanted someone who would take away her burden…tell her everything would be okay. She was scared to let herself trust again. To fall in love…

She stopped herself. No. She couldn't let that happen. Not with a man who would leave. She moved away. "I stopped believing in fairy tales a long time ago."

He arched an eyebrow and showed off a slow, sexy smile. "Are you so sure Prince Charming isn't out there?"

She frowned, wishing she could be as lighthearted about it as he was. "Like I said, I'm not looking."

He leaned forward. "I think you're afraid, Tess Meyers."

"I'm practical," she argued.

"And stubborn."

He moved toward her and she didn't back away, telling herself it was because the room was small.

His head lowered to hers. "And beautiful…and far too tempting."

Tess gave a weak protest, but it died quickly when his mouth covered hers in a soft kiss. He pulled back and she silently begged for more. He didn't disappoint as he wrapped his arms around her, pulling her tight against him, and closed his mouth over hers again.

She released a soft moan as her hands slid up his chest and around his neck as he deepened the kiss. He teased the seam of her lips until she gave him access, then his tongue moved inside, stroking against hers until she made a whimpering sound.

Finally Luke broke off the kiss, but didn't release her. His heated gaze locked on hers. "I need to add *dangerous* to the list."

"Then maybe we shouldn't do this again," she said weakly.

"Yeah, right," he breathed as his head came down and captured her mouth again. His hand caressed her back as he drew her against his hard body. She could feel his desire, but even that didn't frighten her. She wanted Luke Randell.

By the time he released her, he looked as stunned as she felt. "Damn, woman, you make me forget everything...and want everything." His hands cupped her face, his gaze searching hers. "I want you," he confessed, right before his mouth crushed against hers. The kiss was hungry and needy, for both of them.

Somehow Luke managed to push her backward until her legs bumped against the edge of the cot. He drew her down until her head met the wool blanket. Tess opened her eyes to protest against going any further, but when her gaze locked with Luke's her desire soared to new heights.

Luke pulled her shirt from her jeans and put his hands on her bare skin. "Silk," he breathed. He leaned down and kissed her, then trailed his mouth along her jaw, her neck to her breasts.

She gasped, and clutched at his head. "Oh, Luke," she whispered.

He looked at her. "You feel it, too. That happens when we're together. You drive me crazy. I want you so much. Tell me you feel the same."

Tess pushed all caution aside. She wanted Luke, too, if only for a short time. She raised up and placed her mouth against his. "Yes… I want you," she whispered.

He pulled her tight against him as she arched into the kiss, not wanting to lose any contact. Before their passion could be satisfied, his cell phone rang.

He broke off the kiss, but didn't move away.

"You better answer that," she told him.

Finally he pulled the phone from his pocket and stood. Tess tugged her shirt down and drew a calming breath. Her hands were shaking, realizing how far… and how lost she was in Luke's arms.

"This is Luke Randell." He paused and listened. "Yes, Brady Randell is my brother." A long pause as his eyes narrowed. "How bad?"

Tess sat on the edge of the bunk when Luke flipped close his phone. "Well, it looks like I finally get to meet my brother that is, if he survives long enough for me to get to him."

Chapter 7

The next twenty-four hours passed in a blur for Luke.

The call from Brady's commanding officer hadn't divulged much information, only that his brother's plane had crashed during a mission. Brady had to eject from his F-16, but not without injuries. It was touch-and-go for a while, but Brady had survived twenty-four hours before he'd been located, then he'd been taken to Ramstein Base in Germany, then to the second army hospital at Landstuhl. Although he was still critical he was flown home to the States.

It had been Tess who'd taken over and made the necessary calls. The first one to Chance. An hour later Chance and Cade had picked him up and driven him to the airport, but instead of dropping him off, they'd boarded the plane with him.

Luke wasn't used to having this kind of support. He'd been on his own most of his life, but there hadn't been any doubt that both cousins were accompanying him to Walter Reed Hospital in Washington, D.C.

Once they arrived at the hospital, Chance talked with the nurse on duty at the desk. It seemed to take forever, but Luke needed time to gather his thoughts and his emotions.

He might not have liked that Brady had been the son who had a life with their father, but he'd never wanted anything bad to happen to him. And this could be bad. No matter the circumstances, Brady was his brother.

Suddenly that mattered to him.

His cousins walked back to the waiting area. "The nurse is going to get the doctor on the case."

Luke sat down as his thoughts turned to Tess and how she'd been there for him. She'd made him call back Brady's commanding officer to get more information. When Luke was reluctant to make the trip, Tess told him he couldn't ignore the fact he had a brother. And if he didn't go to see Brady, he'd be sorry.

Luke took a breath and released it. Just months ago his life was less complicated—no family, no financial problems. No Tess. His life had been pretty lonely. He felt a strange tightening in his gut. Not anymore.

Chance and Cade stood as the doctor approached. "Mr. Randell?"

"I'm Luke Randell," he said. "These men are my cousins, Chance and Cade Randell.

"I'm Dr. Newberry." They all shook hands. "I'm handling Captain Brady's case. I'm sure your brother will be happy his family is here."

Luke had to ask the dreaded question, "How is my brother, Doctor?"

"He had several injuries, including some internal bleeding, but the surgeons at Landstuhl Hospital got it under control. Also, after he ejected from his plane his leg was shattered on the landing. That, combined with Captain Randell having been exposed to the elements overnight before he was rescued, made his condition more serious."

"How is he now?"

"He's been upgraded to stable. He's still heavily sedated. The surgeons operated on his leg this morning, but that's only the beginning of his recovery. There could be more surgeries, and a lot of therapy to bring his leg back to normal."

Luke swallowed, surprised at the feelings churning through him. "But he's going to be okay?"

The doctor sighed. "He's strong. And barring any complications, he'll survive…but I can't guarantee he'll be able to fly again."

With that announcement, Dr. Newberry took them to the elevator, and they rode up to recovery. "Just one visitor at a time and keep it short."

Luke followed the doctor to the doorway of Brady's room, but he didn't go in right away. He just stood outside and stared at the man lying in the bed. His left leg was elevated as machines monitored his vital signs. A white sheet covered his brother's large frame. A shock of nearly black hair was cut military short. His face was shadowed by a dark beard.

Cade and Chance came up on either side of Luke. "Hey, this is a tough way to meet your brother for the first time," Cade said. "If you'd rather wait…"

"No, I've waited long enough. As you would say, it's time to cowboy up." He stepped through the door. The sounds of the monitor beeping seemed to keep rhythm with the heavy pounding of his own heart.

He walked toward the side of the bed. The stranger lying there had scratches and bruises on his face. A face that strikingly resembled his father's. Luke blew out a breath, trying to slow his pulse. Damn, this was hard.

Chance appeared beside him. "You okay?"

Luke nodded. "I'm not sure what to do."

"You're here," his cousin said. "You two are family. You have to take the good with the bad. He's a Randell, too, and we don't do things the easy way." Chance gave him a half smile. "I'll be just outside if you need me."

Once again Luke was alone. He'd never realized how often he'd faced things solo until he'd spent a good part of the past week with the Randells. And Tess. Now… his brother.

A groan came from the man in the bed as he started shifting around.

Luke was afraid he would hurt himself. "Hey, I think you're supposed to lie still."

The patient opened his eyes, and after a few blinks, Brady's dark gaze glared back at him. "Who the hell are you?"

"Luke… Randell." He motioned over his shoulder.

"Those two guys are our cousins, Chance and Cade Randell."

Brady continued to frown. "If you're here to claim the body, you'll have to wait, I'm not dead yet."

Later that evening, after a long bedtime story, Tess finally got Livy to sleep. She checked in on her father to see that he was down for the night, too. He was exhausted after spending his first day at the seniors' center. They had an exercise program for Alzheimer's patients. Whether the new medication and exercise was helping slow down the disease, only time would only tell. Precious time that could possibly give Ray Meyers the best quality of life. And for her to have her dad with her a little longer.

She went into the kitchen to find Bernice drinking a cup of tea.

"Everyone asleep?"

Tess nodded. "That's what I should be doing, too." She yawned but knew sleep wouldn't come easy, especially not knowing what was going on with Luke.

"He probably can't call you," Bernice said.

It was foolish to act as if she didn't know who her aunt was talking about. "I don't expect a call. Luke's with his brother."

"You could call Chance's wife."

"No, it's too late," Tess told her as she glanced at the clock. "And if there were any news, we'd hear."

The sound of the ringing phone caused her to jump. Tess went to answer it. "Hello."

"Tess," Luke said, his voice was husky.

"Luke." She felt her heart drumming in her chest.

"I'm sorry to call so late."

"No, it's not too late," she told him as a smiling Bernice walked out of the kitchen. "Luke, is everything all right?"

"Better than I first thought. Brady has some serious injuries, but none life threatening. And he's not exactly crazy to see me here."

"He's probably in a lot of pain. Are you going to stay there?"

There was a long pause. "Why, do you miss me?"

Her breath caught. She was afraid to say too much. "Livy wants you to come back."

Another pregnant pause. "Not that I don't care about shortcake, but I want to know about her mother. Tess, do you want me to come back?"

Inside she wanted to take a risk with him. But in the end she could get hurt when he left. "Luke…this isn't wise for either one of us. We have too many other things to deal with."

"I know this isn't the right time. But I keep wishing you were here with me." She could hear the emotion in his voice. "Thank you for talking me into coming."

"Family's important."

He sighed. "I'm beginning to believe that."

The next morning Luke, Chance and Cade headed back to the hospital. He'd only gotten a few hours of sleep after talking with Tess. He knew they shouldn't get involved, but that hadn't stopped his feelings for her. It was the wrong time to think about complicating his life with a relationship…with a woman and a child. He wasn't able to offer her any sort of future.

Luke stopped at the nurses' desk to learn his brother had been moved into a four-man ward. Cade and Chance waited outside while Luke went in.

He found Brady in the bed next to the window. He looked a little better today, but he could see the pain etched around his eyes.

"Morning, Brady," he said.

His brother grimaced as he shifted in the bed. "You still here?"

"I said I'd be back," Luke told him. "I wanted to make sure you're okay."

"Yeah, I'm just great."

"The doctor said you were lucky. You could have died out there." Luke shrugged. "Wherever there is."

"I was on a mission. The destination isn't important. And they got me out." Brady studied him. "I heard you've been looking for me for a while. I didn't have you on my emergency contact list."

"I called your commanding officer last week. Weren't you notified about Sam's will?"

"I was there when Dad's will was read." His gaze narrowed. "Too bad you couldn't even take the time to show up at the funeral."

Luke stiffened. "I wasn't invited."

"You were invited to a lot of things, you just couldn't find the time to come around. I guess Dad finally stopped asking."

"Asking? Sam Randell walked out one day and never came back. He made the choice not to be in my life.

His career and his new family didn't leave any room for me." Luke had told himself he wasn't going to rehash this old topic. "Okay, let's just put it in the past and move on. I came here to see how you were, but there's a lot of unfinished business. Our father left us the Rocking R Ranch."

"I know," Brady said. "Dad told me a while ago."

Luke fought his anger. "In a little over a month Ray Meyers's lease will end. We have to decide if we're going to renew or sell…"

Brady shook his head. "I've already decided," he said. "I'm not selling."

Luke tensed. "Then I guess we'll need to get a lawyer because I can't afford to keep the land. It's more valuable to me if it's developed."

"Out for the almighty dollar, huh, bro?"

"I'm out to survive," Luke countered. "But if you want to buy me out, you're more than welcome. But just be aware, family or no family, I'm not going to give the land away."

Later that evening Luke pulled a beer out of the refrigerator. They'd left Washington that afternoon and arrived home about nine o'clock. That pleased Luke, since he didn't want to see anyone. He had too much thinking to do.

How was he going to manage much longer? He had to come up with something. After he'd talked to his accountant that morning, he discovered that after he'd made financial restitution to all parties involved in the bad real estate deal, he had little left in the bank. He'd been poor before, during the years his mother had to work to support them.

But it was harder to swallow now. He'd worked relentlessly over the years to build financial stability. Six months ago he'd owned a lot of possessions. Maybe he'd been too greedy.

Achieving financial success had been everything in his life. Nothing else had seemed to matter. Now, after just a short time here, he wasn't sure of anything except he and his new brother were already in for a fight.

In the moonlight Tess walked across the yard to the large house. It probably wasn't wise to go and see Luke, but she told herself she was just curious about how things went with Brady.

She glanced down at the T-shirt and cotton skirt she'd changed into after her shower. So what if she wanted to look nice? The one thing she couldn't deny was she and Luke had nearly made love the last time they were together. To get involved with Luke would be a mistake, but she couldn't make herself turn around and run back to her house.

Instead she looked up and saw Luke walk out onto the porch. Her heart began to pound like a galloping horse as she took in his large frame silhouetted in the moonlight—those broad shoulders and a torso that tapered down into a narrow waist. He wore jeans and boots as well as any rancher who was born to the life.

He raised a long-neck beer bottle and took a long drink. He looked tired. Her palms itched with the desire to comfort him.

Suddenly he looked in her direction. "Tess…"

"Hi, Luke," she said as she came closer. "I just wanted to make sure you got back okay."

Luke forced a smile. He was still numb from his trip, but seeing Tess brought back his enthusiasm…and stirred a lot of feelings. "I'm a little tired, but I'm good. Chance and Cade made sure of that. They're more like nursemaids than cousins."

"I'm glad they went with you." She climbed the steps and stood in front of him. The light from the kitchen showed off her soft skin and incredible eyes. Her blond hair curled against her shoulders. The way he liked it. Touchable.

"We couldn't do much but wait around." He remembered the last time he'd seen Tess her mouth was swollen from his kisses, her body was responding to his touch.

He quickly shook away the wayward direction of his thoughts.

"What about you?" she asked in a soft voice. "How do you feel after meeting your brother after all this time?"

"It's strange." He couldn't stop staring at her. He took a step closer. "But I don't want to talk about Brady. I'm glad you came by." He drew her into his arms. "You have no idea how much I've missed you…" Before she could protest, his mouth covered hers.

He felt her hands move upward around his neck. A whimper escaped as he deepened the kiss. By the time he released her, he wanted to carry her upstairs to his bed.

"You feel so good." He kissed her again and again. His hand cupping her breast through her shirt. "All I could think about was what nearly happened between us in the barn."

She looked at him, her own hunger and need showing in her eyes, but she slowly slipped from his arms. "And maybe it's a good thing nothing had happened," she said. "We shouldn't go any further."

He stared at her. She was right, but that didn't stop how he was starting to feel toward her. But she'd hate him for what he needed to do—to sell out to the highest bidder. "You're right, Tess. You deserve more."

"No, Luke, it's not that. We're both at a time in our lives where neither one of us needs more complications. I need to keep my focus on building a future for my family."

Something inside him wanted to argue, but she was speaking the truth. "And that's what you should do."

Suddenly she smiled at him. "And I did. What I really came to tell you is I entered Whiskey in the San Angelo Rodeo this weekend."

He couldn't help but grin, too. "How about that? So you're on your way."

"Well, we haven't won anything yet."

"You will," he encouraged. "You're so good at what you do, and you've got a great horse."

"We'll see," she said, then hesitated. "I guess I'd better get back to the house." Again she hesitated. "Good night, Luke."

He couldn't let her go, not yet.

When she started to turn away, he reached for her

and his mouth came down on hers. His arms circled her waist and brought her against him. He could feel every subtle curve, her heat as her body arched into him. His hands moved to her face, cupping her cheeks as he deepened the kiss. A kiss he never wanted to end. But he knew he was just delaying the inevitable, and he had to let her go.

With the last of his strength, he backed away. His eyes met hers, unable to miss the passion in their depths. Before he could change his mind, he turned and walked inside, praying she wouldn't call him back.

In the end he was disappointed that she didn't.

A week later Luke arrived at the crowded First Community Credit Union Spur Arena in San Angelo. Chance had wanted to see how Whiskey performed and had invited him along. Luke told himself it was to spend time with his cousins, but he, too, was curious to see Tess.

"Hey, there's Hank," Chance said as they walked past the row of pens until they reached the rows of bleachers in the arena. After climbing up several levels, they found where Hank, Travis and Cade were seated together.

Hank greeted him with a handshake. "Luke, nice to see you."

"Good to see you, too."

Luke sat down beside the older man. An air of excitement filled the huge arena as people mingled around looking for seats. Luke glanced toward the numerous pens filled with stock for the rodeo. Colorful banners hung from the rafters, and music mixed with the voices of excited fans.

His thoughts turned to Tess. No doubt she was nervous. Whiskey was a big key to her future. He'd stayed away from her this week, knowing it was for the best, although, he could see her in the corral from the bedroom window as she'd worked with Whiskey.

Chance had stopped by a few times, giving her advice on the training. Luke hated the fact that seeing the two together made him jealous. Not that he thought anything was going on between them. Chance was crazy about his wife. Luke wished he could be the one to help Tess.

He'd always run from women like Tess Meyers—the type who wanted a permanent relationship. That's what he enjoyed about Gina. She was a user, just like he was.

Tess wasn't capable of using anyone. She was honest, independent and…loving. Everything Luke Randell wasn't. He needed to stay away…but yet, here he was.

"Hey, Mr. Luke." Livy's voice broke into his thoughts.

Luke couldn't help but smile, seeing the miniature version of Tess dressed in her jeans, boots and a bright-pink Western shirt. "Well, look who's here."

The child's smile brightened. "My mommy is riding Whiskey in the show. Aunt Bernie and me are gonna cheer for them. Are you gonna, too?"

"You bet." He pulled her into a hug, realizing how much he'd missed her not being around this past week. "I'm going to cheer really loud."

"And she's gonna win. Mr. Chance said so."

Luke glanced toward his cousin and realized that he wasn't in his seat. "Well, Chance should know, huh?"

"You know what else? I'm going to spend the night

with Katie and Ellie 'cause I start school next week. It's a girl night, we're going to do makeup and stuff." Those eyes widened. "I never done that, but Mommy says I'm old enough now." She shook her head, causing her ponytail to swing around. "But it's only cause it's a special 'casion."

"Sounds like you're going to have fun."

Bernice arrived and sat on the row of bleachers just below him. "Livy, give Luke a chance to breathe," she said.

"But I need to tell him a lot of stuff."

"Well, save some for later, he'll be here awhile."

"Okay." The child climbed down to her seat.

"Looks like you've got the attention of a pretty little lady," Hank said.

Luke shrugged. "Livy visits me sometimes," he said, enjoying the child's presence. Strange, for someone who didn't like to keep anyone too close, he suddenly had gotten attached to a lot of people.

"It's kind of hard not to take notice of those lovely lady neighbors."

"Tess carries a heavy load."

Hank nodded. "Yeah, she does. I'm glad you're around to help out. But that's what Texas neighbors do. They look after one another. It's good that you and your brother are coming back home."

"Whoa… I'm not sure what Brady's plans are, but I can't stay. I'm not a rancher, Hank, so I have to find a way to make a living."

Hank frowned. "Maybe there's a way you could do both."

Before Luke could ask Hank what he was talking

about, the announcer came on and had everyone stand. He stood and watched the women on horseback, carrying the American and Texas flags around the arena, then stopped in the center while the crowd sang the National Anthem.

After about ten minutes of announcements, they started the first session, the cutting competition. He quickly turned his attention to the pens and finally located the beautiful bay stallion being led by Tess. She was dressed in a bright-blue Western blouse and dark jeans, and caramel-colored chaps. Her hair was tied back in a ponytail with a black Stetson tugged low on her head.

She was busy talking with Chance, and it looked like he was giving her some last-minute instructions. Suddenly Tess turned toward the bleachers and smiled and waved. His chest tightened, but then he realized she was waving at Livy. He didn't care, he waved back. It was important to him that she know he was here to support her.

When Tess's turn came, she mounted Whiskey. After she was announced, Luke's stomach tightened with nerves as she rode the horse out into the arena.

She looked confident as the competition began and Whiskey went to work. The crowd cheered the duo on as Tess sat in the saddle, the reins slack, her hands on the horn, letting the animal do his job. By the time the two and a half minutes ran out and the buzzer went off, three steers had been cut from the herd.

Luke stuck his fingers in his mouth and let go of a long whistle. Several of the other Randells did the same. Then the score of 74 came up on the board and the crowd roared. Smiling, Tess waved to everyone. He waved back, wondering if she saw him, but he was going to make sure she knew how proud he was of her.

"Come on, Livy. You want to go down and see your mom?"

She cheered. "Can I go, Aunt Bernie?"

"Sure," Bernice said, looking at Luke. "Give her a hug for me."

Holding Livy's tiny hand, he led the way down the steps and along the metal railing until they reached the pen area. That's where they found Tess. When she spotted them, she handed Chance Whiskey's reins and hurried toward them.

"Mommy! You won," Livy called.

"Oh, sweetie, I haven't won yet," she said, then looked at Luke. "Hi."

"Tess, you were great," he told her.

"I think Whiskey deserves some credit, too. Besides, it's only the $3,000 novice division."

"I have a feeling it's just the beginning."

Luke wanted so badly to take her into his arms. And when the last score came up and her name and horse were announced the winner, he got his chance. He reached for her and pulled her into his arms.

"I told you," he whispered, realizing it had been a hell of a long week without her. "You're a winner, Tess."

Chapter 8

Being in Luke's arms, Tess lost all sense of where she was. Until Livy tugged on her arm.

"Hey, Mommy. Is Mr. Luke going to kiss you?"

Tess felt heat rush to her cheeks. What was wrong with her, acting like a teenager.

She quickly pulled away. "Oh, honey, he's just happy I won." She bent down. "But I want a kiss from you."

Her daughter threw her tiny arms around her in a tight embrace and placed a kiss on her cheek. "I love you, Mommy."

"I love you, too, sweetie." She stole a glance at Luke. The good-looking Randell had somehow worked his way into her heart, too. Worse, she didn't seem to know how to stop caring about him.

It wasn't long before her aunt appeared and embraced her. "Oh, honey, Ray's going to be so proud," she said.

Her dad. This was their dream. She wanted him to be here so badly, but she knew it would be too much for him. "As soon as I get Whiskey settled, I'll call him."

"He'd like that."

Tess frowned. "You need me to come home tonight?"

"Oh, no. You have to compete tomorrow." Bernice sent a glance toward Luke. "You stay like you planned and enjoy your victory. You've got your reservations at the hotel. Ray and I will be fine, and Chance is taking Livy to the sleepover with Ellie and Katie."

Livy tugged on her arm. "Don't forget Kelly and Sarah Ann are going to be there, too. And Grandma Ella is going to help watch us."

Tess knew her daughter was excited. This was her first sleepover, and first time away from home. "You sure you don't want me to take you?"

Livy pouted. "Mommy, I'm five. I'm not a baby."

That made Tess a little sad. "Okay, you can go with Chance." After another kiss, her daughter took off with Bernice to find Chance and Hank.

"Don't look so sad," Luke began, "she'll be home tomorrow, wanting to tell you all about it."

"It's her first time away from home." She continued to watch her daughter until she was out of sight. "And her first day of school starts on Tuesday." She took Whiskey's reins and led him down the series of pens, Luke beside her. "I guess I've taken it for granted that she'll always be a baby."

Luke didn't want to leave her. "Kids grow up."

"I know, and she needs me less and less."

"That's because you've raised your daughter to be independent. But Livy will never stop needing you. You're her mother."

They reached the stall area. "Yeah, I am. Oh, boy. If I'm this bad now, how will I act when she goes on her first date? Off to college?" She took Whiskey inside and began to remove his saddle. It was busy work to try to keep her nervousness at bay. Why was Luke hanging around?

Luke knew he should leave, but he couldn't seem to. He looked at Tess, and feelings of possessiveness hit hard. He wasn't going anywhere.

He took the saddle from her and placed it on the stand outside the stall. "What are your plans for tonight?"

"I'm babysitting a horse and catching a few hours' sleep at the motel. Why are you so interested?"

He shrugged. "I was wondering if you could take a break and go to dinner with me?"

Luke drove Tess to a steakhouse not far from the arena. It wasn't the kind of place he normally took a date, but neither one of them were dressed for fine dining.

"The food here is pretty good," Tess said as the waitress walked away with their order. "You didn't need to take me out."

He stared at her. "I wanted to spend time with you, Tess. And I bet it's not often you get out by yourself."

Those blue eyes locked with his. "It's the country,

Luke. We get up early and go to bed early, so we don't go out much." She took a sip of water. "I know that's different from what you were used to in Dallas."

He shrugged. "That's not true, I spent a lot of evenings at home. Most of my socializing was for business."

"Did you socialize a lot with Gina?"

He wanted to be honest with her. "Yes. We met through her father, and we were involved in a project together. For a while we were a couple. But I hadn't seen Gina in months…until she showed up at the ranch."

"She must still have feelings for you if she came here…."

He sighed. "Gina was here because of her father. She and Buck have a new deal in the works and she wanted to know if I was interested in investing."

He paused when the waitress brought their iced tea.

"Well, are you? Interested in investing?"

"Honestly, I'm not sure. I can't deny I would like to make some money. I lost everything just six months ago. That doesn't sit right with me. But it's hard to jump into a project when I have a limited cash flow."

"You act like you're destitute. You own half of a cattle ranch." She smiled. "And a beautiful house filled with antiques."

He was crazy about her smile. He also liked having her all to himself, even if it was just for a short time. "What is it with everyone and old furniture?"

She leaned closer. "For one thing, the craftsmanship a hundred years ago was so much better. And for another thing, good pieces are worth a sizable amount of money."

"I'll try to remember that when I'm looking to pay for my next meal." He needed to think seriously about what he was going to do.

She tossed her head back and laughed. "I doubt you'll ever go hungry. Besides, Bernice would never let you skip a meal."

He couldn't stop staring at her. It wasn't just her beauty that drew him, but the way she touched people… took care of her family, and her animals. And he was comfortable being with Tess. He didn't feel any pressure to try and impress her all the time, although he wanted to. He couldn't remember the last time he could just let everything go, and enjoy himself.

From the first, something inside them had connected, and he wanted more than anything to see where this led.

"I enjoy being with you, Tess," he blurted out.

"I like being with you, too," she admitted, then hesitated. "But I don't have much extra time for things like this. My life is pretty full."

"Yet, we somehow manage to find time to end up together."

She glanced away. "But when your brother comes here, you'll be busy, too." She sat back. "Besides you said so yourself you aren't staying."

"I'm not going anywhere right now." He grasped her hand. "Be truthful, Tess. Would you rather have me stick around?"

"What does it matter?" She looked at him. "Unless you've changed your mind about selling…"

"I can't make a move without Brady's input," he said. "Besides, as much as I've tried to keep my distance, I can't seem to manage that, either. For the past week I nearly went crazy being away from you…. I might not be the best bet right now, but I care about you, Tess, a lot."

She sighed but didn't look away. "I'm not any good at this, Luke. Every time I've trusted my feelings…it hasn't worked out."

His hand squeezed hers. He didn't want to mess this up. "Tess, I'd never intentionally hurt you."

"But what if after those few months are up, you get tired of the simple country life? What if I'm not enough?"

"You are more than enough, and any man would be lucky to have you," he told her, wondering if he would measure up. But he couldn't seem to walk away from her. "Can't we take this one step at a time?"

Before she could give him an answer, the waitress brought their food to the table. The huge steaks didn't look the least bit appetizing.

He found his hunger was for something entirely different than food.

Tess had returned to the arena to make sure Whiskey was settled in for the night. She'd called Bernice to check on Dad and to see if Livy was settled at the party. She turned around and found Luke standing beside the pen. He looked sexy in his Western shirt and creased jeans and spit-shined boots.

She tried to draw air into her lungs, but it was hard. "I guess I'm finished for tonight." She had trouble making eye contact, feeling the electricity sparking between them. "I better get some sleep."

"Sounds like a good idea." He walked alongside her until they reached the door to the parking lot and her truck. "Well, thank you for—"

He stopped her words as he pulled her into his arms and kissed her. By the time he released her, she swayed before she was able to regain her balance.

"No, thank you." He grinned. "I'll follow you to the motel…to make sure you get there safely."

She could only nod as he opened the door to her truck and she slid inside. Trying to slow her heart rate, she watched as he walked to his car.

She was in big trouble.

Ten minutes later Tess pulled into the spot in front of her room. Luke parked a little further away but made it to the door before her. They exchanged a knowing look, and Luke leaned down and brushed a kiss against her lips. Tess knew she wouldn't send him away…not tonight.

With shaky hands Tess managed to work the key card, praying she wasn't making a mistake. She opened the door to the standard-style motel room and walked in. With a bad case of nerves, Tess grabbed the plastic ice bucket.

"I'll get some ice," she said, and he reached for her hand. She froze, suddenly feeling the electrifying heat of his touch.

"We don't need ice, Tess," he said, tossing the bucket aside. "I don't think it's going to help cool us off." He stepped closer and dipped his head to hers.

Tess quickly lost herself in his kiss as his fingers

threaded through her hair. She moved closer as his hands worked their way down her spine. She wound her arms around his neck and snuggled against his body, feeling the outline of his desire.

She moaned as he lifted her, angling her hips against his, applying sweet pressure while he deepened the kiss. It was never like this before. She'd never felt this kind of hunger.

He pulled back and sucked in a breath. "Tess. I can't get enough of you." He anchored his hands to the base of her head and tipped it back.

"I want you," he murmured as he trailed soft kisses across her jaw to her ear. "So you'd better throw me out now if you don't want the same thing."

He paused as his eyes searched hers, waiting for her answer.

Her heart was pounding hard. Even with her doubts, she couldn't let him go. "Oh, Luke. I want you, too."

Luke worked the buttons on her blouse, then stripped it off her shoulders. She gasped when his hands brushed against her skin. He ran his fingers over the lacy edge of her bra, then underneath until his palm pressed against her nipple.

She felt her knees go weak but Luke held her tight. He stroked her sensitized skin and all she could do was let herself feel. By the time Luke laid her on the bed, she surrendered to the passion, and to loving this man.

The sun peeked through the edge of the curtain, shining into Tess's eyes. She gasped and sat up in bed, trying to clear her head of sleep.

Where was she?

She glanced down at her naked body, and her memory slowly returned. She'd spent the night making love with Luke. She glanced around the empty room. He was gone. He'd left without saying goodbye?

Hurt took over as she stood and walked to the chair where her clothes were draped over the back.

So was Luke's shirt.

She picked it up, and slipped it on, catching his familiar essence. She closed her eyes, remembering last night and the man who'd made love to her so tenderly that it brought tears to her eyes. She'd never experienced passion like that with another man.

Suddenly the door opened and Luke walked inside dressed in a white T-shirt and jeans and a sexy smile.

"Man, you look good." He was juggling coffee and muffins. "Good morning." He came toward her and leaned down to place a kiss on her surprised lips. "Thought we should grab some food before we head back to the arena."

Tess tried to hide her awkwardness. "You went for breakfast?"

"Yeah, they have a complimentary continental breakfast for the guests." He set the food on the table and turned back to her. "I knew you wanted to get back to Whiskey early." He pulled her into his arms. "But seeing you looking so sexy in my shirt... I may have to delay the trip."

She felt the heat from his body and the familiar touch of his hands. It would be so easy to let him distract her. She tried to pull away. "I really need to get back to the arena."

Luke refused to let her. "Is this about the competition or what happened between us last night?"

She inhaled and moved away from his intoxicating scent. "I have to stay focused on the ride, Luke. That's why I came here."

He frowned. "And I wasn't invited?"

"No! It's just that—" she brushed back her wild hair, hugging the shirt against her body "—I don't exactly know how to handle this...situation."

Luke wasn't sure he knew, either. He only knew that he didn't want it to end with her. "Last night meant a lot to me, Tess. I'm not going to walk away from you. I've tried, but you keep drawing me back."

"I don't try to."

He smiled. "I know. I almost wish you would." He wondered if she needed him like he needed her. "I want to spend time with you."

"But—"

"I know there's a lot of buts. The ranch and my going back to Dallas and my brother, your father, your daughter..." He hugged her close. "God, Tess. There will always be something. But right now I just want to hang on to this special thing that's between us. Maybe see where it leads us."

Two hours later, back at the arena, Tess saddled Whiskey but was still thinking about Luke. After she'd showered and dressed, he'd dropped her off at the stalls. Then he went back to the ranch to clean up and to check on Bernice and her dad.

She was trying her best not to fall in love with the

man, but it was getting damned difficult. Most of her life she'd never depended on anyone besides her dad. But that had slowly changed when Bernice came into the family, and when she finally let the Randells help out. But there had been no one in her life since she'd been involved with Livy's father. Could she let Luke into her life...and risk sharing her feelings with him?

Tess finished checking Whiskey's tack, then they headed toward the arena. She couldn't help but look around, wanting to see a familiar face. But she knew that Bernice had to stay with her father, and her daughter would be tired after the sleepover. She remembered Luke said he'd be back, but would he make it in time?

"Looks like we're on our own, fella," she said to her mount as the walked along the narrow aisle to the arena.

Suddenly she heard her name called and she searched the crowded stands. Again her name was yelled out and she scanned the faces until she finally located Luke waving at her. She smiled and waved back. Then the man next to Luke stood up and waved at her, too.

Dad. Her dad was here. He came to watch her.

She also saw Bernice and Livy, too. She looked back at Luke. He'd done this for her.

A mistake or not, she couldn't stop how she was feeling. The "damned difficult" just turned to damned impossible.

Smooth Whiskey Doc performed to near perfection. He'd scored a seventy-six in the Saturday session. Once she'd finished her part of the competition, Luke brought her father down to congratulate her. His visit was short, as both he and Livy were tired, so Luke drove her family home. He offered to come back and help her, but she refused his offer.

Two hours later she'd loaded up Whiskey and started the thirty-mile drive home. She found she was anxious to see Luke, too. When she pulled up next to the barn, she was tired, but she had Whiskey to take care of. When she walked around to the back of the trailer she discovered Luke was there already opening the ramp.

"Luke…"

"Thought you could use some help." He dropped the ramp but let her go in and bring the stallion out.

The bay was restless and somewhat excitable, but Tess brought him under control. "I better let him out in the corral for a few hours."

Together they walked the horse to the gate, and Tess took the rope off Whiskey, then let him go. They both watched him for a few minutes in a comfortable silence.

"He did himself proud this weekend," Luke told her. "I guess that means you're on your way."

She shrugged. "It only means something if I decide to travel on the weekends. And the big competition is even more involved. I'm not sure with Dad how I'll be able to handle it." She smiled. "Thanks for bringing him today." Her voice caught. "It meant a lot to me."

"I'm glad. Ray was pretty proud of you." He put an arm around her shoulder. "So am I."

"Thank you."

His silver gaze held hers. "Why don't you go to the house and get some sleep," he suggested. "I know you didn't get much last night." He smiled. "Neither one of us did. Maybe we should take a nap together."

She blushed. "I don't think that's such a good idea. Neither one of will get any rest."

His grin turned downright sexy. "I'm willing to sacrifice." His mouth covered hers, and she lost any argument.

Not that she was going to fight much anyway.

"I call your ten and raise another ten," Luke said the following Friday evening at Chance's house. It was the Randell men's monthly poker game that also included Hank Barrett. Supposedly, he was the champion poker player of the group.

"You sure you want to make that bet, son?" Hank asked.

Hell no, Luke thought, looking down at the spade flush in his hands. This night's gambling had been a bust so far, and this was the best hand he could scrounge up.

He hadn't come to win, though, just to hang out with the cousins. Since Tess had been so busy this week, he hadn't had much to do except relive in his head their night together. Her win was a good thing for her, but had a down side, too. She'd acquired two more horses to train, and had little time for him.

Hank tossed in the needed chips. "I call. Show your stuff."

Luke laid down his flush and watched Hank toss in his two pairs, queens over fours. The cousins hooted with laughter and Chance slapped Luke on the back as he swept up the plastic chips.

"Beginner's luck," Hank murmured with a wink and a smile.

"I think I need another beer," Cade said as he got up from the table. Jared, Wyatt and Dylan followed him into Joy's kitchen, but Chance stayed. "You want another beer?" he asked.

"Thanks, but I have plenty," Luke said.

Chance grinned. "I see your strategy, cuz. Let the others drink enough to cloud their judgment."

Everyone had left at the room except Chance and Hank. The older man was shuffling the cards when he asked, "How is Brady doing?"

Luke shrugged. "He seemed to be doing okay when I called the hospital yesterday. We talked some, but it wasn't much of a conversation."

Chance stretched his arms over his head. "You're still getting used to each other," he said. "I remember when Jarred, Wyatt and Dylan came here. When we learned they were our brothers, it was strained for a long time. But we've managed to become a family.

"I know we haven't kept in touch with you over the years," Chance said as he glanced at Hank. "We had our own things to deal with, although that's not an excuse, we should have hung together. You and Brady are family. Our family."

Those words hit Luke hard and deep. He would have given anything to hear those words years ago. Would have given anything to be part of a family. "After my parents divorced I never wanted to or ever thought I'd come back here."

His cousins' robust voices filtered in from the kitchen but quieted down as they returned to the table.

"Well, you're here now," Hank said. "I believe there's a good reason for you coming back."

Luke wasn't going to lie. "Yeah, it's because I'm broke and have nowhere else to go."

Chance and Hank exchanged a glance before his cousin spoke. "We've all been there. It's hard to lose everything and have to start over again."

Luke stiffened, hating this feeling. "So now you know why I have to sell the ranch." He raised an eyebrow. "Are you interested in buying?"

"Maybe," Chance said. "And maybe we're also interested in investing in it."

"If you say you want me to be a cattle rancher—"

Chance held up a hand. "No, you've made that clear. What we're interested in is the acreage along Mustang Valley."

Hank spoke up. "I've been protecting that herd of ponies for a lot of years. I want to see it continue after I'm gone. I'm thinking the only way I can do that is by buying the land."

"Whoa, Hank. I'm not even sure what that land is worth." Luke wasn't going to give it away, either. "Besides, I've already been approached about developing that area," he sort of fibbed, knowing Gina's father was lurking in the shadows. So it had to be worth a lot.

Hank nodded. "Developers have been after my section of the valley, too. But we've managed to hold on to it."

Chance spoke up then. "We also know that to protect the mustangs in the valley, there has to be a way to generate income in the family business for the next generations. So we need to make some compromises. That's the reason we need you and Brady to join forces with us."

"And do what?"

"We want to develop the property edging the valley."

Luke tried, but failed to hide his shock. "Sorry, did I hear you right?"

Chance nodded. "Yes, you heard right. But although we want to build on our land, that doesn't mean we want to destroy the landscape. The deal you were involved with in Dallas had to do with gated horse property." He glanced at his brothers. "Would something like that work here?"

Luke's mind was reeling with ideas, also Gina's recent proposition. "Of course it would. You could control how much land is developed, regulate the rules of the gated community. For instance, selling as retirement property, and not letting certain vehicles that harm the environment on the property."

Cade spoke first. "That was the first thing we did when we opened the nature retreat. No cars or trucks."

Luke's enthusiasm was growing. "Then carry that rule throughout the gated property, except on designated roads."

The brothers looked thoughtful, then Chance said, "Would you have a look at our nature retreat?"

Luke wasn't sure he knew what was going on. "First of all, I'd want to know what you have planned. Do you want to buy all the Rocking R?"

Chance shook his head. "Just the section that is

across the creek in the valley. That's between Brady, you and Hank. Some acreage from yours and Brady's property, added to the Randells' property that borders the valley will make up the gated community. Of course, we'd like to work out a deal that makes us all partners.

"We could put up most of the capital. We don't have endless funds, so we want you to come up with a idea of what such a project would cost us. And if it's feasible, we would like to hire you as project manager."

A hundred things swarmed in Luke's head. This was like a dream, but soon reality brought things into focus. And were the Randells really just wanting the valley land?

"Hold it. Before we get carried away, I need to think about this. And there's someone who has to give his go-ahead, too. You need Brady to go along."

"The Rocking R has several sections," Chance said. "If Brady decides to give up his military career and wants to ranch, there's enough land so he can raise a small herd and plenty for you, too...to do whatever you want with it."

Immediately Luke thought of Tess's horses. She could stay right here and build her business. Hell, she could even expand. Slow down, he warned himself. Wasn't this how he'd gotten into trouble in Dallas, trusting to easily?

"I'm going to need to talk with Brady, and right now he's not crazy about me being his brother."

Cade stood. "Looks like we'll have to persuade both our cousins that we'll be there for them. That you're part of this family."

Chapter 9

A little more than a week after the show, Tess walked out of the barn. Thanks to Whiskey's performance, she now had two more horses to train. She'd worked them both, along with her own today, and was exhausted but knew the extra money would help out. She needed to be prepared for when her dad needed more care.

Time was running out for her, too. She wasn't sure what was going on with the Rocking R. She had to be prepared for if or when Luke sold the place.

When she'd let him stay with her the night of the horse show, she'd known the facts of life. There hadn't been any declarations of love from him, or any promises to stay in San Angelo. Still, Tess hadn't been able to resist him. He'd charmed her with kindness and thoughtfulness, not to mention his sex appeal. How could she not fall in love with the man?

She'd been walking around in a daze just waiting for him to return. He'd gone to the hospital in Washington again, trying to convince his brother to sell part of the Rocking R. She wanted to hate him for not loving and cherishing the place the way she did. But deep down she knew he cared more than he let on, and there wasn't any choice for him.

But even worse, Luke was walking away from more than just the land, it was his family. Whether he knew it or not, it was going be hard for him to leave the Randells. She hoped if that day came, he'd be sorry to leave her, too.

Tess made her way past Luke's house and down the gravel road where a yellow school bus had just pulled up. She watched with pride as Livy climbed off and waved at the driver before starting toward her. As much as she hated her daughter being away, Livy loved going to school and all the new friends she'd made. Unlike her mother, the five-year-old was a social butterfly.

Livy spotted her and took off running to her. "Mommy, look at my picture. I got a star." She held up the drawing of a large dark horse.

"Wow, that's great."

"It's Whiskey," her daughter said.

"I can tell by his markings. I'll have to hang this one up, for sure."

Hand in hand they started down the road. "I really wanted to give it to Mr. Luke."

Tess's heart sank. Her daughter was so attached to

him. What would happen if he left? "Well, he isn't home yet."

Livy's smile faded. "Is he coming back?"

She nodded. "Remember, he went to see his brother in the hospital."

"I know. He has a broken leg." She glanced up at her mother. "Maybe I should draw him a picture, too."

"That would be nice."

As much as Tess tried to keep her feelings for Luke at bay, he'd managed to sneak into her heart deeper and deeper, even though they hadn't had much time together since the horse show. The day he left for this trip, he pulled her into his arms and gave her a slow, drugging kiss that was filled with promise and hope. By the time he released her, she could barely stand on her own, making her imagine it was possible they could be together. Then two days had passed without a word.

They were just passing the house when a car drove down the road. Luke's BMW. He honked as he pulled into the drive.

Livy jumped up and down. "Mommy, Mr. Luke is home."

Tess couldn't help but smile. "I can see that," she said as Luke climbed out of the car.

He waved and walked toward them. For the first time in a long time, Tess saw a different man. He was dressed in suit trousers and a white shirt with a tie. There was little resemblance of the laid-back cowboy she'd come to know and love.

This man was all about business.

"Hi, Mr. Luke. You're back," Livy cried and she went to him. "I made you a picture 'cause I missed you."

"Hi, shortcake." He hugged the girl. "I missed you, too." He glanced over the picture, "This is great," he said then looked at her. "Hi, Tess."

"Hi, Luke." She felt achy all over, needing to feel his arms around her. "It's good to have you home."

"It's good to be back." He sighed and glanced at his watch.

"Mr. Luke." Livy tugged on his sleeve. "Maybe you can go riding with us. Mommy, can we go?"

"Right now isn't a good time, shortcake," Luke answered. "I have a meeting in a few minutes."

"Oh…" She lowered her head in disappointment.

"We'll make it another day." He knelt down. "Hey, why don't you go hang your picture on my refrigerator? There's tape in the drawer by the phone."

Luke watched Livy until she disappeared into his house. All the way back to the ranch, he'd been dreading talking to Tess. But he owed her an explanation.

"I wanted to walk to you, but I can't now. I've got a meeting with Buck Chilton and Gina."

She looked confused. "Your old business partners?"

He nodded. "Buck has an investment proposition he wants me to look at."

"I thought he was the one who caused you to lose everything before."

He didn't deny it. "I'm just going to listen to what he has to offer. Beside, this time I'd make sure I had control of any project, if we get together."

Her breath caught. "Sounds like you're already decided."

"No, I haven't," he quickly answered. "I have another offer."

"For the ranch? You've had an offer for the Rocking R. Is that what you wanted to talk to me about?"

"The offer is for part of the ranch. And, yes, it's part of the reason." He looked around. "It's hard to explain, Tess, but I also need to hear Chilton out. There are several investors who are interested in reviving my project in Dallas and here at the Rocking R. I'd lost so much before—including my reputation—that I can't just leave things the way they were. Can you understand that?"

"So you'll be moving back to Dallas." The sadness in her eyes tore at him. "Why should I be surprised. Hadn't it been your plan all along?"

He couldn't deny it. "At one time, yes. A lot has happened since then." He still had trouble telling her his biggest fear. "I met you."

A car coming down the drive drew their attention. The luxury vehicle parked at the house, and Gina and Buck climbed out. "Damn. I need to go." He didn't want Gina coming down here.

He looked back at Tess, but she already closed herself off. "Don't let me keep you. You know what they say, Time Is Money."

"It not like that, Tess. But I have to do what's best… for everyone."

"And the hell with your family."

He stiffened. "Just because we have the same last name doesn't make us a family."

* * *

It was after ten o'clock when the business meeting finally broke up. Luke was tired when he went to the kitchen and grabbed a beer. He'd been right about Chilton's proposal. It had been for the Mustang Valley property. Yet, even with the valley land off the table, because it was already promised to Hank, Buck wasn't about to give up. What surprised Luke the most had been the number of investors Chilton had been able to round up for this project.

In return all Luke had to do was contribute his and Brady's share of the land that bordered the valley. What wasn't in the deal was the house and outer buildings and enough acreage to run a small herd if Brady retired to live here.

Luke leaned against the counter and took a drink of his beer. His half brother wasn't crazy about him to begin with, but Brady had listened to Chance's pitch about the Randell Corporation's five-year plan. Would he be willing to listen to Luke about a second offer? Either choice they made, he and Brady had a lot to decide. And somehow they had to agree on it together.

That left Luke a lot to think about before he headed back to Washington. Was the intrigue of Buck's deal only because he wanted to rebuild his reputation in the business? Was the reason he hadn't just accepted the Randell deal because he didn't feel he'd fit in here? He thought back to the little boy who'd been devastated when he lost his home and his father.

Could he really be a part of this family again?

Then there was Tess. His decision affected her, too.

He cared about her and her family. Even if he chose to return to Dallas, he wouldn't abandon her. Her horse-training business was here in this area. She'd needed a place for Ray, for Livy. He was reasonably sure that Brady wouldn't object to her living in the house, and her using the corral and barn.

So if Luke chose Buck's deal and returned to Dallas, that would remove any guilt he felt about selling part of the ranch. Tess would have her dream and he'd have his. Isn't that what he'd worked for? Getting back into the game with the big boys.

Luke's attention went to the refrigerator and the picture hanging crookedly on the door. A funny feeling rushed through him thinking about little Livy. He found he'd looked forward to seeing her every day, sharing things with her and her mother. Strange how in only a few weeks he'd let three women and one old man get under his skin. Not to mention a bunch of rowdy cousins.

"Hiding out?"

He looked around to find Gina standing in the doorway.

"I got thirsty." He raised his bottle of beer.

"I hope you're not having second thoughts."

"Believe me, I'm having more than a few. Buck's offered me a great deal once before, and look how that turned out."

"That isn't going to happen again, not with all your demands in writing."

"It's just good business." Luke wasn't fool enough to make any mistakes this time. He'd never lose everything again. But the gamble was even bigger now. There was Brady to think about. His brother's military career was on the line. Luke had learned that pilots who had to eject from their planes had to go in front of a review board to be deemed fit to fly again. For Brady, he still had a long time to go before that happened, if ever.

Gina came across the room. "I have to say, it'll make me happy if you come back to Dallas." She placed her hands on his chest. "I've missed you."

He removed her hands, hoping that she wasn't offering anything else to sweeten the deal. "It isn't a good idea to mix possible business with pleasure."

"If you're worried about me leaving you again—I won't. I made a big mistake."

He doubted that. If anything, Gina was loyal to herself and maybe her daddy. "I want something different now, Gina. And I'll never work with someone I can't trust."

She glared at him. "It's her, isn't it? That cowgirl."

He wasn't going to give Gina any information about Tess. "This is a business deal, and if I accept it or not, that's all that will be between us." He sighed. "And I believe it's past time to end this meeting."

Her anger was obvious. "I hope you aren't foolish enough to pass up what's right in front of you. Because Daddy is giving you a second chance, and you should take it. So there's only one choice to make." Then she marched out of the room. He heard voices then and the sound of the front door closing.

"If only that were true," he murmured, "life would be so easy." He went to the window and saw the light on in the barn. Tess. He felt his body tighten with need as he recalled their night together. How she felt in his arms. Suddenly he knew. Somehow he needed to find a way back to her.

It was nearly midnight when Tess walked out of the barn, aching with fatigue. She'd groomed Dusty and Lady, cleaned stalls and polished tack, hoping the hard labor would drive everything from her mind and allow her to sleep tonight. Help her forget.

When Tess recognized the shadowy figure coming toward here, she tensed. No, she didn't want to talk with Luke. Not now.

"Tess," he called as he came into the light. "What are you doing out here so late?"

"I was working."

"You need sleep more."

"I can take care of myself, Luke. So don't worry, I'm headed to bed right now." She tried to move around him, but he reached for her.

"Could you give me a minute, Tess?"

She didn't want to listen anymore. "I've heard it all, Luke. We've talked it to death. And in the end you'll go back to Dallas."

"That hasn't been decided yet." He paused. "But that doesn't change the fact that I care about you." He drew her into his arms and kissed her.

She put up a weak protest, but soon surrendered to the sensations he created, to the need, to the desire. She ached for this man, probably always would, but it didn't mean that was a good thing. Not when he wouldn't be there for her, not when money meant more than family.

She broke off the kiss and stumbled backward. "You have every right to sell the ranch, Luke." She blinked back tears. "But I don't have to like it."

"It's only part of the Rocking R. And remember, I'm not in this alone, I have to give Brady the chance to look over all the offers, too."

"He's going along with your plans to develop the land?"

"He's practical, Tess. We can't afford to keep this place going without generating some income." Luke took a step closer. "Tess, I don't want you to have to leave here. No matter what I decide I'd never let that happen."

Tess's chest tightened. "Would that ease your conscience, Luke? Well, don't worry, I can take care of my family. But the Rocking R is more than a just land, it's been in your family for generations. And selling to the highest bidder doesn't seem right. You might have had issues with your father, but don't give away your heritage."

She brushed away a tear. "You've been given a second chance here. A chance to put down roots, to make a real home. That's got to mean something to you. How can you think about selling it to strangers?"

"Maybe because I don't have a choice." He shrugged. "Maybe what I want is out of my reach."

Tess wanted to argue that fact, but he had to make this decision on his own. If he didn't want her, it was better if she let him go now. She shook her head. "Maybe you aren't reaching far enough for that dream."

His eyes were pleading, then quickly he turned angry. "I stopped dreaming a long time ago. They never came true."

Tears clouded her vision. She knew he was talking

about the young boy who left here years ago. "It could this time, Luke. Trust in yourself, in your family. Just don't walk away."

She watched the emotions play across his face. "I'll let you know what's decided about the ranch." His gaze held hers. "Good luck, Tess." He turned and walked off.

Tess hugged herself, the ache in her chest almost unbearable. She had to fight to keep from going after him, knowing in the end if he truly wanted to leave she couldn't stop him. And soon she'd just be a distant memory.

She prayed the same thing would happen for her, that someday she would stop loving Luke. But she knew it was going to take a long time.

Over the next week Luke managed to keep busy. He kept in close touch with the architectural firm that the Randells had hired to draw up tentative plans for the Mustang Valley project, which had been officially named Golden Meadow Estates.

Buck Chilton had been in close touch, also. His architect was due to send him plans by the following week. Luke had flown to Washington to see Brady again, giving him Chilton's offer to go over. He hoped that his brother would be the one to make the final decision, or at least, buy him out of his half of the ranch. Then Luke could go back to his life in Dallas to try to start over.

In his makeshift office in the kitchen, he leaned back in the chair. If the Randell project went ahead, the only thing they'd wanted from Brady or him was the land, and that Luke take the reins as project manager.

And there were always risks in real estate. Thank

goodness the Golden Meadows Estates target market was a wealthier clientele. The corporate type who wanted the quiet ranch life without all the work. All they needed was to load up the horse properties' homes and stables with all the right high-end amenities to impress buyers.

Luke rubbed his eyes. His thoughts turned to Tess. Since last week he'd only managed to sneak a glance at her from the bedroom window when she worked in the corral. He'd also spotted her loading Whiskey into the horse trailer. Later he learned she'd gone to another show. Chance had called and asked if he'd wanted to go, but Luke declined. His cousin later reported back that she'd placed well again.

Luke was happy for Tess. He wished he could have shared in her victory, but she didn't want him there. Her rejection hurt more than he'd thought possible.

He glanced out the window when Chance's truck pulled up. Luke put on a smile and let his cousin inside the kitchen.

"Hi, Luke."

"If you're here to bug me about my answer, I still can't give you one."

Chance frowned at him. "That's not why I came by. Besides, it's only good business sense to look for other options." There was a pause, then Chance asked, "Have you heard anything from Brady?"

"No, but you know he didn't want to sell in the first place. That's probably why he's taking his time. He only let go of the valley land because it wouldn't get developed. He keeps talking about how it was our father's dream to come back here."

Chance took off his hat and placed it on the counter. "That's understandable, this ranch has been in the Randell family for generations. Maybe Brady is thinking about the future, too."

He shrugged. "I don't exactly feel the same way."

"I felt like you for a long time after my dad left us. I wanted nothing that was his. I was going get my own place, make a name for myself. I thought I found the perfect piece of land, the old Kirby place. I lucked out when it went up for auction."

Luke walked to the coffeemaker and filled two mugs and handed one to Chance. "Then I went over one day and found Mrs. Kirby's niece there claiming her inheritance. A very pregnant Joy Spencer, and she just happened to be in labor."

Luke took a slow drink from his cup. "What happened?"

"I didn't have much choice," he said. "I delivered Katie, right there in the barn." There was a faraway look in his cousin's eyes. "I fell in love with that little girl and soon after her mother. I learned that Joy was running from her dead husband's parents. They wanted to take the baby away. So Joy asked me to marry her, and in turn she'd sign over parts of the ranch."

"What did you do?"

He smiled. "Well, obviously I married her."

"Did her in-laws ever find her?"

"Yeah, I walked out on her, thinking I wasn't good enough to be a father." He tensed. "You know, my daddy's reputation and I'd tangled with the law in my youth, so I thought I'd hinder Joy's custody chances. Then I realized I wanted to be Joy's husband and Katie's father." He studied Luke for a moment. "At the end of the day, that's all that really matters. How much do you love each other."

Chance studied Luke. "That's why I stopped by, cuz. You've been cooped up here for nearly a week, trying to figure out what's the best business deal to take. This is what my brothers and I would say is 'a gut call.' You can't think about the money, but what's good for you and Brady. And whether you can live with it."

Luke sighed and went to the window. "I didn't think the memories would be so strong. There are some good ones—then Dad left me and Mom."

"I know that feeling, cuz." Chance stared into his mug. "Jack Randell was a piece of work. But I had Hank and my brothers. You were alone to deal with all the crap." He looked at Luke. "I'd like to think this was your daddy's way of giving you a second chance. A chance to meet your brother and your cousins. I have to say, there nothing like family around. That's something that Hank taught us."

Luke's chest was suddenly tight with emotions. He felt raw and exposed, knowing his cousin could read him so easily.

"And just so you know," Chance began. "My brothers and I didn't offer you this deal because you own some Randell land. We offered you the deal because you and Brady are family. And we want to build a future for us and our children."

A lump seemed to lodge in Luke's throat. He couldn't speak.

"I know we're still strangers to you. We hope that will change. If I've learned anything, cuz, it's that family matters."

Before Luke could answer, he was distracted, seeing a man coming up the back steps. Ray Meyers. Luke opened the screen door and invited him inside. "Ray, good to see you again."

The older man blinked. "Sam?"

Luke exchanged a look with Chance. "No, Ray, Sam was my father, he died. Remember, I'm Luke."

Ray frowned. "Oh, I'm sorry to hear about your daddy's passing." He looked around the kitchen. "One time he told me that he was going to come back here... Someday...bringin' his boys home. Oh, he loved his boys. He talked about you all the time. Even showed me a picture." Tears formed in the old man's eyes. "He was plum sorry about what happened...havin' to leave you."

He wanted to believe that Ray's words weren't just gibberish. "Sam told you that?"

Ray's eyes glazed over, and he looked around, confused. "Do you know where my Theresa went? She said she'd come for me...but I waited and waited..."

Luke and Chance exchanged a look. "Well, she's probably busy with the horses. How about I take you to her?" Luke took Ray by the arm and they walked out the back door.

Luke knew at that moment, no matter what, he'd do everything in his power not to ever uproot the Meyerses. It was their home, as much if not more than his. Just as they stepped off the porch, Tess came running from her house, still dressed in her work clothes of jeans and leather chaps. She looked frazzled, but relieved to see her father.

"Dad," she called. There were tears in her eyes as she hurried toward him.

Luke was hungry for the sight of her. Since she'd been avoiding him, he hadn't seen her close up for too long. She looked tired but as beautiful as ever. Her eyes were still mesmerizing, her scent was still intoxicating, her body was still tantalizing.

"Thank you, Luke. I'm sorry he bothered you."

"He's never a bother, Tess. I'm glad he came for a visit." Luke turned to her father. "You come back anytime, Ray. I want you to tell me more about Sam."

The old man looked at his daughter. "Tess, this here is Sam's boy. Did you know that?"

"Yes, Dad, I know that. Now you need to come home. Bernice has your supper ready."

The older man seemed confused, then he smiled. "My little sister?"

Tess tugged on his arm, "Yes, Bernice is your sister."

Just then Livy came running toward the group. "Grandpa, you got found." She hugged him.

"I don't know what the fuss is about, child," Ray said. "I just went to see Sam's boy."

"Well, now we can go and have supper," Tess said, and tugged her father in the direction of the house. But not before Luke caught her glance. The heated stare sizzled between them before she quickly turned away.

Livy hung back, those big blue eyes looking up at him. "Mr. Luke, Mom said you're working really, really hard and we can't bother you. Are you done yet?"

Luke swallowed hard as crouched down in front of her. "I'm never too busy for you, shortcake. You come by anytime you want."

She rewarded him with a smile. "Jinx wants to come, too."

"Sure, the more the merrier."

She hugged him. "Thanks. Bye, Mr. Luke and Mr. Chance."

Livy caught up with her mother and grandfather, and they walked away together. Luke ached to go with them, to help her. To let Tess know she wasn't alone. That he would be there for her. Instead, he could only stand there, in the middle of the yard, and watch the family he'd always wanted walk away.

Chance came up beside him. "Man, that's a lot for Tess to deal with. I'm glad she's got you here."

"She thinks I'm gonna leave her and go back to Dallas."

"So you gonna prove her wrong?" Chance arched an eyebrow. "Or are you just as stubborn as the rest of us, and can't admit that you're crazy about the woman?"

Luke had never realized how much he could want someone. Or how much it would hurt to watch her walk away.

He had to find a way to make things right.

"I've made a lot of mistakes. She really could do better."

Chance gave him a sideways glance. "You might as well think of a way to win her over, because I'm beginning to believe the Randell men only love once. And it's forever."

Chapter 10

Tess was in the corral, having just finished a session with Whiskey. She'd been busy for days working her four boarded horses. The extra money coming in was great, though. It helped pay for her dad's treatment, and she'd been able to hire part-time help.

Brandon Randell came by after his college classes. He didn't even seem to care about the low pay, because she knew he loved working with the horses. And she was happy to have him.

The extra money also enabled her to spend time with Livy after she got home from school. Yet her nights were filled with loneliness. When she did manage to sleep, she dreamed about Luke and how tenderly he'd made love to her. She would wake up, her body aching for him.

Some nights she'd gone out to the porch and looked toward Luke's house. She'd pushed him away so many times. Would he want her if she showed up at his door?

"Tess…"

She swung around to see Brandon. "Oh, I'm sorry, Brandon. Did you need something?"

"I just asked if you wanted me to work the chestnut today."

"Sure. I did a short workout with her this morning," she said. "But I want to take it slow, she's still pretty green."

The eighteen-year-old grinned. "Okay. Oh, Dad wanted me to tell you that he's doing the roundup next weekend. Is it okay if your herd goes at the same time?"

"That sounds great. I'll be there to help out."

Tess walked Whiskey into the barn, finished for the rest of the afternoon. She led the bay stallion into his stall and began to remove the saddle when she saw Luke coming down the aisle with a young girl, a pretty brunette dressed in jeans and a T-shirt. Tess didn't even have time to prepare for the visitors before they arrived at the stall.

"Tess," Luke said. "This is Shelly Greenly. She's looking for Brandon."

She felt relief and didn't know why. "Hello, Shelly. It's nice to meet you."

"It's an honor to meet you, too. Brandon talks about you all the time."

Tess was a little embarrassed with the praise. "Why, thank you. You can catch Brandon in the corral. He's working one of the horses."

"I promise not to disturb him. I just have to ask him

something. It will only take a minute." She wandered off and through the double doors.

Tess turned back to Luke, trying to eat up the sight of him. He was dressed in business attire, but had on shiny cowboy boots. She quickly glanced away. "You could have taken her straight to Brandon yourself. You don't have to ask permission."

"I didn't want to disturb anyone while they're working. I thought it best to get the okay from you."

"Bringing Brandon's girlfriend here will disturb him no matter what."

Luke couldn't help but smile. He knew the feeling. Just seeing Tess made him ache. "More than likely," he said, then couldn't seem to come up with any more small talk. "Well, I'd better let you get back to work."

"Actually, I'm about finished. It's been nice to have Brandon here. He gives me more free time."

He paused surprised she was interested in talking to him. "I'm glad. You should take time for yourself." His gaze locked on her mouth, until he had to look away. "How's your dad?"

"Same. He has his good days and bad days." She lifted the saddle off the stallion, and Luke took it from her. She removed the bridle. Together, they walked to the tack room. "His time at the seniors' center is one of the highlights of his week."

"Good. Tell Ray I said hi."

"You can tell him yourself, if you want."

He placed the saddle on the stand, then he pinned her with a stare. "I want a lot of things Tess, but some of them aren't possible right now."

She glanced away. "How is your brother?"

"He's good. He wants out of the hospital, but the doctors want to be sure someone is with him." Luke folded his arms across his chest. He caught a whiff of her, the smell of leather, horses, and her own unique scent. He blinked to bring himself back to reality. "I'm going to see him tomorrow, to try and convince him to come here."

"Oh, Luke, that's wonderful. You two will have a chance to get to know each other."

"Or kill each other."

"Or decide what to do with the ranch," she said.

"I think Brady and I have finally come to terms on that," he said. Thanks to Chance, his cousin made him see clearly what was important. Tess. And he'd been working day and night to get things in place.

"Then you're moving back to Dallas."

He came closer. "You seem awfully eager to send me there. What if I don't want to go? What if I want to hang around?"

He watched her swallow. "That's a decision for you to make."

"A little encouragement would go a long way." And he wanted her to understand that he needed to find his way back. "Why don't you come up to the house tonight? We'll talk about it."

She shook her head. "It's not any of my business. Just tell me if and when you need us to move out."

He was angry now. Everything he'd done was because he cared so much about this woman. "Have I ever asked you to leave? Do you truly think I'd push you and your family out of here?"

"You have Brady to think about now," she told him. "He'll have some say about us being here."

"The hell he will," Luke said as he reached for her and brought her closer. "What do I have to say to get you to believe me, Tess?" he asked, his voice low. "Your family will always have a home here."

He saw the tears in her eyes. "Thank you."

He hung on to the last of his resolve as her luminous eyes locked with his. He'd missed so much.

He wanted to devour her right there, taste her sweetness, feel her strength…her love. But he couldn't. Not until he could offer her a lifetime commitment.

"There's so much I want to tell you," he breathed. "How much you mean to me…" His stomach knotted in frustration. "Right now I need to iron things out with Brady."

She hesitated. "And that's the most important thing."

"My feelings for you don't stop just because I found my brother."

"But your family has to come first, just like my family does. We both have responsibilities, Luke. Right now there isn't time for anything else."

The next afternoon Luke stood across the solarium at the rehab center. Brady sat in the wheelchair, reading over the contracts. Luke had to let his brother make up his mind on his own over the land sale to Hank, and about building the gated community for either the Randells or Buck Chilton. And he did.

Finally Brady looked up and motioned for Luke to come over. "I appreciate you sending a copy of the contracts to my lawyer."

Those dark eyes of his brother's were so like their father's. Sometimes it was hard to look at Brady, knowing he'd gotten something else from Sam Randell.

"It's not a problem. You should be careful when you invest."

Brady glanced down at the papers again. "Did I tell you that Gina Chilton paid me a visit?"

Luke straightened. "No, you didn't. That's even low for her. Did she pressure you to selling?"

He raised an eyebrow. "She makes it hard to turn her down."

Luke could just imagine. "I know. I've see her in action."

Brady shrugged as if he wasn't impressed. "I have to tell you I'm impressed with what this Barrett guy is paying for our strip of Rocking R land. Does it have oil on it or what?"

Luke shook his head. "No. Just something he treasures more. Wild mustangs."

For the first time he saw Brady laugh. It made him think they might just have a chance at this brother thing.

Brady sobered. "So you really think we can make some money on this deal with the Randells?"

"In the long term, I do. Chance and I have gone over this several times. They aren't going to compromise the area by overdevelopment. We're keeping a lot of the integrity of the ranch. And as the contract states, the parcels of land in this deal included equal acreage from three ranches, the Circle B, Cade's Moreau Ranch and the Rocking R. When you get released from here, why don't you come and stay with me? I mean at our ranch, at least to see the project get underway."

Brady looked thoughtful. "It looks like I'll need a place to hang out a while." He held out a hand. "I need a pen."

Luke reached into his pocket and gave Brady a pen, but held his breath as his brother signed several copies.

Brady gave everything to Luke. "This doesn't guarantee we're going to be friends. Just business partners."

They shook hands. "Well, partner, what do you say? Do you want to come to the ranch and take a look at your investment?"

"Maybe, but just so you know, I'm not planning to sit in a rocking chair. And as soon as possible, I'll be back in the cockpit."

Luke saw the determination on his brother's face. "Well, until then, I'm looking forward to getting to know my brother."

"Don't get your hopes up."

Luke gritted his teeth as he walked out. "Well, this is going to be a great partnership," he muttered under his breath. Why was he hoping for more?

"Mr. Luke! Mr. Luke!"

Luke went to the back door and looked through the screen at Livy Meyers standing on his porch. His chest tightened seeing the tiny replica of Tess.

"Hey, shortcake." He opening the screen and she walked inside the kitchen. "How are you today?"

She looked up at him with those big blue eyes. "I'm sad 'cause you never come see us anymore. Are you mad at us?"

He crouched down. "Oh, no, Livy. I could never be mad at you. You're my favorite girl."

"But you don't come to my house anymore. Not since that lady came." She wrinkled her nose. "Are you gonna marry her?"

Where had the child gotten that idea? "No, Gina is just someone I used to know in Dallas."

"She's pretty, but not as pretty as Mommy. I hope you like her best. Katie said if you like a lady you kiss a lot, like her mommy and daddy do. I saw you kiss Mommy once. Do you like kissing her?"

"Yes I do, very much. Almost as much as I like kissing you." He leaned forward and kissed her cheek.

She giggled, but quickly sobered. "I want you to love my mommy. Sometimes I hear her cryin' at night." Tears filled the girl's eyes. "I don't want Mommy to be sad." The child wrapped her arms around Luke's neck and sobbed.

"Oh, Livy. I don't want you or your mother to be sad, either. I never meant for that to happen. And I've been working hard to make sure your mommy is happy again…and you, too."

She raised her head and swiped at her tears. "What are you gonna do?"

He shook his head. "I can't tell you because it's a secret. But you can help me surprise your mother."

Her eyes widened and she nodded.

"I want to talk to your mom. And right now she isn't

taking my phone calls." He'd been calling her since he left the hospital with the signed contract from Brady.

"I know. Aunt Bernie said she should let you say your piece before she makes judgments." She frowned. "What does that mean?"

"It means your mommy should listen before she says no."

"She isn't gonna say no 'cause she loves you."

A sudden dryness in Luke's throat made it impossible for him to swallow. "She told you that?"

Livy shook her head. "No, she said that to Aunt Bernie."

"And I want to tell her that I love her, too. So I need your help." He proceeded to explain his plan to the five-year-old, then wrote out a note that Livy was to give to her mother.

With the sweetest kiss, the girl walked out the door, clutching the envelope like a treasure, but stopped on the steps. She turned and looked up at him.

"I've been wishin' real hard every day to have a daddy like you," she said, then swallowed hard. "Have you been wishin' for a little girl like me?"

Luke's heart pounded in his chest. "With all my heart."

"Mommy, are you going riding to Mustang Valley?" Livy asked as Tess stepped off the porch to head to the barn for her afternoon session.

She stopped. "I have work to do, Livy."

Tess had only managed a few hours with the new mare that had arrived two days ago. Work had been her salvation lately. That was until she'd gotten Luke's note yesterday. Then, why had she put on clean clothes and a little makeup?

Her daughter gripped her kitty in her arms. "But you gotta go riding to see Mr. Luke."

The screen door squeaked as Ray came outside. "You gonna go see Sam's boy?" he called to her.

Tess tried to hide the blush heating her face. Did everyone know her business? "Maybe. He probably wants to talk over some business."

"Please, Mommy." Livy jumped up and down. The kitten had enough and leaped out of her arms. "You gotta go see him."

"It is a mighty pretty day for a ride," her father added as he sat down on the porch swing.

Tess wasn't sure what to do. Luke's message played over in her head. *I need to see you. There are too many things left unsaid between us. Luke.*

Truth was she wanted to see him. Maybe it was for the last time, but she needed to keep her wits about her. She told herself it had to do with her future. "Okay, I'll go, just let Aunt Bernie know where I'm headed."

Smiling, the child took off as Tess looked at her father. "Are you okay?"

He smiled. "Yes, I'm fine. You all take good care of me." He went to her. "Maybe you need someone to take of you."

She forced a smile. "You better not let Bernice hear you say that."

He frowned. "It's time, Tess. It's time to let yourself trust someone."

She glanced away. "I don't do well in that department. I'm happier here with you, Bernice and Livy."

"You have a big heart, my girl. You need to share it with someone like Luke."

She swallowed. "Dad, Luke and I are too different. He has a life somewhere else." She wondered how long before he wanted to return to it.

"Bah, that's nonsense. He no more wants to sell this place than he wants to leave you."

Tess was afraid she couldn't hold a man like Luke. "Dad, he's already sold a parcel of land."

Her father looked confused. "Maybe there's a reason for that, Tess. The Rocking R Ranch has several sections, and since he isn't running a herd, maybe he needs the money."

Ray Meyers's loyalty to the Randells was unwavering. She knew Sam hadn't appreciated all the extra things her father had done to keep the place together.

Livy came running out the door. "Aunt Bernie said it's okay to go, Mommy."

Tess looked at her daughter's sly grin. Something was up, and she wasn't sure she wanted to know what it was.

"Give Luke my best," Ray said.

She waved, hating to leave her father. Today was a good day for him. It had been a long time since they'd had a conversation about anything other than his treatment or Livy. It was almost like he was his old self. Of course he wouldn't be for long and she had to remember that. Just as she wouldn't be the same after Luke left here.

Chapter 11

Luke paced back and forth along the creek, among a row of trees, waiting for Tess. He'd ridden in from Hank's side of the valley, even borrowed a mount from the Circle B Ranch. Autumn was in the air and he could already see the changing of the season. When he'd first come here it was summer and Texas hot. Now, with the leaves starting to change, he could see the beauty that everyone was in awe of. There was something magical about this place.

He glanced out toward the meadow. The herd was gone, but he didn't worry about their temporary absence, because he knew this was their home…forever. And the strip of the Rocking R land Luke and Brady had sold Hank would be added to the parcel that was known as Mustang Valley. And it would remain untouched.

From now on this place belonged to the wild ponies that were here long before people had settled here.

Luke sensed someone watching him, and he turned around to see Tess on Whiskey at the top of the ridge. She sat unmoving in the saddle for what seemed forever. His chest tightened with excitement, just watching her. She was an incredible horsewoman.

Tess started down the rise and he walked to meet her. She was beautiful with her curls unbound. She wore jeans and a blue starched blouse. She'd taken special time with herself...for him.

Her horse nudged his hand in greeting. "I glad you could make it."

"You said you needed to see me." She climbed off Whiskey with ease. So graceful and yet strong around the powerful animals.

Tess suddenly felt awkward about coming here. She glanced toward a blanket that was spread out, along with a backpack, then back to Luke.

He was so devastatingly handsome, and he looked more and more as though he belonged here. But did he really want to? "You said you have something to talk to me about."

He leaned forward, and for a split second she thought he was going to kiss her. Or maybe that was her hope.

"Among other things," he told her, then took her hand. "Why don't we sit down and relax?"

She resisted a little. "I don't have much time."

His clear gray eyes bore into her. "Thirty minutes. You've been avoiding my calls for days, I practically had to kidnap you to get some time with you."

He smiled. "If I didn't know better I'd think you were afraid to be alone with me."

"I'm not afraid." She marched to the blanket and sat down, then folded her arms. She could feel herself trembling. "Your note said you wanted to talk."

He strolled over, removed his hat and sat down by the backpack. He took out a bottle of wine. "Chance says this is a good vintage, and it's from a local vineyard." Luke had already uncorked the bottle.

"I don't want any wine."

"Why? Don't you drink?"

"Not often, but I just don't want any right now." She had to keep a clear head.

He studied her for a long time. "You're not—pregnant?"

She felt the heat rise to her face. "No! Oh, no!"

Luke didn't look relieved as his gaze moved down to her flat stomach. "It's crazy, but part of me feels a little disappointed."

Tess glanced away in shock. Why was he doing this to her? "Luke, please, let's not bring up that night." She stood and walked off toward the meadow. She felt the cool breeze against her face, but it didn't help the heat rushing through her body.

Luke came up behind her. "Tess, I didn't mean to upset you. If you don't want to talk about that night, I won't, but I want you to know that I've relived that time we were together, over and over. It was special to me. You're special to me."

She couldn't let herself think about their lovemaking. It hurt too much. "Yes, it was special, but it was a fantasy, Luke. We both knew we had to go back to our lives, back to what's real."

He turned her around. "It doesn't have to be a fantasy, Tess. What if I want to make it real?" His head lowered and his lips touched hers.

Tess sucked in a breath. He took her mouth again, but this time he didn't pull back. He drew her against his body, his heat. Unable to resist, she wrapped her hands around his neck and allowed him to deepen the kiss. When he finally released her, she wasn't able to speak, or even think clearly.

Luke took a step back and ran fingers through his hair. He had to slow this down. "Damn, if you aren't getting me sidetracked. I brought you here because I wanted to tell you about what I've been working on."

He watched her back straighten. "Don't bother. I've already heard you sold this strip of land."

"I did, but for a good reason. The money will help finance my upcoming project."

"So this is what you wanted to tell me? That soon there are going to be houses built along this creek? Well, I don't want to hear about it."

Luke couldn't believe that she wouldn't even listen to him. "That's it, you're not going to give me a chance to explain?"

"What can you tell me, Luke?" She waved her arms around. "That the mustangs will remain safe? Most think of them as a nuisance, and once people move in, the ponies will slowly disappear." She glared. "And you could have prevented it."

He was stunned. Of course six months ago he would

have sold his soul for the right deal. But he wasn't like that anymore. And it hurt that she didn't know him better. "You think so little of me?"

Before Tess could give him an answer, two riders appeared along the rise. They both watched as Hank and Chance made their way toward them.

Luke went to greet the two. "Hi, Hank, Chance."

"Tess, Luke." Hank pushed his hat back. "Sorry to disturb you, but I got call from a neighbor, Merle Townsend about an injured mustang. He's not sure if it's foul play or just the stallions fighting." He glanced around. "Since the herd isn't here, we'll just ride on toward the mesa."

"I'll go with you," Luke volunteered, knowing his time with Tess was over. Probably for good.

"I can go, too," Tess said. "Oh, but I can't ride Whiskey around the herd. He'd stir up those stallions and might get hurt."

Hank stepped in. "Luke, you go on with Chance. I'll stay and keep Tess company until you get back."

Chance's horse shifted. "Merle said it's the palomino stallion, right?"

Hank nodded. "You should be able to spot the blood on the rump, the left side. I'm worried that some kids are using the ponies for target practice."

Luke returned with his horse, his hat pulled down low hiding his eyes. "Ready."

Chance nodded. "Then let's do it, cuz."

Tess watched as Luke mounted up and rode off without even a glance in her direction.

Once they were out of sight, Hank turned to her. "Sorry, we didn't mean to interrupt your afternoon."

Tess nodded. "I should get back to the house, anyway." She started to leave, realizing that Hank had followed her. The spread blanket and the bottle of wine looked like a private time for lovers.

"Luke went to a lot of trouble to make this special." He gave her a sideways glance. "It's a shame you have to take off."

Tess wasn't ready to talk about this. "Believe me, it isn't a good idea for me to stay."

"I might be an old man, Tess, but not so old that I don't remember wanting to be with a special girl."

"It was a bad idea to come here." She didn't want to stay. "I don't have time to wait around."

"It's not really my business, but shouldn't you hear the man out before you turn him down flat?"

"I already heard it. Hank," she blurted out. "Luke sold this strip of land."

"I know. And it cost me a pretty penny to buy it."

She froze. "You're the one who bought the land?"

Hank nodded. "Figured it was the only way to protect the mustangs, and so the grandkids will be able to enjoy this place." He nodded toward the blanket. "So they, too, can come here to ride, or if they want to spend time alone with someone special. Everyone benefits. Luke agreed, but he just needed to get the okay from Brady."

Tess's mind was reeling. "What about his project? The gated community he plans to build?"

"Yeah, we're all involved in that. We lucked out when Luke and Brady chose to throw in with us. The first

Randell Corporation project will break ground in about a month. Of course, there will be a lot of restrictions to protect this valley, and the houses will be far enough away not to disturb the mustangs.

"And Luke's for that?"

"He's a real powerhouse about getting things done. He's already got people in place to start when we get the okay."

Hank saw the confusion in Tess's pretty blue eyes. Life had been rough on her, and she didn't trust easily. "I think Luke always wanted to stay here. To make a home, to have family around. When his father deserted him, he didn't have any other siblings to rely on. And his mother was too wrapped up in bitterness to see her son's loneliness."

He watched Tess blink back tears as she looked out at the meadow.

"At least when my boys lost their parents, they had each other," Hank continued. "And me and Ella to help ease the pain, and make them feel safe and loved." He grinned. "They turned out pretty good, if I do say so myself. I couldn't love them any more if they were my own blood.

"I'm beginning to feel the same about Luke. He's a good man, Tess." He took her hands and held tight. "And in your heart I think you already know that."

Chapter 12

It was nightfall, and he wasn't back yet.

Tess paced the dining room at Luke's house, occasionally stopping to look out the window. She shouldn't be worried. Hank had called earlier and said they'd managed to rope and bring in the wounded mustang. The cousins were celebrating with Luke over his part in the rescue.

So what was she doing waiting for him to come home? Who was to say he'd want to see her now, anyway? She'd pushed him away so many times, and accused him of God knows what. But after she'd finally looked over the architect's plans for Golden Meadow Estates, she realized this was his dream, his plan for all of them. What he'd been trying to tell her all along.

And she'd never given him a chance.

Now it was her turn. She was going to let Luke know how she felt about everything, and her fears, and her feelings for him.

If he'd just come home.

Hugging herself, Tess paced in front of the table where candles were lit, giving the room a soft glow. The wine from earlier was opened, the glasses ready for a toast.

Oh, God, it looked as if she was trying to seduce him. She felt herself begin to tremble, along with a desperate need to run. No. If she left now, she might never get the opportunity to tell Luke how she felt. Tess poured herself a glass and took a drink.

"I thought you didn't want a drink," a deep voice said.

Tess swung around to find Luke standing in the doorway. "I... I changed my mind."

Her gaze took him in. Even though the lights were dim, she could see the fatigue on his handsome face. She fought to keep from running to him. "Did you find the mustang?"

He nodded. "The pony had a big gash on its rump, and even after we roped him, he continued to fight us all the way back to the Circle B Ranch. The vet arrived just as I was leaving."

"That's good," she said.

The room grew silent. Tess only heard the rapid pounding of her heart. She was quickly losing her nerve. "Well, I probably should get home." She put her glass down on the table and started to walk out when Luke took hold of her arm.

"Why are you here, Tess?"

She made the mistake of looking at him. He mesmerized her, just as he had on that day he first came here. Oh, God, she loved him so much.

"I brought back the things from our ride." She nodded toward the table. There was also a copy of the design plans he'd taken along to show her. "I hope you don't mind... I went over the plans. They're wonderful, Luke."

He didn't look impressed. "I'm glad you like them."

"I do." She sighed, hurt and disappointed that he didn't seem to care. What did she expect? "I'm sorry I didn't look at them earlier."

Luke couldn't believe Tess was here. At first he'd thought she was a dream. His gaze roamed over her, then rested on her face again. "At least you had a chance now."

She was so beautiful with her hair in soft curls, and dressed in a T-shirt with a blouse over it that tied around her tiny waist and a flowing skirt.

She sighed. "It's late, I really should get home."

He couldn't let her walk away. "Tess, what are you really doing here?" Wrong thing to say. "I mean I didn't think you wanted..."

She swallowed. "I know. I wasn't eager to listen earlier." Her gaze locked onto his. "I came to apologize. I should have let you explain before I jumped to conclusions. And I thought since our picnic got interrupted you could tell me about your plans now."

All the way home, Luke had wondered how he was going to live next door to this woman who didn't want anything to do with him. When he stepped into the house and saw Tess waiting for him…

His chest constricted. "Do you really want to hear about it, Tess? I know how you feel about developing the land. But the truth is, Brady and I have no choice. It's the only way we can keep a part of the ranch."

He watched the emotions play across her face. "I know, Luke. I was wrong not to give you a chance. This time I'll listen, I promise."

Luke lowered his head, so close he could feel her rapid breathing, inhale her sweet scent. "What if I don't feel like talking right now?"

Her hands touched his jaw. "That's okay, too. I'll just follow your lead."

He bent his head and covered her mouth with a kiss that was long, deep and hungry. He tried to reveal his true feelings to her. How much she meant to him.

Tess wanted him like she'd never wanted another man. By the time he released her, they were both breathless.

"I'm going to live right here on the Rocking R, Tess. I want this to be my home."

"It's where you belong, Luke," she said.

"I know. It took me long enough to realize that. Until I came back, I had no idea." His silver gaze searched her face. "You and your family belong here, too."

She liked the sound of that.

"I have a proposition for you. Once we've built and sold the horse property, how would you feel about being the resident horse trainer?"

Tess tried to hide her disappointment, hoping for

something a little more personal. "Sure, as long as I can train and compete with Whiskey."

"It will take six months before anything is completed, so you may be so famous you won't give me the time of day."

"That would never happen." She couldn't take her eyes from his. "You've always believed in me."

"That's because you're talented, Tess. Your way with horses is incredible."

"Thank you." She was beginning to feel uncomfortable. Maybe that was all he wanted from her. "Thank you, too, for making sure my family can stay on. You'll have to let me know the cost of leasing the barn and corrals."

Tess had to get out of there. She began to back away, but before she could get very far, he reached for her.

"Oh, no you don't, Tess Meyers. You aren't leaving yet. Not until I've said it all." He closed his eyes a moment. "I've worked so hard to find a way to keep all this." He glanced away, then swallowed hard. "Why do you think that is?"

She shrugged. Oh, God, she couldn't breathe.

"You. I'm trying to build a future here. A place for you and your family." He drew in a long breath and released it. "I came here nearly broke. I made some bad choices when I worked in Dallas, and it cost me everything. At least, I thought it was everything. I wasn't a nice man."

He released a breath. "Then I met you and your family, and my cousins. I never had that kind of support or acceptance. You gave me all that and more. I wanted to tell you about the project from the first, but I had to make sure that this deal was the real thing."

"It wouldn't change my feelings for you," she admitted, knowing it was the truth.

"It matters to me. Until the complex is built and sold, it's going to be a little tight financially. But if everything goes as planned, we should be doing pretty well in a few years."

Tears clouded her eyes. She didn't care about the money. "You're going to make it work for yourself… and for Brady."

His eyes narrowed. "That may be, but you're the one I care the most about. I'm doing this for us and *our* future. I love you, Tess."

This time she gasped. "Oh, Luke. I love you, too. I was so worried that I ruined everything. I should have listened to you."

"You didn't ruin anything." He was grinning when he wrapped her in a tight embrace. Then his mouth came down on hers. She didn't remember much after that as the world melted away and there was only this man.

He broke off the kiss, then leaned his forehead against hers. "Does that mean you're gonna take a chance and marry me?"

Tess linked her hands around his neck. "I happen to think you're a sure deal, Lucas Randell. And if that's a proposal, the answer is, Yes. I'll marry you." She pulled his head down to hers in another heated kiss.

"I won't let you down, Tess," he breathed. "You or

Livy. You two are the most important people in my life. I love you both so much."

"I know you won't let us down. I was the one who was afraid to love." She sobered. "I've been running for so long, but I couldn't stop myself when you show up here. I never thought I could love anyone as much as I love you."

Luke hadn't realized how much those words meant to him. His life had been so empty. His mouth found hers in a hungry kiss. He couldn't let her go, and he deepened the kiss until they both needed to take a breath.

"Say it again," he breathed against her ear.

"I love you," she repeated. "Thanks for not giving up on me."

"No worry of that. I'm so crazy about you, I would have come after you." He hugged her and whispered. "And I wanted a family. You and Livy. I couldn't love that little girl more if she were mine. You think she'd let me adopt her?"

More tears threatened. And Tess could only nod. And he kissed her again and again.

"Oh, boy! Oh, boy!" a tiny voice called out.

Luke broke off the kiss and Tess spun around to see Livy dressed in pajamas standing in the doorway.

"Olivia Meyers. What are you doing here?"

The five-year-old tried to look innocent. "I woke up and got scared, Mommy. You weren't in your bed. So I saw the light on here and thought Mr. Luke would help me find you." She walked to Luke and looked up at him with those big eyes. "Are you really going to be my daddy?"

Luke crouched down to the child's level. "If it's all right with you. I've asked your mother to marry me."

She beamed. "I know 'cause I saw you kissing her. It's just like Katie said. You kissed Mommy 'cause you love her the best."

"Yes, I love her best. But I love you a lot, too." He leaned forward and placed a kiss on Livy's cheek. "I still have to ask you something to make this night perfect. I need you, Olivia Meyers, to say you want me to be your daddy."

The child's eyes rounded, and she glanced up at her mother. With Tess's nod, Livy nodded, too. "I've been hopin' you'd be my daddy someday."

Luke drew the tiny child into an embrace. He swallowed the dryness in his throat and managed to say, "And I was hoping someday I'd have a little girl just like you." Those tiny arms around his neck were the sweetest feeling he'd ever had. "I love you, Olivia Randell."

She pulled back, her eyes wide. "Oh, boy. I'm gonna be Sarah Ann and Katie's cousin."

Suddenly they heard Bernice's voice and looked toward the doorway to see the older woman. "Oh, my, Livy. What are you doing here?"

The child rushed to her aunt. "Aunt Bernie, Mommy and me are gonna marry Mr. Luke." She giggled. "I mean my daddy. He's gonna 'dopt me."

Bernice grinned. "Well, I'll be. Seems there's been a lot going on tonight." She hugged the child, then looked at her niece. "Congratulations, I'm so happy for everyone."

"Thank you, Bernice," Luke said.

"Daddy, are we gonna live here in your house? And what about Grandpa and Aunt Bernice? Are they in our family, too?"

Bernice gasped. "Land sakes child, you ask far too many questions."

Luke wanted no doubts with any of his new family. He hugged Tess to his side. "We're all moving into this house." He looked at Bernice. "There are a lot of rooms to fill—for everyone in the family. Besides, I'm planning on having Bernie's famous pancakes at least once a week."

"Yippee," Livy cried. "I get my own room." She paused and looked at Luke. "Will there still be enough room for a baby sister?"

This time Tess gasped. "Okay, young lady, I think it's time for you to head back to bed." She went to her daughter and looked pleadingly at her aunt.

The child relented, kissed everyone goodbye and went out the door. Finally they were alone.

"There's still time to back out," Tess teased. "You're getting quite a family."

"And I'm crazy about every one of them. So I guess I hit the jackpot."

"My dad is going to need extra care."

"And we'll make sure he gets it. If you'd looked over the plans, you might have seen that we added an assisted-care facility."

Her finger trembled as she touched her mouth. "Oh, Luke."

"I never want you to have to put your father someplace far away. He'll be around his family as much as possible. This way he'll always be close by and around the horses he loves."

"Oh, Luke, you're such a sweet man."

"I'm glad you finally noticed." He dipped his head to capture her mouth and let her know his hunger for her.

He finally broke off the kiss. "And right now there're just the two of us," he breathed against her ear. "Maybe we can discuss filling those extra bedrooms with babies."

Tess blushed. "You want children?"

"I want to have a child with you," he stressed. "Just maybe not right away."

"There are so many things we haven't talked about."

"We've already talked about the important things. Love and family."

She smiled. "Maybe we should just enjoy the quiet… and maybe continue our picnic upstairs?"

He touched her face, trying to believe Tess was his. "We definitely have a lot to celebrate."

Epilogue

Luke glanced at Tess as they rode their horses over the rise toward the valley. So much had happened in the past two months. They had been married in a quiet ceremony at a small country church with just family present. Ray had been able to walk his daughter down the aisle, with Livy as the flower girl. Their honeymoon had been a short weekend trip to San Antonio, but it hadn't mattered to them, they were alone and together.

"Oh, look, Luke. The mustangs are here."

"I told you." He walked Dusty down the slope, then stopped by a tree and climbed off. He led the horse to water, and Tess by his side.

The meadow's grass was green after the latest rain, but some of the huge trees along the creek had lost leaves with winter coming.

"I know you're not disturbing the valley, but I thought the noise of machinery and vehicles would scare off the ponies."

"We've tried hard not to disturb anything."

Golden Meadow Estates had broken ground, but not without a lot of help and dedication. Luke was fortunate in that he'd been able to talk two of his former employees into relocating and coming to work for him.

Since it was off season at the Mustang Valley Nature Ranch, some cabins were available for his staff. And many of the construction laborers were staying at the Circle B bunkhouse to help save on costs.

"Have you been able to talk Brady into coming out here? Hank could bring him in one of the golf carts."

Luke shook his head. "He's not ready." His brother had arrived a few weeks ago and moved into the now vacant foreman's cottage. That was the closest Brady would allow him. There had been no talk about Sam Randell…all the years in between and why they hadn't met. "Brady told me to just leave him alone."

Tess turned to him. "He's got a lot to think about, Luke. He could lose his career over this injury." He placed her hand on his arm. "He's in therapy, isn't he?"

"Dylan said he's been taking Brenna to the cottage. Seems our family physical therapist isn't accepting any of his guff. So at least he's doing his workouts."

Tess pulled off her hat and brushed her hair back. She hadn't had much of a chance to get to know her brother-in-law. She did know she didn't like him holed up in the cottage all alone.

"Maybe we should move him into our house. He really shouldn't be by himself right now."

Luke shook his head. "No. What he needs is a kick in the butt. He has no idea how lucky he was to survive the accident." Her husband smiled. "Or we could send Livy to spend time with him."

Tess smiled, too. Brady might be a pain to everyone, but she'd seen how patient he'd been with his new niece. "That might not be such a bad idea."

Luke reached for his wife. "I didn't bring you here to talk about Brady." He kissed her nose. "I brought you here for some alone time." He drew her into his arms, and his mouth came down on hers in a tender kiss that quickly stirred their desire, reminding her of their nearly perfect life.

"Oh, boy, I like how you make a statement," she said, leaning her head against his chest. "I take it you're still happy you married me and inherited a ready-made family."

He pulled back and cupped her face. "I've been alone so long that I can't believe I have all this. You and Livy—" he fought the sudden hoarseness in his voice "—you're my heart."

She blinked back the tears. "And you are mine. I love you."

Luke kissed her again, knowing he'd never get enough of her or her love. He knew now why he'd come back to Mustang Valley. To find what he'd always longed for: to come back home…to have a family.

* * * * *

THE LIONHEARTED
COWBOY RETURNS

To all the men and women in our armed forces, thank you for your service to our country. And to my Tom in the US Army, you make a mother proud. Stay safe and Godspeed.

Chapter 1

He'd been to hell and back, but he'd finally made it…
home.

Jeff Gentry stood on the porch of the foreman's cottage at the Rocking R Ranch. The sun was just coming
up, but he was already feeling the Texas summer heat.
He drew a long breath of the familiar country air, loving the earthy smells of cattle and horses. This place
was where he'd grown up, where he'd been part of a
family. As a kid, it was the first place he'd ever felt safe.

This had been the meaning of home to him, once.
Could it be again?

For the past decade, the U.S. Army had been his
home. Ten years was a long time. During his military
service, he'd traveled the world and seen far too much
destruction and death to resemble the kid who'd left the

ranch at twenty. Now he had his own personal nightmares he needed to forget. And he lived with a particular one that had changed his life for good. He rubbed his thigh, still feeling pain. But, like the doctor had told him, he'd been one of the lucky ones.

He didn't feel so lucky. The last mission had robbed him of his life as he'd known it, and of his future. And now he'd been sent home to figure out his next move. Could he come back to San Angelo and rejoin the Randell family?

"Morning, son."

Jeff turned to see his father approach the porch. He put on a smile. "Hey, Dad."

At fifty-five years old, Wyatt Gentry-Randell was still a formidable man. He walked tall, his spine straight. His muscular frame resulted from years of physical labor handling rodeo stock. He smiled easily, and he was a soft touch when it came to his wife and children.

Years ago, he'd married Maura Wells and taken on her two small children, Jeff and Kelly. The day Wyatt had adopted them had been the best day of Jeff's life. Wyatt had erased a lot of years of painful memories for their mother, for all of them. And two more siblings, Andrew and Rachel, had been added into the mix.

Oh, yeah, he loved this man.

"What brings you out here?" Jeff asked, knowing that most of the family had given him what he'd asked for: space. "Do you need my help with anything?"

Wyatt handed him a mug filled with steaming coffee. "No. I just wanted to spend some time with my son. It's nice to have you home."

Jeff took a sip. "It's good to be back." It wasn't a lie exactly. He enjoyed being here with his parents.

He leaned against the porch railing and looked around the impressive ranch. Every well-cared-for outbuilding had recently been painted glossy white. For over twenty years, twin brothers Wyatt and Dylan had run their rough-stock business here. Not only did Uncle Dylan raise Brahmas, he had a bull-riding school, too. Both were very profitable enterprises, and also came under the umbrella of the Randell Corporation, of which every family member was a paid shareholder.

The corporation had been formed about a dozen years ago by Wyatt and Dylan along with the other four Randell brothers, Chance, Cade, Travis and Jarred, plus two cousins, Luke and Brady. All their properties were involved, including a nature retreat and an authentic working cattle ranch. They'd also built horse-property homes in a gated community that overlooked the famous Mustang Valley where wild ponies roamed freely. That was a big tourist draw.

Even though Jeff and his sister weren't blood, they'd always been considered Randells. And he had no doubt that the family would find a place even for a beat-up old soldier like him in the organization. But that was what he didn't want—pity.

His father's voice broke into his reverie. "We know the last several months have been rough, son. So take all the time you need. Just get used to being home again."

It was hard to hang on to anger when you had that kind of support. Jeff was touched, but he wasn't ready to talk about his time overseas, maybe not for a long time.

If ever. He'd done enough of that after his rescue, during his months of rehab, and it hadn't done a bit of good.

"I appreciate that, but I'm fine." He forced that smile again. "Of course, I should take advantage of this to get out of work. I've never been fond of mucking out stalls."

His father grinned. "It's safe to say we have enough ranch hands to do that task. But maybe you're up to going for a ride with Hank and I this morning?"

Jeff tensed. He wasn't ready to meet up with all the Randell clan. "Where to?"

Wyatt sighed. "A ranch auction." He studied his son. "The Guthrie place."

Jeff couldn't hide his shock at the mention of his childhood friend. "Trevor was having financial trouble?" he managed to ask, knowing it was a crazy question. After his friend's death Lacey would have trouble handling things by herself.

Lacey Haynes Guthrie. Just hearing her name sent a rush through him. Damn, he hated that she still had that effect on him. In school, she was the girl everyone loved, but she'd only had eyes for one man and that was his best friend. Never him—until that one day.

"Why didn't anyone say something sooner?"

His father looked at him. "First, you and your recovery were our main concern. And secondly, we didn't know there were problems until I heard about the auction this morning." He blew out a long breath. "With this economy, so many ranches are in trouble. And Trevor's illness was costly…" His father raised an eyebrow. "Maybe you can talk with Lacey today."

For years Jeff had tried never to think about her. It

seemed like a lifetime ago when they'd all been friends. Best friends. Now Trevor was gone. "I don't know what to say." He released a breath. "How can I explain why I wasn't around?"

"You tell her the truth, son. You were defending our country, and there was your extended stay in the hospital. All those surgeries on your leg. You've gone through a lot. There's no shame in what happened to you."

Jeff closed his eyes, trying to push aside the pain of the past year. "Dad, Lacey doesn't need to hear my problems. She's had enough to deal with." He glanced at his father. "And it's not something I'm ready to talk about yet."

Wyatt nodded. "Okay, we'll honor your decision. But I still think you should get out today." A truck pulled up to the house. "Come on, your granddad's here. And knowing your mom, she's cooked up a storm. If you don't show up, she gives your food to me." He rubbed his flat stomach. "I've already had to loosen my belt a notch."

He hated to worry his parents. "Okay, I'll save you from blueberry-pancake overload."

Jeff smiled and it felt good. His dad kept his pace slow as they walked up toward the house. Breakfast with his parents and Hank would be the easy part. The hard part would be later, seeing Lacey again, knowing he couldn't say or do anything that would ease her loss. Or the fact he hadn't been there for his friend.

Jeff could never forgive himself for that.

Later that morning, Lacey Guthrie walked away when handlers led out her deceased husband's best pair of quarter horses. The coal-black stallion, Rebel Run, and the pretty liver-chestnut filly, Doc's Fancy Girl, were supposed to have been Trevor's best breeding stock. If they were sold off, there was no way she could keep the business going. But today's auction was about survival first.

"Next up for bidding are numbers 107 and 108 in your programs," the auctioneer began. "Anyone from this area knows the bloodlines of these two fine animals. We'll start the bidding on Rebel..."

Fighting tears, Lacey stepped into her kitchen, shut the back door, and leaned her head against the glass pane. She couldn't watch them go. They represented the last of her dreams with Trevor. Their quarter horse ranch. What they'd worked so hard on for the past ten years was never going to come true. What about Colin and Emily?

"Oh, Trevor," she sobbed. "You should be here for us."

"Mom!"

Lacey quickly wiped away the tears and put a smile on her face as she turned around to her eight-year-old son. "What is it, Colin?"

"You can't sell Rebel and Fancy," he said, his fists clenched. "They're Dad's horses."

"We've talked about this, son. I don't have a choice." She went to him and reached out to brush his shaggy blond hair from his forehead. He jerked away.

"Yes, you do," he insisted. "Go out there and stop it. Dad doesn't want you to sell 'em."

"Dad isn't here, honey. And I'm doing what I have to

do to keep our ranch," she told him, knowing her words weren't going to make any difference.

Anger flashed in the boy's eyes, eyes a deep blue so much like his father's. "You didn't love Dad. If you did you wouldn't do this." He turned and ran out, the screen door banging against the porch wall before slamming shut.

Lacey started after him and got to the porch just in time to hear the auctioneer's gavel hit the table as he shouted, "Sold, to the gentleman in the back row."

Lacey looked out into the crowd at the person holding the numbered paddle. Squinting against the sunlight, she glanced over the man's square jaw and the deep-set dark eyes. The cowboy hat shaded most of his face, but there was no mistaking who he was. Her heart raced as she followed his movement through the crowd, closely examining the man she'd remembered from so many years ago. Her gaze moved over his long torso to those broad shoulders.

He might have looked military, but there was a lot of Texas cowboy mixed in. Tall and muscular, he filled out a shirt like no other man she'd seen in a long time.

He glanced over his shoulder. Their eyes met for a second, and Lacey felt that odd feeling, a mixture of longing, sadness and a little anger. Before she could move or even acknowledge him, he turned and walked away.

So, Master Sergeant Jeff Gentry had finally come home.

Jeff couldn't believe it. He didn't even know about his own future, but he owned two horses. He'd only planned to bid to help Lacey get top dollar for them. He couldn't let her lose everything. This ranch had been Trevor's dream for his family. He knew his friend had worked hard to build a reputation.

His father caught up to him. "Do you mind my asking what you plan to do with your quarter horses?"

Jeff shrugged. "Sorry, I guess I didn't think about where I could board them."

Wyatt smiled. "Of course you can bring them to the ranch or maybe take them over to Uncle Chance's place. He's better equipped for training anyway."

Hank walked over to them. Jeff's eighty-five-year-old grandfather was grinning. Still healthy and active, Hank Barrett was the head of the Randell family.

"I'd say you got yourself a fine pair of horses, Jeff." He glanced around. "I'm surprised Chance didn't show up this morning. He's always been impressed with Trevor's stock."

Jeff looked toward the house again. Lacey Guthrie was still on the porch. His breath caught as his hungry gaze moved over her. Tall and slender, she was nearly five foot nine. Her long legs were encased in faded jeans. She'd filled out since high school, and the weight looked good on her. Really good. Her honey-blond hair was thick and silky, hanging to her shoulders in soft waves. Her eyes were grass-green. He remembered her as always smiling, but she was not today. Definitely not the last time he'd seen her, either.

"Do you want to go talk with Lacey?" his dad asked.

Jeff shook his head. "She's busy right now." He pulled his attention away from her. "I'd better go pay for the horses and make arrangement for pick-up." Before his dad or granddad could say anything more, he walked off, unable to hide the limp. He fought the discomfort and pulled out his checkbook as he headed to the cashier. The cost was high, but not nearly what he owed his friend.

Later, Jeff shifted his dad's pickup into four-wheel drive and turned off the gravel road. The oversized tires made the journey easily over the rough terrain along the pathway to the clearing. His spirits began to soar when the familiar lineman's shack came into view. He stopped the truck and climbed out, but didn't go any further as his gaze took in the landscape, the grove of trees and the stream that ran through the Guthrie property.

Hundreds of happy memories of summer days he'd spent here with his friend came rushing back. As kids, he and Trevor would ride their horses up here, wade through the stream, even pretend to fight off villains, rustlers and any bad guy on the most-wanted list. They ran races through the field to see who would win the title that summer as the fastest kid.

Jeff had always won. He was the athletic one. Trevor was the outgoing one, the charmer with animals and people. When it came to girls, Trev had led the way, too. That was how his friend had won Lacey's heart.

He turned his attention to the shack. Their hangout. It was different now. What once was nearly falling down had been rebuilt. Trevor had written saying what he'd planned to do.

Jeff walked across the new porch floor. The door

had new hinges, too. Trying the knob, he discovered it was unlocked. Although the inside was dim, there was light coming through the windows.

"Looks like you did it, Trev," he whispered into the single-room cabin. "You fixed the place up."

Suddenly the emotions were overwhelming. He drew a few breaths and released them slowly as a doctor had once instructed him. Once he'd pulled himself together again, he began to look around.

A small table and a pair of chairs were placed against one wall, on the other were built-in bunk beds. In the corner was a pot-bellied stove. He walked to the kitchen area to find the same old brass water pump arching over the oversized sink.

He touched the aged counter, tracing the familiar initials scratched in the wood. Their names, *Trevor Guthrie, Jeff Gentry,* and then, later, another person had been invited into their sanctum, Lacey Haynes.

When they'd gone to high school, a new declaration had been carved out: *Trevor loves Lacey.* Jeff's finger outlined the heart around their names. The threesome turned into a twosome. Trevor and Lacey never intentionally left him out, but he'd become the third wheel. And he'd found it harder and harder to be around the happy couple. Even dating his own steady girl hadn't changed his feelings for Lacey. But she'd loved Trevor.

Jeff had tried to accept it. After a time, he knew he couldn't stay around. He'd joined the military and was to leave in a few months. It had been a rough summer for all of them, and particularly rocky for the perfect couple. Trevor had asked him to help. Jeff had reluctantly agreed and he'd met Lacey at the cabin. But they hadn't done much talking.

Jeff drew a shaky breath; the pain and joy of being with Lacey still tore at him.

He'd done the unforgivable that day. He'd betrayed his best friend. So the only thing he could do had been to leave and try to forget. He'd heard weeks later of the couple's wedding.

So many years had gone by. So many things had happened over those years. He rubbed his thigh absently.

"What are you doing here?"

Jeff spun around, nearly losing his balance. He gripped the counter as he looked at the young boy standing in the doorway. The kid's hat was cocked low, but there was no hiding his anger. There was no doubt at all that he was Trevor's son.

"Hi, I'm Jeff Gentry. I used to come here when I was a kid."

"This cabin belongs to me and my dad. So you've got to leave."

"I knew your dad, Trevor." He nodded. "You must be Colin."

The boy ignored him. "He's dead."

"I know and I'm sorry. I've been away for a lot of years."

Colin's eyes narrowed. "Dad told me you were in the army, Special Forces. That you're a hero."

Jeff tried not to flinch at the title. "I was just doing my job."

Those questioning blue eyes studied him. "Big deal.

If you were my dad's friend, how come you never came to see him?"

"I was out of the country, serving overseas. As much as I wanted to be here, I had a job to do for the government."

The kid remained silent.

Jeff continued in the awkward stillness. "We wrote back and forth." That sounded lame, even to him. "I had no idea he was so sick until afterwards. I'm here now, so if I can help you—"

The kid reared back. "I don't need your help. 'Cause it's too late." Fighting tears, he ran out of the cabin.

"Wait, Colin." Jeff started after him, but stopped as he spotted a battered Jeep pull up next to his truck. Lacey Guthrie got out and walked up to her son. She didn't look happy with him.

Finally the boy stalked off toward the horse grazing on the grass. The eight-year-old mounted the animal with the ease of a pro, grabbed the reins and reeled him around. Feeling Colin's kick against his ribs, the horse shot off.

Lacey closed her eyes and prayed for strength, then she turned around to deal with the intruder at the cabin door.

Why wasn't she surprised to find Jeff here? So he wanted to reminisce about the past. Too bad he hadn't gotten the urge sooner. The one thing Trevor had wanted during those last days was to see his friend. As far as she was concerned she'd never wanted to see him again.

She blinked away the sudden rush of tears. Why did he have to come back now?

She drew a shuddering breath and worked up the courage to speak. "So, Gentry, you finally made it home."

He stepped off the porch and made his way across the field. His movement was slow and uneven as he finally reached her. "I got here as soon as I could."

She nodded, not wanting to hear another condolence for her loss. "Your parents explained you were out of the country."

He cocked his head and held her gaze. His strong jaw showed a trace of his stubbornness, but his brown eyes gave away his softer side.

And his sexy side. Jeff Gentry had always been the quiet, sexy type. He still was.

"You have to know, Lacey, I'd have given anything to be here for Trevor."

She wasn't going to cry. "I know, but I'm not happy about your trick this morning."

"Trick?"

"You could at least have let me know you were back."

"Yeah, I should have. I've been staying pretty close to home."

The Jeff she remembered never gave much away. Now wasn't much different. "I don't need your help now, Jeff. I don't need you to come and rescue me."

"Who said I was rescuing you?"

She folded her arms across her chest. "You're in the military, Master Sergeant. What do you need with quarter horses?"

"My time's up. I'm a civilian now."

She couldn't hide her shock. "I can't believe it."

He glanced away, but she caught a flash of sadness. "Believe it. I've given my time to my country. I'm ready for a change."

She could see the strain around his eyes. She had a feeling war had taken its toll on him. "Trevor would have loved having you back home."

He looked hesitant. "He wasn't the only one, Lace."

She hated that he called her by her nickname. "Logically, I know that…"

He nodded. "Trevor understood I had a job to do."

She turned and marched to her vehicle. The hurt she felt seemed as intense as losing Trevor all over again. Her biggest problems were that she had to deal with her husband being gone—and Jeff Gentry returning.

Chapter 2

A few hours later, Jeff drove to the Guthrie Ranch. He wasn't going to leave things unsettled. Lacey might not want him around, but too bad, he didn't like the situation any more than she did.

Whether she liked it or not, he was back.

He pulled up in front of the house that had once been Trevor's parents' home.

He'd been here numerous times as a kid. Just as Trevor had been a frequent visitor at the Rocking R.

He went straight to the back porch and knocked on the door. It opened, and behind the screen a little girl about five years old appeared, wearing jeans and a pink-flowered blouse. He was caught off guard for a moment. She favored her mother with that same streaked blond hair and big eyes. The fight inside him suddenly died.

"Who are you?" the child asked.

"Jeff Gentry." He smiled. "I'm a friend of your mom and dad. Who are you?"

"Emily Susan Guthrie." She shook her head. "You can't see my daddy, he died."

Jeff leaned down, bracing his hands on his thighs. "I know, and I'm sorry, Emily."

She seemed to brighten a little. "My daddy used to call me Emmy Sue," she announced proudly.

"That's cute. Is your mother here?"

"She's down at the barn, feeding the horses. I have to stay here and watch TV. She only lets Colin help her 'cause he's older."

"I bet when you're older, she'll let you help, too."

"I used to help my daddy. He said I was his best girl."

Jeff could still remember years ago how Wyatt used to call his younger sister Kelly 'Princess.' "I bet you were. And I bet your daddy would be happy that you're minding your mom, too."

She nodded eagerly. "And I'm not s'posed to let anybody in the house when she's not here."

At least one of this family's members was talking to him. "That's a good thing. I'll just go down to the barn and see your mother there."

The child looked disappointed. "'Kay. Bye." She shut the door.

Jeff made his way down the steps, wishing he could spend the afternoon watching television, too. Instead he had to try and think of what to say to Lacey to convince her to accept some help.

He owed Trevor that much.

* * *

"Mom, I'm finished feeding the horses," Colin called as he came out of Fancy's stall. "Am I done now?"

Lacey looked around the nearly empty horse barn. Thanks to the successful auction that morning, there were only five horses left, and two more would soon be gone.

She pointed to the leather bridles tossed over the railing. "Just take those back to the tack room and you can go to the house, but I don't want you to bother your sister."

Her son grabbed the tack off the railing and started down the center aisle. "You always blame me for all the trouble."

"That's because you can't leave Emily alone. I mean it, Colin, don't go near her. You're already in trouble for riding off today without asking."

"Fine, I'll just go to my room." He went into the tack room, then came out seconds later. She knew he hadn't had time to put away the bridles properly, but it wasn't worth the argument; she'd just do it herself later.

It had been a long day and she was tired. The auction had taken a lot out of her. At least the money made today would finally pay off Trevor's medical bills, and the ranch would be solvent for the next year. After that, she wasn't sure what she'd do. She knew she couldn't continue the breeding business without a stud. She'd kept her chestnut broodmare, Bonnie. She just needed a stallion.

She looked toward the barn door where her son had stopped to talk with someone. Jeff Gentry. Great. She didn't need any more of him today, but by the looks of it, she wasn't going to get her wish.

She watched as he started down the aisle. Large and powerfully built from years of military life, he roamed efficiently. Her gaze moved over him and noticed a slow gait and a slight limp. Had he been hurt? She hadn't heard anything about any injuries.

He made a stop at Reb's stall and began to get acquainted with the stallion. Much like Trevor, Jeff had a knack with animals, maybe more so than with people.

It had surprised her and everyone else when he'd announced that he'd joined the military. Even though college hadn't worked out for him, she'd always thought he'd partner with his dad and uncle in the rough-stock business. His decision to go into the army had affected a lot of people, including her. She had a feeling his return would affect just as many.

No, she couldn't let it affect her. Not after all this time and after everything she'd gone through.

Jeff gave Reb's muzzle one more pat, then started toward her. A strange sensation surged through her and all she could do was watch him. He was a good-looking man, but so was Trevor, although the two friends couldn't have been more different. Trevor was blond with hazel eyes, while Jeff had dark-brown hair and brooding coffee-colored eyes.

She thought back, recalling their conversation earlier. How could she have talked to him that way? Even with the hurt and months of loneliness since Trevor's death, she had no right to blame Jeff. He hadn't caused the virus that had damaged her husband's heart. Yet she couldn't bring herself to apologize for her actions. They had too much history for that. Jeff hadn't only walked away from Trevor all those years ago, he'd walked away from her, too. With not even a care, or as much as a backward glance. Jeff Gentry never realized the pain and hurt he'd caused her. It had been Trevor who'd picked up the pieces.

Lacey drew a breath and released it. Now, ten years later, she knew it was finally time to let it go.

"I take it you're here for your horses."

Jeff paused to regroup for his talk with Lacey. He wasn't going to let her brush him off. He could do attitude with the best of 'em. "First, I want to settle something."

"Settle what?"

"Can we cut this out? I get you're angry at me for just showing up."

She threw him a surprised look. "Why don't we just chalk it up to a bad day?" Her gaze locked with his. "You ever felt your world was suddenly crashing down around you?"

Jeff gripped the stall railing, shifting his weight onto his good leg. "Hell, yes, once or twice," he answered, flashing back to the painful days during his long recovery.

He'd only heard of Trevor's illness right after surgery when he was flat on his back, fighting his own hell. His friend was dying and he couldn't help him. He'd sent word to Lacey, but by the looks of it, that hadn't been enough.

"Trevor wouldn't want you wasting time being so angry," he said.

Those pretty green eyes narrowed. "Cut me a little slack, Gentry. I had to give up a lot today."

"I'm not cutting you anything. You can't fall apart now. You have kids who need you."

She shot him a look. "Who are you to tell me what I need to do? You weren't here. It might not be reasonable to blame that on you, but he was your best friend."

He tried not to flinch. "The military doesn't care about friendships, Lace. And neither did the terrorists I was fighting. There were times I couldn't even contact my parents."

He closed his eyes for a moment as he took a breath. The last he'd heard from Trevor, he'd said everything was fine. That had been about a month before he'd been deployed on his last mission. Then everything had changed.

He shook away his wayward thoughts.

"Lacey, you've got to know, if it were humanly possible, I would have found a way to be here for him."

He couldn't take his eyes off her. She'd always been pretty, and that had only been enhanced with age. "For you, too."

"I didn't need your help, then or now," she said stubbornly.

"That's just too bad," he retorted.

She froze at his words, then snapped out of the daze. "Look around, Gentry, there isn't much left."

Jeff moved closer, feeling fatigue in every step. He ignored it. "That's why you need me."

She said something very unladylike, grabbed a feed pail and started down the aisle. Jeff reached for her arm and turned her around. "Tell me, Lacey. How bad are things?"

"That's none of your business." She started off again.

Jeff went after her, pushing hard to keep up. She went into the tack room.

"Is Rebel Run your only stud?"

Lacey busied herself hanging up the bridles. "As of this morning he's *your* stud."

So she didn't have any business left. Great. "Okay, here's the deal. I need a place to board my horses. I'd like to leave Rebel and Fancy here. I'll pay you a fair price."

She looked shocked. "You're kidding, right?"

"Since when have you known me to kid around?" He paused and waited for her answer, but got none. "Okay, here's the clincher. I need a place to stay." He released a breath. "And I want to rent the cabin."

Lacey ran her sleeve over her brow, pushing her worn hat off her forehead. She threw up a silent prayer this day would end, along with all the craziness. She didn't want this man messing in her life.

Lacey looked back at Jeff. "The Randells own more property around here than anyone. You can take Rebel over to your uncle's place, put him out to stud there."

He gave a shrug. "I have my reasons. So, you want to take me up on my offer? The money couldn't hurt."

"All right, the horses can stay."

He nodded. "You should think about boarding other

horses, too. Bring in another half dozen and you'd make a good income."

She shook her head. "I can't work at the market and handle more animals without help."

"Then hire someone," he said. "Until then, I'll come by and help out."

She jammed her hands on her hips. "If this is your trick way of rescuing me, I don't want it."

His dark gaze settled on her face. "It's the other way around, Lace. You're the one rescuing me."

The next morning about 6:00 a.m., Jeff walked in the back door of his parents' house and found his mother standing at the stove cooking breakfast. The aroma of coffee and bacon hit him.

Maura Gentry looked up and smiled. With her auburn hair and green eyes, she had always been pretty, and that hadn't changed over the ten years he'd been away. Even though she'd come to the Rocking R a city girl, she'd fitted into ranch life as if born to it.

"Morning, honey." She eyed him closely, unable to hide her concern.

"Hi, Mom. Something smells good." He walked to the table and pulled out a chair. The kitchen had always been the heart of this home. It had also been remodeled a few times. The cabinets were maple with dark granite countertops and the latest stainless-steel appliances. The floor was the original honey hardwood. He'd loved growing up in this house.

She set a plate on the table. "I made sweet rolls."

He picked one up and took a bite. "You keep this up and I'm going to gain ten pounds."

"You could use some extra weight."

He frowned and took another bite. After he swallowed, he asked, "Where's Dad?"

"He's with Dylan. The new bull arrived earlier. He should be here soon." She brought over a plate piled high with bacon. Just then the back door opened and his dad walked in. He hung his hat on the hook on the wall, then nodded to his son before he went to his wife and kissed her.

He came to the table and pulled out a chair. "Mornin', son."

"Morning, Dad."

"You've got to see this bull, Jeff. Dylan's named him Rough Ride." His father beamed. "We both think he's going to make quite a reputation on the circuit."

Maura Gentry brought a dish of scrambled eggs and joined them. "Just so long as the two of you stay away from him, I'm happy."

Wyatt frowned. "Are you saying I'm too old to climb on a bull?"

"No, I'm saying you're too smart. So don't make me out a liar. Save the ride for those twenty-something kids who need to impress the girls." She picked up a fork. "You can impress me in other ways."

Jeff should have been used to his parents' flirting. Since the moment they'd met it had been like that between them.

His dad winked. "I'll do my best." He looked at his

son. "You thought about what you're going to do with the horses?"

Jeff shrugged. "Only that I'm going to leave them at Lacey's and pay her to board them."

"So you've got no plans to go into the breeding business?" his dad asked.

Jeff scooped up a forkful of eggs. "Still thinking on that one. I need to find a place to live first."

His parents exchanged a look, then turned to him. His mother spoke. "You know you can stay in the cottage here as long as you want. There's no hurry to leave."

"I need to be closer to the Guthrie place. That's why I'm planning to move up to the cabin."

His dad swallowed his food. "What cabin?"

"The one where Trevor and I used to hang out."

His mother frowned. "That old lineman's shack? It was nearly falling down years ago."

Jeff took a drink of his orange juice. He understood his parents' concern. "Trevor must have put some work into it, because it's in good shape now."

His mother didn't look convinced. "Jeff, do you think it's a good idea to move so far away? It's pretty isolated there."

He'd been isolated in a lot worse places…the hills of Afghanistan, the deserts of Iraq. "Mom, it's only a few miles from the ranch house. Besides, I like the quiet."

"Haven't we left you alone?" she asked. "I only worry about you because of the…accident. You haven't been walking again that long." Her eyes filled with worry. "You've only been home ten days."

He didn't want to hurt either one of them. "I've had months of physical therapy. Yes, both of you have given me space while I've been here, and I appreciate it. But I'm too old to live at home. Mainly, I've got to come to grips with what I'm going to do with the rest of my life. I never dreamed it would be anything but the military. I hadn't planned to retire for another ten years."

This time his father spoke up. "I know you'd be happier in the army, son, I only wish that were an option."

Jeff shook his head. "Not if I can't do what I was trained for." And now that a terrorist sniper had changed everything for him, he had to make a different kind of life. "Right now, I need some time."

His mother started to talk, but his dad stopped her. "Maura, our son is a man. He needs to make his own decisions. Whatever that is, Jeff, we're proud of you."

The praise from Wyatt Gentry meant more to Jeff than any medal he'd received from that last mission.

Maura nodded. "I guess it's the best solution for you both. Lacey can use your help, too." His mother reached for his hand and smiled. "I think you can be a big help to each other."

The next day Hank Barrett drove up the road toward the cabin. He knew he probably shouldn't have come here without an invitation, but he might never get one. So he'd come to see Jeff on his own.

Along with age came some privileges.

He'd stopped by the Guthrie Ranch and talked with Lacey. She'd been in the corral working with the horses. He'd stood back and watched and had been impressed with her talent. He'd always thought it had been Trevor who had had the skill with the horses, but Lacey knew her way around those animals, too. Maybe Jeff's idea wasn't so bad. Those two could help each other.

He grinned. Who knows? Lacey Guthrie might even finally take notice of his grandson. At least, maybe she could help Jeff get through the rough time.

Avoiding several mesquite bushes, Hank continued toward the cabin on the hill. He parked and climbed out, then grabbed two shopping bags filled with things Maura and Ella had sent with him.

He made his way to the porch when Jeff came out. "Granddad. What are you doing here?"

"It was either me comin' here, or your mother and grandmother. And they'd probably be hanging ruffled curtains in the windows. So you got the best of the deal, me."

Jeff chuckled and took the bags.

"That's food, and in there are some towels. There's a cooler in the back of the truck."

"I'll get it later," Jeff said. "Come inside."

Hank walked through the door first. The place wasn't much bigger than a horse stall, but it was a lot cleaner.

The bunk against the wall was made up with white sheets and a green army blanket tucked in neatly on all sides. Two pairs of cowboy boots stood at the end. The one thing that looked out of place was a single crutch next to the door, reminding him of the months of pain and anguish his grandson had gone through during his time in the hospital.

Sadness hit Hank as he ambled over to the only place

to sit down. He pulled out a chair. "So, looks like you've made the place real homey."

"It's not so bad."

"Sure, I believe you, but you know your mother isn't going to feel the same. An outside latrine and no shower isn't what they'd call civilized. So if you feel the need to get under a warm spray, come by the house."

Jeff couldn't help but smile. He always enjoyed Hank. Getting a grandfather was one of the best things about being adopted into the family.

"I'm going to rig up a portable shower out back."

"Good thing the weather is warm." The old man grew serious. "You know I have to report back to the ladies on how you're getting on. And I've learnt never to cross the women in this family, not if I ever want to eat again."

Jeff smiled. "Then you tell them that if I survived the deserts and the jungle, the Texas prairie isn't going to hurt me."

Grinning, Hank nodded. "I told 'em you'd be just fine."

"What else brings you up here, Granddad?"

Hank pushed his hat back off his forehead. "Well, I had this idea I wanted to run by you."

"I hope it doesn't have anything to do with moving home."

"No, I think if this is where you want to be, then it's the right place for you. My idea has something to do with Randell Corporation."

"And this concerns me how?"

"Just hear me out," Hank coaxed. "You know how

we have guests that come to the ranch on vacation and want to work. They like the cowboy way of things."

"And it's always made money, too."

"I was thinking this year, at summer's end, I'd like to do an old-fashioned cattle drive. All guests on horseback, and we even have a chuck wagon with a cook to make the meals just like they did a hundred years ago. We can start at Chance's place and drive the cattle across to your dad's ranch. Then go on to Uncle Jarred and Aunt Dana's and onto Cade's lands, then finally end up at the Circle B. I have the quarters to house the guests."

"Sounds like you'd be going around in a circle."

"Almost. But we'd stay on private property, and if something does happen, we're not far from help." Hank raised an eyebrow. "So, what do you think?"

"Sounds good to me." Jeff was surprised his dad hadn't said anything. "How do the brothers like it?"

"I'll tell them eventually, but right now I want the grandkids on board first. And I want you to be in charge."

Jeff was caught off guard by this. "I can't do it."

"Why? You've been in the military for years, in charge of men, giving orders."

"I haven't been on a horse in a long time. Secondly, I don't even know if I can still ride."

"Sure you can. It's something you don't forget, especially since you were so good it. You could out-ride any of your cousins." Hank smiled. "Even then you strove to be the best."

Jeff knew he had drive. He'd proven it many times

in the army, and it had saved his life more times than he could count. "That was before." He rubbed his thigh.

"Before what? The accident?" Hank shook his head. "You're just as good as before."

"The army doesn't think so," Jeff said bitterly. "They seem to think you need both legs to be a soldier."

Chapter 3

Early in the morning, Jeff closed Fancy's gate. It had been a long time since he'd mucked out a stall. He didn't like it any better than he had as a kid.

He'd only been a horse owner for a few days, but he needed the physical work. Outside of his daily workouts, he'd been pretty sedentary lately, unlike the days when he used to take five-mile runs every morning. He couldn't handle that—yet.

He sat down on the bench next to the stall gate and rubbed his knee. Maybe he'd been pushing it. But that was how he did everything—to the hilt. He'd never held back, and he wasn't going to now.

"What's wrong with your leg?"

Jeff looked up find Colin standing nearby. Was the

kid just lurking around, waiting to give him a bad time? "I'm just tired."

Those blue eyes narrowed. "You get shot in the army?"

Jeff gripped the railing and pulled himself up to stand. "Yeah, you could say that."

"Does it hurt?"

He didn't want to talk about this. "Sometimes. What are you doing out here?"

"Mom said I should help you. What do you want me to do?"

"What do you usually do?"

"Dad used to let me exercise the horses, but Mom only wants me to clean stalls."

"How about we do the cleaning first, then we'll see about the riding part."

If the boy was surprised at the answer, he didn't show it. "Whatever."

"Okay, let's start with the first two stalls. I need fresh straw spread out on the floors."

"Why? There aren't any horses."

"You've got a lot of questions, son. In the army, you don't ask, you just do."

"I'm too young to be in the army."

Jeff smiled. "Guess you're right. But there are two mares arriving tomorrow."

Thanks to his Uncle Chance spreading the word about the Guthrie Ranch being open for boarding and training, they already had their first two horses. The only problem was he wasn't sure he could handle it without help. "If you do a good job, we'll talk about wages."

The boy blinked. "You gonna *pay* me?"

Jeff nodded. "This is hard work. I'd like you to help out a few hours in the mornings. I need to learn my way around here. It's been a while since I handled horses. So, are you available?"

The kid couldn't hide his surprise. "Yeah. Do I get to help work the horses, too?"

"We need to talk to your mom about that. But from what I saw the other day, you're an experienced rider."

Colin puffed out his chest. "Since I was four years old. I'll be nine next month."

He liked the boy sharing that with him. "We still have to talk to your mom."

"Talk to me about what?"

They both turned around to find Lacey dressed in her uniform for her job at the supermarket. She came down the aisle. Her hair was pulled back into a serviceable ponytail, showing off her high cheekbones and bright-green eyes. Damn, if she didn't get his blood going.

He finally found his voice. "I've asked Colin if he wants to help me for a few hours a day. I was going to pay him."

"Can I, Mom?" The boy was excited. "Can I work with the horses?"

Lacey didn't look pleased with the idea. "We'll talk about it later. Why don't you go up to the house and wash up, Colin? Mindy's here to watch you and Emily while I go to work."

"Ah, Mom," he argued. "Why can't I help with the horses like I did with Dad?"

"Colin," Jeff began. "Your mom and I need to discuss this," he suggested, realizing his mistake of not telling Lacey about his idea first.

The boy's enthusiasm quickly died, and he turned and marched off.

Once alone, Lacey turned back to him, anger furrowing her eyebrows. "If you're trying to win my son over, you'll probably do it, especially when you dangle horses in his face."

"I wouldn't have, if I'd known how disrespectful he is to you. Why do you let him talk to you that way?"

Lacey didn't need this today. She'd purposely avoided Jeff since he'd been coming in the mornings. She hadn't liked the feelings he'd created in her whenever he was around. Feelings she'd had to kill off years ago. "Colin has had a rough time since his dad's death."

"Most kids do, but you still need to rein the boy in."

"What makes you the expert?"

"I acted like a jerk at his age, too. Someone needs to take him in hand, and that means stop coddling him."

Her eyes widened. "He's only eight years old."

"Almost nine," he corrected her.

"He's not an army recruit, Jeff. He's still a little boy who's just lost his daddy."

"He also needs to learn respect for you. I don't think Trevor would have let him talk to you that way."

At the mention of her husband's name, sadness hit her. From the day Colin had been born, father and son had been inseparable. "Trevor would have handled it differently."

Jeff stiffened. "Sorry, I'm not Trevor."

Lacey tried to keep calm, but having Jeff around

was making everything difficult. "Look, Gentry. We might be thrown together temporarily, but my family is *my* concern. Not yours. I'd appreciate it if you'd let me decide what's good for my son."

Jeff's dark gaze watched her for what seemed like an eternity. "Agreed," he finally said. "But there's something else we need to discuss."

She studied the man she'd practically grown up with. They'd shared childish secrets, survived adolescence, and he'd been her husband's best friend.

Her first lover.

Lacey glanced away. No, she couldn't think about that anymore. She couldn't let him know that it had been on her mind, either. Easy to say, harder to do when she'd been noticing the man far too much. The first thing she had to do was stop being so uptight whenever he was around.

"What…what do you want to talk about?" she asked.

"I think I've solved your problem with the ranch. Have you thought about taking on a partner?"

The next day Jeff stood back and gave the new portable shower a nod of approval. Not bad. The five-gallon container hung from a tree branch, directly over the canvas cubicle. At least now he could wash his entire body at one time. The hot summer sun would warm up the spring water quickly.

"So this is what you army guys call roughing it."

Jeff swung around, nearly losing his balance on the uneven ground, to find his cousin. A grinning Brandon Randell was dressed in the standard cowboy uniform of boots, jeans and a long-sleeved shirt to protect him from the Texas sun. He held the reins of his black quarter horse, Shadow.

"Well, I'll be damned." They exchanged a hearty hug. "What brings you out of the city, Detective Randell?" He glanced over his shoulder at the black stallion. "Just happened to be out for a ride?"

"I stopped by Hank's, and he told me you were staying up here." Brandon shrugged. "So Shadow and I cut through a couple of neighboring pastures and here we are. By car it would have been about a twenty-mile drive."

"So you did some trespassing," Jeff teased.

"I just tell people I'm on sheriff's business." Brandon jammed his hands on his hips. "Besides, I need to come see how my cousin's doing."

Jeff had no doubt that Brandon had been sent to check on him. "Not bad," he told him. "I've lived in worse conditions. Best of all, I'm enjoying the peace and quiet."

Brandon smiled. "Surely you're not saying the Randell clan is too much for you?"

"I can handle them in small doses. Dad's been running interference for me."

"Take it from me, cuz, it's not going to stop a Randell. You know, eventually they're going to come looking for you." Brandon's smile disappeared. "Just know it's only because we all care about you. Man, it's good to have you home."

"It's good to be back." Jeff relaxed a little. He'd always gotten along with the oldest cousin. When Jeff, his mother and sister had first come here years ago, it had been Brandon's mother, Abby, who'd helped them find a place to live. They also shared the fact that their mothers had come from abusive backgrounds, and Randell men had come to their rescue.

Brandon led his horse to the creek for some water, and examined the shower structure. "Not bad. I guess you couldn't stand your own stink, huh?"

They both laughed. It felt good to Jeff. "You could say that."

Brandon was like all the Randell men—tall and broad-shouldered, with dark hair and eyes. There was also the distinguishing cleft chin that marked nearly all the male Randells. Brandon had surprised everyone after college by going into law enforcement instead of ranching. He was a detective with the sheriff's office.

"Granddad Hank said you bought two of the Guthrie's quarter horses at the auction and you're boarding them there."

"It seemed simpler to keep them there." Jeff started back up the rise toward the cabin. The hot afternoon sun beat down on his T-shirt-covered back, and his leg was tired from his long day. "The past year was rough on Lacey, or she would never have sold off her best quarter horses."

Brandon tipped his hat back. "I was sorry to hear about Trevor. Man, he was so young." Brandon shook his head. "And leaving a wife and young kids."

They reached the small porch partly shaded by a tree. "I heard you're a married man now. Congratulations."

"Thanks. When you're up to it, maybe you can meet Nora and Zach."

Jeff nodded. He wasn't making any promises.

"It's good you're around to help her," Brandon told him. "Lacey can use a friend."

Friend. He hadn't been much of one when Trevor had needed him. So far, he hadn't been doing well on that front with Lacey either. "I don't know how much good I can do." Jeff hated to admit to any kind of weakness. "Sometimes I think I have enough to deal with just taking care of myself."

Brandon paused. "Seems to me you've got a pretty good start. It takes time to adjust to your new life. You've started already, living up here alone."

Jeff frowned. "Alone? I think I've had more visitors here than I did at the house."

"Comes with the territory in this family. You wouldn't remember that because you've been gone so long."

"I guess I like my privacy."

"Isolating yourself isn't a good idea," Brandon pointed out.

Jeff wanted to argue, but instead he walked inside the cabin. The place was stifling. He grabbed two sodas from the cooler under the sink and went back outside to where Brandon sat under the shade.

"Thanks," his cousin said as he took the can and popped the top.

Careful of his leg, Jeff eased down beside him. Looking out at the horse grazing by the creek, he enjoyed the hint of a breeze from under the tree.

Brandon turned to him. "Look, Jeff. You have a right to live wherever you want. I'm the last one to preach, since I avoided the family ranch for years." His cousin gave him a sideways glance. "And I didn't have anything as life-changing as losing a leg happen."

Jeff flinched. Since being home, he hadn't talked about his loss, not even with his parents. Yet it seemed easier with Brandon. "I lost more than a leg. I lost my career. My identity. Special Forces was who I was." He looked down at his soda can. "Man, you'd think this was a beer, as much cryin' as I'm doing."

"I'm glad you're talking about it," his cousin said. "But you're wrong, Jeff. You might have lost your leg, and a career, but no, not your identity. There's a lot more to you, cuz, than being a soldier. And you have a family who loves you and we'll support you any way we can."

Jeff took a long drink of the sugary soda, trying to get rid of the lump in his throat. He couldn't lose it now. "Well, when you discover where I fit in, let me know."

"I think you've already found it. You own two fine quarter horses and you're working with one of the prettiest and best trainers in these parts."

Jeff stiffened. He couldn't think of Lacey in that way, not anymore. "She's also my best friend's widow."

"So that's what's bothering you?"

"No," Jeff denied quickly. "What's bothering me is that I wasn't here when Trevor needed me. Now Lacey needs me."

"So that's why you bought two of her horses. To help her out?" Brandon stared out toward the pasture. "So are you going to be partners?" He turned to Jeff. "Are you going into the horse-breeding business?"

Jeff shrugged. "I'm not sure I can do more than clean stalls and feed the stock."

"Why not?" Brandon asked. "Years ago you were an exceptionally good horseman." Brandon smiled. "As I remember, you even broke a few mounts that summer we worked together."

That seemed like another lifetime ago. "I haven't been on a horse since I got back."

Brandon nodded and glanced down at the leg. "Seems to me if you can drive a vehicle, riding a horse shouldn't be difficult for a Special Forces guy. How much of your leg had to be amputated?"

His cousin had finally cut out the finesse, causing Jeff to tense before he forced himself to relax. "A few inches below the knee."

Brandon nodded. "I bet being in the military, you got the most hi-tech prosthesis."

He had. What the heck—he'd show Brandon. Jeff tugged his pant leg up, revealing his Justin short roper boot and the titanium limb that was connected to a plastic boot that covered his knee. "It's hard getting used to it. The hardest part is even after months, I still feel the loss, but it's been less and less. They call it phantom pain."

"I can't say I know how you feel, because I don't. But look at it this way; you nearly lost your life on that last mission. Just think how your mom and dad would be suffering if you hadn't made it back alive. All of us would be." Brandon's throat worked hard. "I never fought in a war, but I've known life-and-death situations. Far too many close calls over the years. Whatever you decide to do, I hope it's around here. I'd like to get to know you again." He broke out into a big grin. "I've never known a genuine hero."

Lacey was about at the end of her patience. When she got hold of Colin he was going to be grounded until the end of summer. If he lived that long.

She pulled the truck off the road and up toward the cabin. The last thing she wanted to do was disturb Jeff, but there wasn't any choice. Her son was missing and she had to find him.

She parked next to the familiar truck and headed up the rise, hoping Colin was here. Had Jeff been right? Did her son need a firmer hand? This was all new to her. She'd never had to worry about Colin's behavior before. She knew he'd been angry since his father's death, but it had only gotten worse. As much as she hated to, she needed to ask for help.

Lacey came around the side of the shack and found two men sitting on the edge of the porch. She recognized Brandon Randell right away. She hesitated to disturb them, but maybe the sheriff's detective could help, too. They were engrossed in conversation as she approached the porch. She saw they were both concentrating on Jeff's leg. She got closer and could see that it wasn't his leg, but a metal prosthesis. She gasped.

Both men turned toward her, and Jeff quickly pulled down his pant leg.

Brandon stood. "Lacey." He walked toward her and took her hand. "It's good to see you again."

"Hi, Brandon." She tried to gather her thoughts, but it was difficult. She glanced at Jeff, then started backing up. "I didn't mean to disturb you. I should go."

Jeff got to his feet and started after her. "Lacey, wait."

She did as he asked, but couldn't look at him. Oh, God, his leg. All this time she'd been harping on at him about not being around. What must he have gone through? She blinked at sudden tears.

Jeff's gaze narrowed. "Did you need me for something, Lacey?"

She opened her mouth, but her words were lost. What could she say?

"Lacey? What's wrong?"

Suddenly she remembered her reason for coming here. "I can't find Colin. I think he's run away."

Chapter 4

When Jeff drew Lacey into his arms, he couldn't think about anything but calming her. Not how her soft and delicate body felt against his, or how many years he'd ached to hold her close like this. It was heaven and hell.

Right now he needed to concentrate on the problem at hand. He released her. "It's going to be okay, Lacey. We'll find Colin."

"When was the last time you saw your son?" Brandon asked, breaking into the moment.

Lacey's eyes widened. "It sounds terrible, but I'm not sure. When he came in from doing morning chores, we argued." She glanced at Jeff. "He talked again about working with the horses. I got upset with his attitude so I sent him upstairs." She brushed her hair back from her face. "About noon, I fixed him a sandwich and took it up to him, hoping we could work it out." She blinked back fresh tears. "He was gone."

"What about Emily?" Jeff asked. "Did she see him leave?"

Lacey shook her head. "She's been at her friend's house all day."

Jeff watched as she tried to stay in control. "Did you check the barn?" he asked. "Maybe he was just hiding out."

She folded her arms. "I checked and found his horse gone, too. I don't know how I missed him. I was in the kitchen most of the morning. He must have walked Buddy around the front of the house so I wouldn't see him leave." Her lower lip quivered. "He wanted to get away from me that badly."

"He's had a rough year, Lacey," Brandon said. "But we're going to find him." He frowned. "Are you sure you've checked all the places he would go?"

She nodded. "That's why I came up here. This was where he used to come with Trevor."

Jeff's gut tightened. "Had he been upset that I moved in?"

She began wringing her hands. "I don't know any more. Colin seems to be mad at everything and everyone lately. He hated that I had to sell Rebel and Fancy."

Jeff pulled out his cell phone. "I'll call Dad and get some of the family out looking for him."

Brandon also reached for his radio and made a call to Granddad Hank. Jeff knew that the Randells wouldn't hesitate to help in the search, especially for a lost child.

Brandon hung up. "I think we'll come up with

enough manpower to search for a few hours. If we don't find him by then, we'll handle it as a runaway. I'll need a picture of Colin and I'll alert the sheriff of the situation." He held up a hand. "It's just a precaution for now."

Lacey wiped her eyes and nodded. "I have a school photo in my purse." She walked off to the truck.

Brandon faced Jeff. "I can make better time if I borrow your pickup."

"Sure, the keys are on the console," Jeff agreed. "What about your horse?"

"Could you put Shadow in the lean-to? I'll send a ranch hand up to get him."

Lacey returned and handed Brandon the wallet-sized picture of Colin.

"Good-looking boy." Brandon smiled as he examined the photo. "I know it's useless to tell you to go home and wait, so I won't."

"We'll go look together." Jeff nodded to Lacey. He hated feeling helpless. Hell, his job in the military had been tracking people.

Brandon walked to the truck and took off. Once alone, Jeff glanced at Lacey and caught her looking at him. It just wasn't the way he'd always hoped she would.

He might as well get it out in the open. "I haven't been on a horse since I lost my leg." There, he'd said it. "But we can search a lot of territory by truck. We both know the area pretty well."

Stunned, Lacey watched as Jeff started off toward the creek. Focusing her attention on his stride, she finally noticed the slight limp. She closed her eyes, thinking about all he must have gone through. Especially the pain.

Oh, God. The terrible things she'd said to him. All the time he'd been in a hospital, going through his own hell. No one had said a word to her and Trevor about it.

Well, there were going to be words now. She caught up with him as he took hold of Shadow's reins.

"Why didn't you tell me?"

He didn't look at her as he led the large animal up the slight rise toward the cabin. "What was there to say, Lacey? Oh, by the way, I lost a leg during my last mission." He shot her a glare. "There are thousands of men and women who've come home in worse shape them me. I only lost the lower part of my leg. Some lost both, some lost arms…so I'm one of the fortunate ones."

"You are," she told him. "You made it home." She hesitated. "But, Jeff, I said some awful things to you."

"So because now you know I'm an amputee you're going to be nicer to me?"

She cringed. "No. I just couldn't understand why you weren't here. I thought you stayed away because you just couldn't face coming back to see Trevor."

"Forget it, Lacey. I deserved it. I didn't come and see Trevor as much as I should have. But don't ever doubt that I loved him like a brother. I'll always regret that I couldn't be here for him, or you."

Lacey stiffened. Had Jeff ever regretted not being there for her ten years ago?

They made it to the rough wood lean-to, and Jeff tied the horse to the post, then flipped the stirrup over the saddle and began to loosen the cinch. Once finished, he pulled the saddle off the horse and put it on the railing.

"Deep down I knew that," she said, wondering how much her husband had wanted to see his friend. "I guess I wanted you there to ease Trevor's fears." She felt her emotions stirring again. "You were the level-headed one, never afraid of anything."

Jeff's dark gaze met hers. "Hell, Lacey, we're all afraid sometime. And I'm afraid right now that my moving up here might have pushed Colin away more."

Lacey shook her head. She was the one feeling threatened that Jeff was back, and living so close. "No, my son has been angry for a long time. He misses his dad. At one time we were a close family."

Jeff studied her. "Of course. You and Trevor have loved each other since high school."

She avoided his gaze. There had been many rough patches in their marriage, but what was the point of dredging that up now?

He patted the horse. "You were the perfect couple."

"We all know how looks can be deceiving," she said quietly.

For the past two hours, Jeff had driven around the area, going everywhere possible. If Colin was on horseback, he doubted they'd find him along the road. He called Brandon, who informed them that several of the Randells were out looking for the boy. The only problem was that nightfall was closing in on the search efforts.

Jeff pulled Lacey's Jeep up beside the cabin. They

got down as Lacey took out her cell phone and called back to her house.

He walked to the cabin, praying that the boy had come to his senses and was waiting for them inside. When he saw the empty room he knew from experience that there was a possibility Colin could be in trouble. He sincerely hoped the child was just plain stubborn.

Lacey appeared behind him. "Brandon told me that there's quite a group of people at my house." She sighed, leaning against the table. "I can't face them, Jeff."

He felt completely helpless. He wasn't used to standing around and doing nothing. "Are you sure there isn't anywhere else the boy could be? Did he and Trevor go riding anywhere special?"

She shook her head.

"Did he ever mention a name? A landmark?"

She shook her head, but then her eyes began to widen. "Wait! There was a place that Trevor took Colin camping."

"Where?"

"I'm not sure, only that it's on the property." She paused. "And they called it their secret place. I didn't want to intrude, so I never pushed for a location."

Jeff tried to remember all the places he'd gone with Trevor when they were kids. They'd both loved to investigate everything, and they'd pretty much had free rein of the ranch. Suddenly he recalled a place along the back of the Guthrie property. A rock formation. It was so cool; they'd sworn never to tell anyone. He guessed Trevor had never even told Lacey.

"Did Trevor ever mention a place called Three Rock Ridge?"

She looked thoughtful. "I did overhear him mention that name once. Oh, Jeff, do you think Colin went there?"

His spirits brightened, too. "I'm not sure, but I'm going to find out." He walked through the door, around to the lean-to and Brandon's horse. After tossing the blanket over Shadow's back, he reached for the saddle before Lacey showed up.

"What are you doing?" she asked.

"I'm going to find Colin," he told her.

"You can't, Jeff. I'll call Brandon."

He turned to her. "Why? Don't you think I'm capable of finding your son?"

"It's not that," she said, then paused. "It's just you've only gotten out of the hospital—"

"And I don't have a leg anymore so I can't possibly do anything," he finished for her flatly.

"No, that's not what I meant." She gripped his hand. "You said it yourself, you haven't been on a horse in a long time. What if something happens to you out there?"

"Nothing is going to happen to me, I know where I'm going."

"Then wait for Brandon," she pleaded.

"I'm asking you to trust me on this. We don't have time to lose, Lace. We're running out of daylight, fast."

Jeff continued to tighten the cinch, adjusting the stirrups before leading the horse out. He slipped his right foot into the stirrup, grabbed the pommel and pulled himself up into the saddle. His heart raced as he glanced down at his left leg and guided it into the other stirrup. There was no doubt that it felt strange, but he quickly took control of the spirited animal. He tugged on the reins, putting the horse through long-remembered commands.

He looked down at her. "Tell Brandon I'm heading northeast about two miles from here. I have my cell phone and I'll call you when I get there."

Lacey came up to the horse and placed her hand on his leg, just above his knee. "Jeff…"

Her touch bothered him more than he wanted it to. He'd hoped over the years that his feelings for her had faded. They obviously hadn't. "I'll bring your son back, Lacey. I promise."

"You don't have to do this," she insisted.

She had no idea. "Yes, I do. I owe this to Trevor."

Thirty minutes later, Jeff's muscles were tensed, and fatigue had set in. Man, he seemed to have forgotten his years of training. He'd run off without even a flashlight on him. Great, he could see the headlines now: Special Forces Soldier Gets Lost While Looking for Missing Boy.

As the sun began to set behind the trees, he finally came up to the familiar rock formation. So far, there was no sign of the boy—then he smelled the smoke. A campfire. He swung his leg over the back of the horse, and carefully climbed down. Once he got his footing, he led the animal to the other side of the boulders.

He stopped, and his heart lurched at the sight of the boy sitting by a small campfire in the clearing. His saddle and blanket were arranged in a makeshift bed. Nearby, his horse, Buddy, was hobbled and grazing in a patch of grass. So the kid knew how to take care of himself.

Jeff stepped out into the open. "Looks like all the comforts of home."

Colin jumped up, looking guilty, then turned on the attitude. "What are you doing here?"

"I'll give you three guesses." With a tug on Shadow's reins, he walked into camp. "You have to know how worried your mom is."

The boy shrugged and sat down. "She treats me like a baby."

"Maybe that's because you keep acting like one," Jeff pointed out. "Pulling this stunt wasn't a wise choice."

Colin threw him a killer look. "She won't let me do *anything*."

"Like I said, you have to prove yourself first. And your actions lately haven't been exactly mature."

"What do you know? You're not my dad." He turned away, his eyes filled with tears.

"I know, Colin, but can't I be your friend? To start with, I know why you're acting like this."

"You don't know nothin'."

"I do, because I acted the same way when my mother brought me here to live, and my dad wasn't in my life," Jeff explained.

"Did he die?" Colin asked curiously.

Jeff shook his head. "No, he went to prison." He hadn't thought about his biological father, Darren

Wells, in years. "But that didn't mean I didn't want him around. Boys need their dads."

He saw the boy blink at tears. "Well, I don't need one anymore."

Jeff's chest tightened, knowing what Colin was going through. "Yeah, I can see that." He glanced around. "By the looks of it, you're doing fine on your own. Are you planning on living off the land?"

"No. I just need to think about things."

"Anything I can help you with?"

The boy shook his head.

Jeff released a breath and motioned to the log. "Would you mind if I sit for a while? My leg isn't used to riding yet." He rubbed his thigh, happy he'd accomplished the task, then took a seat on the log.

"What's wrong with your leg?" Those eyes, so like Trevor's, studied him. "Did you get wounded or something?"

"Yes, I did, but the doctors couldn't save it."

The boy swallowed. "You mean you don't have a leg?"

There was no more hiding for him. "They removed it just below my knee."

"Wow," the boy sighed in wonder. "Can I see?"

Jeff couldn't help but be taken aback. Colin was definitely Trevor's son. He reached down and tugged up his pant leg, once again exposing the metal post.

Colin leaned closer to examine it. "Does it hurt?"

"Sometimes. It's been nine months, but I'm still learning to walk with the prosthesis."

"Cool. Do you ever take it off?"

Jeff nodded. "When I shower and sleep."

"Will you take it off now?"

Okay, this was more than he'd expected. He hadn't shown anyone this besides medical personnel. He examined the boy's wide-eyed look. Jeff realized Colin wouldn't judge him, or even make fun of him. He was just curious.

"I'll make a deal with you. I'll call your mother and you tell her you're safe, and then I'll show you."

Colin groaned. "She's going to be mad. And she'll ground me until school starts."

"What you did was wrong and dangerous. So you've got to deal with that."

The boy nodded. "Okay, but you've got to stay with me here until morning."

Jeff gave him his best stern look, thinking about the hard ground.

"It's already too dark to go back now," Colin pointed out.

The boy was too smart for his own good. "I'll say one thing, kid, you remind me far too much of your dad. He used to get me into trouble, too."

Colin flashed a bright grin. Jeff was suddenly taken back twenty years. He had a feeling Trevor would have loved this idea.

Early the next morning, Lacey waited at the cabin for her son's return. She had been against letting Colin stay out there, but Jeff had assured her they were both safe. Yet one night out didn't solve their problems, not with her son, and not for the future.

Lacey drew a breath and paced the small cabin. How was she going to handle this? Colin couldn't get off without a punishment. She sighed. "Oh, Trevor, what do I do? I'm not sure if I can handle raising a boy on my own."

At the sink, she glanced out of the window toward the pasture. Still no one. She looked down at her hand resting on the counter and the letters carved in the wood.

She smiled and began tracing the chiseled-out letters, remembering all those years ago. She'd been new in San Angelo when Trevor Guthrie had come up to her in seventh grade and introduced himself. There had never been anything shy about him. From that moment they'd become friends. In high school things changed and they became a couple. From the first, Trevor had been her friend, protector and so much more.

She traced the other name. Jeff. "Jeff Gentry," she breathed.

He was as opposite from Trevor as you could get. She would label him the strong, silent type, along with dark and dangerously handsome. The two boys had been best friends from an early age. Then she'd moved in. There were times when she wondered if Jeff had resented her for that.

Sometimes she'd caught him looking at her. Nothing that had ever spooked her, but his gaze just caused strange feelings inside her. Then, after graduation, Jeff's plans had been to go away to college. The only thing Trevor ever wanted had been to take over his father's horse-breeding business. She'd also spent a lot of her time at the ranch, helping him with the training while taking college courses locally.

She and Trevor had gotten even closer that year. He talked about marriage. After having lived through her own parents' divorce, Lacey had wanted to wait a while. They'd argued about it a lot, eventually breaking up.

During that time, Jeff came home from college for the summer. He'd contacted her and asked her to meet him at the cabin. Lacey went, surprised at the change in him. He'd filled out, literally turning into a man.

When he started pitching to her about what a great guy Trevor was, she'd gotten angry, telling him that she needed some time and space. She'd told him she wanted to date other guys since she'd never had a chance to before. Feeling furious that Trevor had sent Jeff to plead his case, she'd slipped her arms around him and kissed him. To this day she couldn't believe she'd done something so crazy. What she did remember was that it had been an unbelievable kiss. By the time Jeff had released her, she could barely stand without swaying.

"Lace, this is wrong," he had told her, but he still had kissed her again. Soon they couldn't get enough of one another and had ended up making love on the single bunk. Lacey had suddenly realized her strong feelings for Jeff.

But afterward Jeff could barely look at her. He'd told her he was sorry about what happened. When she'd tried to tell him that *she* wasn't sorry, he'd informed her he was going into the military. Then he'd left the cabin, and she'd stayed and cried her eyes out.

Over the next few weeks, Jeff had been scarcely

around and she'd been miserable. She was in love with a man who wanted nothing to do with her.

Jeff had finally left town without even seeing her. Trevor came to see her, though. In her pain, she'd realized that he was the one who truly loved her—and so three months later she'd married him.

Over the years Jeff had only made it home about half a dozen times. She'd made excuses not to see him. Trevor had kept in touch by e-mail or gone to visit Jeff on base a few times, but that had only lasted those first couple of years. Then there'd been nothing from him at all.

Her marriage with Trevor had gone through some rough times. Lacey hated the fact that what had happened that summer could have caused her husband pain. Trevor was a good man. The man who'd stood by her. Lacey had tried to be a good wife to make up for what was lacking in their marriage.

But there would always be that summer. That night she and Jeff had betrayed Trevor.

"Mom?"

Lacey swung around to see Colin standing at the door. Her heart began to pound hard. He was safe. She rushed to him. "Oh, Colin." She didn't want to think about the possibility she could have lost him. She held him tightly as Jeff walked through the door.

"Thank you," she managed. "Thank you for bringing my son back."

Jeff nodded. "Colin, I believe you have something to say to your mother."

The boy lowered his head and began to murmur.

Jeff came in. "Speak up, son, so she can hear you."

Colin raised his head, his blue eyes sad. "I'm sorry I ran away, Mom, and that I worried you. I won't do it again."

Lacey glanced at Jeff then back at her son. "Yes, you did worry me, Colin. How can I trust you when you run away because things don't go your way? And there were so many people out looking for you."

"I know. It was a stupid thing to do. Jeff said I need to act my age and help you more 'cause you have a lot on your shoulders."

She tried not to act surprised at her son's newfound understanding. "Well, not any more than I can handle."

"I'm going to do more," he promised. "If you say it's okay, I'll help Jeff with the horses and clean out the stalls."

"Sounds like a good idea. And it looks like that's all you'll be doing since you'll be serving a two-week punishment. That means you can't ride Buddy, or any other horse." She started to leave but stopped. "And no video games or television, either." Lacey walked out, hearing her son's groans.

"I warned you," Jeff told him. "Never make your mother worry."

"I bet Mom's tougher than being in the army."

She heard a laugh from Jeff, before he said, "No way, your mom's much better. No sergeant I ever knew gave me hugs and kisses."

Chapter 5

Early one morning the following week, Jeff arrived at the Guthrie Ranch. When he got out of the truck, he spotted a horse and rider in the corral.

The air in his lungs seemed to stop as he watched the vision on horseback. It was Lacey riding Fancy. She sat atop the beautiful liver-chestnut filly, her shoulders and hands relaxed as her long jeans-clad legs easily controlled the horse's movements.

Jeff stood on the bottom rung of the railing, unable to take his eyes off her. Her blouse hung open, revealing a tank top underneath. A honey-blond ponytail was pulled through the back of a Texas Longhorns baseball cap and swinging freely while she rode around the arena, putting the animal through its paces.

He'd had no idea she could ride like this. When

Lacey had moved here, she and her divorced mother had lived in town. As kids they all rode, Lacey usually doubled up with Trevor, so Jeff had never got to see her hidden talents. He studied her closely, enjoying her grace and ability. This wasn't something you could teach a person.

"Hey, Jeff."

Hearing Colin call out his name got Lacey's attention, too. The private show was over.

"Hey, kid." Jeff got off the railing and went through the corral gate. "Morning, Lacey," he called to her as he walked into the arena.

She climbed off Fancy and led the horse toward him. "Good morning," she returned, looking embarrassed, as if she'd been caught doing something wrong. "I didn't expect you so early."

"I thought I'd get started before the day heated up," he said, feeling the warmth already, though it had nothing to do with the sun. "Why didn't you tell me you could ride like that?"

She shrugged, but before she could speak, Colin showed up and took over the conversation. "Mom used to show horses. Dad said she has talent."

"Colin," Lacey began. "Aren't you supposed to be in the house watching your sister?"

"Ah, Mom. I want to help Jeff."

"And you will, but your punishment isn't over yet. You still have another week."

Colin looked at Jeff for support. "Sorry, buddy. I can't help you on this one. You did the crime and now you have to do the time."

The boy nodded. "Are you still going to pay me to work with you next week?"

Jeff stole a glance at Lacey. "I have to discuss it with your mother first."

The boy looked at his mother and began to say something, but stopped when she raised her hand.

"Not now, Colin," she said. "I told you my decision will be made when I see how you handle yourself in the next seven days."

The boy nodded. "Okay, I'll watch Emily and clean my room. Then I'll do the dishes." With a wave, he ran off toward the house.

Jeff watched Colin leave and smiled. "Darn, the boy works all the angles, doesn't he?"

"I guess you can say, 'like father, like son,'" she said, finding herself smiling, too. "Together they would gang up on me and I didn't stand a chance."

He looked at her. "How's he been this past week?"

"Not too bad. He has his moments."

"If you want I'll talk to him again," he offered.

She shook her head. "No, thanks, I can handle my children." She turned and tugged on Fancy's reins as she headed toward the barn.

Jeff caught up with her. "Hey, I didn't mean to cause a problem."

"Look, Jeff. Emily and Colin are *my* responsibility. I'm the one who's raising them, so I'm the one who disciplines them."

Lacey had tried to stay away from the barn whenever Jeff came around. She didn't want to confront her feelings since his return. It had been more than she wanted to admit. The one thing she could do was keep him out of her personal life.

She opened Fancy's stall and put her inside, then began removing the tack. What was wrong with her? Jeff had found her runaway son, and bought two of her horses. Now, he was paying to board them here.

But what she didn't want was another man handling everything for her. Not again.

She looked up from her task to find him leaning against the open stall gate. He looked too good at six in the morning, with his fitted green army T-shirt and worn jeans. That was the problem, she was noticing far too much about Jeff Gentry. Still, that wasn't a reason to be rude.

"Sorry, I shouldn't have said that. You went out and found Colin and you're helping me out here."

"I don't want your *gratitude,* Lace. What I need is a partner."

Jeff had always liked the Guthries' kitchen. The maple table was placed in the center of the bright-yellow room. The cabinets were a knotty pine with fifties-style brown Formica covering the counters. The white appliances weren't in much better shape. Nothing had changed since they were kids.

Had Trevor done poorly with the business? The outside of the house could use some paint, although the barn and corrals were in great shape.

Lacey filled two cups at the coffeemaker, then brought them to the table and sat down. He took a seat across from her.

She sighed. "I thought we already settled this. I can't afford to continue with the breeding business. I can't take that much time away from the kids."

"You could if you quit your job in town."

She shook her head. "I need the health insurance, especially for the kids. My hours are cut to the bare minimum to even qualify for it at the supermarket as it is. I can't afford to buy it on my own."

"You could if we got a group policy for the business. I believe we only need three employees." He shrugged. "We can hire someone to help out, for feeding and exercising the horses. With help we can bring in more boarders. That means more monthly income."

Jeff paused to watch her. Good. She was thinking about it.

"What do you want me to do?" she asked.

"I want you to do what you're good at, the training. I had no idea you were so accomplished."

"Trevor was the one with the talent." She shrugged. "He taught me. When I got good enough, I began working with the horses on my own."

"From what I've seen, lady, I'd say you were damn good."

"I've had some success. Trevor was the one who built the reputation. I'm afraid that people won't be as willing to trust me without him here."

"They will when they see you ride."

"We need horses for that to happen, and we only have three. Since Bonnie is Rebel's dam that eliminates her."

"Would you be opposed to talking with my Uncle Chance?"

She blinked in surprise. "Chance Randell?"

He nodded. "Maybe we can work a business deal with him. Granddad said he's impressed with Rebel and Fancy. There's also my Aunt Tess. Of course, she's more involved with the training end of it."

Lacey had admired Tess Meyers Randell for years. "She's one of the top trainers in Texas. How many reining champions has she bred and trained?"

"I'm not sure. But I know Brandon used to help her when she only had one horse. In the past few years, she's cut her business down considerably. I bet she'll be willing to give us some pointers."

Lacey studied Jeff. Suddenly he wanted to go into the quarter horse business. "Jeff, why are you really doing this? I mean, why not eliminate me as competition and team up with your uncle?"

He took a long drink from his mug. "To be honest, I want to stay out of the family business for now."

Did he have any idea how lucky he was? "They're your family, Jeff. They love you. They just want to help you."

His eyes narrowed. "I like to do things on my own."

Stubborn man. "You just said you wanted me as a partner."

"I want to prove to myself I can make it on my own. But I need your help and talent, too, Lace." He glanced away. "I'm not sure I can handle the hours on horseback."

She doubted that. "You'd be surprised, Jeff. You've always been able to do anything you put your mind to."

He sucked in a breath. "I'm not the same man you once knew."

Had she ever really known Jeff? "None of us are the same."

He studied her, but didn't say anything.

"But I know what courage it took to get up on that horse the night you went off to find Colin."

She saw the flash of pain in his eyes as he got to his feet. "I need to get to work." He started toward the door. "I'm going over to Chance's place. I just need you to tell me you'll give the partnership a try."

She was crazy, no, insane, even to think about risking any more with this man, especially her heart. She couldn't speak, because even with the risks, something made her want to take this chance, rationalizing that this would be for Colin and Emily. But deep down, she wanted it for herself, too.

She looked at Jeff and nodded. "I'll think about it."

Later that day, Jeff pulled up to the restored Victorian house at the Randell ranch. Chance was the eldest of the three Randell brothers, then came Cade and Travis. Years ago when their father, Jack, had been sent away for cattle rustling, Chance had tried to keep them all together, but the courts wouldn't allow a minor to take responsibility for his siblings. That's when widower Hank Barrett had stepped in and become their foster parent. They'd been family ever since, even adding Jack's three illegitimate sons, Jarred, Wyatt and Dylan, to the clan.

Chance came out of the back door followed by his petite wife, Joy. The couple had been happily married for years and it showed. Like Jeff's own parents, they were crazy about each other.

Chance hurried down the steps. "Hey, nephew, it's about time you came out of hiding." He gathered Jeff in a tight hug. "It's good to have you home."

"I'm taking it slow," Jeff managed, not having realized how emotional he'd feel at seeing his uncle again.

Chance stood back and looked him over. "Not too bad. I heard you got shot up pretty good."

Jeff didn't want to talk about it at the moment. "I survived."

There was a flash of sadness across Chance's face. "Sorry about the leg." Just as quickly he brightened. "You can't keep a Randell down for long, though."

Jeff laughed, covering up the still-vivid memories of his months in the hospital. "No, I guess you can't."

Joy, a pretty blonde, then came up and offered him a hug, too. "I'm glad you're home safe, Jeff. I know your mom is over the moon."

"If her cooking up a storm is any indication, yes, I'd say she's happy to have me back."

Joy made Jeff promise to stop by for supper one night, before returning to the house.

They watched her leave, then Chance turned to him. "I talked to your dad and he said you bought two Guthrie quarter horses."

"Yeah, Rebel Run and Doc's Fancy Girl."

Chance let out a long whistle. "Man, I tried to get my hands on that pair a while back." He frowned. "I take it Lacey Guthrie is having a rough time."

Jeff nodded. "Yeah, I'm hoping that's going to change. I've asked her to be a partner."

His uncle didn't look surprised. "So what are your plans?"

"That depends on you. Seems I'm going to need some stud service."

Chance laughed as he shoved his cowboy hat off his forehead. His sandy-brown hair was streaked with gray. "This sounds interesting."

Jeff explained the situation as they headed toward the large barn. Chance Randell's quarter horses were top grade around the area. He didn't train them for show, only as riding mounts and some cutting horses.

"We need to build up our barn stock," Jeff told him as they went into the cool barn. "I want Lacey to continue to do the training, but we need foals. How do you feel about making a deal? Give me stud service for Bonnie. In trade, Rebel will cover two of your mares."

"That sounds like a possibility." Chance rubbed the back of his neck. "Another is why not just sell Rebel's semen?"

Jeff began to realize that ten years in the military wasn't going to help him in this new venture. "I hadn't thought that far ahead, but that's an idea."

"Jeff, I'll do whatever I can to help you out." Chance grinned. "And it wouldn't be a hardship at all to get a couple of foals sired by Rebel."

"So it's a deal?"

His uncle held out his hand. "Welcome to the horse-breeding business."

The next afternoon at the cabin, Jeff was tired, not to mention hot and dirty from his morning at the Guthrie Ranch. He needed a shower in the worst way.

After stripping off his clothes and prosthesis, he

grabbed his crutch, a towel and shaving kit, then made his way down to the creek. The intense heat was peaking, but he kept his focus on the thought of the cool, clear water. Too bad it wasn't deep enough to swim in. With the crutch under his arm for support, he reached the large rock he'd moved a few days ago so he could sit down to wash.

With a sigh, he then scooped up creek water with an old pan he'd found in the cabin, and poured it over his head. The cold water made him gasp, then smile. Heaven. After a few more scoops, he grabbed a bar of soap and began to scrub the filth off his body. Once lathered up, he reached for his crutch, stood and made his way to the shower. Inside the canvas flap, he reached up and opened the valve and let the trickling water rinse him off.

He was starting to feel like a new man.

Lacey closed the Jeep's door and walked up the hill to the cabin. She'd been trying to reach Jeff by cell phone, but there wasn't any answer. It kept going straight to voice mail. And she needed to talk to him right away, before he started making any permanent plans for the business.

There wasn't going to be a partnership, because there wasn't going to be a ranch. Not since today's mail had brought a notice from the bank, stating a payment was due in two weeks. The sum was an unbelievable amount. She didn't recall any loan that was due. Nor did she have that kind of money to pay it off. There had to be a mistake.

During a call to the bank and a long discussion with a Mr. Dixon, she had learned Trevor had taken out the loan about eighteen months ago. What hurt the most was that her husband hadn't even discussed it with her. He'd even forged her name on the loan papers. He'd used the ranch as collateral to borrow for the business.

She didn't have a way to come up with the money to pay off the loan. She was going to lose her home.

What was she going to tell Jeff? Pride wouldn't allow her to say her own husband didn't trust her enough to share their troubles. She had to come up with another reason to pull out of their partnership.

She struggled with threatening tears. For the first time in nearly a year she'd started to hope again. She was going to get to do what she truly enjoyed, train horses and provide security for her kids. Now, once again, she had to fight to keep a roof over her family's head.

At the cabin, she found the door partly opened. "Jeff?" With no answer, she peered inside. The neatly organized room was empty and Jeff was nowhere in sight. She started to leave when she caught sight of a pair of jeans at the end of the bunk alongside his boots, one still with the metal prosthesis attached to it.

Sadness washed over her as she thought about the agony Jeff had to have gone through. She didn't know any details about his accident, but it must have been life-or-death for the doctors to remove his leg. She felt a tear on her cheek and brushed it away. So much had changed in just a year. While Trevor had been fighting to live, it seemed Jeff had been, too. Was he just trying to make up for the past, for not being here when his best friend was dying?

Lacey had carried the guilt as well. But this was different. She wasn't Jeff's responsibility. Maybe finding the loan papers was the disconnection she needed. She couldn't let Jeff get drawn any closer to her.

Lacey walked out of the cabin. She had to get out of here before Jeff came back, but she couldn't leave without making sure he was okay. Halfway to the creek she saw the top of his head in a portable shower. How did he do that, standing on one leg?

It wasn't her business. She quietly backed away, hoping he hadn't noticed her. Before she got back up the slope, she heard a curse and looked over her shoulder. The shower had collapsed to the ground, taking Jeff with it.

She rushed toward the creek and knelt down beside him. "Jeff! Jeff, are you okay?" She worked to open the canvas flap.

His head shot up with a groan. "Lace? What the hell are you doing here?"

"I was looking for you. You need me to help you."

"No, I don't need your help. Just go."

His short hair was spiky, his face unshaven. He looked good in a rough-guy sort of way. "I can handle it."

"I can't leave you like this." She looked around and saw an abandoned crutch by the stream. "At least let me help you up."

"No!" He sat up and the canvas fell, exposing his muscular chest and washboard abs. He pointed to the spot just out of his reach. "Just hand me the crutch and leave."

Don't think about this gorgeous man, she told herself. She finally tore her gaze away and went to get what he asked for. "Someone's got to help you to the cabin."

His dark eyes locked with hers. "Then you're going to be waiting a long time, lady."

"You are the most bull-headed man," she sighed.

"And you are one seriously stubborn woman. I can do this myself."

"And I'm going to make sure that you don't hurt yourself any further." She glanced down at his body. She gasped. He was naked. Of course he was—he'd been showering!

Her eyes met his narrow gaze. "That's right, Lace. You're going to get an eyeful if you hang around much longer."

She swallowed as she realized she was practically lying on top of the man. She could feel his heat, the hardness of his body. "I only want to help you," she managed.

"And I'm telling you, I don't need it." His gaze darkened even more as it lowered to her mouth. "Unless you want to take care of my other needs."

"Hey, you two."

They both turned as Brandon came toward them. "And here I was worried about you." He grinned. "I can see you're both in good hands."

Chapter 6

Damn. The last thing Jeff wanted was an audience.

"Not funny. Why don't you both leave? I've got this under control."

He glared at Brandon, hoping he'd understand and take Lacey with him, but neither one of them moved.

Lacey looked at Jeff. "Since Brandon's here to help you, I'll go." She turned and marched off.

Once he heard the truck start, he breathed a sigh and, naked as the day he was born, got up onto his knees. "Grab me that towel, would you?"

"Not a problem." Brandon did as he asked and handed it to him with a grin. "Anything to keep from looking at your skinny butt."

Jeff couldn't help but smile. "You were always jealous 'cause the girls liked mine better in jeans."

"What is this, high school?"

Sometimes he wished it was. Life was so much simpler. With the towel secured around his waist, Jeff reached for the crutch, then pulled himself up with ease. Once he got his balance, they headed to the cabin.

Jeff walked inside with Brandon following him. "So you want to tell me what was going on with Lacey?" his cousin asked.

"Nothing. She just showed up." Jeff sat down on the bunk and slipped on a pair of boxers, then his jeans. Securing the prosthesis boot over his stump, he stood and pulled them up. After buttoning the fly, he walked to the kitchen area and took two cold cans of soda from the cooler, and handed Brandon one. "Just like you did."

"We're cousins. Do I need an excuse to stop by?"

Jeff studied him awhile. "Are you going to tell me I should move home where someone can take care of me?"

Brandon cocked an eyebrow. "Why should I do that? You seemed to handle things." He took a drink of soda. "And besides, you've got Lacey showing up to check on you."

Jeff glanced away. "Ending up butt-naked on the ground isn't the way to impress a woman."

Brandon's smile grew bigger. "That depends on how you want to impress her."

Jeff stared. He wasn't going to go there. He'd stepped over the line once before, never again. "She's my friend's wife."

"Was," his cousin corrected. "Trevor's been gone nearly a year."

Jeff was surprised at Brandon's suggestion. He shook his head. "It wouldn't be right."

"Says who?"

"Me." He turned and looked out of the window above the sink. He loved this view. Would he ever get over the guilt? "I can't think about this now."

"Why, because you lost a leg?"

Jeff's fingers gripped the counter. "That's part of it. Another is I don't exactly have a career."

"None of that will matter to the right woman." He paused. "Not to someone like Lacey. She cares about you, Jeff, and if you're honest you care about her, too."

"Of course I do, she and Trevor were my friends." He couldn't just blurt out his feelings for Lacey. "My main focus is trying to figure out how I'm going to fit in here." He turned to his cousin. "In case you haven't noticed, my life has changed drastically in the past year."

Brandon nodded. "And know that we're your family and we love you. We're just happy to have you back."

Brandon watched him for a few seconds. "That brings me to why I stopped by. I want you to meet my wife, Nora. We'd like you to come to dinner."

Jeff didn't want to do the single-guy-comes-to-dinner thing. "I don't know if I'm ready."

"You'll never be ready. Just jump in. Hey, it's not a big family dinner, only Nora, myself and Zach." Brandon looked thoughtful. "If you don't want to come alone, bring Lacey and her kids. Colin is about Zach's age."

Bring Lacey as his date? That could change things between them. Not that there was anything between them, or ever would be. He suddenly flashed back to the creek and how it felt having her body pressed against his. A thrill raced through him, but he shook it off.

"I don't know if I'm ready to get close to a woman."

Brandon gave him an incredulous look. "From what I saw out there between the two of you, I'd say you're pretty much there already."

Hours later, Lacey was still pacing the office at the house. Colin was up in his room and Emily was in the family room playing with her dolls.

That gave her too much time to wonder about the bank's next move. Would they evict her in two weeks? Would she have time to find a place for the horses, as well as an apartment? She began to shake, knowing she couldn't do anything to stop her world from falling apart. She'd already used most of the auction money to cover Trevor's hospital bills.

Anger and fear took over. "Oh, Trevor, how could you leave me with this mess?"

"Lacey?"

She turned around to find Jeff standing in the doorway. What was he doing here? "Jeff."

"Your back door was open and I called out, Colin let me in," he explained. "What was so important you needed to see me about?"

Now that he was here, she was quickly losing her nerve. "Oh… I didn't mean you had to rush over."

"That's not how you were acting a few hours ago."

He was right. "I just needed to tell you I've decided against the partnership."

His expression didn't change. "So what made you change your mind?"

She shrugged, unable to look him in the eye. "It's just a lot of work, and we're not sure it will pay off. I'll be taking a big chance. We both would. You should go into business with your uncle."

She was hoping he would get angry and walk out. Instead, he came further into the one-time pantry, which had been converted into an office. "What are you really afraid of, Lace?"

Those dark eyes bored into hers, not letting her hide. "A lot of things, Jeff. Businesses fail all the time. We could lose everything, and I can't afford that. I have my children to think about."

"I thought that was one of the reasons you considered doing the partnership? So your kids would have their mother around, and a chance at a better life."

She didn't have an answer so she shrugged. "I may just sell the ranch altogether."

"The hell you will," he said and took her shoulders. "Tell me the truth, Lacey. Is it me? You afraid I can't pull my weight?"

His strong grip held her close, making it hard for her to think, to talk. "No, Jeff! This has nothing to do with you."

"Then prove it. Trust me to make this work."

"Trust?" she questioned. "I don't know if I can, ever again. Not after what Trevor—" She closed her eyes, hating her weakness.

He released her. "Trevor? What did he do?"

She shook her head. "Nothing that concerns you. I'll deal with it."

Jeff didn't budge, taking up too much space. His scent engulfing her.

"Like you told me this morning," he began. "I'm not leaving until I know you're okay."

When she didn't offer to tell him, he looked over the desk as if he had every right, then picked up the bank notice.

"Give me that," she demanded as she tried to take it away.

His strength won out. Lacey gave up and he read the paper. "How long have you had this?"

She sighed. "It came today."

"Is this why you had the auction?"

Lacey shook her head. "The money that made was for medical bills and the little that left is for the ranch operation. This took me by surprise." She took a breath. "It seems Trevor took out the loan. He had kept money in an account to make the monthly installments, but there's not enough for the upcoming balloon payment. He never told me," she said in a whisper.

Jeff wanted to believe his friend had a good reason for doing something like this without his wife's knowledge, but it was hard. The problem now was paying it off so she and the kids wouldn't lose anything.

The amount wasn't so large he couldn't handle it himself. He'd saved a lot in the military, but he knew without asking that Lacey wouldn't take his help.

"Let me talk with the bank." He found the name of the guy. "This Mr. Dixon."

"I tried and it didn't do any good."

"If he knows that we're going to partner in a business, maybe he'll agree to more affordable payments spread out over time."

She shook her head. "Jeff, no. This is my problem."

"If we become partners then it's both of ours."

She blinked. "You still want to be my partner?"

Seeing her sadness, his chest tightened. "I wouldn't have asked you if it's not what I wanted." Jeff found himself reaching out and brushing away the moisture from her cheek. "Lace, I'm not going to let you and your kids lose the ranch."

She quickly pulled herself together. "Thank you for that, but there might not be a choice."

"There's always a choice. We just have to come up with a plan."

"How can I?" she asked. "I've already sold most of my stock. My job in town doesn't pay enough to qualify for refinance."

"It's going to be all right, Lace." He couldn't seem to resist drawing her into his arms. His hand pressed her head against his chest as he absorbed her sadness and fear. "I promise. You're not going to have to move anywhere. We'll find a way to keep the ranch going."

She raised her head. Her eyes filled with tears. She looked beautiful. Without thinking he leaned down and pressed his lips against her forehead. The touch was so fleeting that he didn't think she felt it until she gasped. Her pretty green eyes darkened, but she didn't pull away.

Neither did he. As hard as he tried to think about the

loan problem and the future of the ranch, he couldn't. He wasn't able to think at all as he lowered his head and brushed his mouth over hers. She gave a breathy sigh. God help him, he went back for more.

Then he heard, "Hey, Mom."

Jeff jerked back just in time, as Colin poked his head inside the doorway. "I'm hungry."

"So fix yourself a sandwich," Lacey told him.

Colin gave them both another long look, then finally left.

Jeff turned back to Lacey, and seeing her flushed face, guilt once again washed over him. He had no right to kiss her. Not now, not even back then. "I need to go." Grabbing the paper from the desk, he walked out. Even hearing her call his name didn't stop him because if he went back, he'd break all the rules. Again.

Two mornings later, Lacey stood outside the bank in downtown San Angelo. She checked her watch again, knowing she had to be at work in a little over an hour.

Where was Jeff?

She thought back to the other day at the house and his kiss. She'd been telling herself ever since that it had just been a reassuring kiss. Just a soft brush of his lips over hers. She shivered. The effect had been far more devastating, stirring up feelings she had no business feeling.

She wanted more. What had gotten into her? Not since that summer when she'd broken up with Trevor had she ever thought about another man. Not any man, only Jeff Gentry. And look where that had gotten her.

Well, not this time. She couldn't let this happen. No

matter the feelings he'd caused, she wasn't ready. Her life was enough of a mess, and he had his own problems. Adjusting to a new life as well as losing his leg was enough to handle. Not that that bothered her. But they both had too many other complications to deal with.

She closed her eyes. Even now, she still couldn't believe Trevor was gone. He'd been such a big part of her life since adolescence. So had Jeff. Although Trevor had been the one who'd stayed for her. But now, she found herself fantasizing about Jeff.

"Sorry I'm late."

Lacey swung around to see the man in question. "Oh, hi."

Her heart raced as she looked over the handsome man dressed in a white collared shirt, dark trousers and shiny black boots. He was carrying a leather folder.

She groaned. "You look so nice. I should have worn something smarter."

He put on a smile and took her arm. "You look fine. Let's go get that loan."

Inside Mr. Dixon's small office, Jeff tried to relax as the loan officer went over his business proposal.

The young man behind the desk looked as if he was barely out of college. "This looks very impressive, Mr. Gentry," he said as he sat back in his chair. "On paper. But these are hard times."

Jeff leaned forward. This guy was going to be a hard sell, but he had ten years of military training. "Farmers and ranchers go through rough times, it's a fact of life. I know because my family ranches. And you also know that Mrs. Guthrie's land is worth thirty times the amount of her loan. I'm bringing in stock, and Lacey is going to do the training in this business venture."

"It's still a risk."

"What risk? Our stock combined is worth this much."

Dixon straightened. "Are you willing to put up the horses as collateral?"

"No," Lacey jumped in. "I can't agree to that."

Jeff didn't know much about loans, but shouldn't the land be enough? "It'll be okay, Lace." He turned back to Dixon. "I need to make a quick call." He stood and moved across the room, punching in numbers.

His uncle answered. "Chance Randell."

Jeff explained to him what was going on. Chance listened then asked to give him ten minutes and he'd get back to him.

Mr. Dixon reluctantly granted them the time, then he called to get some coffee. Soon a secretary came in, along with another man.

Mr. Dixon stood immediately. "Mr. Handley," he greeted the visitor eagerly.

The older gentleman ignored the loan officer and walked directly to Lacey and Jeff. "Hello, I'm Bert Handley, the bank manager. You must be Mrs. Guthrie and Mr. Gentry."

"Yes, sir, we are," Jeff said.

Mr. Handley turned to Lacey. "I'm sorry to hear about the loss of your husband, Mrs. Guthrie. I wish we had known sooner."

"Thank you, Mr. Handley," Lacey said. "That's why we're here. Since my husband's death, I can't handle the terms of the loan."

The bank manager smiled. "Then we'd best work something out."

"We've been working on that, Mr. Handley," Dixon said quickly. "They're going to put up their stock as collateral."

Bert Handley walked behind the desk and glanced over the loan papers. The older man frowned. "I don't see a reason why the ranch itself can't be enough to secure a loan."

Dixon was nervous. "It's just that with a new business venture and no assured income, I thought—"

Handley shook his head as he turned the page. "With these excellent credit scores, surely we can come up with a better interest rate." He glanced at Dixon. "Larry, why don't I take care of this? I've been a friend of the family for years." He smiled at Jeff. "I gave Chance Randell his first loan."

At the mention of the well-known Randell name, Dixon excused himself and left the room.

Handley looked back and forth between the two. "I like to think we're still a neighborhood bank. Since the circumstances with your husband have changed, I'm sure we can also adjust the terms of the loan with a better interest rate for the two of you."

"No, Mr. Handley. This is my debt and I don't want Mr. Gentry liable for any of it."

The man looked over his reading glasses. "This is a business loan, Mrs. Guthrie. I need both your names on it and both of you are to be responsible for it."

Jeff felt Lacey tense. "Would you excuse us a moment?" At the man's nod, he took Lacey outside the small office and into the hall. "You can pay the money, I don't care, Lace, but we need to get the loan first."

She crossed her arms over her chest. "I won't have you take care of this for me, Jeff."

"Okay, what do we do? Walk away? You lose the ranch and move into town?"

He saw the determination on her face. "No. I plan to sell you the cabin and the acreage around it."

Jeff didn't even need to think about it. "Fine, when we're rich and famous, I'll sell it back to you. That section of land is valuable and the cabin belongs to Colin."

She nodded. "Thank you."

"Don't thank me yet, we could still lose our shirts."

She smiled. "Now I feel like we're equal partners."

And suddenly he was a landowner. "Then let's go have Mr. Handley draw up the papers."

Chapter 7

That evening, Lacey arrived home from work with the kids in tow to find Jeff on the porch. She was tired and still in her uniform when she came up the steps.

"Hi, Jeff," Emily greeted him, her blue eyes lit up with excitement. "What are you doing here? It's dark outside and the horses are sleeping."

He leaned down to her. "I know. I just need to talk to your mother for a few minutes."

"Okay." She looked to her mother. "Mom, he needs to talk to you."

Lacey didn't want to talk to anyone. All she wanted was a long hot bath, a glass of wine and no interruptions. But it didn't look like that would happen. "Give me a minute.

"Colin, take your sister upstairs and start her bath. And don't leave the water running this time."

Her son grumbled something, but then looked at Jeff. "Okay, Mom." He took Emily's hand and they disappeared inside.

She turned to Jeff. "Was there something else we need to talk about?"

"If you have a few minutes. We were so rushed this morning. I wanted to make sure you're okay with everything."

"Come in." She went inside, leading him through the kitchen and pantry, then into the small office.

She turned and faced Jeff. He looked freshly showered and shaved with a crisply starched Western shirt and jeans. Maybe he was going out.

He pulled a paper from his back pocket. "I spoke with my dad's lawyer after you went to work and he came up with an agreement for us. If you want you can have your attorney go over it." He frowned at her. "I figured that everything would be fifty-fifty. I own stock; you have the stables and the experience for training."

"You now own part of the ranch." She hated giving that up or anything that actually threatened her kids' future.

"Temporarily. Until the loan is paid off."

She looked down at the papers. She also didn't have an attorney. "Can you give me a few days to look it over?"

"Sure." He hesitated. "Lacey, we don't have to go through with this. I don't want your land. I'm fine with investing in the business without it."

His dark gaze held hers. She felt a rush go through her, making it hard to concentrate. "I know, but I can't let you take all the risk."

He smiled at her and her heart tripped.

"I don't think this is a risk at all. Our stock is top-rate. It will be slow going at first, but once we start advertising about your training, things will pick up."

She still wasn't sure that would mean anything to anyone.

"We should come up with a name," he suggested. "I thought we could use our initials. G&G Quarter Horses. Lacey Guthrie, trainer."

She suddenly felt more of Trevor fading from her life and Jeff intruding in it. "The name will change?"

He paused. "Not the ranch, just the business. Maybe both our names could help us, with my dad and uncle in rough-stock business. The Gentry name is pretty well known."

He was right, she thought.

"Don't forget we have Chance Randell as our pitchman. And if we get a few more boarders we can hire that stablehand we talked about."

Her head was spinning. "You've been thinking about this a lot."

"Just since we talked to Mr. Handley." He grinned. "This is going to work, Lace. Our partnership."

She couldn't help but get caught up in his excitement. "You make me want to believe it."

"Believe it. This is your future, too." He checked his watch. "I wish we had more time to talk, but I have to go."

Why did it bother her that he seemed anxious to leave? "You have a hot date?" she blurted out. Oh, no, she sounded so desperate.

Jeff looked confused at her question. "I'm meeting Brandon, Jay and my brother, Drew." He sighed. "They talked me into going out for a drink. It's kind of a welcome-home celebration. I'm meeting them at a place called the Horseman's Club."

It was an upscale country-western bar, also known as the best hook-up place in the area. "That should be nice."

"I'll let you know tomorrow," he said. "I'm not much for big crowds, drinking or dancing."

What about pretty women in tight jeans with the big...buckles? she wanted to scream. "Well, I won't hold you up." She headed to the door. "I guess I'll see you tomorrow, just not so early."

Jeff stopped. "I'll be here at my usual time. Chance is coming by, he wants to talk to us about which stallion would be best to cover Bonnie."

"So soon?"

He shifted his hat in his hands. "Is there any reason to wait?"

"No, I guess not," Lacey agreed, once again feeling the excitement. They were truly going to be partners. Why was that bothering her so much? *Because Jeff Gentry would be a part of her life.*

Two hours later, the cousins sat at a corner table in the large bar as a Kenny Chesney song played in the background. For a weeknight, the place was crowded with people. His single brother, Drew, and Brandon's younger brother, Jay, were taking advantage of the abundance of girls and were out on the dance floor.

Jeff took a sip of the beer he'd been nursing the past hour, then looked across the table at Brandon drinking cola. He was the designated driver.

"You're not having much fun, are you?" his cousin asked.

"It's not bad. I've just never been big on the club scene."

"Do you think I picked this place?" His cousin smiled as he nodded toward the dance floor. "Blame it on Drew and Jay. It was their idea. Nora wasn't exactly crazy about it, either. Not that she has anything to worry about."

Jeff envied Brandon. The man had found love with someone special and his life seemed to be going great. He thought about Lacey. He would rather be with her, going over some ideas for the business. A few nights ago he hadn't been thinking about business when he'd held her close, when he'd kissed her. Those feelings hadn't changed over the years.

"Hey, how's the new partnership going?" Brandon asked, drawing Jeff back to the present.

He nodded. "Good. Uncle Chance has agreed to help out."

Grinning, his cousin shook his head. "You've been in the military so long, I didn't think you'd ever come home. Now, you're a horse-breeder."

Home. It had been a while since Jeff had thought about San Angelo as home. Nor had he thought he'd end up partners with his best friend's widow. "I didn't have much choice. I was forced into finding a new career." He found himself smiling, too. "But so far I'm enjoying it."

"And a pretty woman doesn't hurt, either."

Jeff shook his head. "There's nothing going on between Lacey and me," he said, knowing he wouldn't go there again.

Brandon grinned. "If you say so. Just so you know, there's plenty of room in Mustang Valley for another Randell."

"Yeah, this family has changed so much, and you're the first of our generation to get married. You have a son, too."

Brandon leaned forward and lowered his voice. "And there'll be another Randell soon. We're not saying anything yet, but Nora's pregnant."

A pang of jealousy hit Jeff, surprising him. "That's great news." For a split second, he let himself think about the possibility of having his own wife and child. Lacey immediately came to mind, but he quickly pushed aside the fleeting dream.

"Keep it quiet for a while. We haven't told Mom and Dad yet."

"You can trust me, I only give my name, rank and serial number," Jeff said wryly.

They were both laughing when their younger brothers returned. "Hey, what's so funny?" Drew asked.

Brandon shook his head. "It's a private joke."

Drew pulled out his chair and sat down. In his early twenties, Andrew resembled Wyatt with his dark hair, but he had lighter eyes like their mom. "Well, here's something that's not so private. Granddad Hank's cattle drive." Drew looked at his older brother. "And he's insisting that Jeff's going to be the trail boss."

Jeff shifted in his chair. "A couple of weeks back, he mentioned something about it, but I didn't think anything had been finalized yet."

This time it was Jay who spoke up. "Oh, no, you know Granddad. He has it all planned out. He's even had Aunt Josie put it up on the Web site, advertising it for Labor Day weekend. The first Annual Randell Ranch Cattle Drive. Seems there's a lot of interest, too. One thing I know for sure, Hank wants this to be headed by the grandkids. He said he wants the next generation of Randells to show what they're made of."

Brandon smiled. "I believe Hank's just thrown out a challenge. Sounds like fun. What about you, Jeff, you planning on going?"

"I haven't told Hank one way or the other." He wasn't sure if he could do it, but the idea sounded intriguing. He was interested in finding out more details. "I'm not sure I'm in shape for it."

"Then get in shape," his brother told him. "Put in some time on horseback. We've got some fence you can ride."

Jay glanced at his brother Brandon. "You probably could use the exercise, too."

Brandon pulled in his flat stomach. "What do you mean? I'm in great shape." He looked at Jeff. "We've got about five weeks to pull this together. You can come by the ranch on my days off. We'll chase some cows around."

The younger brothers broke up with laughter. "I can't wait to see this," Jay said.

Jeff suddenly felt the stirring of competition. He found he liked that. "Cuz," he said to Brandon, "looks like we have to show these two how it's done. If you can spare a few dozen steers and bring them up to the cabin, we can hone our skills. There's plenty of grass and water to keep them happy."

"You're telling me," Jay said. "The Guthrie place has the best underground spring in the area. If Lacey ever wants to sell us some water, we'd be interested in buying. In fact I would love to have that acreage to run my own herd."

Jeff had never paid much attention to the water shortage, but that could be another source of income. "If and when you're serious I'll talk it over with Lacey."

Jay grinned. "Man, oh, man, you're home less than a month and you've bought a couple of quality quarter horses and got a pretty partner, to boot. How did you get so lucky?"

A few weeks ago, Jeff hadn't felt so lucky, but things were starting to look better. He thought about Lacey again. No, a *lot* better.

There was a tap on his shoulder and Jeff turned to find a pretty brunette. She was very young, and decked out in tight jeans and a fitted Western shirt. "You want to dance, cowboy?"

Jeff held his panic in check. He'd never been the best dancer to begin with, but now…he wasn't sure if he could do this.

Before he could answer, his brother spoke up. "Why would you want to dance with this old guy?" Drew stood. "I'm younger and much better-looking." He took the young girl's hand and tugged her toward the dance floor. She didn't look as if she were disappointed at all with the switch. When the music changed to a ballad, Jay got up and snagged a partner, leaving Brandon and Jeff alone once more.

Brandon leaned forward. "She was a little on the young side. But it's nice to know you can still attract them." He shrugged. "Of course, it's not the same if it's not the right woman."

Jeff recalled his kiss with Lacey and his body stirred to life. She'd always had that effect on him. Hell, he was crazy about her; that hadn't changed since the day they'd met.

Jeff looked at his cousin. There was no use lying about it. "There's only been one woman for me."

Brandon nodded, knowing who he was talking about. "Then don't you think it's about time you went after her?"

The next morning, Chance Randell arrived at the Guthrie place. Nervous, Lacey climbed off Fancy as Jeff walked into the corral with his uncle. She'd never officially met Chance, only heard about him from Jeff and, of course, from quarter-horse circles. She wiped her forehead on her sleeve and went to greet them.

"Lacey, this is my Uncle Chance."

"It's a pleasure to meet you, Mr. Randell."

The handsome older man took her outstretched hand and shook it firmly. "Please, it's Chance. May I call you Lacey?"

"Of course." She glanced at Jeff, then back to his uncle. "Jeff said you're interested in Rebel."

Chance nodded, but his attention was on the liver-chestnut filly. "Of course, my wife threatened to leave me if I brought home another horse. So I'm glad Jeff got them."

Lacey smiled. "And I'm happy that saved your marriage."

He winked at her. "It wouldn't be the first time I've been sent to the barn over the years." His expert eye and hands moved over the filly, letting out a soft whistle. "She's a beauty."

Jeff smiled. "I'm trying to convince Lacey to train her seriously. To get her name out there."

"Are you training her?" Chance asked.

Lacey nodded. "Last year, Trevor and I entered Fancy in a local reining competition, but I haven't had much time for training lately." .

"That's all changed since the partnership," Jeff began. "You should see these two working together."

"It's not my expertise," Chance said and turned to Jeff. "That would be Tess's area, but I bet she wouldn't mind stopping by to have a look."

"I might ask her," Jeff agreed.

Chance nodded. "So let's see this stallion I've heard so much about."

They walked into the barn. Lacey stayed back, but Chance refused to let her lag behind, asking her questions about the layout of the place and complimenting her on the operation. After all the work she and Trevor had put in, that made her feel good.

They reached Rebel's stall and the stallion whinnied in excitement. Chance immediately went inside. With Lacey's coaxing, the horse allowed the older Randell to look him over.

"You say Bonnie is Rebel's dam?"

"Yes," Lacey answered. "He's a two-year-old, sired by Johnny Reb."

"He's a good-looking horse. Your husband knew what he was doing." Chance looked at her. "I'm sorry to bring up your recent loss."

"Not a problem. My husband would have liked you saying how much you're impressed with his horses." She wasn't sad at the mention of Trevor's name. He'd left a legacy in his horses. "I think the best way to honor him is to keep this bloodline going."

Chance nodded. "Then if it's all right with you, I want to bring Rebel to my place and introduce him to two of my mares. I prefer to do live cover, but if there's any risk of injury to the stallion, we'll go AI. My foreman, Terry Hansen, handles most of the breeding and he takes all the precautions, and I'll be there, too. But it's up to you."

"I don't have a problem with it." Lacey looked at Jeff. "What do you think?"

"I think we should pack Rebel up and go introduce him to the ladies."

Later that day, Jeff had Rebel loaded in the trailer and headed to the Randell Quarter Horse Ranch. He wasn't surprised that Lacey wanted to come along. After all, they needed to decide on the stallion they wanted to breed with Bonnie.

With the kids off with the babysitter, it felt strange to have Lacey to himself. Not that it mattered, there wasn't anything going on between them but their connection to the business. He thought back to their kiss. Could he even classify what had happened between them as a kiss? A simple brush of his mouth against hers. It was enough to remind him of years ago, and that one stolen afternoon. Only he'd be crazy to think about getting another chance with her. His hand rubbed his thigh, quickly reminding him of his limitation.

What he needed to do was help plan her and the kids' future. He stole a glance across the cab to watch the quiet woman leaning against the headrest, her eyes closed. She looked tired, but it didn't take away from her beauty or the fact that he couldn't stop desiring her.

His gaze darted back to the road. "Something wrong?"

She sighed. "I don't like to leave Colin and Emily. I spend too much time away at work as it is."

"Colin and Emily could have come along. They both know how to act around horses." He meant it. They were good kids.

She shook her head. "This is business, Jeff, so I prefer to treat it professionally. Besides, I'll be busy getting Rebel settled. That might not be an easy job. He hasn't been out of his barn before. You saw how he fought getting into the trailer."

Jeff turned off the highway. "So you're along to mother him?"

She tried not to smile. "This is his first time."

Jeff pulled the truck up beside the barn. "Don't worry, it'll come natural to him."

There was a playful expression on her face. "You mean what comes natural to all males?"

He turned in time to see her pink face before she quickly climbed out of the cab. Had she been thinking about their one time together as well?

He shut off the engine and got out, too. They met at the back of the trailer. He pulled his hat down to shield his face from the sunlight.

She was working the gate when he stopped her. "I'll do it," he told her. "I can handle the heavy stuff."

Lacey stood back as he dropped the ramp. "I should bring him out." Anything to put some space between her and Jeff. She couldn't think about him as a man. Yeah, right. Jeff Gentry was definitely a hundred-percent male.

She touched Rebel's rump then ran a soothing hand along his flank, whispering reassuring words. She took hold of his lead rope and coaxed him to back up, aware of the narrow ramp, but Jeff was there guiding her.

Rebel was finally out and definitely excited about his new surroundings. She held him securely, but the mare at a nearby corral was calling to him. The stallion showed evidence that he was very interested in the attention.

It took the two of them and a stable hand to get Rebel into a separate barn and stall. Before Jeff could get out of the way, the horse had kicked him. He cursed several times and limped out.

Lacey went to him. "I should have warned you about him. Did he hurt you?"

He grimaced in pain. "I'll live," he said, rubbing his leg. "Wouldn't you know it, he got my one good leg!"

Chapter 8

Getting kicked by a horse wasn't funny, and Jeff wasn't laughing. It had really hurt, but he hadn't been going to drop his jeans to show everyone the bruise. Now there wasn't a choice as he lay on the examining table in the emergency room two hours later. His leg was throbbing like crazy. What worried him was the horse's hoof had caught him right above the knee. What riled him the most was that he hadn't been able to move fast enough to get out of the way.

"I said I was fine," he told Lacey, looking at his uncle for support. Chance's expression told him he wasn't getting any.

"Hey, I've been kicked a hundred times," Chance said. "It's nothing to mess with."

Lacey folded her arms. "Maybe if you'd gotten

kicked in your hard head, we wouldn't have to be here at all."

"Very funny," Jeff said, seeing the worry on her face. "I'm fine." He turned to his uncle. "So don't call Mom or Dad. I don't want them to worry over nothing." He'd hate for them to go through that pain again.

Chance agreed. "Then stop complaining and let the doctor look at you."

Jeff sighed and relented. "Okay. Now, will you two stop hovering? I can handle this myself."

Before they could argue the point, the doctor came in, carrying his chart. "Mr. Gentry?"

"Yes, that's me."

"I'm Doctor Stoner." He shook Jeff's hand, then glanced at the chart. "So you were kicked by a horse?" Without waiting for an answer, he turned to Lacey. "Are you Mrs. Gentry?"

Lacey blinked. "No, I'm a…friend. His uncle and I brought him in."

"It's always good to be cautious in these matters. I should examine the patient, so I'll have to ask you both to leave."

"Of course." Lacey glanced over her shoulder at Jeff as she went to the door. "We'll be outside," she told him.

He waved them away. "I'll be sure to holler if I need anything." He wasn't willing to strip down in front of Lacey. Not that he hadn't dreamed of it for years, but not like this. Not with only one leg. Nope, those dreams had long since died.

* * *

For the next thirty minutes, Lacey paced in the waiting area while Chance sat in one of the many plastic chairs, pretending to read a discarded newspaper.

"Do you think you should call his parents?" she asked, wondering what was taking so long.

He shook his head. "That's up to Jeff. He'll call them if it's anything serious."

"Do you think it is?"

Chance shrugged. "It's a pretty deep bruise. I don't think anything is broken, but that's why we're here, to find out."

She nodded, wishing his reassurance would calm her. "I'm worried there might be some damage to his knee. I don't know much about the situation with the leg he lost, but doesn't he need his good one? I mean, both his legs are good, of course, it's just…" She only knew what Jeff had told Colin the night he'd found her son. That he'd lost part of his calf and his foot.

"Lacey, let's not borrow trouble. Jeff was able to walk in here and he'll probably walk out of here with two good knees."

"He was limping pretty badly."

"He favored it a bit," Chance corrected.

"I never should have let him handle Rebel."

Chance stood and walked to her. "That stallion is his horse. More importantly, Jeff needs to handle things on his own. I think the last thing he wants is to be treated like an invalid. He's gone through a lot and he's already come so far." He raised an eyebrow. "If you care about him as much as I think you do, don't let him see your worry. He might mistake it for doubt."

She gasped. "I don't doubt him."

Chance winked. "Good, because I don't think my nephew thinks of you as a mother."

She couldn't stop her blush. "It doesn't keep me from worrying about him."

"Of course not, we all do. Trouble is, Jeff spent the last ten years in the army doing heroic things. That all ended when he lost his leg. Although we think he's no less of a man, he needs to prove it to himself."

A pretty redheaded nurse walked toward them. Smiling, Chance went to greet her and pulled her into a tight embrace. "How's my pretty niece?"

"I'd be fine, if I could keep you Randells out of the ER." She looked at Lacey. "Hi, you must be Lacey Guthrie, I'm Brandon's wife, Nora. It's nice to finally meet you. Only I'm sorry it's here."

Lacey smiled. "It's nice to meet you, too. How's Jeff?"

"Being just as disagreeable as the rest of the Randells who've been patients here. He's fine, though, and very lucky there wasn't any damage to his knee. The doctor will have instructions and medication for him." She frowned, then lowered her voice. "I doubt it's a good idea for Jeff to stay alone up at the cabin."

Chance nodded. "Not a problem, but I might need Brandon's help with this."

"That can be arranged if needed." Nora laughed. "Jeff should be dressed now." She turned to Lacey. "Once he's feeling better, I hope you both will come to the house for dinner, and bring your kids."

Lacey nodded. She liked Nora. "Thank you. That would be nice."

Nora hugged Chance once again and walked off, then returned pushing Jeff out in a wheelchair. He didn't look happy.

"Can we get out of here?" he grumbled.

"Should I take you home with me, or to your parents?" Chance asked.

"Neither, to the cabin," he said.

His uncle shook his head. "That's not an option."

"I'm not going to Mom and Dad's place. I only have to stay off my leg for a few days. I can handle that on my own."

Lacey watched the two Randell men glare at each other and she found herself speaking up. "You can stay with me."

Twenty-four hours later, Lacey knew one thing for sure. Jeff Gentry was the worst patient ever. He had rejected any and all help from her.

Of course, the drugs had him sleeping a lot. That was definitely a good thing. Chance had gone to get some clothes from the cabin and brought them by. Jeff had moved into the small sewing room at the end of the hall upstairs. There was only a pull-out sofa, but he said it was fine. She'd also stayed home from work the previous night thinking he'd need her. He hadn't.

After supper, her kids went to watch some television while she fixed a supper plate for the patient. Jeff needed to eat. Taking pills on an empty stomach wasn't a good thing. She set a slice of meat loaf and a baked potato on the tray, added a roll and some iced tea, then carried it up the wide staircase to Jeff's room.

The fourth and seventh steps creaked. That was just one of the many repairs that needed to be made in the century-old house. But in spite of it being overdue for a fresh coat of paint and the plumbing rattling, she loved the place.

Lacey made her way down the long hall and heard voices. At first she thought it was the TV but soon realized it was her daughter. She stopped outside Jeff's bedroom.

"See, my dolly has an owie on her knee, too. Does yours hurt really, really bad?"

Jeff had never had anything against kids, but he wanted to be alone to wallow in his own misery. "Not much," he answered.

"Did they put a big Band-Aid on it?" she asked. "Mommy has kitty cat Band-Aids if you want one."

He nearly smiled. Okay, so she was cute. "That's all right, thanks. I'm good."

"'Kay." She nodded. "I'm sorry Rebel kicked you." She shook her head, sending her ponytail swinging back and forth. "He didn't mean to. I think he got scared 'cause he had to go away. I get scared sometimes when I have to leave my mommy. Do you get scared?"

Those big blue eyes studied him. "Sometimes."

"My daddy got scared." She swallowed. "When he was sick, he cried 'cause he was going to miss me, Mommy and Colin. He went away to heaven." She blinked back tears. "I miss him."

He felt his chest tighten painfully. "We all do, sweetie."

He reached out and touched her arm. That must have been an invitation because the next thing he knew the tiny girl was curled up against him, clutching her doll. He found all he could do was wrap his arms around her small frame.

"Shh, Emily. It's okay." His voice was rough with emotion. "I know your daddy wouldn't want you to be sad. He would want you to be happy."

She looked up and wiped her eyes. "That's what Mommy says. But sometimes I get sad."

"Well, you come to me and I'll tell you some funny stories about your daddy and you'll laugh."

He needed to remember those good times, too. "Really?"

"Really."

Jeff glanced at the doorway and saw Lacey watching them. Great. How long had she been there? By the look on her face, she'd heard it all.

"I thought you might be hungry," she said, and carried the tray inside. "Emily, weren't you watching your favorite show?"

"I want to talk to Jeff. He's going to tell me stories about Daddy. He says I'll laugh so much that I won't think about being sad."

"Well, if anyone knows stories, it's Jeff. But I think it's time to say goodnight."

In a flash those tiny arms wrapped about his neck and she kissed his cheek. "Goodnight, Jeff." Her warm breath brushed his face, making him realize all that he had missed being a soldier. "Happy dreams. That's what my daddy used to say."

"'Night, sweetie. Happy dreams to you, too."

"I'll be in your room in a bit, Emily," Lacey said to her daughter. "So get into bed."

She put the tray on the desk and went to straighten the blanket over Jeff. He hated her fussing, even though he knew it was ungrateful of him. "You don't have to do this, Lacey."

"I only brought you supper."

He sighed. "Go to your daughter."

Those green eyes met his as she leaned in close. "Do you need anything before I go?"

He could think of a million things he wanted from her. He shook his head. "I'll probably sleep," he lied.

She glanced down at his jeans. "You should take off your pants, you'd be more comfortable."

Yeah, that would do the trick. "I'm fine, Lacey. Now, go."

"Okay, Mr. Tough Guy." She brought the food tray to the bed, tossed him a grin, then walked out. When the door closed, he released a long breath. He wasn't going to survive this. He popped a pill into his mouth and took a hearty drink of water, hoping he'd be able to sleep. More importantly, that he wouldn't dream of Lacey.

Hours later, Lacey jerked awake and sat up in bed. She'd heard a noise. In the pitch-blackness, she pulled back the sheet and got up. Since Trevor's death, she'd left her bedroom door open, wanting to be able to hear the kids if they needed her.

She checked their rooms, but both Colin and Emily were sound asleep. She glanced at the door at the end of the hall. No, she wasn't about to disturb him. Before she was able to turn to go back to her bed she heard the sound again. It was coming from Jeff's room.

Without hesitation she opened the door, allowing the hall light to illuminate the bed where he was thrashing around in the tangled sheets. He cried out again. She went to his side and called his name. She gripped his arm and immediately felt the sweat. "Jeff, wake up."

He tried to push her away. "No, don't." His expression was a grimace.

"Jeff, you're dreaming. Wake up," she called, but finished with a gasp as he grabbed her and pinned her down on the mattress.

He leaned over her, breathing hard. In the shadowy darkness, he looked disorientated as he tried to focus. "Lace? Oh, God. What happened?"

Too aware of his body on hers, she was suddenly breathless. "You cried out. I thought you were in pain."

"You have no idea."

She shivered. "Are you okay, can I get you anything?"

"Many things," he told her. "But I don't think you want to hear what they are." He finally rolled off her and dropped back onto the pillow. "Go back to bed, Lace. I'm not in the mood to talk."

She missed the feel of him. What was wrong with her, that she couldn't resist this man? "Were you having a nightmare?"

Although she wasn't touching him, she felt him tense and sat up. "Was it about the accident?"

"First of all," he began, "it wasn't an accident. It was the enemy's job to kill me. Just like it was mine to do everything possible to get them first." There was a long pause. "I lost."

"That's not true. I hear you saved the lives of several men."

"So my uncle has been doing some talking. I was in the army, Lacey, I was doing my job. What I'd been trained to do."

"Don't you dare make it sound like it was nothing, Jeff Gentry." She felt as though she was on a soapbox. "You went in under heavy fire to get those men out of harm's way."

His head snapped around to her. "In the end, they had to carry *me* out."

"And you all made it out alive. You have to look at the positive, Jeff. You came home alive. You may have lost part of your leg, but for those of us who care about you, what's important is that you're still around." She couldn't help but think about Trevor. "I think you were pretty lucky."

When he didn't say anything, she started to stand. "What's the use? You're not going to believe me, and I don't have to listen to your self-pity."

He grabbed her arm and stopped her from leaving. "Don't go, Lace."

The gentleness of his touch surprised her. "Why shouldn't I? Everything I say is wrong."

"It's not. It's just being in the hospital today brought back bad memories."

"I understand that, Jeff, but don't turn on your friends. I'm just trying to help." She saw his sweat-stained T-shirt outlining his muscular chest. She was tempted to put her palm against his skin, wanting a connection with him again.

"I know it doesn't seem like it, but I appreciate it."

She got up and went to his duffel bag. She pulled out a pair of sweatpants and a T-shirt. "You should change out of your clothes and try and get some sleep."

"I'm not one of your kids, Lace," he said.

"Then stop acting like one." She tossed the shirt at him.

He cursed as he fought with the damp T-shirt but managed to get it off. She couldn't help but study the impressive body, the toned arms and chest, the flat stomach. A lot different from the young boy she once knew.

He caught her surveillance of his semi-naked body. "Shouldn't I get to return the favor?"

She was shocked at his words, then suddenly realized she was only wearing a pair of boxer shorts and a tank top. "Sorry, I just ran in here when you called out."

"No need to apologize."

Jeff shifted in the bed, knowing he had to be crazy not to get her out of here. He'd been working so hard to resist her that he'd used up all his energy, and yet he still wanted her. And now he had no fight left.

"You should have gotten out of your clothes earlier," she said, her voice a shaky whisper. "I mean, sleeping in jeans can't be comfortable."

"I didn't need to take them off."

Her hair caught against her cheek as she glanced away.

Jeff reached out and drew her back down on the bed.

His pulse raced out of control as he cupped the back of her neck. In the shadowed light he watched her eyes widen, but when she didn't resist, he gave a gentle tug.

His lips brushed over hers and she gasped, but didn't pull away. He took it as a go, and closed his mouth over hers. His lungs tightened as he fought to breathe, but who needed air anyway? He deepened the kiss as he pulled her close, crushing her against his chest. His long wait was finally over; Lacey was in his arms at last.

With soft whimpering sounds, her lips parted and he swept his tongue inside, tasting her sweetness. Her hands went around his neck and she clung to him as they drank from each other.

He broke off the kiss, but went to work on her neck, feeling her shivers. He raised his head and looked down at her. "Tell me to stop, Lace."

She opened her mouth and hesitated, then finally said, "I can't." Her breath rushed out as she lifted up and placed her mouth against his.

He swiftly shifted the position as he rolled his body over hers. She moved under him, causing him to groan.

"Damn it, woman. You're not making this easy."

"Jeff," she gasped as she pushed him onto his back and began kissing him. He enjoyed the assault until she started to unfasten his belt.

He finally came to his senses and broke off the kiss. He pressed his head against her forehead, feeling their hearts pounding in unison.

"We can't do this again," he said, somehow finding the breath to speak.

Jeff rolled away and sat up. What was he thinking?

He couldn't make love to Lacey. He couldn't let her see him this way.

"Jeff." She touched his back. "If it's because of your leg…it doesn't make any difference to me."

He nearly jackknifed off the bed. "I don't want to talk about this, Lace."

She didn't move. He had to get rid of her, whatever it took.

"Of course, what do you expect when you come into a man's bedroom in the middle of the night?"

She blinked at his cruel words, but it worked. She got up. "Go to hell, Gentry." The door slammed behind her as she left.

"I'm in it right now," he whispered to the empty room.

Chapter 9

The next morning, right after breakfast, Lacey gathered the kids and went to work in the barn. Colin and Emily cleaned out the stalls and fed the horses, with the promise that she'd take them riding later.

As hard and as long as she'd worked, it couldn't erase what had happened with Jeff last night. Good Lord, what had possessed her? First of all, she had no business being in his room in the middle of the night. Definitely, she shouldn't have gotten into the position of ending up in bed with him. She closed her eyes a moment, recalling years ago when Jeff had rejected her the first time.

You'd think she'd learn her lesson.

She straightened and began to smooth the straw. Well, it wasn't going to happen again. Getting Gentry out of her house was going to be her main goal.

Coming out of Fancy's stall, Lacey saw Hank Barrett walk down the aisle toward her. He was probably here to see his grandson. Good. Maybe he'd take Jeff home with him.

Hank smiled as he tipped his hat. "Mornin', Lacey."

"Hello, Hank."

"I'm sorry to come calling so early, but I hear Jeff got a little too close to his new stallion yesterday."

"He did, but he won't be happy that you heard about the accident."

Hank shook his head. "It's amazing how much pride a man's got, isn't it? And the Randell men seem to have more than most."

How true. "Would you believe he's been the perfect houseguest?"

They both laughed and it felt good to Lacey.

"That's not the intense young man I remember." He sobered. "Years in the military have had a lot to do with that. It's hard to accept change sometimes. I'm hoping I can help."

"Well, you're welcome to try. Jeff is upstairs in the room at the end of the hall."

Hank started to walk off, then stopped. "If I haven't said it before, thank you for all you're doing for him."

"We're partners, and friends." The last part was what she needed to concentrate on, and nothing more. It was getting harder and harder, not because she didn't like him, but because she was beginning to care too much.

Jeff was tired of lying around, but he had to agree with the doctor, it had helped the swelling go down on his knee. It was feeling much better today, yet, he wasn't sure he could handle even one more night here. Not with Lacey playing nurse. No matter what, he was headed back to the cabin tomorrow. At least there he would have some privacy.

Although no one had come to see him this morning. Only Colin, when he'd brought breakfast. Since he'd wakened, he managed to make it to the bathroom for a shower, but on coming out he'd noticed the house was silent.

Good. Dressed in a pair of sweats, he'd removed his prosthesis and was able to relax on the bed. He leaned back and closed his eyes, but memories of last night came flooding back. Kissing Lacey, and feeling the softness of her body pressed against him. The way she'd put her hands on him, eager to please.

He shifted on the bed. What if he hadn't stopped her? He didn't want to see her reaction when she saw what was left of his leg. He didn't know if he could handle that.

There was a knock on the door, and he tossed the sheet over his legs. "Come in."

Hank peered in and smiled. "I hear you tangled with a stallion."

"Hi, Granddad. Uncle Chance told you, didn't he?"

Hank shook his head. "It was Nora. But you should have let your parents know."

"It's nothing. I got bruised."

"That's what Nora said. And that you needed to stay off of it for a few days."

"Which means my time will be up tomorrow and I'll be gone. So there isn't anything to worry about."

"Did I say I was worried? I needed to talk to you, that's all."

"Have a seat."

Hank pulled a chair over to the bed. "I came to see if you've given any more thought to the cattle drive? I still want you to head it up."

Jeff still had doubts. "Wouldn't Jay or Drew be better?"

"With your background, I believe you can keep everyone in line. And believe me, your cousins can get out of hand real fast. I want one person in charge. You."

He felt honored. "I haven't herded cattle in a long time."

"So? You'll have several men helping to do that. We already have twenty-six want-to-be-wranglers signed up and paying for this experience. I've assembled a team of the cousins. The next generation of Randells, including your brother, Drew, and your sister, Kelly. There's at least a dozen."

"It sounds tempting," Jeff told him. "I haven't spent any length of time in the saddle in years."

"You have time to get in shape."

"I'll never be in perfect shape again, Hank."

"Yes, you will. In fact, right now, you're in better shape than most. Jeff, you're the boy who overcame an abusive father. And the man who always strived for perfection. None of us are perfect, son. We're only human." Hank laid his hand on Jeff's stump. "You have to accept this, but it's not all that you are. If you believe anything, believe this. You are the man you always were, because that comes from within here. Your heart." Hank's work-roughened fingers touched his chest. "Please, don't let what happened to you change that."

Jeff swallowed. "I'll try not to."

Hank nodded. "Good. You'll be my trail boss, then?"

It was hard to say no to this man. "Yes, sir."

His grandfather grinned. "That's what I like, a man who shows respect to his elders."

There was a knock on the door, and Emily peeked inside and gave them her best smile. "Hi, Jeff. Hi, Mr. Hank." She strolled in. Today she was dressed in jeans and a T-shirt that looked pretty dirty. "Did you come over to see Jeff's owie?" she asked Hank.

"Yes, I did, and to ask him to help with a cattle drive."

Another head poked through the door. Colin. "A cattle drive! Who's going on a cattle drive?"

Hank looked from the children to Jeff. "You know, Brandon is bringing Zach along. Colin's about the same age."

"Would you like to go?" Hank asked.

The boy's eyes lit up. "Wow! A real cattle drive. Could I?"

"You need to ask your mother," Jeff quickly added, not sure that Lacey wanted anything to do with him after last night.

The door opened wider and Lacey came in. "Ask me what?"

Jeff hadn't seen her since the night before, and he found his hunger for her hadn't diminished any. She had on her standard work jeans and an unbuttoned blouse over a tank top. Most of her hair had come loose from her ponytail, yet she looked sexy and capable.

Hank handled the explanation. "We're talking about the cattle drive."

Lacey didn't know what was going on. She'd come up to invite Hank to stay for lunch, but she hadn't expected to find a party going on in Jeff's room. She couldn't help but notice that, although Jeff had the sheet covering his legs, he wasn't wearing his prosthesis. Trying not to seem too inquisitive, she saw that he still had a lot of his leg. She glanced at his face, their gazes held, and she tried to relay to him that she didn't think of him any differently.

Hank once again broke into her thoughts. "I just had a thought," he said. "Lacey, can you cook?"

"She's great," Colin chimed in. "She can cook everything. Beef stew is my favorite."

She shook her head, coming back to the present. "Well, we're not having stew for lunch," she told her son. "But you're welcome to stay, Hank."

The older man's face lit up in a big grin. "I'd love to, and we can discuss this idea I have."

Lacey would have preferred it if Jeff had stayed up in his room, but with the aid of his crutches, he found his way down to the kitchen. That wasn't so bad, until the kids stole Hank away to show him something and they were left alone.

She tried to stay busy putting together sandwiches from the cold cuts she had in the refrigerator. When she brought plates to the table, Jeff reached for her hand and she couldn't move.

The sudden strength and heat of his touch startled her. She finally looked into his eyes. "What?"

"I'm sorry," he said. "I was out of line last night. I had no right to treat you like I did."

She took a ragged breath. She hadn't expected this, or the feelings that still lingered between them. "I have to take some of the blame. I should have left sooner."

He shook his head. "I took advantage of you, your vulnerability. It hasn't been that long since Trevor died."

She nodded, but inside she knew she hadn't been thinking about her husband when she'd been in Jeff's arms. "Sometimes it feels like he's been gone a lifetime." She nodded toward the door. "Then other times, I expect him to walk in the door any minute."

With a nod, Jeff released her hand. "The last thing I want to do is tarnish his memory." His gaze bored into hers. "We're partners now. I don't want to mess that up. So you don't have to worry about me…overstepping again."

Well, wasn't that just like a man, making all the decisions, as if *her* feelings didn't count. She leaned toward him. "In case you haven't noticed, Jeff Gentry, I'm all grown up. I can make my own decisions whether I leave or I stay. Most of all, I don't need to be protected from things. That was something Trevor never realized, and now, I'm getting the same from you. I also make my own choices." She turned and went to the refrigerator.

Jeff was at a loss, but before he found his voice, Hank returned with the kids. His granddad was smiling as Emily tugged him into the room, but not before he caught Jeff looking at Lacey and sent him a wink.

Well, darn. How had his life gotten so complicated?

"Mom, did you know that Mr. Hank doesn't have any little granddaughters my age?"

"No, I didn't." She looked at Hank. "I hear you've got a great-grandson. Zach, isn't it?"

Hank nodded. "A nice boy. But my other grandchildren seem to be taking a long time to settle down and get married."

Jeff wasn't going to get involved in this conversation.

Emily climbed into the chair beside Hank. "How many grandkids do you have?"

"Sixteen at last count, but I got a suspicion there's more coming soon."

Those big blue eyes lit up. "That's a lot. My grandpa only has two, and he lives far, far away in Flora."

"Florida," Lacey corrected.

"Florida," Emily repeated. "Maybe you need a little girl for your family."

"That's not a bad idea." Hank glanced at Lacey. "Would you and the kids be available around Labor Day? I'm in need of a cook for our cattle drive."

Jeff bit back a groan, seeing the surprised look on Lacey's face.

"Granddad, Lacey can't want—"

"Excuse me." Lacey interrupted as she came to the table. "I can answer for myself." She sent him a warning look before turning to Hank. "Exactly what would this job entail?"

"Well, I've found a replica of a chuck wagon, but I

decided it would be easier to switch to a truck and re-frigerated trailer." He held up a hand. "This is one of the areas we're going to update with propane stoves and grills along with a motorized vehicle. I've also been informed that the addition of portable toilets along the trail would be appreciated by the women."

"How many other women are going along?"

"There's Jeff's sister, Kelly, and you." He smiled down at Emily. "This sweet one. And I'm hoping to get Nora to ride along in the wagon. It would be nice to have a nurse along to patch up any minor scratches and cuts. There will also be a generator to keep the food cold and plenty of fresh water. And the trail isn't so far out in the wilderness that we can't get to you within thirty minutes."

Hank announced the pay for the job, and her eyes widened.

Jeff sat up straight. "I didn't know we were getting paid for this."

Hank shot him a smile. "You're family, so you already get your share from the corporation. That's the reason I came up with this, to promote more family income." He turned back to Lacey. "What do you say, Lacey? Are you interested?"

"I'll have horses to care for."

"If that's your only concern, I'll have a couple of the ranch hands take care of them for the duration," Hank countered.

Jeff watched as the kids got into the act. "Please, Mom, I want to go," Colin said. "Can I ride with the herd?"

Emily joined in, too. "Mom, I want to ride with you in the wagon. Please, say we can we go."

Lacey looked at Jeff. "I don't think the question is whether I go. Hank needs a trail boss. And he hasn't got an answer from you yet."

All eyes turned to him. Great. If he didn't know better, he'd swear this was a set-up.

Emily climbed down from her chair and came to him. "You got to go, Jeff. It's no fun without you." She climbed up onto his lap and sat there as if she belonged. "Your owie will be better, too."

"Yeah, my owie is much better. And I've already told Hank that I'll go."

He was rewarded with a big smile from the little girl. He felt his heart swell, realizing what he'd missed being away. His friend had had the life he could only dream about. He stole a glance at Lacey, knowing he couldn't have what was never his.

By week's end, things had gotten back to normal—if normal was avoiding each other. Jeff had gotten what he wanted and had moved back into the cabin. To be left alone. Funny thing was he missed the kids, but most of all, he missed Lacey.

Today though, they were together and on their way to Chance's place to check on Rebel. The stallion had performed his task, but they were waiting to see if the mares were pregnant before the horse made the trip back home.

The kids climbed out of the back of his truck. They stayed with their mother, waiting for him. Jeff tried not to think about the idea of them as a family, but it was hard not to.

"Come on, Chance said he'd be in the corral."

They all walked off toward the covered area. Although the late-afternoon Texas heat was stifling, once inside the temperature was much cooler. They went to the railing and saw two horses being ridden around the large arena.

You couldn't help but be impressed by the beautiful quarter horses. A glistening black stallion pranced as if he already knew how special he was. The other was a smaller roan filly.

"Look, Mommy," Emily said, pointing to the horses. "She's so pretty."

"Yes, she is," Lacey answered.

Jeff didn't miss the longing in her voice.

"Can I have a horse like her when I get older?" the little girl asked.

"I can't promise you that, Emily."

"I bet you could train her, Mom." Colin jumped into the conversation.

"I bet you could, too."

They all turned to find Chance Randell behind them. He shook Jeff's hand. "Hello, kids. So you like my new additions?"

"They're pretty," Emily said.

"They're much more than that." He nodded. "The stallion is Ace in the Hole. He's a descendant of my first quarter horse, Ace High. He was the reason I wanted this place, to build my dream of breeding quarter horses."

"Looks like you got it," Lacey said.

Chance grinned. "I got so much more. This place came with bonuses—my wife, Joy, and a baby girl, Katie Rose."

Jeff glanced at Lacey. She didn't have any idea how much he longed for the same kind of life. Her gaze caught his and he looked away. "Is Ace in the Hole for sale?"

Chance seemed to be caught off guard. He pushed his hat back and studied Jeff. "That all depends. What would your plans be for him?"

"I need a good saddle horse. Also another stallion in the barn wouldn't hurt." He looked at Lacey. "What do you think, Lace? Would Ace make a good addition?"

Lacey studied the handsome horse, trying not to act surprised that Jeff asked for her opinion. "Any horse bred by Chance Randell doesn't need my approval."

Jeff grinned. "So, Uncle, are you willing to part with him?"

Chance pushed back his hat. "I don't know if I should. That would be feeding the competition." He tried to hide his smile. "But I guess we can make some sort of deal."

"And maybe a family discount?" Jeff asked.

His uncle slapped him on his back. "You are definitely a Randell." They both laughed.

Lacey liked seeing this side of Jeff. It reminded her of their youth and those carefree days.

Planting the kids on the railing, Chance escorted Lacey and Jeff inside the arena. While Chance and Jeff went to see Ace, Lacey kept her attention on the filly.

"She's a beauty, isn't she? And a fast learner." The young rider climbed down and raised his fingers to his hat in greeting. "Hello, I'm Will Hansen. My dad is Chance's breeder and trainer."

"Lacey Guthrie." She patted the horse's neck and the animal bobbed its head, enjoying the attention. "What's her name?"

"Summer Mist. We call her Misty."

The filly nudged her when she stopped the stroking. "So you like that, do you, girl?"

The two men joined them. "Looks like someone else has found a horse," Jeff said.

She froze. "Oh, no. She's just so sweet. Besides, we can't afford another horse."

Chance smiled. "Since she's my youngest daughter's horse, Misty's not for sale anyway. Ellie's away in England on a student-exchange program. But I wanted you to see her, and ask if you'd be willing to work with her."

Lacey was taken aback. "But you train your own horses."

"Saddle and cutters, mostly." Chance rubbed the horse's muzzle. "She's special. Ellie wants Misty to compete in reining." He turned back to Lacey. "And I think you'd be the best person for the job."

Jeff came up behind her, placing his arm across her shoulders as if he did it all the time. "Looks like you've started your training business."

Chapter 10

An hour later, they'dset a fair price for the horse's training and made arrangements for Misty to be moved to the Guthrie Ranch. Jeff gathered the kids to the truck and asked if they wanted to go out to supper in town. Hearing the cheers, he smiled and they headed for a popular pizza place at the edge of town.

After everyone had ordered their favorite food, Jeff handed out coins to Emily and Colin with instructions that the older brother watch his little sister. Reluctantly, Colin guided Emily to the rows of video games while Jeff carried two iced teas to the booth in the corner.

This wouldn't be the place he'd choose to take Lacey, but he liked them all being together. Not that this was a date, but he'd take any time he could get with her. It had been a long week without her and the kids. Yeah, he'd definitely missed Emily and Colin, too.

Since he'd insisted on leaving their house, he'd spent lonely evenings up at the cabin, with Chance checking on him now and then. He'd only seen Lacey when he'd gone to the ranch to work. At the end of the day, she hadn't even invited him to stay for supper. Not that he blamed her for holding back on the invitations, not after the way he'd acted as her houseguest. His idea of keeping his distance had well and truly backfired on him.

He placed the drinks on the table and sat down. "While the kids are busy at the machines, I want to talk to you."

She looked at him with those big green eyes, causing him to lose his train of thought.

"Things moved pretty fast today at Chance's place and I want to make sure you're okay with training Misty."

She leaned back. "It's going to be tight, and it will take time away from Fancy, but I'd like to go for it."

"I'll help as much as I can," he told her, hoping she wouldn't rebuff him. "Maybe it's time you quit your job at the market."

Her expression changed so quickly he had to clarify his reasons. "Before you start to argue, I've checked into group insurance packages, and with the extra money from the horses we're boarding, and now your training, we can afford it. I have the feeling that once people know you're working with one of Chance's horses, other owners will take notice of your talents." He glanced away. "I also talked with Will Hansen about working part-time for us. That will free up more time for you. He can also do the exercising and grooming."

Lacey was silent for a long time. "What about health insurance for the kids?"

"It's affordable since we've formed a partnership and it's all in the package I mentioned."

Lacey was silent for a long time, then said, "Seems like you've been making a lot of plans. I wish you had come to me about hiring Will."

"I didn't hire him, yet. I told him I had to check with my partner first."

She nodded. "I appreciate that. One of the big problems Trevor and I had was when he tried to handle everything on his own. We all know how that worked out." She looked so sad. "All I ask from you, Jeff, is that I get a say in making the decisions."

He never wanted to cause her pain again. "I promise, Lace. I want this to work between us."

Jeff pulled his truck up to the cabin. He shut off the engine and the outdoors suddenly went dark, but he waited for his eyes to adjust to the moonlight shining over the shack.

Home sweet home.

He definitely needed a generator. No, what he really needed was his own place. Even though he officially owned this land, he'd always intended to give it back to Lacey. That hadn't stopped him from thinking about building a bigger place, a house on the prime piece of land. It would be across the creek, on the rise overlooking the area.

Of course, his granddad Hank owned one of the sweetest spots, Mustang Valley. A home to protect his wild ponies. It was also the site of Randell Nature Retreat for guests who wanted to enjoy the peace and quiet. Jeff glanced around. Even in the dark, he knew this place could attract people, too. He just wasn't sure he wanted to share it with strangers.

He made his way to the porch, but didn't go inside. The night heat kept him from being in a hurry. Though he valued his solitude, he found he missed the kids' noisy chatter.

He mostly missed Lacey. The way she looked, the way she smelled, especially that fresh citrus fragrance of her hair. Even after she worked with the horses, it still lingered on her. His body stirred, and he didn't like it. His entire adult life he'd been disciplined, except when it came to Lacey.

He heard a noise and tensed. It came from the side of the cabin where he kept the trash bin. He unlocked the door, grabbing a flashlight off the counter and the handgun from the shelf. He wasn't sure what he'd encounter.

Hesitantly, he stepped off the porch and rounded the corner. His flashlight illuminated the area next to the cans. That was where he found the mangiest dog he'd ever seen. His brown and sable fur was matted and dirty, and worse, he was all skin and bones. The animal gave him a soulful look as he wagged his tail.

"Aren't you a sad-looking thing?" He slipped the sidearm in the waistband of his jeans, knelt down and held out his hand. Country roads were a dumping ground for unwanted pets.

With its ears pinned back, the mutt took a tentative step and sniffed his hand. "You could use a good meal."

Jeff went inside the cabin, lit the lanterns so he could see what he was doing, then began rummaging around the cupboard to see what he had to feed the animal. Way in the back of the top shelf he found a can of stew. He pulled it out and something fell down. Looking closer, he discovered it was some kind of book or ledger. He set it on the counter, then opened the can for his intruder. After he dumped the stew into a bowl, he set it on the porch, along with a towel for the dog to sleep on. If he was still there in the morning, then he'd decide what to do. Until then the animal wasn't coming inside. He closed the door and looked at the lone bunk.

Solitude. Wasn't that what he'd wanted since coming home? Sure. He should be used to being alone.

He sat down at the table and rubbed a hand over his face. Tonight he was restless. His thoughts turned to his friend and Jeff got a sudden ache in his chest, making it hard for him to breathe. He missed Trevor, missed the years they could have had together if he hadn't been so hung up on Lacey. Yet how could he have come back when he coveted someone else's wife?

He went to turn off the lantern when he saw the notebook on the counter. It was probably left over from the years the Guthries ran cattle through here and kept track.

He opened it and discovered it wasn't that at all. It was a journal, written by Trevor.

Jeff sank back into the chair, adjusted the lantern and turned to the first page. It was dated nearly ten years ago. He read through a few of the early entries. Trevor's wedding. The day Jeff left for the army. The births of his children. His breath caught as he flipped to the last page and found a letter addressed to him, dated August tenth—nearly a year ago.

> *Jeff,*
> *So you found my journal. Why am I not surprised you came back to the cabin? It's been a long time, friend. Even though I should be angry that you haven't been around much, I missed those times when we could just escape up here. The hours we sat by the creek and talked about life.*
>
> *Oh, it was so simple back then. Our biggest problem was how to stay out of trouble in class or with our parents. Boy, we learned a lot together, but a lot we had to find out on our own. I miss you, friend.*

Another entry a week later.

> *Jeff,*
> *Today is a bad time for me. I received some news from my doctor. It wasn't good. I didn't handle it well, so I had Lacey drive me up here for a few hours. She always understands when I need time by myself. It's funny how this place always gave me that peace. Most of all, I feel close to you here. You have no idea how badly I want you to come through that door.*

Three days later.

Jeff,
This morning, I was told that I'm dying. Funny,
isn't it? I'm barely thirty, I catch a cold and a
virus damages my heart. There's nothing they can
do but put me on a donor list, and they're not opti-
mistic that I have the time to wait for a new heart.
So I came up here and cried like a baby.
    I need you, friend. I wish I had your strength
to help me through this. I know you can't drop
everything just to be with me and I have to deal
with that. Even worse, I also have to deal with the
fact that I'll be leaving Lacey and the kids alone.
They're my life.

Jeff had to put the book down at that moment. He
didn't think he could read any more about the life he'd
envied for so long. What kind of friend did that make
him?

The next morning, Jeff pulled up next to the barn
two hours late. Since Will had started work today, he
wasn't worried that Lacey was left to do it all.

He wouldn't be worth much today, anyway, since
he hadn't slept last night. He'd ended up sitting on the
porch, thinking about Trevor, trying to put the past to
rest, letting a silly mutt keep him company. There were
still so many unanswered questions. He didn't understand everything that Trevor had been trying to say.

Did he know of his betrayal with Lacey? They were

so young and stupid back then. And in the end Lacey had chosen Trevor over him. She'd married him.

Jeff stepped down from the truck and looked back inside to see the dog, hesitating to get out. He knew the feeling.

After the dog had been checked out at the vet and had an extra-long bath and flea dip, the border-collie mix didn't look too bad. And he had a home now.

"Come on, boy. There are a couple of kids that'll be crazy about you." He reached for the leash and helped the too-thin animal down to the ground.

He walked into the corral and saw Lacey working Fancy. This had become one of the highlights of his day, watching her with the filly. His thoughts also flashed to Trevor's journal. He'd kept calling Jeff *friend.* How could that be? Jeff had broken the code of honor when he'd made love to Lacey. Even if it were ten years ago, he knew the feelings for her were still there. For him anyway.

Lacey looked in his direction, then rode over to the railing.

"Who's your friend?"

He tipped his hat back. "Not sure, he paid a visit to the cabin last night." He glanced down at the dog sitting next to him. "I took him to my cousin Lindsey's veterinary office to have him checked out. Then we went to the groomer's."

Lacey climbed down from the horse and tied the reins to the railing. She examined the dog closely. "He's one pathetic-looking animal."

Jeff didn't think he looked so bad. "You should have

seen him earlier. His coat was so matted they had to trim it short. He's also missed a few meals."

Lacey knelt down and held out her hand. The dog took a tentative step closer, sniffed and then licked it. "What's his name?"

Jeff shrugged. "Don't know. Should I ask him?"

"Very funny, Gentry. You have to call him something."

"I'm not even sure I'll keep him."

She frowned. "You can't take him to the pound."

"Oh, a doggie," Emily cried and came running.

Jeff held up a hand. "Easy, Emily, I'm not sure how he'll act around kids."

The child ignored him and began petting the dog. The mutt just looked up at the girl with those big soulful eyes. It was instant love.

Jeff glanced at the smile on Lacey's face. He knew the feeling.

Colin joined them. "Hey, whose dog? Man, he sure is ugly."

"He's Jeff's," Emily said. "And he's not ugly. He's just sad. I wish we could have a dog."

Jeff looked at Lacey.

"Oh, no, your friend is not staying here," she said. "I have enough to take care of."

"But, Mom, we'll take care of him," Emily said. "He can sleep in my room."

Colin spoke up. "Oh, no. He'll get lost in all your stuffed animals. And you'll dress him up."

As if the animal understood, he shot a look at Colin. "He can stay in my room," the boy said.

Jeff caught another warning look from Lacey. "How about he stays with me for now? It gets lonely up at the cabin."

"You can move back to our house," Emily suggested.

He didn't miss Lacey's uneasiness. "I think old Lonesome here and I need to stay at the cabin for now."

"I like that name," Colin said. "Can we play with Lonesome now?"

"If it's okay with your mother."

She nodded.

They cheered and took the leather leash from Jeff. "I have food and water dishes in the truck," he called to them. "Keep him out on the porch, I'm not sure he's housebroken."

The happy kids took off with the suddenly perky dog.

"You are such a phony," Lacey began. "Mr. Tough, ex-military guy, takes in strays."

He liked her teasing. His pulse began to race as his gaze moved to her lips. That wasn't all he enjoyed about her. "It takes one to know one, Lace. You took *me* in."

She didn't seem to have a comeback for that. "I'd better get back to work."

He nodded and followed her to the barn. He was wanting like hell to fit in here again. He wanted a home. But so much depended on Lacey. He knew the one thing he didn't want was to be just one of her strays.

Two weeks passed before Jeff and Lacey were able to get out to Brandon and Nora's place. The ranch had once been his cousin's maternal grandfather's spread with a small section that bordered Mustang Valley. Brandon had inherited it along with his two siblings, and they'd ended up dividing the land and the cattle operation between the three of them. Brandon had chosen law enforcement as a career, but had moved his new wife and her son, Zach, to the ranch about a year ago.

Jeff pulled up just as Nora and Brandon came out of the two-story yellow-and-white house to greet them.

He was used to the impressive Randell Ranch, but Lacey was busy taking in the numerous outbuildings and the pristine white fencing, not to mention the large house.

"This is unbelievable," Lacey said.

"Someday the Guthrie Ranch will look like this." He climbed out of the truck and came around to her side as Brandon came up to them.

They shook hands. "You made it."

Nora welcomed Lacey with a hug. "I'm so glad we finally got together." She turned to the kids. "These must be your children."

Emily stepped forward with a smile. "I'm Emily, and this is my brother, Colin. I'm five and he's eight, but he'll be nine on his birthday in two weeks."

Nora leaned down. "Well, I'm Nora and I'm happy to meet you both," she told them. "My son, Zach, is helping to get the horses saddled. We thought we'd ride out to Mustang Valley today and have a picnic."

"Cool!" Colin cheered. "Will we see wild mustangs?"

"If we're lucky."

They all headed toward the corral where there were six mounts ready for the ride. Although Zach was the same age as Colin, he wasn't as tall. The dark-haired boy was friendly, and finally Lacey's son began to open up.

"Okay, let's head out," Brandon said.

Zach showed Colin to his horse, Bandit, and Emily to the small mare named Sugar. A strange feeling took over as Jeff helped adjust the stirrups for Emily. This was a family outing. Over the past month, he'd gotten close to these kids. He glanced at Lacey. Their mother was a different story. Since that night in the bedroom, she had kept her distance.

Jeff glanced at Brandon to see him pull his wife close and kiss her. "Nora's going to drive out and meet us there," he told everyone as he touched her slightly rounded stomach. "She's expecting a baby and we're not taking any chances with our little one."

Brandon mounted his gelding, then they all tossed a wave to Nora and headed out of the corral toward the trail. Jeff rode up beside Lacey. "I haven't ridden out here since I was a kid." He sat up in the saddle, feeling good about how easily he handled the horse. "Trevor and I came out here once and we camped out with Brandon and his dad. We should have invited you along."

Lacey smiled. "I hadn't moved to San Angelo by then. Besides, were girls even invited?"

Jeff stole a look at the beautiful woman riding beside him. "At ten years old, we weren't into girls yet." Not until the day Lacey Haynes walked into their seventh-grade class. "We might have made an exception for you, though."

Lacey tugged on her horse's reins as they rode to the ridge and looked down at the rich, grassy valley where several trees lined the rocky-bottom creek. Ancient oaks dotted the slopes, nearly hiding the nature cabins from view.

Jeff stopped beside her. "It's still as pretty as I remember." He leaned on the saddle horn and took it all in. "Over the years, Hank added the cabins when they started up the nature retreat. To preserve the area, and protect the mustangs, there aren't any vehicles allowed in the area. They use golf carts to bring in guests, or they ride in on horseback."

"This is incredible." She looked at him. "I thought the area around our cabin was pretty, but this—"

"Hey, I love that old cabin."

Brandon rode up. "How do you like it so far?"

"It's beautiful," Lacey said.

Brandon sighed. "Yeah, I never get tired of the view."

"I want to see the mustangs," Emily said.

"We will," Brandon promised. "First, we eat lunch. If we're quiet the mustangs will show up. Well, we'd better get moving. Nora's waiting at the cabin over on the ridge."

"Then let's go," Jeff said. "I'm suddenly hungry."

They took off across the valley to the cabin where Nora had tables set up on the porch. A tray of sandwiches and salads were waiting. After washing the dirt off, they sat down on the cabin porch and enjoyed the family meal. The kids were chatting away. The boys even included Emily, who seemed to be mesmerized by Zach.

"Look, the mustangs," the girl cried and turned to her mom. "Can we go see them?"

"I don't know, honey, we might scare them off."

Brandon stood. "I think we could get a little closer if we're quiet."

The kids followed Brandon and Nora as they walked down toward the creek. Jeff watched Lacey begin to pick up the lunch mess, but he stopped her.

"We'll do this later, you're coming with me."

She tried to argue, but he grabbed her hand and walked her down the slope. Once they reached the grove of trees, they paused as a mare and her filly wandered into view. Emily was trying hard to keep quiet but she was dancing around with excitement.

"Oh, Jeff. Look at them." Lacey glanced over her shoulder to him. "I wish I had a camera."

He moved in close, inhaling her fresh scent. "I guess I'll just have to bring you back here."

She turned again. "I'll hold you to that." She studied him with those sweet green eyes. "I bet you brought a lot of girls here."

He shook his head. "I never did." He only wanted to share this with Lacey. "I would have brought you, but I doubted you'd have come."

She turned around. They were standing close, her back against a tree. Normally, he'd take advantage of the situation, but the kids were too close.

"You never asked me," she said.

His heart skipped and began to pound in double time. "I'm asking you now."

Chapter 11

Later that night, back at his cabin, Jeff sat outside on the porch, Lonesome lying at his feet. The dog hadn't left his side since he'd returned home.

Jeff knew the feeling. After spending the day with Lacey, he hadn't wanted to leave her, either. How could he have said those things to her? He recalled Trevor's words from his journal. *Lacey's my life.*

Maybe coming back home was a mistake. The wanting hadn't stopped. All the longing for her over the past years had never gone away. Yet actually having Lacey as his seemed like a dream—albeit an impossible one. He couldn't exactly ask Trevor's permission.

The sound of an engine interrupted his solitude. He stood as Lacey's truck pulled up. Panic hit him as he stood and she got out. Was something wrong?

She walked up to the porch. All he saw was her silhouette in the shadows. "Lacey, what's wrong? Is it the kids?" He knew they had stayed for a sleepover at Brandon and Nora's house.

She shook her head. "I wanted to see you."

His heart didn't slow as she stepped closer. "See me about what?"

"Can't I just want to be here?"

"Sure. I can understand you're lonely without the kids—"

"Did you mean what you said today?" she interrupted. "Did you want to ask me out?"

Suddenly he felt as if everything was going too fast, but he couldn't lie to her. "Yes."

She didn't hesitate and wrapped her arms around him.

Oh, God, he couldn't deal with this. "Lacey, maybe we should talk about this…tomorrow." It killed him, but he slipped from her embrace.

She looked up. "You want me to go?"

He was trembling, he wanted her so badly. "It might be better if you did." He thought about what had happened all those years ago, and how guilty he'd felt.

Inside he was praying she wouldn't leave. He couldn't resist, and pressed a kiss against her forehead, then her eyelids, moving downward to the corner of her tempting mouth. "Lace, we can't start this…"

"Why, Jeff? We already know it'll be good between us."

"It would be too good," he breathed. "I'm not the man for you, I'm still trying to figure things out. To accept who I am."

"I've accepted you, Jeff." Her hand covered his. "But it seems like you're not ready to accept me, or the possibility of us."

It seemed impossible even to think they could finally be together. He'd waited so long.

She pulled away. "Thank you for the perfect day, Jeff. I'll leave."

He held on to her. "Don't go, Lace." He drew her close. "But you'd better be sure."

"I don't want to think about the past or the future right now. I just want this moment with you." Her voice lowered. "Make love to me, Jeff."

He lost it. He leaned down and captured her mouth, ending her words. He only wanted to hear her sounds of pleasure. If nothing else, he was going to make sure she felt that tonight.

He broke off the kiss and swung her up into his arms. Inside, with only one lantern lit, the cabin was dim. It was also warm, but he wanted to make love to her in a bed. Even if it was just a bunk.

He put her down next to the single bed, happy he'd removed the top bunk. "God, Lace, I've thought about this since I left your house. When you came into my room."

She touched his face. "This time, I'm not leaving, Jeff. I want to share everything with you tonight." She tugged his T-shirt over his head, then went for the drawstring on his sweats.

Stopping her, he forced a smile. "Ladies first." When he had undressed her, she stood, allowing him to take her all in.

"Now, it's your turn," she insisted.

He released a breath, and sat down on the bed, then reached under the leg of his sweatpants. He removed his prosthesis and set it aside. His heart was pounding, his fears were about to overpower him, but he kept his focus on her eyes.

"The other night, I didn't want you to stop," she admitted. "I definitely don't want to stop now."

Jeff closed his eyes as she kissed him. He didn't want to bring up the past. There was no guilt here. This time it was only about them. "I don't want to stop either." He just wasn't sure if he could pull it off. He hadn't made love in a long time, not since before he'd been wounded.

Her questioning gaze locked with his. Then her hands went to his sweatpants and slowly began tugging them down his body, until finally they were off. She tossed the clothes on the floor, but her gaze never left his body.

"You are one beautiful man, Jeff Gentry. You always were."

He was glad the light in the cabin was dim. He didn't like being on display, even before he'd lost his leg. Yet, he didn't want to shy away from Lacey. "You're the one who's beautiful."

She kissed him again. Her fingers traced over his skin. "I have a lot of scars, too, Jeff. I've had babies."

"I don't see anything but perfection," he told her honestly.

Her gaze moved over him as her hand brushed down his leg. He tensed, holding his breath as she stroked his knee, then further down to where his leg used to be.

"From what I can see, you're pretty much perfect, too." Her gaze returned to his face. "Except maybe your ears stick out a little." She leaned over and kissed him on his surprised mouth.

He quickly flipped her on her back. "Maybe we can find something we're perfect at together." He took her mouth in a hungry kiss. One night with her wouldn't satisfy him. He needed a lifetime with this woman, and he knew that wouldn't even be enough.

The next morning wasn't awkward at all because Jeff didn't stay in the bed. It had been years since he'd analyzed his feelings for Lacey. He didn't want to find regret in her eyes, so he decided to get up and give her time to herself.

After pulling on his prosthesis and sweatpants, he'd started for the door when he saw the journal on the counter. Damn that book. Damn Trevor for even writing anything to him.

He went outside, where he and Lonesome made their way down to the creek. But all he could think about was the woman he'd left in his bed. The woman he loved. But would she ever be his? His biggest fear was that she would always belong to his best friend.

Regret and sadness rushed over Lacey as Jeff walked out of the cabin, the click of the door latch seeming to signal the finality on her previous life with Trevor. She hadn't given one thought to her husband during the night. It had been the first time in years she'd been able to think about Jeff without guilt.

It had been Jeff who'd brought her pleasure such as she'd never known. It had been Jeff who'd worshiped her body with his touch, praised her with hushed promises of passion.

Lacey brushed away a tear, recalling all those years ago. Had Jeff loved her back then? If she had asked him, would he have stayed and accepted his responsibility for their afternoon of passion? She'd never know. He'd left without a second glance. He'd left not knowing she'd gotten pregnant with his child. A baby she'd lost before she'd gotten the chance to hold, to nurture it. She'd lost them both. If it hadn't been for Trevor...

She wiped away another tear. No, she wouldn't let Jeff hurt her again. She wouldn't make any more mistakes. She had her children to think about.

Lacey sat up, reached for her clothes and began to dress. Once her boots were on, she combed her fingers through her hair as she headed for the door, and with as much dignity as she could manage, she walked out.

Outside, the sun made her squint as she looked around. Even if he wanted to be alone, she couldn't just leave without saying anything. She wasn't that much of a coward. She walked toward the creek, where she spotted Jeff sitting under the trees on a rock.

He hadn't put on a shirt, given his quick departure, and he looked sexy. She hated that she still wanted this man. But she was grown now and didn't expect any confessions of love.

The dog caught sight of her and came running. She knelt down to pet the animal as Jeff stood and then walked up the hill.

They stared at each other, and then she finally spoke. "Morning."

"Good morning." He glanced around as if he were nervous. "I can fix us some breakfast if you're hungry."

Lacey didn't want food. She wanted the same thing she'd wanted ten years ago. For him to take her into his arms and tell her that he wanted her again and wanted to make things work out between them. But he didn't and she had to face that fact.

"This is strange for me, Gentry. I've never done the morning-after regret thing." She drew a breath and rushed on. "No, that's wrong. Didn't we have this same awkward moment about ten years ago? Only that time you walked out on me."

He looked miserable as he came closer. "Lacey, I couldn't regret anything if I tried, not then or now." He hesitated then, and confessed, "I don't know where to go from here, Lace."

"We don't have to go anywhere, Jeff." She took his hand. "If you're worried I expect something because we had sex last night—don't."

"That's not what I meant. I'm not sure if you're ready for this. Trevor's only been gone a few months."

"It's ten months, and don't bring Trevor into this."

"How can I not? You were married to him. He was my best friend."

"Yes, he was my husband," she said. "But I didn't betray him, Jeff. Not last night, or ten years ago when we made love. So don't try and make me feel guilty."

She could see that she wasn't getting through to him. She was crazy to think they'd renewed their past feelings. It was evident who he was loyal to. Had she just been the pawn between the two men?

She turned to leave, but he reached for her. "Please, Lacey, I need to make you understand. I want things to be different."

She fought with as much pride as she could hold on to and broke his hold on her arm. "Oh, I understand all right. We need to forget last night ever happened, just like the last time."

He started to speak, but didn't.

And that was all Lacey had to say. She turned and marched to the truck. Trouble was, how did she erase the fact that she'd fallen in love with Jeff Gentry all over again?

By afternoon, Jeff was on his fourth beer. He usually didn't drink, mainly because he didn't like not being in control. And because his biological father had been a drunk and got abusive. But at this moment, he didn't care about any of that.

As he popped another tab and took a long drink, he placed his feet up along the porch railing. Lonesome, lying in the spot next to his chair, suddenly took off barking. Jeff looked toward the pasture and blinked. Cows. The sound of mooing filled his aching head.

"What on earth?" He stood and walked around the cabin. Off in the distance there were about two dozen head of Herefords coming his way. Behind the herd were two riders, Brandon, of course, and his brother, Jay.

The cows were directed to the larger grassy pasture,

and when his cousins rode his way, Jeff noticed Brandon was leading another saddled mount. "Oh, no, not today," he groaned.

"Hey, cuz," Brandon called with a big grin. "You ready to go to work?"

"You ever thought about giving a guy some warning?"

Brandon leaned against the saddle horn. "So you can ditch me? No way, cowboy." He turned to his brother. "You can head back, Jay. I have this under control."

Jay grinned. "Have fun."

Jeff watched the younger Randell take off and Brandon climbed off his horse as the cattle settled down to graze in the high grass. He came toward Jeff, pulling off his gloves. "So, you going to offer me a drink and tell me about it?"

Great. "Tell you about what?"

Brandon frowned. "Lacey shows up to pick up the kids looking like she's lost her best friend, then says she's taking them to see Trevor's parents in Florida."

"What?" He couldn't let her go. "When is she leaving?"

"She's already left." Brandon frowned. "She didn't tell you?"

Jeff shook his head. He didn't deserve to know anything about her. "No."

"You'd think partners would tell each other these things." Brandon walked the horses toward the lean-to and tied their reins to the post. "What happened yesterday, Jeff? Everything seemed great between you two. Did you fight?"

They walked around to the front of the cabin. Brandon started to go inside, then stopped. "This place is like an oven." Grabbing a couple of waters, they headed toward the shade of the creek with two fold-up lawn chairs.

"Okay, you dropped Lacey off last night and everything was okay between you two."

"Later, she came out to the cabin."

Brandon's mouth broke into a grin, then faded. "You didn't send her home, did you?"

Jeff glanced away. "I should have."

"Well, finally," Brandon said, his smile returning. "I take it you two…got together?"

Jeff leaned forward, his elbows on his knees. "I told her that maybe it was a mistake, it might be too soon for her."

Brandon groaned. "You actually got a chance with her, and you tell her that?" His cousin sprang to his feet. "I was wrong. No man would ever turn away a woman like Lacey."

"I'm not like you. I'm not a Randell."

"The hell you aren't. You're as much a part of this family as I am. Damn it, man, you've proved that by screwing up so royally. Most men in this family love their women forever. That could be because Jack was such a womanizer." He stared at Jeff. "So how long have you loved Lacey?"

Jeff shrugged, mumbling, "Since seventh grade."

Brandon shook his head. "Did she even have breasts then?"

All at once Jeff threw back his head and laughed. "Who can remember?"

"Well, remember this, she came to you last night. So that means she has feelings for you."

"You don't understand, Lacey and I have history." He looked at Brandon. "Before I went into the army, I came up here to talk to her, to say goodbye. We made love."

Brandon whistled softly. "What about Trevor?"

"No, she and Trevor had broken up that summer. The problem was he'd been the one who begged me to talk to her, to help them get back together."

Brandon leaned forward. "Instead, you broke the guy code and slept with your friend's girl."

Jeff nodded.

"Come on, Jeff. It might have been a lousy thing to do ten years ago, but everything worked out. Trevor got the girl, and you went into the military. Now, it's your chance, fair and square. I'd say that Lacey coming here last night was a pretty good indication she wants to be with you."

"What if it's just because she's lonely, and I'm convenient?"

"This isn't about your leg, is it? Oh, I know what it is." He snapped his fingers. "She cringed during sex because of your leg."

Jeff could still feel Lacey's hands on his injured leg, touching him where he was the most vulnerable. Her trust and caring had just enhanced their lovemaking.

"No, I just don't know if I'm the man she needs in her life." And there were the kids. Not that he didn't love them already, but could he be the dad they needed?

"You think because you're missing part of your leg you can't have a life? Can't have the woman you love? A family?" Brandon didn't wait for an answer. "So I should tell my son, Zach, that because he's diabetic he can't go after what he wants?"

"Of course not," Jeff argued, hating that his cousin knew him so well.

"Good, because I'm never going to let Zach give up on anything. Unlike you, who won't fight for what you want. Come on, man, you have a second chance, don't use being an amputee as an excuse." Brandon stood and started toward the cabin. "We better get to work and herd some cattle before the drive. Unless you think you can't handle it."

Jeff wasn't looking forward to sitting on a horse most of the day, but he needed to build up his leg strength, and get used to long hours in the saddle.

He grabbed two more bottles of water from the cooler and they headed to the horses. "Okay, what if I go after Lacey and it doesn't work out?"

Brandon climbed on his gelding. "There are no guarantees with love, but you can't win, Jeff, if you don't try. I can't tell you how many times, even when Nora pushed me away, that I kept going back. I couldn't give up. I loved her too much. For heaven's sake, Jeff, Lacey came here last night. That means she's decided she wants to give a relationship with you a try."

Jeff's spirits soared with hope, but just as quickly sank. He needed to talk to Lacey. He swung his leg over his horse. "I know I'll probably be sorry I asked, but do you have any suggestions on how to win her back?"

Lacey was happy to be home. It had been a long, miserable week, and she'd missed Jeff more than she wanted to admit. Even though Trevor's parents had showed them a good time, the kids had missed home, too. They wouldn't stop talking about Jeff. Even the Guthries figured out that he had become a big part of their lives. They'd always liked Trevor's friend, and in so many words gave Lacey their blessing to move on with her life. Would they feel that way if they knew the truth about what had happened ten years ago between them?

After a week, Lacey knew she had to return to Texas. Even though Jeff didn't want her, she had a ranch and a business to run. She had to face her partner sometime.

That was the problem. Over and over she'd relived her night with Jeff. And now, somehow, she had to put that out of her mind and find a way to be able to work with him.

Since she would have to spend three days on the cattle drive with the man, she'd better figure it out fast. Luckily, they wouldn't be alone much, and she wasn't riding with the herd. She only had to get to the designated spots and serve meals for the twenty riders. She would have help, Nora and Jeff's sister, Kelly.

At 5:00 a.m. that morning, she and a pair of excited kids headed for the Circle B Ranch where the first Annual Randell Ranch Cattle Drive was set to begin.

She walked into the main dining hall, already crowded with eager guests. She and the kids got in line and filled their plates and went to sit with Nora and Zach.

"Good, you're here," Nora said. "Jeff wants to have a quick meeting before they take off."

She didn't want to talk to Jeff. "But we're just driving out to the first stop on the trail."

Nora frowned, glanced at the kids talking at the table, and then took Lacey's hand. "Come with me."

Lacey reluctantly got up and followed her new friend to the empty side of the room. "Brandon told me what happened between you and Jeff before you left town." She raised a hand. "I don't need details. I do know it's easy to do crazy things when it comes to the Randell men." There was concern on Nora's face. "Maybe if you and Jeff talk—"

"No," Lacey interrupted. "I've made a fool of myself over him more than once and Jeff's made it clear how he feels."

"Okay, but so you know, he regrets how things turned out."

Her heart raced. "So do I. I never should have gone to the cabin. I won't make that mistake again."

"You still want to go on this trip, don't you?"

"Of course, the kids are looking forward to it. And I told Hank I would go. It's too late to replace me." She blinked back tears. "And I'm not going to dump this all on you with you being pregnant."

"Lacey."

She froze on hearing Jeff call her name. She turned as he walked toward her. He was dressed in his standard Western shirt and jeans covered in a pair of black leather chaps. His hat was pulled down on his forehead, his expression serious. She could also see the other women in the room staring at him.

He managed a half smile. "I'm glad you're back. Did you have a good visit with the Guthries?"

Suddenly the room emptied. "Yes. They send their regards."

His eyes connected with hers. "Lacey, I know I'm the reason you left."

She jerked her gaze away. "Don't flatter yourself, Gentry. I had this trip planned for a while," she fibbed. Seeing his hurt, she nearly apologized but held her nerve. "Nora said you needed to talk to me about the cattle drive."

He pulled off a sheet of paper from the clipboard. "Here's the schedule and a map. I could vary it, but I'm hoping not by much." His dark gaze met hers again. "I'm sorry, Lacey. The last thing I wanted to do was hurt you."

She took a shaky breath. "I hurt myself, Jeff. But at least I was honest about my feelings. Excuse me, I need to help get Colin ready to leave."

She started off, but Jeff reached for her arm, forcing her to look at him. "If I owe you anything, Lacey, it's honesty, and I hope you're ready for it. Because when we return from this trip, we're going to deal with us."

Lacey watched him walk away. Honesty. She doubted that Jeff Gentry knew the meaning of the word—not now or ten years ago when he'd walked away from her. He'd never stayed to see if she was okay, or if she could possibly be pregnant with his child.

Chapter 12

So far the first day of the cattle drive hadn't gone too badly.

Jeff rubbed his thigh as he sat in the saddle. He turned to watch the wranglers on horseback as they rode drag behind the herd. They'd made good time through the morning. The only mishap had been when one man went after a runaway calf. He got his horse tangled up in some mesquite. Two of the experienced ranch hands took control and got him out. Luckily, the horse only had minor scratches.

Cousin Lindsey had been waiting for them when they arrived at the chuck wagon for lunch. After cleaning the horse's wounds, she then deemed the gelding well enough to go on.

If anything could deter him from becoming a cattleman, today had been the day. Yet he did want the ranch life, and the more time he'd spent with his Uncle Chance and working with Lacey, he knew raising quarter horses was what he wanted to do. He still had a lot to learn about the breeding business. Luckily, he had a lot to draw on among the Randells, including his dad and uncle. They all ran a successful company.

That was what he wanted to make of G&G Quarter Horses—a success. Eventually he wanted to expand, even build his own place. He'd already been checking out a way to grow the business to make it as much Gentry as Guthrie.

Right now everything at the ranch had Trevor's stamp on it. Not that he wanted to take anything away from his friend, but he needed to make his own mark. That could happen soon, but he still had to talk to Jay before he could go to Lacey with the idea of leasing some pasture land, and even selling some of the ranch's spring water.

His thoughts turned to the woman who had been on his mind and in his heart forever. What if he'd already blown it, and she never forgave him? He shut his eyes, unable to stop thinking about the night she'd showed up at the cabin. Even before he'd lost his leg, he'd never been one to let anyone get too close, except Trevor and Lacey. It scared the hell out of him.

He cursed himself for his own insecurities about the past and for letting her leave that morning. If he got another chance, he definitely wouldn't do it again.

"Hey, there's no sleeping on the job," Brandon called as he rode up next to him.

They fell into an easy pace alongside the herd. "I'm the boss here," Jeff joked.

"If you say so." Smiling, his cousin glanced around. "How are you doing?"

"Not too bad, outside of the heat, and the fact I'll probably be sore later, but the leg doesn't seem to be giving me any trouble." He rubbed his thigh again. "I hate saying this, but you were right about putting in time on horseback the past two weeks."

Brandon nodded. "Good. Have you had a chance to talk to Lacey?"

He shook his head. "This isn't the best place for a serious talk."

"You can be subtle, but let her know you're not letting her get away."

"When did you turn into such a matchmaker?"

Brandon shrugged. "Nora, I guess. I never knew I could be this happy. So don't give up on Lacey."

Jeff knew how hard his cousin had worked to win Nora. She might have loved the sheriff's deputy who'd rescued her more than once, but her abusive ex-husband had made her extremely leery of trusting again.

"Catch you later," his cousin said as he kicked his horse's side and shot off, then met up with nine-year-old Zach. Watching the two together, Jeff could see they were truly father and son.

He drew a ragged breath. Could he be that for Lacey's kids? They seemed to like him enough, but how would they feel about him loving their mother? Taking their dad's place in the house? Whoa. Maybe he should get another opinion. He caught sight of Lacey's son on his horse riding with Brandon and Zach.

Jeff pressed his heels into his horse and pulled up beside the boy. "Hey, Colin, you want to ride up ahead with me? We'll scout out the trail."

"Cool," the boy said.

Yeah, Jeff thought it was cool, too. Would the boy feel that way after he pled his case?

"Brandon, could you and Zach watch things for a while?" Jeff asked.

"Sure." His cousin looked down at his son. "We can handle it, can't we, Zach?"

The boy nodded. "Sure." Brandon waved them off.

The pair picked up the pace and headed down the old service road, no longer used except to check on the cattle.

Jeff glanced overhead at the scattered clouds. "I hope it's not going to rain. We'll have a lot of wet wranglers."

Colin didn't laugh.

"Is there something wrong, son?"

The boy shrugged. "Mom's been sad. And I don't know why she suddenly made us go to Papa and Grandma Guthrie's."

Jeff shifted in the saddle. "You ever think maybe your mom was tired and needed some time away?" He'd bet he was the cause of Lacey's misery. He hated that, but it also gave him a spark of hope.

"Yeah, but she's crying again like she did after Dad died."

Okay, Jeff didn't like that.

The boy looked at him. "Maybe if you talk to her she'll feel better."

Jeff nodded, praying he got the chance. "I think I'm the reason she's sad. I hurt her feelings and said some things I didn't mean."

"Can't you say you're sorry?"

"She doesn't exactly want to talk to me right now. I was hoping you could help me."

The boy turned his serious blue-eyed gaze toward him, reminding him so much of Trevor. "How?"

"I care about her, Colin, a lot." He released a long breath. "And I want to be more than just friends with your mom," he rushed out.

The boy didn't look at him. "You mean get married like Zach's mom and Brandon?"

Jeff tried to relax with the gentle sway of the horse. "Yeah, but I want you to know, I'm not taking your father's place. Trevor Guthrie was the best man I ever knew and I was honored to be his friend." Jeff smiled through his sadness. "He raised two fine children, too. I'd be lucky if you'd let me share your life."

The boy looked him in the eye. "You mean you love us?"

Jeff swallowed as the realization hit him. "Yeah, I do."

Colin looked down at his reins. "Before Dad died, he told me some things." Tears filled the boy's eyes. "He asked me never to forget him, and to take care of Mom and Emily."

Jeff nodded. That was a big job for a little boy.

"Dad said that if I needed help with anything, I could ask you."

"I wish I could have been around more," Jeff told him.

Colin shook his head. "Dad said your life was the army. Someone had to keep our country safe, and you were the best man for the job."

Jeff's throat tightened so he could barely speak. "I tried, but I've had regrets, too. I didn't make it home in time to see your dad before he died. I only hope you let me hang around to be there for you and your sister."

The boy thought for a while. "You think we could go back to Three Rock Ridge sometime?"

Jeff's chest swelled. "Sure. Anytime."

Colin finally smiled. "So how are you going to get Mom not to be mad at you, so you can marry her?"

Jeff couldn't help but grin. "That's exactly what I need your help with."

It was just before dusk by the time Lacey and Nora finished feeding forty hungry trail hands. They were tired, but at least they didn't have to worry about clean-up. Hank had taken care of that by hiring some college kids.

Of course, they still needed be up at 5:00 a.m. She and Nora would spend the night in the trailer so they could get ready for an early breakfast. She was enjoying every minute of the trip.

Nora stretched her arms over her head. "I'll miss having Brandon next to me, but not enough to sleep on the hard ground."

Lacey smiled. "Yeah, a single bunk with a mattress is sounding pretty good to me right now."

She glanced over the camp as night began to fall. The sound of the calves mooing and laughter around the campfire was peaceful. She caught a glimpse of Colin with Zach, and they even had Emily with them.

Off in the distance, she caught sight of three riders on horseback coming into camp. She wasn't surprised to see Hank, Chance and Wyatt. They were greeted with enthusiasm by everyone. After a few minutes, Hank wandered over to them and hugged them both.

"How's it going?"

Lacey shrugged. "No one's complained about the food."

"All I've heard was praise about your stew and homemade rolls. They enjoyed Nora's pies, too." He winked at his grandson's wife before she wandered away.

"Well, we're sticking with the basics, hoping to please everyone. Tomorrow night, we'll grill hamburgers and I'll make some baked beans."

Hank studied her a moment. "I was hoping you'd find some time to enjoy this trip. That's the reason I hired the helpers."

"I'm not overworked, Hank," she protested, knowing she'd stayed busy to avoid Jeff. "You're paying me to do a job."

"You still can have some fun," he insisted as the sound of a strumming guitar drew their attention. "Come on," Hank coaxed. "Let's go enjoy the music." He took Lacey's hand and pulled her over to the fire ring where she sat down on a log beside her kids.

She was caught off guard to see Jeff was the one who was playing, and then she recalled years back when both Trevor and Jeff had attempted to learn the instrument.

It wasn't long before the group threw out song requests. The first was "Home on the Range," and another, "Yellow Rose of Texas." Jeff really got the crowd going as he then went into a Garth Brooks favorite and everyone broke into applause and cheers.

Once the group quieted, Jeff began to strum again, quietly. The few women in the group sighed when Jeff began singing a George Strait ballad, "The Man in Love with You."

Lacey glanced away. She didn't need this. She didn't want this from him. Yet she quickly got lost in the words.

Jeff had never been the kind of man to draw attention, but he had everyone's now, including hers. Finally he looked at her, and his eyes told her his feelings as he sang the last note.

Silence fell over the group as their gaze met momentarily. Her heart drummed against her chest, wondering if everyone could hear. Then the spell was broken as someone called out another song title.

Jeff began to play and she did the cowardly thing: got up and walked away.

"I never said it would be easy," Brandon conceded after the group broke up.

Jeff shook his head. "It was a crazy idea."

"Men do crazy things for the women they love."

Jeff swung around to see his dad standing behind him.

"The important thing is, son, keep trying." The older man raised an eyebrow. "I can't tell you how many times I could have cut my losses and walked away from your mom, but love kept me coming back."

"Yeah, but this is different from you and Mom."

"That might be, but I'd say you have an advantage over me. It's said people who've been in happy marriages are more willing to marry again." Wyatt shrugged. "Of course, if you feel you couldn't be a good husband to Lacey or a father to her kids…"

Jeff really didn't know, and yet… "I want the chance to try."

"All I can say is don't let it slip away," his father advised.

The next morning, Lacey felt disappointed when Jeff didn't come through the chow line at breakfast. Instead he sent Brandon because he was too busy.

"Well, I can be busy, too," she murmured while loading up the trailer to move to the next location. Already bored, Emily had left earlier when her best friend Megan and her mother had picked her up for a sleepover.

Lacey now had time to go home for a quick shower and a change of clothes before she was due at the next location for lunch. She climbed into the truck and watched as the last of the riders and cattle moved on down the trail. All but one lone cowboy.

Jeff had hung back. With everyone out of camp, he checked to see nothing was left behind, then kicked dirt over the cool campfire before he climbed on his mount. Surprisingly, he did it with ease as he swung his leg over the back of the horse. He sat straight in the saddle and took control of the animal, in spite of the fact he hadn't ridden for years and was missing part of a leg. Lacey's stomach tightened as she remembered their night together. They were good and bad memories at the same time.

"He's one of those men who are hard to get off your mind."

Lacey turned to see that Nora had climbed into the cab, catching her in the act of staring. "I've always cared about Jeff, he was my husband's best friend." She rushed on. "We were all friends back then."

Nora raised a hand. "That's good. Friends, then lovers."

Lacey was a little shocked at her blunt assessment. "That's the problem, we stepped over that line twice, and I think the baggage we both have ruined everything."

Nora frowned. "You can't tell me you two didn't sizzle."

They had. Even the first time when they'd been practically teenagers. Her stomach did a flip remembering their lovemaking the second time. Even better. "That doesn't automatically say we're meant for each other." At least Jeff didn't think so, Lacey thought as she started the engine and drove over the uneven terrain.

That didn't stop Nora. "Look, Lacey, I saw the condition of Jeff's leg at the hospital. He's a lucky man that he healed so quickly. And he's accomplished a lot so far." She motioned toward the rider and herd. "I'm not an expert on amputees, but he's probably loaded down with insecurities, especially when it comes to being able to please a woman. To feel like a whole man."

Lacey couldn't stop the rush of memories of their night together, or the blush.

Nora smiled. "He's just like all the other proud and stubborn Randells. Think about this, Lacey. Is the man worth another chance?"

By the second day of the cattle drive, Jeff's body had begun to feel the effects of his hours in the saddle. It was a good thing they'd arrived at camp, and so far there'd been no mishaps with any of the riders. They'd completed a count on the herd and discovered six cows missing. He sent out three of the experienced ranch hands, and within an hour they'd rounded up the steers.

He wasn't about to leave anyone behind, man, woman or bovine, even if he had to go search on his own. Maybe that would get his mind off Lacey. Yeah, right. It didn't seem to be working.

He rode around the herd that had settled down for the night. Thanks to the recent rains, they had full stock water troughs and plenty of summer grass to keep them happy. He glanced back toward camp and saw smoke coming from the grills. It was their last night on the trail, and they were going to have steak for supper.

The group of men and the few women deserved it. They'd worked hard. There wasn't a city slicker in the bunch, which made his job easier. Although he did miss not having a shower, a shave and good sleep for three days. Most of all he missed talking with Lacey. Yet, he couldn't state his case until they were off the cattle drive. Once home, he needed to make plans. He couldn't go to Lacey and ask her to share his life if he didn't have anything to offer her and the kids. He had to talk with Jay to see if he was serious about leasing the land.

He wanted to be more than just Lacey's business partner.

Jeff walked his gelding back into camp and climbed off. He was hungry, but first he had to check out the area. They had to make sure the bush was cleared so there wouldn't be any accidents or mishaps.

He caught Colin walking toward one of the portable outhouses for the guests. He tensed, knowing that cool structures were a perfect spot for creatures to get out of the heat.

Jeff stopped one of the ranch hands. "Have you swept the camp for snakes?"

The kid shrugged. "That's Marty's job today."

Jeff didn't wait to track Marty down. He took off for the outhouse just as Colin pulled open the door. The second he saw the kid freeze, he slowed his pace, hearing the rattling sound loud and clear.

"Don't move, Colin," he instructed in a low voice. He knew that, as a Texan, Trevor would have taught his son about snakes.

"Jeff…" the boy managed.

"I'm right here, son." Jeff stepped a little closer to get a better look. Not good, the snake was cornered, and passing Colin was his only way out. Jeff couldn't tell how long the snake was, so he couldn't judge the striking distance.

Jeff felt someone behind him. Brandon.

"Do you have your gun with you?" Jeff asked, not moving.

"I grabbed your shotgun."

The idea didn't sound as good as he first thought. "Better not take the chance, I could miss. The best bet is to slam the door closed before the snake can strike."

"Tell me what to do," Brandon asked.

Jeff motioned for his cousin to go to the side of the outhouse door. Then Jeff slowly moved into position to get the boy to safety. With a nod, Brandon threw himself against the metal door and it slammed shut with a bang. At the same time Jeff pushed Colin to the ground, landing on top of the boy.

With the door safely closed, Jeff rolled over, feeling his bad leg hit the hard ground at a funny angle. But his first concern was the boy. He rose up. "You okay, son? The snake didn't get you?"

Colin managed to shake his head, fighting tears. "I'm okay."

"Good." Jeff rolled over onto his back and sat up. Rolling up his pant leg, he exposed his prosthesis while he shifted the rubber boot back into place over his knee, and then tugged his jeans back down.

Colin was watching him. "Did you get hurt?"

Jeff smiled wryly as he put his hat back on. "No, I just zigged when I should have zagged." He got to his feet as Lacey came running toward them. "Go to your mom, Colin." He gave the boy a shove and turned back to Brandon.

Grinning, his cousin tossed Jeff the shotgun. "Want to impress your girl?"

"You're real funny," he said, then took aim. "Ready," he called and Brandon opened the door. Within seconds the snake was history and with the help of a knife, it became a trophy. That brought several of the group to see what was going on. After a few slaps on the back to both Brandon and Jeff, everyone wandered back to camp.

Jeff was headed there himself when he heard his name called. He turned, knowing it was Lacey.

"Jeff, thank you. If you hadn't been there, Colin could have been bitten." Tears welled in her eyes. "I don't know what I would have done—"

He reached out and pulled her into his arms, loving the feel of her softness against him. "Ah, Lacey, don't. Don't play the what-if game. Colin's fine now. And I think he'll remember to check for snakes from now on." He searched her face, hungry for the sight of her. He'd missed her so much. It would be so easy to lean down and taste her sweet mouth. "You be careful, too."

She nodded, but didn't move. "I will." She swallowed and he could see the rapid pulse in her neck. "I guess I should go start supper." She gave him a half smile. "You've earned the biggest steak."

She went to leave, then stopped. Before he knew her plans, she leaned in and kissed his cheek. She paused as her gaze locked with his. "Thanks again, Jeff." She ran off.

Suddenly he broke into a big grin. "Just wait until we get back, Lacey Guthrie," he breathed. "I'm coming for you. This time I'm not letting you get away with a kiss on the cheek, and I'm definitely not letting you go."

Chapter 13

The next day around noon, they arrived at their destination, the Circle B Ranch. All steers and wranglers were accounted for. Jeff rose up in the saddle from about fifty yards out and spotted his dad, Uncle Cade and Uncle Chance waiting at the pens ready to separate the herd, the mamas from their calves.

There were more ranch hands to take over so the guests could go to their quarters, clean up and rest for the celebration later, although some of them wanted the full experience and planned to stay and help with the branding.

Jeff was going to pass this time. His job as trail boss was completed and he was headed to the cabin. After three nights on the hard ground, his single bunk looked pretty good to him. He planned to come back here tonight, and if he was lucky he'd have a date.

After he'd taken care of his horse, he walked over to the food trailer and Lacey. Colin was the first to see him.

"Hi, Jeff," the boy called.

Jeff tugged on the boy's hat. "Hi, Colin. You did a great job on the drive. Your dad would have been proud."

The kid's face lit up. "Thanks. It was fun, but I think I like working with horses better."

Jeff leaned forward. "So do I."

They both laughed as Emily joined in. "Mom said when I get older I can ride with the herd like Colin did."

Jeff couldn't resist the little girl and lifted her into his arms. "Well, you let me know when that is, and I'll help you practice herding cows."

Her blue eyes widened as she looked over her shoulder. "Mom, Jeff's going to teach me."

Lacey stopped her chores. "That's nice, Em. But right now you need to gather your things from the truck so we can go home."

"You'd better get busy." He set the girl down and the two kids took off.

Finally alone with Lacey, he turned to her. "Are you coming to the party later?"

Lacey shook her head. "I haven't worked Fancy in days."

"Will's been doing a pretty good job with the filly. Of course, he's not you, but Fancy seems to like him."

"Thank you both for handling things while I was away. That's the reason I need to stay home tonight."

Jeff wasn't going to let it go. "How about I come by

and help you? The two of us can get it done faster and you can rest. You worked hard during the drive and deserve to have some fun."

Lacey didn't need to spend any more time with the man. "You don't have to do this, Jeff." She glanced away. "We made a mistake that night, and somehow we need to move past it and go on."

"Is that what you want? Just to forget everything?"

She could never do that. God help her, he would always have a piece of her heart. "It's for the best."

She just needed a way to stop loving him, to get things back to there being just business between them.

"We're not going to the party," Lacey said to her son hours later after they'd finished chores. "We're all tired from the trip and we need to spend a quiet night at home."

"But you've got to go, Mom. Jeff will be there. I know Mr. Hank will want to thank you, too."

"I'm sure he'll understand why I can't make it tonight. Besides, you kids start back to school tomorrow."

"We can go, too. Zach's going with his parents."

"Zach is a Randell. They're family."

Colin looked agitated. "We can be Randells, too, if you'd just go."

Lacey's head shot up to look at her son. "Colin, why would you say that?"

"Because Jeff told me—" He stopped. "Oh, never mind." He started out of the room.

"Colin Trevor Guthrie, you come back here."

"Oh, boy, you're in trouble," Emily whispered as

her brother marched past her and stood in front of his mother.

"Please explain to me what you meant by that."

The boy released a long breath. "Jeff told me he wants to win you back."

She raised her hand. "Jeff talked to you about this?"

"Yeah, he asked me how I felt about him wanting to marry you."

Emily squealed and Lacey was speechless. Jeff wanted to marry her!

The boy went on to say, "He said he wouldn't take our daddy's place, but wanted to know if I'd mind if he helped raise us and married you."

Emily marched up to them. "Hey, he didn't ask *me*."

Colin glared at his sister. "Don't you want Jeff to be our new dad?"

She nodded. "Oh, Mom, please say yes. Jeff tells me stories about Daddy. He reads to me and he even kissed my dolly goodnight. I want him to be my new daddy so you're not sad anymore."

Lacey fought her rising hope. "Oh, honey, I'm not sad, I have you and Colin."

"Is it because Jeff doesn't have a leg?" Colin asked.

Lacey gasped. "Of course not. That doesn't matter to me." She looked back and forth between her kids. "What about your dad?"

"Dad told me Jeff was like a brother to him," Colin said. "Remember how he always talked about him?" Her son studied her. "Do you love Jeff?"

Her kids' gazes were leveled on her, waiting for an answer. "I loved your dad. You know that, don't you?"

They both nodded. "Can't you love Jeff, too?" Colin added.

"Yeah, Mom," Emily confirmed. "So put on a pretty dress and go to the party and tell him." She smiled. "Just like Beauty and the Beast, you can dance with him."

Colin groaned at his sister's fairytale reference, but didn't say anything.

Lacey felt her own excitement building. Her heart pounded with hope and fear as she looked at her children. "Kids, I might need to go to the party by myself."

Music played in the background as Jeff walked along the patio. He took another drink of water. He didn't want anything clouding his thoughts or senses.

He watched as couples two-stepped around the makeshift dance floor. Most of them were Randells, and none of the women were Lacey. He wasn't sure she would even show up, and his hopes were fading that he could say all the right things to finally win her over.

"Jeff?"

Hearing Lacey's voice, Jeff turned so quickly that he stumbled a little, reminding himself of his limitations. But once he saw her, he wasn't backing away.

He smiled. "You made it."

She nodded. "I found a sitter at the last minute."

"I'm glad." He looked over the woman he usually saw in jeans and T-shirts. Tonight she had on a long white gauzy skirt with a turquoise Indian print blouse which exposed her delicate shoulders, and a chain belt hugged her small waist. "Can I get you something to drink?"

"Thank you, maybe later. You could ask me to dance."

He swallowed. "I'm not sure I can keep up."

The music ended and a soft ballad replaced the quick beat. She took him by the hand and led him away from the crowded patio to the garden. She stepped onto the manicured lawn. "This looks like a good spot to practice."

Jeff didn't hesitate to draw her into his arms. The top of her head rested against his chin. With a love song in the background, his arms tightened and he pulled her against him so her breasts were pressed to his chest. She fitted perfectly. He couldn't speak, too afraid to break the spell between them.

About halfway through the song, Lacey pulled back and looked up at him. "I missed you when I was in Florida."

"I've missed you, too. Since the second you left the cabin that morning." His eyes searched her face. "Please believe me when I say I regret all the stupid things I said to you. It wasn't you, it was my insecurities talking." He stopped as the moonlight played across her face. "You're so beautiful."

"Keep talking. It sounds good so far."

He stopped moving. "I don't exactly feel like talking right now."

Jeff pulled Lacey back into his arms, then lowered his mouth to hers. At first he tried to go slow, but she tempted him so the kiss turned hungry and sparks went off. By the time he lifted his head they were both breathless.

"Oh, Lace. As much as I like where this is headed,

this isn't the place. And there's too much I want to say to you." He wanted more than just a few stolen nights. He had to let her know he wanted them to truly be partners, in every way. "Okay, can we at least take this somewhere more private?"

Lacey felt as giddy as a teenager. At first, she'd thought she was crazy to get talked into this, but she couldn't deny her feelings for Jeff any longer. "Just to talk?"

"We definitely need to begin there," he said. "Because I want this to be a beginning for us, Lacey. I want more than a business partnership."

Her spirits quickly lifted. "I want that, too."

Jeff's mouth spread into a sexy grin. "Hold that thought. I need to tell Brandon I'm leaving." He grabbed her hand and walked her back to the edge of the patio. "I'll be right back." He gave her one last kiss and hurried off.

Lacey couldn't stop smiling as she watched several of the guests dancing. One of them was Jay Randell, busy talking with several young girls. He spotted her and waved, then came over to her. "Hey, Lacey, how about a dance?"

She smiled. "Sorry, all my dances are taken tonight."

Jay raised an eyebrow. "So Jeff finally won you over."

She nodded. Did everyone know what had been going on between them? "We're working on things."

"That's more good news to make my day. My loan was approved, so if you're agreeable we can go ahead and discuss the land lease."

Lacey frowned. "What are you talking about?"

"I guess Jeff hasn't told you about my offer to lease the acreage up by the cabin."

Lacey shook her head and remained calm.

"Hey, I bet he's planning to surprise you."

It hadn't taken Jeff long to find Brandon. After hearing Jeff's explanation of his early departure, his cousin gave his blessing, along with a key to a cabin in Mustang Valley.

"You're going to need help to convince her you're the man for her," he teased, then grew serious. "Tell her what's in your heart, Jeff. It'll work out."

Jeff went to find Lacey. He saw her standing with Jay and felt a pang of jealousy at the sight of his cousin talking to his girl. When he arrived, she wasn't smiling any longer.

"Sorry I took so long," he said, but Lacey didn't seem happy to see him.

"Guess what, Jeff?" she began. "Jay's been telling me an interesting story about a plan to lease my land."

Jeff glared at Jay. "It was just an idea he mentioned in passing. That's all."

Jay raised a hand in defense. "Hey, I didn't mean to cause trouble," he said, and was wise enough to make a quick departure. "I'd better go."

Lacey turned and started toward the parking area. Jeff caught up with her at her truck. At least they could talk privately. "I thought we were going to talk, Lace."

"Seems as if you've already discussed things with Jay, so you don't need me. You men are all alike." She didn't need to bring up Trevor's name, because they both knew who she was referring to.

"I know you think I went behind your back, but I didn't," he denied. "It was an idea Jay threw out a few weeks ago. I didn't know he was even serious until today."

"I still wanted a say in it."

He straightened, feeling anger building. "Then you shouldn't have run off to Florida." It had really hurt that she hadn't called him. "Business partners don't just walk away from one another."

"Look who's talking about running off! You're pretty good at it, too. Ten years ago you couldn't get away from me fast enough."

He didn't look away. "It was for the best. You and Trevor got back together."

She brushed her pretty blond hair off her shoulders. "So that's what you told yourself to make it all right? What about me? You gave no thought to *my* feelings. Did you think I made love to you to make Trevor jealous?"

"Of course not." He took a step closer and she backed away. "I cared about you then and I care about you now."

She hugged herself. "How can I believe that when you never contacted me? To find out if I was okay." Angry tears welled in her eyes. "I wasn't, Jeff. I wasn't okay. I was pregnant."

A baby. Jeff felt the shock down to the pit of his stomach. "Oh, God." He reached for her and gripped her arms. "You were pregnant? Why didn't you tell me?"

"You'd already left for the army." She brushed away

a tear. "You deserved to know, but before I convinced myself to write you, I'd miscarried."

The pain hurt so badly, he couldn't concentrate on her words. Lacey had been pregnant. With his child. "You still should have told me."

"Why? What would you have done? Offered to marry me?"

In a heartbeat. "Yes, I'd have married you."

She stiffened. "Funny, you didn't seem to want to be anywhere near me back then."

"I thought I was doing the right thing. You were Trevor's girl."

Another tear slid down her cheek. "That afternoon, I thought I was Jeff's girl." She wiped away the tears. "But I learnt fast what I meant to you."

He'd thought he'd been doing the right thing by leaving. "Did Trevor know about us? About the baby?"

She shook her head. "No. I couldn't hurt him. He was such a good friend. And he loved me enough to still want to marry me."

Totally stunned by her revelation, Jeff could only stand there as Lacey walked away without a backward glance.

Hours later, Jeff still hurt.

It was after midnight when he arrived back at the cabin. He'd been driving around, going over and over what Lacey had said to him. Her words had felt like a kick in his gut. They hurt worse than the bullet that had shattered his leg. She couldn't have been any plainer than that, taking away the last of his hopes to win her back.

He didn't blame Lacey. He'd walked away from her twice.

He went into the cabin and lit the lantern, then opened the windows to try and cool the place as Lonesome came to greet him.

Jeff sat down at the table and leaned forward to pet the dog. "Oh, buddy, I've messed everything up, when all I wanted to do was help her out. Instead I got too involved and ended up falling in love with her all over again." He knew that was a lie before the words came out of his mouth. He'd *always* loved her.

The thought of her being all alone and pregnant just about killed him. Back then he'd been so young and stupid. He should have known there'd been a chance it could happen. But he hadn't thought about that. All he'd wanted was to get out of town, to forget that she belonged to another man. His best friend.

He went to get a bottle of water and noticed Trevor's journal on the counter. He picked it up and carried it back to the table. "Hey, friend, I'm in trouble now." He closed his eyes momentarily, not knowing if he wanted to read more, and knowing he'd let his friend down, too. He needed some kind of closeness to the man who'd shared his childhood and loved the same woman. He opened the book to where he'd left off the other day.

It was dated a week before Trevor's death.

Jeff,
I don't know how much time I have left. Even the doctors can't say, only that they're still hoping for a miracle. I want to believe, too, but it's hard.

And it's hard to keep up a front with Colin and Emily. Damn, they're too young to be without their dad. My boy needs a man around to help him. My daughter is practically a baby.

So my friend, I'm calling in all favors. I need you to be there for them now. And Lacey. She acts tough, but she'll be hurting. I've been blessed these past ten years to have a wife who loves me and kids that make me so proud. The only thing is I won't be around to protect them and see how they turn out.

I know this is a big deal to ask of you, but I can't trust my family with anyone else. And you have all those Randell aunts, uncles and cousins, so share them with the Guthrie clan. We always said we were like brothers, now prove it. It shouldn't be a problem since they're all so easy to love.

Jeff felt tears on his cheeks and he wiped them away as he turned the page.

There's one last thing, friend. I've been lucky to have married Lacey and shared a life with her, but I know you always had a piece of her heart, too. Come home, Jeff. You need your family, and Lacey and the kids need you.

Goodbye, old friend,
Trevor

Chapter 14

The next day was likeany other day, Lacey told herself. The kids had gone back to school that morning. Thank goodness, because they had too many questions about Jeff. Questions she couldn't answer.

Once they'd boarded the bus, she headed to the barn and to her job training Fancy. Something inside her made her hope that Jeff would come by. But why would he? Not after what had been said last night. All she could see was the pain etched on his face when he'd learned about the baby.

Was it possible to move on? To continue working together?

At lunch time, Lacey went to the house but wasn't hungry and ended up sitting on the porch, drinking iced tea. She closed her eyes, thinking back to only a year ago.

Trevor would have been with her. No, he hadn't had much time for her, not the last few years, anyway. It was clear that the ranch problems had taken a toll. Maybe if he had shared those troubles with her they would have been closer. Trevor had called it "protecting her." And he'd protected her far too often. It had left them nearly bankrupt and caused problems in their marriage.

How could she think that she could work with Jeff? It was even crazier to think she could start a relationship with him without the past intruding on them. Maybe she shouldn't have told him about the baby. But it had finally needed to come out.

That news had hurt him. She didn't need to relive the pain again, either. She had no choice but to move on without Jeff. Not that she'd ever had him, then or now.

She started to go inside when she spotted a truck coming down the road. Her breath caught as she recognized the dusty vehicle. Jeff's truck. It came to a stop next to the corral, and he climbed out.

She stood, her heart pounding against her ribs as he walked to the porch, but didn't come up the steps. "Hello, Lace."

She had to swallow before speaking. "Jeff. I didn't expect you today."

"For the moment we still have a partnership. There are some matters that need to be cleared up."

"I don't think we have anything else to say."

"That's where you're wrong, Lace." He came up the

stairs as he pulled a manila envelope from his back pocket. "Here's the deed to the cabin property."

She backed away. "No, I can't take it, Jeff. I don't have the money to pay you back."

His gaze softened. "You still think that I bought the property for an investment? No. I bought it to help you and the kids, but yeah, to help myself, too. Truth is, I needed a purpose to get up out of bed, to want to work again. Buying your horses that day got me thinking about a future. So you see, Lacey, I needed you as much as you needed me." He paused, watching her. "It was always my intention to include you in all decisions. I never purposely tried to leave you out."

She swallowed hard, ashamed of her reaction to Jay's offer. "I know. I was surprised and angry."

He nodded. "But the important thing is I want you to know that I would never have left town if I'd known you were pregnant. I would have done anything for my child."

Lacey fought her emotions. "It's strange to talk about the baby after all this time. Afterwards, I just buried the memories and tried to move on and build a life with Trevor."

She looked at Jeff, seeing he was struggling with his emotions, too.

"Oh, God, Lace, I'm so sorry." When he reached for her, she went willingly into his tight embrace. After all these years they had the right to share their pain. "I'd give anything to have been here for you."

She let the tears fall. "I wish you had been here, too. So badly."

He drew back and looked at her. There were tears in his eyes. "How far along were you?"

"Eleven weeks. The doctor said it happens sometimes. It wasn't anyone's fault."

Her gaze met his, seeing his doubt. "We can't blame ourselves, Jeff."

"I need to know one thing… Did you want my baby?"

She nodded. "Yes, Jeff, I wanted our child." She glanced away. "I wanted a part of you."

He lowered his forehead to hers. "Oh, Lace, I want that, too. I dreamt about it for years, but you were Trevor's wife."

"I'm not his wife any longer," she surprised herself by saying. "No more guilt about the past."

Jeff finally smiled. "You have no idea." He drew her back into his arms and lowered his mouth to hers in a searing kiss. She melted against him, reliving every dream she'd ever had about this man.

He broke off the kiss. "As much as I want to continue kissing you, and more, I need you to come with me first."

He tugged on her arm and she resisted. "I can't, the kids are due home from school."

He smiled. "I think there might be a Randell around to help with that." He pulled out his cell and punched in a number. "Nothing is going to stop us this time."

After getting Hank to come by to take care of the kids, Jeff drove Lacey to the cabin. It seemed like everything began there, and it was time to put it to rest before they started their beginning.

He leaned down and kissed her quickly, then got out and hurried around to her side to help her out of the truck.

"Come on, I want to show you something." They continued to walk past the cabin about a hundred yards. The late summer breeze was tolerable and there were mature oaks around the building site that promised shade from the heat.

He stopped on the edge of the ridge and looked out at the pasture. There were survey stakes in the ground to mark off the large house he'd planned to build here.

His pulse sped up seeing Lacey standing beside him with the sun highlighting her hair. She was dressed in those slim-fitting jeans that made her legs look a mile long. She had her hands on her hips as if she were ready to take on the world. He loved all that attitude.

He was suddenly anxious, hoping she'd go for the idea. "I confess I kept this from you, but I wanted it to be a surprise."

She looked at him. "What is all this?"

"I want to build a home here." He paused and drew air in. He could smell her and he took a step back, trying to keep his head. He nearly stumbled. She reached for him and her touch was searing.

"So you're going to stay?"

He nodded. "I want to make a life here, Lace. It's something I've dreamed about for a long time. If I'd been honest with you that day in the cabin all those years ago, maybe you would have married *me*." He gripped her hand. "It nearly killed me to leave, but I thought you loved Trevor, otherwise you couldn't have pried me away."

Lacey's green eyes stared back at him. "I know that now."

He forced a smile. "We can't go back, Lace, and question the decisions we made in the past. I thought I was doing the right thing."

"I know."

"I also want you to know I've always loved you, Lace. I've never stopped, and never will. I'm not talking about friendship. It's not enough after kissing you, making love to you," he breathed. "So, I'm asking you to give this gimpy ex-soldier another chance."

Her gaze searched his face as he tried to control his excitement. "Hey, I happen to love this gimpy ex-solder!"

He grinned. "You don't know how happy that makes me, because I happen to love this talented horse trainer. Her beauty, her kindness and how she fills out a pair of jeans." He kissed her again and again, feeling his body stirring. With a groan, he tore his mouth away and rested his head against her forehead. "I love you, Lace."

Tears rushed from her eyes. "Oh, Jeff, I love you, too."

He shivered at the words he'd always longed to hear. "The important thing is we found each other. And I'm not planning on losing you again."

"I don't want to forget the past, either."

"Of course not," he said. "There are too many good parts, and we can't forget Trevor. We both loved him." Jeff thought back to the journal. He hadn't wanted to bring it up today, but like everything else from now on he would share it with Lacey as soon as he could. This moment was theirs. Alone.

He reached for her hands, because he had to touch her. "Today is our beginning, Lace. I want it to be our start together. That's why I want this house for us, and the kids, too." He stopped and drew a calming breath, trying to find just the right words. "Funny, I've thought about this moment so many times…"

Lacey squeezed his hands. "Just say what's in your heart, Jeff. That's all I need to hear."

He nodded. "I need to do this right." He slowly got down on one knee. "You've always had my heart, Lacey Guthrie. I want to build a life together with Colin and Emily, and maybe another child, too. Will you marry me?"

A tear ran down her cheek. "Oh, yes, Jeff. Yes! I'll marry you." She pulled him up and went into his arms as his mouth took hers in a hungry kiss that only made him want her more.

Finally it was Lacey who broke off the kiss. "Oh, Colin and Emily."

"Granddad Hank can handle them, and we'll tell them later." He knew he already had a couple of allies. He started to tug her toward the cabin. "Right now, I want their mother to myself for a little while." He stopped and looked at her. "I know it will never replace the child we lost, but I want another baby with you."

She smiled and touched his face. "Oh, Jeff, I want to have your baby," she said softly. "You'd be a great dad, and you've already won Colin and Emily over."

He paused and his throat worked hard. She trusted him enough to share her kids with him. "You're sure the kids will be okay with us getting married?"

With a nod, she moved closer and kissed him sweetly. "And so is their mother."

Her trust meant everything to him. He pulled her to his side. "I still have Brandon's key to the cabin in Mustang Valley. I'll call Hank and see if he can play granddad until bedtime."

"Sounds like a good idea," Lacey agreed. "But I think we should be home in time to tuck them into bed. And after that, their mother's going to need your full attention."

"I like the way you think." They walked toward his truck. "Wait until later. I've got some more surprises for you."

Jeff glanced back at the cabin, knowing that he and Lacey had a lot more to talk about, to forgive, to share and to plan, but tonight it was for just them.

And all the good memories they were going to make. They were going to get their chance at a future. Together.

Epilogue

Nearly a year later, Jeff looked up at the completed two-story, stone and cedar structure. Large oak trees framed the new Gentry home, and the rolling hillside made a perfect backdrop to complete the picture.

His heart swelled with love and pride, remembering the day six months ago when he'd married Lacey. They'd waited until after the one-year anniversary of Trevor's death before they became a true family.

He still had trouble believing he'd won Lacey's heart. Not too long ago he'd been a lonely soldier who couldn't fit in. Now he was a husband and father to a couple of great kids, living in a new house, getting a new beginning.

They'd only moved into the house two months ago, and were barely unpacked. But they were home. It was the Gentry home.

Will Jensen worked full-time now and lived in the apartment over the barn. Jay was renting the main house. He'd wanted to be closer to his herd.

Lacey went along with it, knowing the Guthrie house belonged to Colin and Emily, as did the ranch. All Jeff and Lacey owned was the section of land around the cabin. It was enough to eventually build a covered arena and barn closer to the house. That was further in the future.

Right now they were comfortable having Will help with the training. And they'd already welcomed the newest addition to the family, a colt from Bonnie and Ace, named Trevor's Pride. They wanted the kids to know their father lived on through the horses he loved.

Jeff thought of his friend a lot. He'd always miss him, but every day he got to see Colin looking so much like his father. Jeff would do everything to keep that memory alive.

He'd also shared Trevor's journal with Lacey. They'd laughed and cried together, cherishing their happy childhood, the years of friendship that they'd never forget.

Jeff found he loved working with horses, too. Maybe because he had the best partner—not only in the business but in life. He smiled. Yeah, he was one lucky guy.

"Hey, soldier, you looking for someone?"

He turned to see his wife coming toward him. She looked beautiful first thing in the morning, her sunny blond hair pulled away from her pretty face, those green eyes that smoldered when he loved her. He drew a breath as his gaze moved on to the worn jeans and fitted shirt. She was a pure Texas country girl. And she was his.

"I think I found her," he said and greeted her with a kiss that lingered awhile.

Lacey had never been so happy and she couldn't wait to share the reason with Jeff. "I like that greeting."

"There's always more where that came from," he assured her. "You heading over to the barn?"

"No, Will can handle things for a few hours."

Today wasn't about breeding or training. She had other plans for her husband. "You and I are going to play hooky. The kids have a half day of school, so later we're going to meet Brandon and Nora and their brood at Mustang Valley."

He pulled her close. "So that gives us a few hours to kill." He raised an eyebrow. "Got any ideas?"

She laughed, trying to hide her nervousness. "First I'd like to talk to you." She took his hand and together they walked to the creek that ran behind their house, but she went nearer to the cabin. This had been where they'd fallen in love.

He sobered and waited for her to speak. With a shaky hand, she reached into her back pocket and pulled out the pregnancy test stick. "It's positive."

He looked down at it with a shocked expression.

She smiled, knowing they'd been planning a baby since they'd moved into the house. They just didn't expect it would happen so soon. "I'm pregnant."

"A baby? We're having a baby?"

She nodded. "I believe it happened the first night

in our new bedroom, on that wonderful new mattress. Or maybe it was the next morning in our new double shower, or—"

Jeff finally came out of his shock and kissed his wife. When he tore his mouth away, he was breathless. "I love you, Lace." He closed his eyes, thanking God for this blessing. "I'm going to take care of you this time. Nothing's going to happen."

She touched his jaw. "I know you will, Jeff. And I'm going to be careful, too. I'm done riding for now."

"And you're not lifting anything heavy." He grasped her hands. "I wish I could help you more."

She smiled. "Okay, when the time comes, I'll let you handle the labor."

"I would if I could."

"Right, Mr. Tough Guy. You'd crumble in minutes."

"I probably would, but I'm going to be there with you, every moment." He broke out into a big grin. "Damn. We're going to have a baby." He pulled her into his arms and kissed her again and again.

"So you starting something, cowboy?" she asked. "Just remember we only have a few hours before the kids get home." She grinned. "So you'd better take me back to the house and see if we can be creative in another room."

"Sounds like a great way to celebrate."

Jeff glanced one last time at the cabin. It was time to move on. He turned back to his wife and together they walked toward their future. Being away had only made him appreciate everything he had, especially now, having his family around him. He was a Randell, after all. This was where he belonged, with the woman he'd always love.

He was home. For good.

* * * * *

*Harrison McCord was sure he was the rightful owner
of the Dawson Family Ranch. And delivering Daisy
Dawson's baby on the side of the road was a mere
diversion. Still, when Daisy found out his intentions,
instead of pushing him away, she invited him in, figuring
he'd start to see her in a whole new light. But what if
she started seeing him that way, as well?*

*Read on for a sneak preview of the next
book in Melissa Senate's
Dawson Family Ranch miniseries,*
Wyoming Special Delivery.

Daisy went over to the bassinet and lifted out Tony,
cradling him against her. "Of course. There's lots
more video, but another time. The footage of what the
ranch looked like before Noah started rebuilding to the
day I helped put up the grand reopening banner—it's
amazing."

Harrison wasn't sure he wanted to see any of that. No,
he knew he didn't. This was all too much. "Well, I'll be
in touch about that tour."

*That's it. Keep it nice and impersonal. "Be in touch"
was a sure distance maker.*

She eyed him and lifted her chin. "Oh—I almost
forgot! I have a favor to ask, Harrison."

Gulp. How was he supposed to emotionally distance
himself by doing her a favor?

She smiled that dazzling smile. The one that drew him like nothing else could. "If you're not busy around five o'clock or so, I'd love your help in putting together the rocking cradle my brother Rex ordered for Tony. It arrived yesterday, and I tried to put it together, but it has directions a mile long that I can't make heads or tails of. Don't tell my brother Axel I said this—he's a wizard at GPS, maps and terrain—but give him instructions and he holds the paper upside down."

Ah. This was almost a relief. He'd put together the cradle alone. No chitchat. No old family movies. Just him, a set of instructions and five thousand various pieces of cradle. "I'm actually pretty handy. Sure, I can help you."

"Perfect," she said. "See you at fiveish."

A few minutes later, as he stood on the porch watching her walk back up the path, he had a feeling he was at a serious disadvantage in this deal.

Because the farther away she got, the more he wanted to chase after her and just keep talking. Which sent off serious warning bells. That Harrison might actually more than just like Daisy Dawson already—and it was only day one of the deal.

Don't miss
Wyoming Special Delivery *by Melissa Senate,*
available April 2020 wherever
Harlequin Special Edition books and ebooks are sold.

Harlequin.com

WE HOPE YOU ENJOYED
THIS BOOK FROM

HARLEQUIN
SPECIAL
EDITION

Believe in love. Overcome obstacles. Find happiness.

Relate to finding comfort and strength in the
support of loved ones and enjoy the journey
no matter what life throws your way.

6 NEW BOOKS AVAILABLE EVERY MONTH!

Willow Emery approached her brother and sister-in-law's two-story home in Brooklyn, New York, with a deep sense of foreboding. The white paint on the front door of the yellow-brick building was cracked and peeling, the windows covered with grime. She swallowed hard, hating that her three-year-old niece, Lucy, lived in such deplorable conditions.

Steeling her resolve, she straightened her shoulders. This time, she wouldn't be dissuaded so easily. Her older brother, Alex, and his wife, Debra, had to agree that Lucy deserved better.

Squeak. Squeak. The rusty gate moving in the breeze caused a chill to ripple through her. Why was it open? She hurried forward and her stomach knotted when she found the front door hanging ajar. The tiny hairs on the back of her neck lifted in alarm and a shiver ran down her spine.

Something was wrong. Very wrong.

Thunk. The loud sound startled her. Was that a door closing? Or something worse? Her heart pounded in her chest and her mouth went dry. Following her gut instincts, Willow quickly pushed the front door open and crossed the threshold. Bile rose in her throat as she strained to listen. "Alex? Lucy?"

There was no answer, only the echo of soft hiccuping sobs.

"Lucy!" Reaching the living room, she stumbled to an abrupt halt, her feet seemingly glued to the floor. Lucy was kneeling near her mother, crying. Alex and Debra were lying facedown, unmoving and not breathing, blood seeping out from beneath them.

Were those bullet holes between their shoulder blades? *No! Alex!* A wave of nausea had her placing a hand over her stomach.

Remembering the thud gave her pause. She glanced furtively over her shoulder toward the single bedroom on the main floor. The door was closed. What if the gunman was still here? Waiting? Hiding?

Don't miss
Copycat Killer *by Laura Scott,*
available April 2020 wherever
Love Inspired Suspense books and ebooks are sold.

LoveInspired.com

Heartfelt or suspenseful, inspiring or passionate, Harlequin has your happily-ever-after.

With new books published
every month, you are sure to find the
satisfying escape you know you deserve.

SIGN UP FOR THE HARLEQUIN NEWSLETTER

Be the first to hear about great new
reads and exciting offers!

Harlequin.com/newsletters

Love Harlequin romance?

DISCOVER.

Be the first to find out about promotions,
news and exclusive content!

f Facebook.com/HarlequinBooks

Twitter.com/HarlequinBooks

Instagram.com/HarlequinBooks

P Pinterest.com/HarlequinBooks

ReaderService.com

EXPLORE.

Sign up for the Harlequin e-newsletter and
download a free book from any series at
TryHarlequin.com

CONNECT.

Join our Harlequin community to
share your thoughts and connect
with other romance readers!
Facebook.com/groups/HarlequinConnection

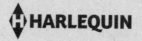